SECOND PASS

SECOND PASS

Book Two of The Grid Saga

To Tony
with Best Wishes from
Jfovert — (ROD)
9th april 2021

J. J. Overton

ISBN- 1978100973
ISBN- 9781978100978

For Sandra, David and Chris, and this time, for the other people who have made my life significant. This includes Doug and Mary Horton, David and Violet Davies, and others far too numerous to mention, who have had a bearing on my writing.

Acknowledgments

Grateful thanks to my excellent team of beta readers, Sandra Horton, Connor Horton, Mike Williams, Pauline Weston and Heather Harper. Thanks also to Brenden Hindhaugh and Andy Docking for their encouragement and the laughter.

Glossary.

Wasiri-Poya. The world where all things began. The home of the Wasiri-Chanchiya.

Wasiri-Chanchiya. The people from the beginning of time.

Thar-Thellin Spiral. The home Galaxy of the Wasiri Chanchiyans.

Stessar Tharon. The double star system containing Wasiri-Poya.

Stessar Tharon 7. Position of Wasiri-Poya in the Stessar Tharon system.

Wasari. More than a single person of the Wasiri-Chanchiya.

Wasaru. A single person of the Wasiri-Chanchiya.

The Second One. The name the Wasiri Chanchiya have given planet Earth.

The Hnioss. The Council of the Interface of Worlds, who oversee the administration of the known and the emerging worlds.

Ahra-Than. One of the lands on the planet, Wasiri-Poya. The Hnion reside in Ahra-Than.

Hnion. An individual member of the Hnioss.

Krel-Rahn. Preceptor of the Hnioss.

Lan-Si-Nu. Grid Commander. He is a Wasaru.

Fen-Nu and Thal-Nar. Close companions of Lan-Si-Nu.

Sar-Theit-Nos. The greatest of the Grid Travellers of ancient times.

The Great Annals. The entire body of knowledge and exploration recorded by the Travellers of the Grid.

∿ The Symbol standing for The First One, Wasiri-Poya, in Wasiri-Chanchiyan.

Phaelon 23057C. Wasiri-Chanchiyan for the Milky Way galaxy.

Chakrakan. A rogue planet, a one-time sister planet to Earth. Moved in ancient times from its twin planet position for the safety of the planet Earth. Chakrakan is known as Nibiru to the people of Earth.

Hnirath of Science. A Mastership of learning on Wasiri-Poya.

1

2,370 BCE, The Land Of Havilah

The sounds of drunken laughter and a terrified scream echoed across the city which was lit by flaming torches and the light of the Moon. Conditions had been deteriorating ever since the ancestors migrated down the River Pishon, one of the four rivers flowing from the land where all things began. Now fear was part of every night and violence was always close at hand.

The Keeper, Sho'mer, was a wise man whose task it was to make and keep records of events. Sho'mer's father and grandfather, who were both the record keeper before him, recounted stories from their younger years, but conditions for them had been gentle compared to today. Anarchy had become widespread; Murder and rape were rife and few people could be trusted. The Keeper feared for the future. He wrote of the anger and hatred that flowed like a foul stench across the land of Havilah and the surrounding countries. Adding to the uncertainties was a light that had appeared near the Sun in recent times. Sho'mer and the other wise men discussed the light. Instead of being faint and difficult to see through the fibrous leaf acting as a shield to protect their eyes, the light in the sky was now brighter and growing in size. The wise men talked with trepidation about what it portended.

Sho'mer, who was also a stonemason, went across the square to speak to the elder whose task was to record the progression of

1

the light in the sky. When Sho'mer questioned him about whether he knew why the light was there, the elder looked evasive and said that most likely it would go away as quickly as it had come. Sho'mer, being dissatisfied with the answer, went in search of it elsewhere.

A day occurred when he was in conversation with some men from the desert, who had arrived on camels. He heard that there was a man in a place far off who, with the help of his sons, had been building a great vessel. So the story went, he had been building the vessel for many years and in recent times he had seen the tides where he lived rising in their ebb and flow. As that was occurring the light in the sky grew steadily brighter. Word was that the old man insisted the First Cause had spoken to him.

Word of this man's activity was spreading everywhere, but as people considered he was mad, they laughed at his activities. He was telling people that unless they changed their ways there would be a catastrophe. The people held him in derision and jeered when he walked amongst them in the marketplace gathering food.

Sho'mer was interested in what the man was saying about the light in the sky, so he gathered his meagre belongings into an animal skin, hoisted it onto his back and started the journey to find out from the man himself what he thought was happening.

Eventually, after weeks of travel over difficult terrain, Sho'mer reached the place where the man was building the vessel. As he reached a hill near the coastline, he could smell the saltiness of the sea on a breeze that blew over the brow of the hill. The sea birds flying overhead sang to him of the deep ocean that he had heard of but never seen. He could hear its movement before ever he saw it and he could taste salt on his lips.

When he topped the rise, he crouched down and peered over the crest. Sho'mer saw the builders working on the strange vessel on the shore below. It was a busy but orderly scene. There were great piles of timber, trimmed of all branches, ready for use on a great box-like structure. A few younger men were doing the heavy work, lugging the timber to wooden scaffolding for lifting into position. There were large cauldrons suspended over fires some distance away from the timber, and from them, steam arose, and the smell of tar hung in the air. An elderly, heavily bearded man was standing to one side at a table, consulting a plan incised into a clay tablet.

Sho'mer heard part of the conversation as he approached. The old man was pointing out where a feature on the superstructure needed strengthening.

"That's the way it should be. It is how the voice I heard told me how to make it and we must follow what I have been told exactly so that we will survive."

The old man turned at the sound of a footfall.

"What brings you here, stranger?"

Sho'mer said that, ever since he had heard about the vessel from some nomadic travellers, he had been interested in it and wanted to help.

"You are welcome my friend, we have much work to do and, I fear, little time to do it." The old man looked up into the sky and shaded his eyes with his hands against the sunlight.

"See, it is happening just as we have been told." The old man pointed to the object in the sky.

He called for refreshments, which the wife of one of the younger men brought over, and he told Sho'mer to put his bag down, to sit, and refresh himself.

*   *   *

3

Building work was nearly complete and all, including the women, took a hand in applying the hot tar to the hull to make it waterproof. During those final stages Sho'mer, the Keeper, learned more about why the vessel needed building.

The family of the older man showed Sho'mer great hospitality. It did not take long for the old man to grow to love the Keeper almost as one of his own sons. In the evening times when they were sitting around a fire, the builder of the vessel would recount the progress they had made during the day. Sometimes he delighted to tell them how the proportions they had been given were important for the vessel's stability, and that they had adhered to the proportions rigidly. During those hours, Sho'mer carried on with his calling as keeper of records, writing the information on parchment with ink made from soot mixed with acacia gum.

Eventually a day came when the seas became fierce and rain lashed the land unmercifully. Torrents of floodwater ran down over the beach and into the sea in great gushing runnels. The elderly man said he had been told that it was time for everyone to board the vessel. Before they did, they stood firm against the tempestuous wind and looked into the sky through the wild weather and saw that the light had grown into a great orb that was almost overhead. They entered the vessel along with the multitude of livestock bedded down on straw in many separate stalls on the different levels that were reached by ramps and then the heavy outer door shut solidly, as if blown by a mighty wind, sealing them inside.

When a few hours had passed, they felt movement as the great vessel lifted from its building position and rocked with the movement of the wind and the water.

Sho'mer made a detailed record of the momentous voyage for the benefit of his ancestors. He felt compelled to continue writing while they were afloat, telling of the privations they faced and their great joy at the first sighting of land after months at the mercy of fierce winds and mountainous waves.

After the vessel grounded on high land, Sho'mer looked into the sky and wrote about the recession of the great orb and about their life in the new land where there was lush vegetation and every other commodity they needed. Sho'mer settled on the peaceful land and took as his wife one of the daughters of the old man.

For safekeeping, he kept the words he had written in a cedarwood box and placed in it the tools of metal that he used as a stonemason; a square, a set of compasses and a mallet made of beech wood.

The generation of the voyagers passed with Sho'mer the Keeper's death. He was the last survivor of the voyage. The box he left, with its contents, became revered by his descendants who, in the male line, also became the Keeper. In time, with migration and war and rivalries of kingships that came and went, the cedarwood box and its contents became lost. All that remained was the rumour of a sacred box and the story of a deluge.

2

The Black Alaskan wolf, Tomahawk Shahn of Offchurch, stood abruptly. He brushed by Dearden's leg and walked slowly to the floor to ceiling window, where he stood, listening. He looked into the night, attracted by a movement. Dearden frowned at the unusual behaviour when Tomahawk, full-grown and black, raised his muzzle and howled. The primeval sound from the icy wilderness made the hairs on Dearden's neck rise. Tomahawk edged closer to the window and sat alone, fixed on what he could see outside. The others in the great hall laughed at the performance and apart from Dearden and Red Cloud, they carried on chatting against the soft background of easy music.

Red tapped Possum Chaser's shoulder. She looked up and saw him nod his head in the direction of the window where Tomahawk was sitting. She followed Red's gaze but could see nothing because of the reflection shining in her eyes from one of the table lamps. Red walked to the window and stood at Tomahawk's side, looking out into the night. The others in the room knew Red was a loner, so other than Dearden and Possum Chaser, they took no notice.

Red often picked up what other people missed. As well as seeing the topmost branches of the trees at the outer edge of the forest moving in the strengthening northerly wind, he had seen three tall silhouettes moving in the starlight. He kept his eyes on them as they walked slowly toward the house, one leading the way and two following. They stopped beyond the outbuildings where it was darkest and appeared to be looking into the house. Red turned to face Possum Chaser and nodded his head just sufficient for her to see. From his clenched fist behind his back, he raised three fingers. She saw the signal and smiled in answer. They had talked through the possibilities of this happening. He returned to his seat and shifted it around to face the door. Possum Chaser clutched his hand tightly. They settled in to wait . . .

* * *

Peace had descended onto Dearden Hall and Leofwin's Hundred, a remnant of the Forest of Arden belonging to the hall. But the area in the proximity of Leofwin's Hundred would never be normal. The Hub, the building the Anglo-Saxons had called the House of the West Wind, lying deep in the forest, was the strangest place on Earth.

Jem Dearden, as a way of showing his appreciation for the way his friends pulled together during The Manhattan Affair, had organised a celebration. The table in the great hall was loaded with food to cater for all tastes and some of the drinks were expensive enough to make the Ritz envious.

Bill Templestone arrived with a case of 1992 Domaine La Grave Bordeaux and he put it at the side of the room where it was cool. Dearden indicated Templestone's favourite winged armchair and he settled himself in as Dearden put three more newly split logs onto the fire. As the logs started to blaze, flames arose and cast a rich flickering glow around the room.

Dearden brushed some ash onto a shovel and put it into a bucket at the side of the Norman fireplace then sat next to

Rowan, waiting for the others to arrive. The tension of the previous months drifted away. Frieda Heskin brought more bottles up from the cellar to add to Templestone's Bordeaux, a Pencarrow Martinborough Pinot Noir, and two bottles of 2003 Chateau de Malle Sauternes.

"Where did you get the wine, Bill?" Dearden asked, studying the label on the Bordeaux. He thought it must have made a big hole in Templestone's wallet.

"Courtesy of a cellar in Wyvern Hardewicke. What was Raegenhere's loss is our gain."

The others began to arrive and the Great Hall became the scene of light-hearted banter, recollection of times past and the promise of times to come. Dearden was standing in his favourite place, leaning against the massive stonework of the fireplace. There was laughter, the lights were low and the buffet food and the wine were good. Red Cloud was sitting in a chair with Possum Chaser on the floor, her back resting against his legs. They were tense. Tomahawk was alert and stood by them. Wynter was telling the others about one of his experiences back in the Bronx where he bested one of the up-and-coming thugs. He was getting to the punch line when they heard the outer door to Dearden Hall opening. Being heavy and ancient, it grated on its hinges, which reminded Dearden that they needed oiling, and then the door closed. The room went quiet. From the other side of the closed door to the great hall, they heard Frieda Heskin shriek and her husband Gil shouting something like "What the bloody hell . . ." and then they went quiet.

Dearden and Doughty snapped into action, leaving Wynter and the Bronx forgotten, ready to hit whoever it was outside first, and ask questions afterwards. Julia Linden-Barthorpe shifted quickly away from Dearden and Doughty, prepared to take the oncoming threat from the flank with Shotokan.

Templestone crossed the room to Rowan and Esma and stood in front of them. He still had the Smith and Wesson with him, unlike the others whose weapons were back in the gun cupboard. He stood in the classic shooter's stance, the .38 in a two-handed grip. Which was when the heavy door swung open and the aliens stood in the doorway. Flames from the burning logs in the fireplace at the far end of the room guttered and flared in the chill breeze from the open door and uncertainty gripped the room.

It was bizarre – the three aliens from the Hub standing on the threshold as if it was a normal thing for them to do. They were too tall for the door and had to bend low to come into the great hall. The one at the back shut the door gently behind him and the three of them walked in silently with huge strides until they stood side by side in front of Dearden. He was unafraid when he saw them this time. He knew they had good intentions because of how they helped Rowan when she was lying near death inside the Hub with a crossbow bolt in her back, but he felt way out of his depth.

The door at the side of the great hall opened and Harry Stanway came in from his room upstairs and stopped in his tracks. His smile, which was permanent most times, disappeared and he crossed quickly to Templestone when he saw him with the raised .38. He pushed the weapon down so it was aimed at the floor.

"There's no need for that," Harry said.

"Be it on your head." Templestone kept his eyes on what was going on and stuck the gun into his belt. He folded his arms defiantly and stayed in front of Rowan and Esma.

Possum Chaser pushed Red Cloud forward but stayed where she was herself. He cautiously approached the aliens, followed by Tomahawk, and lifted his hand in the traditional Lakota Sioux gesture of welcome. The leader of the three aliens did the same in return and his face creased in what Red took for a smile.

Tomahawk moved up close to the aliens, sniffed at the one in front, then sat on his haunches at the side of the strangers as if they were on equal terms.

For Dearden and his colleagues, apart from Harry, it took almost two hours for the tension to ease off. When the people of Earth realised that the aliens were not a threat, the conversation became intense and loaded with questions. The event became something to hold onto, to lay down in memory. It was a turning point for the people of Earth gathered in Dearden Hall. Monumental as the situation was, however, Dearden and the others eventually succumbed to sleep.

Language was no problem. The aliens explained that they and their ancestors had been around Hampton in Arden and southern England for a long while. During that time, their race had picked up English. The occasional word was medieval, some were even Anglo-Saxon, showing how long their race had access to the planet Earth. They said that the learning of Earth's languages became easier after Marconi invented radio, to which they had avidly listened.

Harry spent time with the leader, who went by the name, Lan-Si-Nu. Together they discussed the operation of the Hub.

"The Node is nearly ready for us to return to our galaxy," Lan-Si-Nu said. He was impressed with what Harry Stanway had achieved with calibrating the temporal and spatial shift modes. "To make it fully capable what we need to do is this . . ." and Lan-Si-Nu, who was a brilliant draughtsman and engineer, sketched out and detailed some alterations that were necessary.

Harry brought his laptop down from his room and went online sourcing materials. He felt strange sitting next to the giant, who exuded an acrid smell. Lan-Si-Nu took the laptop and his fingers flew over the keys. He explained to Harry that he was looking for a particular metal in the periodic table. It was needed to replace components that had broken down. The metal had a crystalline structure with a particular resonant quality that altered in the molecular state when it was energised. When placed in a circuit, it had a memory function that was unsurpassed.

"It is needed to process all of the data involved with an intergalactic shift through many nodes across the grid," Lan-Si-Nu explained.

Julia chose her time to speak to Dearden about a phone call she had from Trent Jackson just before the aliens came into the great hall.

"Trent found a separate note tucked into the manual. It's written in a derivation of the alien script. Someone way in the past must have inserted it into the manual. Trent managed to translate most of it. He said it's a warning, and to tread carefully."

Over the following weeks, they had regular contact with the aliens. Dearden talked at length to the one named Fen-Nu. He learned that they came from a far distant galaxy. Their world sounded like Wasiri-Poya, which translated as 'The Dawn World', and they were the Wasiri-Chanchiya, 'The Dawn People'. Dearden understood the 'Dawn' part of the name to have the sense of 'beginnings', giving the name of the people the sense that they were 'The People at the Beginning of Time'. The place they came from was 'The World at the Beginning of Time'. They were enjoyable weeks and it was a time of great learning for Dearden and the others, and much planning for the Dawn People. One day Lan-Si-Nu invited Dearden and Harry to the Hub.

"It is you and Harry Stanway we want to see, Jem. No-one else must come."

Dearden talked to Harry about the secrecy and they concluded that something of vital importance had occurred. Lan-Si-Nu met them at the lower entrance door.

"Come in." He indicated the vast interior with a sweep of his arm and they stepped inside. "Jem, Harry, we are very near to leaving for our home, but before we go I must tell you more about the Grid and the Portal, which is the part of this building that you call the Hub." The outer door shut silently behind them. Although Dearden was familiar with the Hub he felt out of place in it, in the presence of the tall alien.

"You are familiar with the four levels above where we stand now. We have our living space off the room where examples from different worlds we have visited are on display. What I must tell you is that there are functioning levels below ground. For the time being, you are not allowed to go below ground."

"Why not, we have made great strides understanding the function of the Hub," Harry challenged.

"Yes and we recognise that you have made it possible for us to return to our home world. For that we are grateful, but what lies below ground belongs to a higher level of physics than the Hub. You see, our ancestors built the levels of the Hub that are above ground many thousands of your years ago. We have been travelling the Grid since the stars of your galaxy were closer to one another."

Harry asked, "What does lie below?"

"About three point-seven million of your years ago, an important breakthrough was made in the application of dimensional science. Our scientists had long postulated the existence of parallel universes, sometimes events occurred by accident where, for a fraction of time, a universe in close dimensional proximity to ours overlapped. The events were made manifest by odd coincidences occurring that challenged our perception of reality. Glimpses of other beings or even scenes that were unexplained made us realise that a veil between the dimensions sometimes lifts for a fraction of time. You may have noticed occurrences similar to that yourselves."

"Are you saying that what lies in the lower levels allows us to see into those other dimensions?

"Patience, Harry, I am explaining. Our scientists investigating particle physics discovered what could be translated into your language as the Super Quantum, where entangled particles were perceived to exist in multiple dimensions of reality. It is a strange twist of existence and the discovery pointed forward to further research that took place over many years. Eventually, it became possible to peer into the other realities."

Harry began to walk to the stairs going down.

"Harry!"

He stopped. It was the first time they heard Lan-Si-Nu raise his voice. It wasn't in anger, but it was authoritative.

"What lies down there is the means to transfer to those alternative realities; you are definitely not ready for that."

*   *   *

All too soon, the day came when the Wasiri-Chanchiya programmed the nodes on the route over the grid for their journey
back to the World at the Beginning of Time. Lan-Si-Nu gave
Dearden an object that he called the Key. He showed where it
fitted into a slot in the control panel of the Hub and said that it
was how Dearden could contact the Dawn People if ever there
was a need to do so.

One of the last things Lan-Si-Nu told them was that in time,
if the people of Earth were seen as worthy by the Hnioss, they
would be able to follow suit and travel to remarkable places.

"Worthy by the what?" Dearden asked.

The Hnioss. It is the Council of the Interface of Worlds, the
representatives of those who travel the grid

"How will we prove worthy to the Hnioss?" Harry grinned
as he said the word.

"Do not treat the Hnioss with disrespect, Harry." Again, the
authoritative tone came into Lan-Si-Nu's voice.

"You and your colleagues, or your descendants will be invited
to go before the Grand Council. Your planet and its peoples are
being closely observed."

Dearden grimaced. "What are the standards we are being
judged by?"

"How you deal with each other. You must learn how to deal
with your own race before being allowed to go further afield."

"Then we have a long way to go."

"Maybe not as long as you think." With that, Lan-Si-Nu
stood, and the aliens walked off into the forest, to go through the
Hub on their journey home.

* * *

There was a prolonged silence in Dearden Hall. Although the presence of Lan-Si-Nu and his two colleagues had been brief in the lives of Dearden and the others, they were momentous times that had seen the first interaction between people of Earth and a race from a different galaxy. Now they were no longer present an acute sadness descended that was difficult to shake off. Even Tomahawk was subdued. Over the following days, apart from Templestone and Harry, who remained at Dearden Hall, most of the group of friends drifted apart and went back to their previous lives.

Jem and Rowan occasionally walked into Leofwin's Hundred, to the place where the trees were most dense, beyond Shadow Brook and the mighty oak, Old Jack. In the clearing at the bottom of the hill topped by the Hub they would pass leisurely hours enjoying the wine and food that Frieda Heskin had prepared. It was a time for reminiscing about Heanton in the Arden, Earl Leofwin of Mercia and the others back in Rowan's time.

Dearden still found it difficult to comprehend how he and Rowan of Maldon came together. How a temporal shift opened up at the Hub and he, Doughty and Julia Linden-Barthorpe went through to the Anglo-Saxon settlement. It had been almost a chance meeting in a village in the Forest of Arden, a few months, but paradoxically, a long, long while ago. Sometimes, unbidden and unwanted, the thoughts intruded about how he would have lost her, but for the aliens' intervention.

Now and again, they invited Bill Templestone on their rambles, but most times he kept out of the way in the apartment where he lived above Dearden's stained glass studio. From time to time, during the evening, he went out. He never said where he was going. Occasionally Jem and Rowan heard him coming back in the early hours of the morning and Rowan said that she thought Bill was seeing a woman.

Dearden liked having the older man about. He was good company and their friendship went back a long way in SHaFT, the Shock and Force Team for justice. Templestone had been good to Jem years ago after his father died, and now Dearden wanted to repay him, so Bill managed the stained-glass business in one of the outbuildings. He earned a decent wage and lived in the apartment above the studio, free of charge.

Harry Stanway had moved in too. Dearden had a fatherly interest in the young man, so Harry had a self-contained flat upstairs in one of the wings of Dearden Hall and the flat had an extra room fitted out as a laboratory. It was where Harry conducted his research into cutting edge science between the hours of nine and five. He was strict with his time and applied himself thoroughly to his projects, driven by an inner determination to produce results. Dearden said that he could do all the research he wanted, with two provisos. The first that he didn't blow the place up and the second, that he kept Dearden up to date with his findings. Jem Dearden possessed a lively curiosity for innovative science, and the output, mostly theoretical, from Harry's lab kept his interest satisfied. Sometimes they talked about the aliens. The Wasiri-Chanchiya were never far from the minds of those who had met them during those extraordinary few weeks.

It had been a roller-coaster time for Dearden since he inherited Dearden Hall. Now he was glad things had slowed down. The quieter pace of life for all those who had been involved with the

Hub, the House of the West Wind, as the Anglo-Saxons called it, had given him time to retrench and get on with an ordinary life. Dearden jealously protected the peace and his newfound privacy with Rowan.

*   *   *

They were near the forest, at the place where they chopped wood for the fire.

"You have got a funny face, Jem." Rowan laughed, looking at the wood chippings from the axe in his hair. He didn't know whether to take her seriously, so he laughed with her.

"As long as you love my ugly face, I don't care," he said, as Rowan brushed the chippings out of his hair. He laid the woods-man's axe down with its handle resting against the pile of logs ready for the fire in the great hall. It was hard work but exhilarating and he was ready for the lager Rowan had brought from the fridge. She was adapting well to the different way of life. She had a can to herself, and after popping the ring-pull she drank, and enjoyed the taste.

"We are doing well," Rowan said, looking at the results of the work. She picked up the axe and felt its weight.

"Almost done," he said putting his arm around her and pulling her close. Her golden hair touched his cheek and he caught the faint scent of Jasmine. Rowan broke away with a smile and went to the pile of logs Jem had cut to length with the chainsaw.

She picked up one of the logs and placed it on the tree stump they used as a chopping base. "My turn, I have another go." She grasped the woodsman's axe with both hands. Earlier she took a turn with the axe and Jem stood to one side after showing her how to split the logs by striking in line with the grain. He was surprised at her stamina when she wielded the axe. Her resourcefulness continually surprised him.

Tomahawk came and sat on his foot. The wolf liked to get close. The creature had stopped growing and his paws, that only months ago seemed too large for his body, were now in perfect proportion. He was impressively big. Just as Red Cloud at BW Breeders had warned, he sometimes went on the wild side. His primeval nature surfaced at unexpected times and sometimes on demand, as it had in the storm drain in Manhattan. With Julia Linden-Barthorpe, Tomahawk had helped Dearden and Doughty when they were seconds from death.

Tomahawk Shahn of Offchurch was jealous of the two people he lived with and he often demanded the attention of one or the other. It was not a master and mistress arrangement, it was a hierarchy. Tomahawk was the boss and he protected Jem and Rowan as if they were part of the pack.

3

Twenty miles to the south of Dearden Hall, in Warwick's market square, Cyrus Crowe ran his art and antique dealership. He had a shop, with its frontage facing the square and there was a large warehouse at the back, accessed through a door marked private.

Apart from art and antiques, Crowe had other ways of raising cash, which he carried on in the darkness of night. Its secret nature was maintained by men in his pay. Word on the grapevine was that Crowe would stab his mother in the back and twist the knife when it was in. Crowe's attitude was similar to his namesake, Corvus Corone, the carrion crow, because he raked through any available pickings to satisfy his appetite, which, in Crowe's case was for hard cash.

Crowe had dark coloured skin that hinted at Latin ancestry and his hair was jet black and Brilliantined so that it shone. He was quick in his movements, quick with his temper and his unpredictability matched the volcano near the village of his ancestors. There was no direct evidence, but once in a while things would go missing during the night from other dealers' outlets. There might be a trail of broken glass or spaces where choice items had been on display, but always no clue about who might be the perpetrator of the crime. On the darker side, two unsolved murders, antique dealers both, were said on the grapevine to be his responsibility and there was an undercurrent detectable in his personality that gave people the creeps.

Crowe advertised house clearances. Whenever he entered a property to rummage through the contents for a clearance, he felt the same as when he bought a lottery ticket. There was inner excitement at the possibility of finding a masterpiece, or some bygone relic unrecognised by its owners for its great value. To him, attics were special, because, over successive generations of a family living in a house, the attic would become the repository of surplus items. Being out of sight, the items would be forgotten and lie in a time warp as they gathered dust over the years. An older generation would die, and those inheriting the house would be oblivious to the value increasing above their heads. One day, with a house move contemplated, a dealer like Crowe might arrive on the doorstep by arrangement.

One Monday he answered the phone and spoke to Barry West, who was the son of James West, a retired headmaster. The headmaster had recently died and his son asked Crowe if he would clear the contents of his father's house in Temple Balsall before it went on the market. Crowe arranged to go to St Mary's Lane to view the contents. As usual, he only showed marginal interest as he walked from room to room. This strategy set the punter up not to expect too much from the deal. Crowe was inwardly totalling the value of the items he passed by. There were some quality antique pieces and he knew that he would sell them for a good profit.

Now the question . . .

"Anything in the attic?"

"I don't know, you'd better have a look. I want it cleared before the house goes on the market and the garden shed needs clearinging too."

"I'll start with the attic."

Barry West stood at the foot of the stepladders under the entrance to the roof void, and Crowe slid the trapdoor to one side. His spotlight pierced the darkness and he clambered into the familiar musty smell of forgotten belongings. To Crowe, it possessed the aura of expensive perfume. Dior and silk with champagne came to his mind. Someone had boarded the floor to take the weight of everything that was in the attic. The beam of the spotlight picked up all manner of bric-a-brac, old games, toys of a bygone era and jigsaw puzzles in cardboard boxes that had deteriorated through the seasonal extremes of heat and cold.

At the far end of the attic, there was a trunk, a brown painted metal sea-going trunk with 'White Star Line' stencilled on it in white. There was a trail of footprints in the dust on the uneven floorboards leading up to it. Crowe thought that the trunk would be desirable, particularly with the name stencilled on it. Probably it would be the most profitable item in the whole house. He walked over to it, shining the spotlight on its top and sides. As he got close to it, he saw the word TITANIC stencilled in bold letters on the end that had previously been hidden. His heart lurched with anticipation and he turned to see if West had seen his quick movements of excitement. This was an unusual find, unique and no doubt very valuable. He went back down the steps from the attic with a figure in mind for the job lot.

Within a week the house was empty. Crowe and his assistant, Garth Wilde, had been cleaning and re-polishing the furniture and some of it was on display in the showroom. The jigsaw puzzles and games were on shelves in the shop. Crowe's attention turned to the White Star Line trunk.

It was locked, so Crowe called Wilde, who had a feeling for locks, to see if he could release the latch. Wilde took two probes from a small drawer in his toolkit. He inserted one into the hole in the lock, fiddled around with it for a minute before shaking his head and trying with the other probe, which was the bigger of the two. Five more seconds and the lock grated open. Crowe, standing close, shoved Wilde aside and lifted the lid. The hinges protested through the accumulation of rust. Wilde seemed too interested and Crowe, suspicious of the man's motives, told him in definite terms to clear off and carry on with what he was doing in the workshop.

A number of books were lying on top of pages of handwritten and typed paper and large envelopes, which were stacked in untidy piles. The books were academic, and much of what Crowe saw was beyond his level of learning. There were books on astronomy and astrophysics, freemasonry and masonic rites, and there was a version of the Bible that included the Tetragrammaton on its title page. By its side was a large, leather bound Bible of the Old Testament written in Hebrew.

Initially, Crowe was disappointed but then, amongst the papers below the books, he saw the words, MOST SECRET. They were stamped in bold red ink on the front of a stiff buff-coloured cardboard binder held together with string. The MOST SECRET words arrested Crowe's attention and caused him to stare at the contents of the trunk with increased interest. He unwound the string from the buttons on the outside of the binders. There were papers inside which were also stamped MOST SECRET. That the words were black told him the documents were copies of the originals. Crowe put the sheets back in the folder and shut the lid of the trunk. He looked around to make sure Wilde hadn't seen what he had found and dragged the old Titanic trunk into his office.

He locked the door behind him and after opening the trunk he removed the books and put them on top of his desk. He tried to be systematic as he removed the papers underneath, quickly reading headings and underlined type as he proceeded. On one of the sheets he read about a place called the 'Knights' Sanctuary' and its custodian, whose home, apparently, was Keeper's Cottage in Temple Balsall. A large brown envelope came next. There was a thick wad of paper inside, the old foolscap size, some folded, some creased and some torn, all of them aged to an off-white colour. Crowe spread them out on his desk. All of the sheets bore writing in black ink. It was a firm, confident hand in which some of the ink had faded, but was still legible.

The topmost sheet had the heading, Conclusion. The text spoke of an ancient Hebrew scroll which described a cataclysmic event. There was a warning written in capitals about a similar event yet to take place, but the writing finished abruptly. There were no details about what the forthcoming event was to be, or when it would occur.

Crowe was immediately alert. He backtracked with his finger past the cataclysm warning. He read the words again, *ancient Hebrew scroll* and went to the cupboard where he kept the brandy. He took a slug straight from the bottle as he tried to come to terms with the fact that he may have stumbled across a once in a lifetime find. He tipped the trunk on its side, raked the contents out and shuffled through the pile of papers looking for the scroll.

There was page after page of mathematics, complex diagrams with circles, ellipses and straight lines. There were large brown envelopes and bundles of paper tied with string, but no scroll. He sat down and contemplated the possibilities, trying to work out what to do next.

The contents of the trunk appeared to be someone's research into a place in Temple Balsall called the Knights' Sanctuary, which in itself didn't interest Crowe. What he wanted was the scroll. At the forefront of his mind was its potential value. He already had a customer for it, a Saudi prince with money dripping like oil from his pockets, who was fanatical about Hebrew history, which was odd for an Arab. The ancient scroll would raise a princely sum from him. Crowe had visions of Monte Carlo. He could berth a yacht there and sail to exotic places. The excitement had tired him, so he closed the lid of the trunk, locked his office and went home.

* * *

Crowe went online and Googled the search string *Knights' Sanctuary*. It produced over five and a quarter million hits. He put the two words into quotation marks and reduced the results to just over four million. The most popular of the results referred to fantasy web pages with links to online games. No results referred to an actual place called the Knights' Sanctuary. What did keep showing up in the results were the Knights Templar. Crowe disregarded that and bookmarked the search.

He went to www.mapsforfree and checked out Temple Balsall on a large-scale Adventurer map of the area. There was a public house called The Cuttle, a few residential streets off the main road, and a group of buildings called the Hartlow Hill Craft Centre. Isolated houses were dotted about; some of them important enough to be named on the map. There was a church, St. Mary the Virgin and close to it he saw the Knights' Sanctuary. Amongst the other buildings named on the map was Keeper's Cottage. Crowe's mind worked on the possibilities. The Keeper had cropped up a number of times in the MOST SECRET documents.

There was a problem. The majority of the contents of the White Star Line trunk were highly academic. The math was too difficult for Crowe to understand. To make progress with the information that was probably still most secret, he had to get someone involved who would be able to understand the complexities and keep his mouth shut about what he was reading. If Crowe could find the right man, he would have to give him a cut of the profits in exchange for his silence and there could be money to be made from the *secret* documents in the communist bloc.

Crowe decided to begin his search for the Hebrew scroll at Keeper's Cottage. He sat back in his chair and figured out a plan. He would ask the Keeper's permission to look inside the Knights' Sanctuary. As a reason to do that he could spin a tale about being involved with a research project about Temple Balsall and the Knight's Templars. Of course, for his project, he would need to describe the interior of the Sanctuary. Easy. Once inside the Sanctuary he could look for the artefact and once he had gained the Keeper's confidence he could return any time to continue his 'research' if he needed to.

*   *   *

He pulled up outside the detached cottage and went to the door on which there was a large iron knocker. As he approached it, he noticed some lettering, שומר, cut into the keystone at the centre of the porch. An incised stone at head-height in the wall to the right read 'Keeper's Cottage'. He rapped twice and the noise echoed inside the building. He rapped twice and the noise echoed inside the building. As he lifted the knocker again the door suddenly opened, wrenching it out of his hand, and it hit its base with a solid thump.

A medium sized individual, probably in his eighties, stood there. Crowe introduced himself with a false name. He tried to be polite when he asked the man if he was the custodian of the Knights' Sanctuary, but the elderly man asked why he wanted to know. Crowe told him about his 'research project'.

"The building is private. No-one is allowed inside, other than a certain few," the old man said.

"How do I get to be amongst the certain few?"

"You don't. Now, please leave." The man stepped back abruptly and shut the door in Crowe's face. He was unprepared for the response and walked away, feeling slighted and boiling with rage.

"If that's the way you want it, you old bastard, we'll play a different game," he muttered, under his breath. He would have to up the stakes to get into the Sanctuary, but to keep his hands clean someone else would have to do the job for him, and it would need to be done in the darkness of night.

4

Emotion rarely affected William Henry Templestone. There was something of the old school about him, drawn from his tough upbringing. His father had been on the Arctic convoys in the Second World War, on the Murmansk run where it was hell on earth. The experiences of the father permeated the son and prepared young Templestone for whatever life threw at him.

Templestone's roots lay in the ancient village of Temple Balsall, in the heart of rural Warwickshire. 'Bill', to all who knew him, was the only son of Andrew Templestone and Sophie Montarion. As Templestone's name suggests, coupled with the place where generations of them had lived, there was a family tradition that their ancestors had connections to the Knights Templar, but what the connection was had been lost over the passage of time.

Every so often Templestone would go back to his old stamping ground and meet with his circle of friends. He had never moved far away from his place of birth because Warwickshire had everything he needed. It had the flat plains that had been chosen for Second World War airfield locations and as a counterpoint, the rolling hills of Burton Dassett, and the sharp incline of Edge Hill, with the village of Radway in its shadow.

One particular afternoon when the weather was fair Templestone's roots were calling. He headed off to Temple Balsall in his

Morris Minor Traveller. He decided that he would call in at the Cuttle for a while to catch up with local news and relax in the familiar surroundings. The landlord, Joe Fox, was an old friend who, like Bill, hadn't moved far away from his roots. After the Cuttle, he would call in on David Sancerre.

After talking to Joe Fox, Templestone sat in a corner of The Cuttle to read for half an hour while he had a drink. He was always reading a book, generally crime and detection, or a tough-guy taking on the world. He settled into Lee Child's latest Jack Reacher novel.

The session in the Cuttle turned out to be longer than he anticipated because he drifted off to sleep. Someone moving a cask in the cellar startled him awake. He looked at his watch through eyes fuzzy with sleep and swore under his breath. Two hours had gone by and night had fallen. He found the last page he remembered reading, turned over the corner and hurried out of the pub to catch up with David Sancerre, who lived at Keeper's Cottage. There was a short cut to Sancerre's house in Church Lane. It cut through grounds shared by the church of Saint Mary the Virgin, and the Knights' Sanctuary.

The Knight's Sanctuary lay behind a tall yew hedge with notices dotted about warning that it was Private, and to Keep Out. Templestone remembered from his younger years that there had always been secrecy surrounding the Sanctuary. It had intrigued him and in his early teens he pestered his father to tell him more. Apparently, people met in the building beyond the tall hedge. Rumour was that fabulous wealth had been brought back from the Crusades and that, as a result, hundreds of years later, a trust fund that never ran out of money was managed from the Sanctuary.

Templestone recalled thinking how odd it was when his father told him how someone who might be hard-pressed finan-
cially would find cash through the door in a plain envelope at the
right time. These occurrences only took place within the boundary of Temple Balsall and the beneficiaries were only the families
that were long established in the village.

People did not want to upset the balance of events, so they
left well alone and kept very quiet about the occasional shower of
good fortune. As they had done for centuries, without hindrance,
there were occasions when shadowy figures late at night made
their way through the gap in the yew hedge and through the
Gothic arch into the Sanctuary.

Templestone had a torch in his pocket, essential now his eyesight
had started to deteriorate. It began to rain as he switched on the
torch, so he walked faster as he went through the Lych-gate into
the churchyard and shone the torch on the pathway up ahead.
It wound through the encroaching trees and gravestones, then
alongside the yew hedge where there was a gap and a gate where
the path divided, one leading left through the gate to the Knights'
Sanctuary and the other straight on toward Sancerre's cottage.

Templestone looked at the gap in the hedge and saw that
the gate was open. He stopped to latch it and as he shone his
torch on the catch, a movement up ahead in the darkness at the
Sanctuary caught his eye. He shone the torch toward the porch
and could see that the large oak entrance door was open and
moving in the breeze. He walked to the doorway and saw newly
damaged wood on the frame where it had been forced.

Alert for trouble, he felt for his Smith and Wesson in his
pocket. With the problems that the team had faced in previous
months, it was better with him than in a gun cupboard. He eased

himself silently around the door without opening it further. The penetrating cold and damp inside the building struck him and he shivered. He shone the torch ahead and it penetrated the darkness as he walked up the centre aisle. He reached the far end of the large meeting hall where there were two other rooms, one to the right and another to the left. One of them was a robing room, with cupboards built against a wall. The other was a storage place for wooden crates and other bric-a-brac. There was no intruder.

Templestone began walking back up the centre aisle. Just ahead, a water droplet fell through the torchlight. He shone the torch into the roof void and the beam picked out the structural timbers of a hammer-beam roof, massive and intricate. Another water droplet came from a spot where the earthenware tiles beyond the roof timbers were darker than the surrounding ones, where they had been discoloured by the seepage of water. The dripping water was pooling on one of the stone floor-slabs and trickling down a joint at its edge.

The damage to the tiles must have happened recently, Templestone thought, otherwise, Sancerre would have got repair work under way. And it was fortunate that the water wasn't falling onto the misericords each side of the centre aisle; it would have ruined the patina developed over the years on the ancient timber.

Templestone had a bad feel about the situation. The open door was worrying. He pulled it shut behind him. The building looked secure from the outside. As long as no one tried the latch, all would be fine. Templestone hurried through the rain the few hundred yards to Keeper's Cottage.

*   *   *

Sancerre's front door was ajar and there was no light coming from inside. Templestone gingerly pushed the door open with his foot and shone the torch around the room. The .38 was leading at arm's length and Templestone was ready.

"David," he called his friend's name just once. He fancied he heard a movement, but if Sancerre was in the cottage he would have answered straight away. Templestone carried on into the room. It was a male preserve, no feminine touches of any kind. David was a confirmed bachelor. There were no added touches of comfort. It was austere . . . cold even. Templestone saw the familiar leather armchairs, old but expensive, the cushions dented by the sitter. There was a stone-flagged floor, its harshness softened by rugs. In the centre of the room, a large dining table, dark with age, had eight carved chairs around it. A carved mantel topped a stone fireplace and the fire was alight in the hearth. A brass coal scuttle was tipped over, a bad sign, particularly with the coal scattered over Sancerre's expensive hearth rug.

Templestone picked his way around the coal, his eyes trying to pierce the dark beyond the light of the torch. He walked warily into the room at the back. He had a sense of foreboding, but the solid feel of the .38 reassured him as he went further into the cottage.

In the back room, the torchlight picked up empty spaces in the sideboard. The drawers were on the floor, their contents scattered about. Templestone wondered if whoever it was who had been searching found what they were looking for. Using a handkerchief on the catch, he cautiously opened an under-stairs cupboard door. A vacuum cleaner, brooms, and bottles of cleaning materials were scattered around the floor-space. Sancerre would never have put the objects away in that state. Templestone shut the cupboard door and moved on into the kitchen.

The window was open, letting in cold air . . . the intruder's escape route. The way to the rest of the house upstairs led off the kitchen through a pale green ledged and braced door. Templestone opened it and climbed a set of steep and narrow stairs. He shone the torch around the landing.

There were four doors, three shut and one half-open. Walking to the open door, he could see the white porcelain of a wash-hand basin at the far end of the room. There was a familiar smell from inside, like a butcher's shop. He steeled himself to look in the room.

Sancerre was there, lying spread-eagled on the floor, his blood sprayed over the walls. It was still spreading from his body. Templestone's pulse jacked up a notch. He was used to seeing violent death, but seeing his elderly friend lying on the floor seeping blood as a result of violence first brought grief, then anger and thoughts of vengeance.

Templestone had to force himself to be objective. The murder was recent because the blood had not coagulated. There was a knife sticking out of the victim's chest in the region of the heart. He used his handkerchief again, covered his fingers with it to save leaving fingerprints on the skin. He gently touched Sancerre's carotid artery. There was no pulse.

He shone the torch around the bathroom. The bolt on the door was hanging loosely, still held by one remaining screw, and the catch-plate was on the floor, along with splintered wood and the rest of the screws that had fastened it to the doorframe. It looked as though Sancerre had been cornered and had locked himself in the bathroom trying to escape his attacker. There was nothing to explain the reason for the attack, or who the murderer was.

Templestone moved out of the bathroom, Smith and Wesson out front. He stealthily walked along the landing and used his handkerchief on the door handles to open them. The first two were bedrooms and harboured no surprises. As he came to the closed door of the last room, he was ready. Dearden said that at times Templestone had a kamikaze streak. When his adrenaline was up he didn't care what challenge he faced. If the assailant was still at the cottage he had to be in the room the other side of this last door and he would have to get out of it past the full chamber of the Smith and Wesson.

Twisting the handle so the door was just open Templestone kicked the door hard so that it hit a chair inside the room, then he went in quickly, gun and torch leading, but there was no intruder.

He went back to the body. The knife thrust was straight in, but there didn't appear to be any other wounds. There was evidence of a struggle, a chrome receptacle was lying on the floor, with its contents scattered about.

Templestone's torchlight reflected on a metal object, barely visible, clutched in Sancerre's right hand. It was bright and mostly concealed by his fingers. On first glance, Templestone thought it was a ring until he looked closer. He took the handkerchief out of his pocket and put the gun away so that his hands were free.

Rigor mortis had not yet set in so the fingers opened easily. Templestone felt mean as he took the object from his old friend's hand and gently closed it again. The purpose of the object was not obvious. In size, it was about three inches long and one end was bulkier than the other. The narrow end had a series of notches on it, spaced out irregularly around its circumference.

He pocketed the item and made his way back down to the kitchen. A plant pot was lying on its side in a sink below the open window. The soil from it was soaking up water from a dripping tap. Templestone turned the tap off. It looked as though the killer must have heard him coming into Keeper's Cottage – or seen him with the gun – and escaped out of the window, knocking the plant pot over in the process.

Templestone shone the torch into the back garden. He could see nothing suspicious, but as the beam of the torch picked out the furthest corner of the garden, there was a scrabbling noise behind a bush and a dark hooded shape heaved itself over a fence at the back. Templestone aimed and fired but the killer got over the fence too soon and the slug smacked through the wood and whined off harmlessly. There was the sound of running, a car door slammed. An engine started and tyres screeched as a car sped off.

*   *   *

There were two things on Templestone's mind. Three if he counted the gnawing pain inside at the loss of his friend. The attacker needed apprehending, and the door of the Knights' Sanctuary needed locking. If he was able to do so, Sancerre would have ensured the security of the Sanctuary, and Templestone knew he guarded that jealously. He went to the under-stairs cupboard again and picked up a small bag of tools. He scouted around and found some fine masonry nails to do some repairs to the seasoned oak of the door frame at the Knight's Sanctuary. He remembered there were two bunches of keys, one for Keeper's Cottage and one for the Sanctuary. They were kept on hooks screwed into a beam in the front room. Using his handkerchief to hold them, he took both sets and locked the door to the cottage on his way out.

On his way to the Sanctuary, Templestone attempted to visualise what had happened. The murderer had been looking for something in the Sanctuary. He broke in, leaving the woodwork of the door frame damaged. He couldn't find what he was looking for, but he knew that Sancerre was the custodian of the Sanctuary and that he lived at Keeper's Cottage, so he went to confront him. Sancerre had been determined not to give his attacker what he wanted, so he fled upstairs and locked himself in the bathroom. Things went wrong, maybe the attacker, when he broke into the bathroom, couldn't get what he wanted and killed the old man in a fit of rage. Templestone felt anger welling up inside again.

At the Sanctuary, he made some quick repairs to the door frame, locked the door and quickly retraced his steps to Keeper's Cottage. When he was back there, he keyed his mobile phone. After two rings, Sir Willoughby Pierpoint answered.

5

After Templestone rang off, Pierpoint hurried to the cellar under Ireton Grange. He had moved out of the cottage in Radway to Ireton Grange, in the same village of Radway, after it came up for sale and his need for space had outgrown the cottage. Something Templestone mentioned in the phone call had rung an alarm in Pierpoint's mind. It was urgent, way back in the past. He had inherited a vast amount of information from the S.A., the 'Special Agency', which was the precursor to SHaFT. He was modernising the filing system, but it was so antiquated that it was taking an inordinate amount of time to get the information in the steel filing cabinets digitised.

There had been an incident in the past that he recalled was something to do with Temple Balsall. As Pierpoint went down the steps to the cavernous underground room, some of the details of the Temple Balsall affair came back to him. He found a reference to it in the old Roto-Index system that referenced the steel filing cabinets. He looked at his watch. Ten minutes since Templestone's call. He crossed the room to one of the filing cabinets, cursing the antiquated system for its inefficiency.

The bulky folder he found had a note clipped to it with 'Temple Balsall, Ongoing' in large letters. Although he last set eyes on it years ago, he recognised it immediately because it had created such an impression at the time. Pierpoint unwound the string holding the covers together and scanned the report on top of the pile of papers inside. It summarised a SHaFT investigation in the nineteen-seventies and the report had been cut-off mid-sentence. Clipped to the report were papers outlining supporting evidence.

Underneath the folder, clipped to another sheaf of papers discoloured with age, was a sheet that bore the date 27th of August 1939, only a few days before the outbreak of the Second World War. As he scanned the information, Pierpoint knew that Templestone had inadvertently stumbled onto something of great significance. Sheet after sheet inside the cardboard covers had a red diagonal stamp, 'MOST SECRET', across the text. Pierpoint remembered reading the 1939 pages for the first time back in the seventies, and back then thinking how unusual it had been that the information was hushed up.

Within days of the original SHaFT information being written, the Nazi onslaught into Poland occurred and with it, the threat to the rest of Europe. Understandably, the Temple Balsall issue faded into the background when preparations for conflict took precedence.

A sheet of handwritten mathematics in faded black ink, with the signature, Prof. Charles Villiers at the bottom of the sheet, was amongst the bundle of papers. There was a sentence at the bottom of the page, outlining Professor Villiers' conclusion about the mathematics. Pierpoint was a reasonably competent mathematician, but the calculations on the sheet were serious maths that he could barely understand. Closing the folder, he went upstairs quickly and put the folder on his desk ready to read when he returned from meeting Templestone.

*　　*　　*

Within twenty-five minutes of talking to Templestone on the phone, Pierpoint was on his way to meet him at the victim's house in Temple Balsall. He tried to set his mind in order, but it was difficult because of the issues raised by the contents of the folder. He had only scanned a portion of it, but what he read made him act with urgency. It was the same back in the nineteen seventies when the Temple Balsall issue was one of a number of archived cases that were still open. At the time, his investigations prodded a sensitive area of government. He had a visit from a government minister who ordered a shut-down of the Temple Balsall investigation. Pierpoint was damn sure they wouldn't shut it down this time, almost forty years later. He was pleased Templestone had opened up the issue again. Times were more critical now and age had made him one hell of a lot more stubborn.

Sir Willoughby Pierpoint was usually a careful driver but this time he stepped on the gas. The trees and hedges of the route away from Radway took him past the tall wire security fence of the MoD site at Kineton where SHaFT had its Headquarters in Dump 4. Pierpoint looked ahead over the tall hedges as he drove, looking for the gleam of oncoming headlights, which would be the only reason to slow down. Ordinarily, he would think that the way he was driving at present on the public roads was insane, but there was no time to lose on this occasion and he pushed the Bentley Mulsanne to the limit of safety.

* * *

In Keeper's Cottage, Templestone heard a car approaching at speed. It pulled up outside and Templestone went to meet Pierpoint.

"You've stirred the Hornet's nest here haven't you Bill?" Pierpoint said, as he flung open the Bentley's door.

"Have I, do you know something I don't?" Templestone asked as he led the way into the Cottage and up the stairs.

"I know plenty you don't on this one, Bill," Pierpoint said, as they reached the head of the stairs. "There's an old file that's two inches thick on an investigation that was centred on Temple Balsall years ago. You'll have to come back to my place. There are things we have to set in motion. I want your opinion before we do. First, we need to seal Keeper's Cottage off, and the Knights' Sanctuary. The lads will be here any minute." Pierpoint took a quick look around the bathroom. His gaze lingered on Sancerre's body.

"Poor chap, the only thing that might mitigate his death is that it may have come at the right time."

"Did I hear you right?" Templestone said, angrily.

"You did. What has happened might have forced this whole thing out into the open, but I'll tell you more when we get to my place."

As they got downstairs, Templestone heard the sound of V8 vehicles rapidly approaching. Within a minute they were pulling up outside. Templestone and Pierpoint went out to meet the SHaFT team who arrived in full black combats. Directed by Pierpoint they cordoned the area off and set up an armed patrol around Keeper's Cottage and the Knight's Sanctuary. As soon as the area was secure, Pierpoint left Temple Balsall for Ireton Grange, with Templestone following in his Morris Minor Traveller.

When they arrived at Pierpoint's house they went straight to his air-conditioned office. There were no windows. The door, although overlaid with walnut, had a high-carbon steel and Kevlar core; the lock was state of the art. Pierpoint was privy to information that was sensitive to the extreme and needed cutting-edge security. The door to his office was specially commissioned. It wasn't the only way in and out of Pierpoint's office. Ireton Grange took its name from Major General Henry Ireton who fought with the Parliamentarians at the battle of Edge Hill. Edge Hill, with a village of the same name on its summit, is a steep escarpment which is a few hundred yards from Radway. Some of the larger manor houses, like Ireton Grange, had priest's holes and tunnels built into them as a means of hiding and escape. One of those tunnels led off from behind a cunningly disguised panel in Pierpoint's office, and it led to the church.

Pierpoint tipped two brandies out, one for himself and one for Templestone and they took them neat.

"If I'd been there earlier I would have prevented Sancerre's death."

"I'm sure you would," Pierpoint knew that Templestone was still formidable. "The Custodian was targeted because someone wanted something from him and the reason he died was that Sancerre didn't intend him to have it. I want to show you something."

Pierpoint indicated for Templestone to sit at his desk, and he opened the Temple Balsall folder. He slid the topmost sheet over to Templestone, who noticed the *Ongoing* stamp. After the first few paragraphs he looked at Pierpoint, who was engrossed in reading some of the other pages.

"Is this for real?" Templestone asked.

"It most likely is. I first read that page a number of years back and it had the same effect on me back then as it's had on you. First, I want your opinion about whether you think it is real or not; whether it could even be possible. If it is for real, we all have serious problems. I need someone else's thoughts on this information; that's why you're here, but first I'll give you some background to the case."

*   *   *

Pierpoint brought Templestone into the picture about his involvement with the case when it re-emerged in the seventies. He pointed out the Prof. Charles Villiers signature dated 27th of August 1939.

"Villiers had started his research before the second world war. Even if the authorities back then had listened to him, there was nothing they could have done about the threat Villiers was warning them about because they didn't have the technology. I don't want to be pessimistic but there's probably nothing that can be done even now, sixty years later, if it's true."

"*If* it's true." Templestone carried on reading the next sheet Pierpoint passed to him.

"Of course, the Second World War intervened and that's one reason this case was forgotten and gathered dust," Pierpoint said.

"It's the last thing that should have been gathering dust, war or not."

"Maybe. Once we've read the entire folder we'll have a better idea of what went on. We shall see. The point is, back in the seventies the Callaghan government got wind of SHaFT re-opening the Temple Balsall case and they shut the investigation down. They must have known something we didn't and wanted it hushed up. What interested me was what I read in Villiers' notes about an impending cataclysm."

"He mentions cataclysm and catastrophe a number of times," Templestone said, taking another sip of brandy. "The point is, as the saying goes, there's no smoke without fire. This information coupled with Sancerre's death gives me a bad feeling." He eyed up the thickness of the folder. "I think it's going to be a long night,"

Pierpoint stood. He turned to the page he remembered from years ago, the one where Villiers had named the threat and told how he had warned the government about it. He looked at the word, Nibiru. He recalled hearing, before the government forced them to abandon their investigation, that Villiers was involved with a branch of cutting edge research that was highly classified.

It had been difficult to believe that the device he heard Villiers was working on was even possible. Pierpoint recalled the sleepless nights that he had after he heard a rumour about the invention. The obliteration of Hiroshima and Nagasaki had been just over twenty-five years previously and that was insane enough.

Pierpoint reached for the phone and told his estate manager, Mike Tennant, that unless there was a dire emergency he and Templestone weren't to be disturbed by anyone over the following day. They decided to finish, to be fresh for the task next morning.

Pierpoint lay awake in bed. The wind was disturbing the trees nearby and gusting around the gables facing Kineton Plain. The noise of the wind and Templestone's words about having a bad feeling about the way things were shaping up was making sleep impossible. An idea occurred to him. It was elusive, based on a conversation years ago about Villiers' invention. The source had been impeccable. He might be able to develop the idea into a plan in case Villiers' warning about Nibiru's return turned out to be true. He turned on the table lamp at the side of his bed. On top of a pile of books he had a notepad and a biro. He wrote his thoughts down while they were fresh in his mind and he would investigate the possibilities with the utmost urgency.

*   *   *

Ireton Grange had extensive lands attached. Some of it was cultivated and provided vegetables. There was a spinney set with Scot's Pine that Pierpoint intended to replace with native broadleaf trees. Behind a hedged-off area, there was a shady place, an arbour almost totally enclosed by a tall box hedge and an old climbing rose with a scent of musk when it was in flower. It was chilly but refreshing and the two men found it invigorating after spending half the night poring over the folder and comparing notes. Templestone had eventually given up during the early hours and went up to one of the guest rooms to snatch a few hours' sleep. He left Pierpoint trying to make sense of information on a number of sheets of foolscap with headings underlined in red.

By eight o'clock the following morning Templestone and Pierpoint were out in the garden, wrapped in heavy coats. The breeze off Kineton Plain ruffled the sheaf of papers, causing Pierpoint to turn back to the sheet he was reading for the third time, his eyes closed again and he jerked himself awake. He forced himself to read on because of the urgency of the words. He stabbed his finger on one of the sentences half way through the document.

"I can't make head or tale of the figures on this sheet." He held the sheet of calculations up. "Villiers wrote that the origin of the information was an artefact in the Knights Templars protection when they returned to England after one of the Crusades." Pierpoint gathered the sheets he had read and passed them to Templestone.

"Apparently, there were times the Templars literally guarded the artefact with their lives after it came from the Holy Land. Another thing, Bill, why this folder of information that's been gathering dust over the past sixty years has been hushed up officially is extraordinary. Villiers made sure the government knew of it. For some reason, they were worried about his message getting out. But there's an over-riding factor that strikes me, the whole episode is so detailed that it has the ring of truth."

Templestone nodded and looked at the sky. He picked up a pebble and threw it into a nearby water feature with a fountain. It splashed into the pool, which was large and deep. The ripples spread, moving outward, gaining momentum as they spread.

Templestone quietly said, "What if the information about a coming catastrophe relating to Nibiru is true? The government in nineteen thirty-nine couldn't have had a solution and war was imminent. They obviously thought that what the document revealed was a threat, hence the most secret stamp. As I see it, they had three choices, either they didn't want to face the inevitable, or they had an agenda to keep it quiet, or the threat of war took precedence. If resources had been pooled and Villiers had headed up a research team, at least they may have come up with a solution."

"What we have to remember is that Chamberlain had come from Munich waving his agreement saying there would be peace in our time. Despite that, the nations were squaring up for war and all available resources were going into that. If anything looked against the national interest, the government would have hidden it, regardless of content. The problem is that after the war ended the threat remained hidden."

Templestone asked, "So what else do you know about the documents?"

"Well, quite early on in the whole affair Villiers implied that the major source of his information about the warning of the catastrophe lay in the Knights' Sanctuary. It looks as though all the math on these sheets was Villiers' attempt to either prove or disprove the threat." Pierpoint sorted through the sheets he had read and chose one in particular. "Here it is. This sheet came before all the math," he looked up at Templestone, who was frowning with concentration. "Villiers says here that all of his work is based on information in the Knights' Sanctuary. He is convinced it is dependable. In the next paragraph, he says that because no member of Parliament would listen to him, he would go to the public gallery in the House of Commons to make sure the whole house heard the warning." Pierpoint tapped the sheet of paper.

"Villiers did just that. I remember reading this sheet of information in the nineteen seventies investigation. We scrutinised Hansard to see if he succeeded. He did. The entry was written up as a disturbance in the public gallery. Apparently, the chamber laughed and heckled the poor chap out. People considered he was a madman, but the threat was recorded in the daily proceedings of Parliament."

Templestone wondered how he would deal with such a situation. "Villiers had some strength of character to carry on his research, faced with all the ridicule."

Pierpoint nodded his agreement and shivered as a chill wind blew down from the massiveness of Edge Hill. He had tried to keep himself awake by choosing to be outside in the weather that started chill but sunny, but he gave up on that. "He must have believed that there was a threat, to be so persistent." He shivered. "Let's go where it's warmer." He got up from the garden seat.

The Sun disappeared behind clouds. The forecast was for unsettled weather, maybe even snow later. They made their way back into the warmth of Ireton Grange and picked up from where they left off outside.

By the time nine thirty came around they were not much further forward. Pierpoint was wading methodically through the rest of the folder sheet by sheet. Templestone had a sheet of paper with mathematical symbols in tabular form in front of him.

"We need help with this," he said to Pierpoint. "I don't have a hope of understanding it. Maybe if we could unravel the math it would help us understand what the whole folder's about, and whether we really need to worry about it."

"What do you suggest Bill?"

"That we get Harry Stanway involved."

"Harry Stanway's a useful young chap. He got Jem and Mitch out of a dire situation in Manhattan with some clever work . . . OK, Bill, get him on board. We need to establish whether the research Villiers was working on was based on fact or myth. If it was based on fact, the sooner we pick up from where his research broke off, the better," Pierpoint held up the unfinished page of mathematics. A calculation on the page was only half-complete and there was a blot of ink on the same line. "Let's hope we're not too late," he said, standing quickly.

6

"**D**id you find anything?" Crowe asked, as Garth Wilde came in through the door. There was no preamble, no pleasantries. His attitude was true to form.

"Find anything? No, I bloody didn't." Wilde had something on his mind and avoided Crowe's eyes as he spoke. He looked flushed as if he had been running. "I got into the Sanctuary with this *crow*bar," Wilde emphasised the first syllable and held up the iron bar with two prongs on it.

"Are you taking the piss?" Crowe asked. He was sensitive about his name and looked at Wilde and the tool malevolently.

"No, I'm just telling you." Wilde felt he wanted to retract the words when he saw the coldness in Crowe's eyes. He sounded nervous as he carried on with his explanation. "The old building's big inside and there's a few places I could see where stuff may be hidden, a couple of rooms are at the far end from the door. I looked in them, had a poke around but couldn't find anything."

"Go on."

Wilde looked for a chair, dragged it round and sat down. "I went to where you said the old man lived. I knocked the door and asked him if he knows where the thing is that's supposed to be hidden inside the old barn."

"You what?" Crowe stormed, "You bloody idiot, I told you not to go anywhere near his house. What happened then?" Wilde flinched as spittle landed on his face from the irate Crowe. He wiped it off with his sleeve.

"Well, the old sod must have got suspicious and asked me why I wanted to know. I told him I know someone who might be interested in buying it." Crowe's mouth dropped open.

"Come on, make my day." More spittle. "Then you told him my name I suppose." Wilde looked around, suddenly very unsure of himself.

"I didn't. What d'you take me for . . . I pushed past him into his house. I needed to look around to see if what you're after was there. It's an old place, beams everywhere, lots of places to hide things. He asked me what I was doing. When I went into the back room he grabbed my sleeve and told me to get out. He said he was going to call the police."

Crowe felt himself go cold and he paced the room. "What did the old guy do then?"

"He didn't do anything because I got my blade out and told him to tell me where the scroll's hidden. He ran upstairs, moved quick for an old geezer, I'll give him that."

Crowe stopped pacing. Wilde's account was deteriorating.

"And what happened then?" Crowe asked, quietly. He had a feeling he didn't want to know.

"I went after him. He'd locked himself in the bathroom."

Crowe put his head in his hands. "Tell me something good will you."

Wilde's foot started tapping rapidly. When he answered his voice was weak.

"I shouldered the bathroom door and got inside. I thought he'd got a weapon so I stuck him."

Wilde had gone pale.

"What do you mean, stuck him?"

"The old guy's dead –"

"Dead? NO . . . you stupid, stupid bastard."

"That's not all," Wilde spoke easily now. The worst was over and he needed to get the rest of the incident off his chest, like a confessional. "Someone else came in the house. I heard him calling from the front door, I had to get out quick."

"You didn't stick him as well?" Crowe asked. Wilde ignored him and carried on the explanation.

"It was an old guy who had a torch and a gun. I got out the window. You could tell the bloke could handle himself by how he held the gun."

"Pity he didn't use it on you," Crowe said. His voice sounded pinched. "And?"

"I got to the top of the garden and hid."

"Did the guy with the gun see you?"

"No, but I saw him. I got a good look at his face"

"The one good thing of your evening," Crowe muttered. "Come on then, tell me more."

"The guy with the gun came back downstairs and shone his torch around the garden so I got over the fence. He took a shot at me, but he missed."

"Pity . . . listen to me and give me a straight answer. Did he see you when you were getting out of the garden?"

"He probably didn't, it was dark."

"*Probably* didn't see you? Great. You don't know if he saw you or not. A simple job to get into the Sanctuary to find the damn scroll and you end up killing the man who would have led us to it. You need to watch your back now Wilde."

"Before you go off on one Crowe, after I got over the fence I cleared off in the car. I pulled into a layby to think things through, waited about an hour. I wanted to take another look around the house for the thing you're after. All hell had broken loose. There was crime scene tape and armed men about who were dressed all over in black. The old guy with the gun and a smart looking guy came out of the cottage and drove off separately. The old chap was in a classic car with a wood framework at the back. The other must be a rich bastard because he was in a Bentley. When they drove off, I left it a minute then followed them. They went to a big place in Radway. It had *Ireton Grange* on one of the gateposts.

"So, you've managed to salvage something out of the mess, but now we're on the back foot. I am sick of you, Wilde. You are a complete liability." Crowe paced again. "This is what we'll do. Listen, and get this right. Get hold of Dan Blundell and Bernie Crosher. Say there's a job to do and I want them here, tonight, got it?" Crowe involved others in keeping his own hands clean, which is where Blundell and Crosher came in.

On his mobile phone Wilde spoke to Blundell, and then to Crosher. He outlined the boss's plan.

* * *

In Pierpoint's study Templestone was wading through the sheets of foolscap from the folder. As Pierpoint finished with them he passed them over. Templestone tried Harry Stanway's mobile phone, but getting no answer he rang Dearden instead, saying that something urgent had come up that he needed to talk through, but that he needed to speak to Harry about it as well, urgently.

"Harry's gone over to Offchurch to see Esma, she's staying with Possum Chaser and Red Cloud. He'll be back later. What's up, Bill?"

"I'm starting back in a few minutes. It's too complex over the phone . . . I'll tell you when I get back, I won't be long."

Templestone rang off. Dearden looked at his watch, nine forty-seven. He was teaching Rowan to read modern English, and she liked to hear the stories he read to her when they were sitting on a settee pulled near the fire in the great hall.

Rowan saw the frown on his face. He looked concerned.

"Is Bill in trouble?"

"I'm not sure, but he sounded worried. He's starting back from Will Pierpoint's house now." Dearden checked the time, nine-fifty. "He'll be about an hour and then we'll know what it's about."

7

The object Templestone had taken from Sancerre's hand and put in his trouser pocket dug in his side as he walked to the Morris. He put it with the Smith and Wesson in a gun safe he'd had fabricated under a pull-up piece of carpet in the front passenger foot well.

Templestone hated using motorways so he chose the slower route from Ireton Grange to Hampton in Arden, which would take him through Warwick. He was on the Lighthorne Road, coming near to the Fosse Way when he saw a four by four coming up rapidly behind him with its lights full on. It overtook, to the flashing of lights and a sustained blast on the horn from a car coming in the opposite direction.

Templestone's concentration was on the road ahead rather than on the idiot at the side of him, but in his peripheral vision he saw the passenger's face staring at him. At the T-junction up ahead, the four by four turned right onto the Fosse Way. Fifty yards down the road, there was a sharp left to Moreton Morrell, the way Templestone was going. The four by four accelerated rapidly down the road with a dark cloud of turbocharged exhaust.

After Moreton Morrell the road became isolated and tree-lined. Wiggerland Wood lay to the left and right near the T-junction with the Banbury road. There was a gravelled pull-in on the left before the junction. The four by four was there, parked well off the road. There was someone lying on the ground and another person was flagging Templestone down. He indicated and pulled over. Switched off, leaving the keys in the ignition, and hurried over to see what was wrong.

"What's up?" he asked the individual standing by the man on the ground.

"He went for a run-out in the wood and collapsed when he got back." Templestone nodded and knelt down at the side of the man on the ground. For the second time in twenty-four hours, his fingers searched for a pulse. He looked at his watch to check the beats per minute. It was ten fifteen when he began the count. The man's pulse was strong and regular.

The man suddenly turned to Templestone and winked. Before he could react, the man standing grabbed him from behind, held his arms in a vice-like grip and dragged him to his feet. The man he thought was unconscious leapt to his feet and rounded on him.

"We meet again. Where's the gun this time?" the voice said from behind. Templestone inwardly cursed his stupidity falling for the ruse; it was Sancerre's attacker gripping his arms. Templestone wasn't a man to be intimidated. If he got angered inside he controlled it. He always used his anger when the time was right, but he couldn't resist starting to weaken the opposition.

"You're the coward I met last night," he said to the guy he couldn't see.

"I'll show you who's the coward." Wilde drew his hand back to hit Templestone in the kidneys.

"Back off Wilde, Crowe wants him unharmed," Blundell threatened. Crosher knocked Wilde's fist down. Templestone stored the name, Wilde, Sancerre's murderer. He would deal with him later. For the time being he went along with what they wanted him to do, particularly after Blundell pulled a Mauser out of his coat pocket and aimed it unwaveringly at his head. Templestone could tell the man knew how to use it.

Blundell indicated for Templestone to get into the four by four. "Get in the back by Bernie," he indicated the door with a wave of the gun. Crosher opened the door and slid over to make room for Templestone, who got in leaving the door open. Blundell slammed it shut then got in and started up. Crosher produced his own gun.

"Do anything I don't like and you'll get kneecapped." Templestone looked at him straight and level and saw the gun wavering. Crosher's Achilles heel was nerves. Wilde got into the front passenger seat and belted up.

"What's the plan, Bernie?" Templestone asked the man at his side.

"You'll see soon enough, so shut your mouth." Templestone could see Crosher's face in the rear-view mirror on the windscreen. It was blotched and red. His eyes looked rheumy, probably too much drink, and he stunk of sweat.

Templestone studied the back of the individual doing the driving. Medium build, close-cropped black hair, aftershave. He looked after himself better than Crosher did. The strongest one of the three in a showdown. The one to take out first if he had the opportunity and the space to do it. Dan, Crosher called him.

Take the strongest out first was what made Templestone formidable when he headed up some of SHaFT's toughest assignments. He had retired from that now, but not long ago he did it without blinking.

Thirty minutes after Templestone was overpowered, they passed around a traffic island with five exits and took the road leading to Shrewley. Within a few hundred yards, they took a right down Case lane, which was wide enough for one vehicle. They came eventually to a stone-pillared gateway. An ornate stone panel let into a curved wall at the entrance bore the name, Alderhanger.

Blundell drove the vehicle down a gravelled driveway with lawns each side. He arrived at a gravelled car park at the front of a square three-storey Georgian house. Outbuildings lay on the left and the furthest side of a car park and the four by four pulled up in front of one of them. It was a dilapidated building compared to the rest, white painted sometime in the past but now it had mould down the walls where water had leaked from the guttering. Blundell switched off, got out of the vehicle and came to the rear where Templestone was sitting.

"Out." The gun was there again. Templestone recognised it as a Mauser C96 Broomhandle, an antique that chambered 10 rounds. It was accurate in the right hands because of the long barrel. Templestone wasn't going to argue with the Broomhandle, at least not yet, so he got out. The man he encountered the previous night, the killer, Garth Wilde, walked to the blue back door of the house, knocked and went in.

"Over there." Blundell was short on words. He indicated a door in the outbuilding. It had the remnants of maroon paint clinging to the weathered timber surface. Crosher reached the door first and undid a padlock on a heavy chain. With one hand he thumbed an iron lever, which lifted a latch on the inside of the door, while with his other hand he pushed the door where a sheet-metal plate reinforced its weakness. Crosher went inside, fumbled for a switch and flicked the light on. It cast a feeble glow into the large room where there was a lot of darkness. Templestone was pleased about the darkness. He could use it as a weapon.

There were a number of wooden stalls, and iron rings, at one time used for tethering horses, were fastened to the wall. A faint animal smell still hung in the air.

"Tie him to one of those rings well away from the door," Blundell said to Crosher, getting some rope off a hook on the wall. Crosher gave Templestone a shove in the back making him stumble. He grabbed one of the posts at the end of the stall to stop himself falling. He kept his anger in check until payback time, particularly Wilde's payback time for what he had done to Sancerre.

Bernie Crosher tied Templestone to one of the iron rings while Blundell covered him with the pistol. He stood back looking at the captive. Crosher saw a man in his sixties, square-jawed, close-cropped black hair turning silver-grey at the sides. Templestone's brown eyes were weighing them up. Crosher looked away from the eyes, they were cold.

"I don't like his eyes," he whispered in Blundell's ear.

"You might get a chance to put them out. We'll ask Crowe what he wants us to do with the nosey old bastard." Blundell turned to Templestone, "You're lucky," I'm going to leave the light on in case you have nightmares. Crowe's evil when he gets crossed." Blundell spat on the floor close to Templestone, and they went out the door. The chain was fastened outside and Templestone heard their footsteps and their laughter as they walked off in the direction of the house.

8

Dearden checked his watch, almost eleven o'clock. Rowan saw his frown and felt his tension. An hour and ten minutes had gone by since Templestone's phone call.

"Bill should have been here by now," he said. It was unusual for Templestone to be late. He was more often early than late. Lateness was out of character. Rowan sensed Jem's unease but she was still unable to understand how precise an arrival time could be with modern transport.

"How far is he coming?" she asked.

"Pierpoint's house is an hour away at the most." Dearden looked at his watch again, "He's ten minutes late and he said there was something urgent to tell us."

"To be ten minutes late on a journey is nothing." Rowan tried to work out journey times with reference to travel by horse.

"If Bill said he would be here within an hour he would be. You don't know Priest like I do. With him an hour is an hour. Something's wrong. I'm going to look for him"

Rowan heard the sound of a motorbike coming down the long drive to Dearden Hall. She went to the window.

"It's Harry, back from seeing Esma," she said. Rowan liked Harry's readiness to smile and his light-hearted attitude to life. She was pleased Esma and Harry were seeing each other.

"She'll be coming back on the pillion with him one of these times," Dearden said. Esma, originally Rowan's handmaid, had changed. She grabbed twenty-first-century life with both hands. It had given her a delicious sense of freedom. Dearden was explaining what a pillion was to Rowan when Harry came into the Great Hall.

"You're just in time to come with me, Harry."

"Where to?"

"To find Bill. He phoned well over an hour ago and said he had something urgent he needed to talk through with us, but he hasn't arrived."

"He might have broken down."

"Maybe, but I doubt it with the way he keeps that old car of his serviced. I don't like it, Harry. We'd better get moving."

"I'm coming with you," Rowan said.

Dearden looked at Harry and shrugged as she ran upstairs. They heard hangers sliding along the rail in her wardrobe and she came down in a black leather jacket, red scarf, jeans and trainers.

"I'm ready," she said. Dearden never ceased to be attracted to Rowan. It was mutual. They gave each other a slight flash of the eyes. Dearden went to the sideboard and unlocked a steel lined drawer containing his 9mm Beretta. He checked the magazine and put a spare box of cartridges in his pocket.

He put on a heavy jacket after he noticed the yellow colour of the sky through the window. The weather forecast had mentioned snow.

"OK, let's go."

Dearden knew Templestone disliked Motorway driving because his eyes and his road craft weren't what they used to be. Because of that, Dearden anticipated he would take the most direct country route from Radway because of the urgency of his news. That would take him through Moreton Morrell, Warwick and then Knowle.

*   *   *

Rowan was up front in the Range Rover with Dearden. Harry was in the back. They were approaching the turn leading to Moreton Morrell when they saw Templestone's Morris Minor Traveller at the pull-in at the side of the road.

Dearden skidded to a halt by Templestone's vehicle, leapt out and looked through the window of the car. Rowan and Harry were out just as quick. There was no one inside, and the Morris was unlocked. Dearden called out toward the woodland but there was no answer other than the echo of his voice.

"The keys are still in," Harry said.

"I've seen them." Dearden took the keys from the ignition and walked round to the side of the car nearest the scrub leading into Wiggerland Wood. Rowan came up close. She tapped the pocket where she had seen him put the Beretta.

"You may need that," she said.

He nodded. "If Bill stopped for a leak he wouldn't have gone far into the wood. We'd better see if he's in there."

9

Templestone looked around the old stable and started assessing the security of the building. He looked for a way to get rid of the rope that bound his wrists behind him. There was a hefty knot where it was tied to the ring on the wall. With his hands tied behind his back he was unable to reach high enough to undo the knot. There were a few narrow grimy windows about a foot in height and three feet wide near the ceiling. Swathes of dusty cobwebs hung over them. The meagre light filtering through the grime picked out a few of the details in the stable.

There were the wooden partitions, fixed at right angles to the back wall, forming stalls where horses had at one time been tethered. Trampled down straw was still strewn over the floor and a large cartwheel with a metal rim was resting upright against the boards of the stall where he had been secured. His eyes looked past it to the door. The light was shining in from outside through gaps between distorted planking. On his way in Templestone had assessed the strength of the door. The grain of the planking had opened up because the layers of protective paint had flaked off and the cycles of rain and sun had weakened the timber. A swift kick would separate the planks from the rails and braces, so his escape would be easy, once he was free from the rope.

He looked for what he could use as a weapon. There were some rusty nails; panel pins that were too small to do any damage. They were on a shelf created by an extra thickness of brickwork built up against the wall to a height of about four feet. An engineer's file lay on top of the bricks. It was further along than the nails and was out of reach. The file was rusty, but promising as a weapon and it could be lethal. It looked about twelve inches long including the pointed tang. Bill, who was an engineer, recognised the cutting surface of the tool, which gave it the name of a bastard-cut file. He smiled at the name.

He looked past the cartwheel. A wooden peg protruded at an upward angle from a vertical beam at the end of the wooden stall where he was tied. Hooked over the peg was a large leather collar, probably once used by a draught horse. A length of rusty chain forged with large links and swivels was hanging on the same peg. It would have some force if he swung it onto Wilde's head. There was enough equipment lying about that he could use. The bastard file, with its pointed tang, would do as his primary weapon. The chain would do in his other hand, in case two came in through the door.

He had to escape from the rope tying his wrists. He analysed his immediate surroundings and did a double take on the metal rim of the cartwheel. The metal band around the rim was thin in places, heavily abraded during its time on the roads. The corner of the metal was sharp, well able to slice through the rope and he could reach the cartwheel easily.

Templestone stood and went up close to the cartwheel. He examined the corner of the iron band where the flat met the edge. In places it was razor sharp. He gauged the portion of the iron band that was at the height of his wrists, turned his back to the wheel and felt for the edge with his left forefinger.

As he started to saw through the rope it reminded him of the time Dearden had done the same thing on a SHaFT mission in Tierra del Fuego. There had been a sharp piece of protruding rock and Dearden used it to attack the rope binding his wrists. It had taken him some time to cut through it and then he had come over to Templestone.

"Priest, it's your turn now," Dearden had whispered in his ear. It took five minutes for Dearden to undo the ropes and for them to escape in a stolen helicopter with Templestone at the controls. This time there was no Dearden and no helicopter.

The cutting was going well until he heard footsteps coming over from the house. He crept over to the wall at the back of the stall, settled down and looked unconcerned.

The chain securing the door rattled. Templestone imagined they sounded like the description of Marley's Ghost dragging his chains of torment in Dickens' book, 'A Christmas Carol.' He smiled at the thought and the humour of how he could use it to his advantage. How his voice would sound outside the door. He moaned from deep down in his throat, thinking himself to be Marley's ghost moaning to the accompaniment of the rattling chains. Scrooge had been petrified waiting for the spectre approaching the other side of the door to enter his London garret. Whoever was outside the door to the stable would wonder what it was they held captive inside.

Crowe had sent Garth Wilde to the stable to see if the prisoner was softening up. He was fumbling with the padlock when he heard the animal noise inside the stable. Wilde hesitated and looked behind him. It didn't help that he kept visualising the man he had killed lying at a grotesque angle in the bathroom. He could shake neither the memory nor the guilt.

The prisoner in the stable frightened Wilde. The man gave the impression he was in charge even though he was tied up. What gave Wilde the creeps were the feelings of hatred he could almost grab hold of coming from the prisoner's eyes.

Wilde hesitated as he put the key in the padlock. He turned it. The chain dropped free and he took a deep breath. His heart was hammering as he opened the door with sufficient gap to look inside. He peeped at the prisoner, sitting in the semi-darkness with his back to the wall, and there were the eyes again. Wilde fancied the man was looking inside him.

"What do you keep bloody staring at?" he challenged.

"You," Templestone replied, "And how weak you are. Cowards run from their crimes at night and last night you ran after you killed Sancerre."

"I didn't mean to kill him—"

"You did . . . and I know your type, runners. I avoid them like the plague."

"What is it you want?"

"Your name . . . do you have a name, or are you a no-one, as well as a man with no guts?"

"Wilde . . . I'm Garth Wilde," he said, uncertainly.

"Wilde . . . Mmm." Templestone's voice softened as he played the man. "Garth, what were you looking for in Sancerre's house?"

Wilde sniffed. "Crowe's seen some information about a valuable old record in Temple Balsall."

"And you went to find it . . . but didn't." The harsh voice again, "You're a failure, Wilde. You didn't find what you were looking for and you killed a defenceless old man." Wilde's face betrayed his inner torment. "Work with me Garth and I'll see what I can do. On the other hand, work against me and you'll end up dead." Templestone nodded his head. Wilde looked at Templestone and then his fear of Cyrus Crowe generated some resolve.

"Hold on. You're here because you saw me at the house, simple as that."

"Wrong again. I didn't see you." Templestone looked at the door when he heard someone approaching. A broad shaft of sunlight illuminated the floor and a shadow passed into it. The individual whose shadow it was came through the door. He had a wiry frame. His voice gave away that he originated from London. It was Crowe, and he asked Templestone his name,

"My name?" Templestone made Crowe wait for his response. The answer came in a quiet voice. "My name . . . is Death." Crowe frowned as he tried to take in what the prisoner meant. Templestone saw the frown. Score, one-nil, the rule applied, uncertainty. A wait of a few seconds.

"Ok, have it your way, we'll establish what your name is later. What do you know about the Temple Balsall papers?"

"The daily ones are delivered in the morning; the evening ones come in the evening. Depending on where you live, the evening one comes through the letterbox between half past four and half past five. What else do you want to know?"

Crowe stepped forward a couple of paces.

"Don't try to be clever with me, old man. I want to know about Keeper's Cottage and the Knights' Sanctuary. There's an ancient scroll hidden somewhere in the Sanctuary and I want it. What do you know?"

"What I know is that it's an interesting legend. That's all it is. The item you're talking about doesn't exist."

"Then why was it that after your colleague from Radway went to Keeper's Cottage last night, a heavy mob armed to the teeth arrived in double quick time. They came to cover something up. What is it?"

"I made a phone call after your thug killed one of my friends and then some other close friends arrived. Like you said, they're a heavy mob. They'll be looking for me right now. Do you know something?"

"What?"

"They won't stop until they find me. Oh, and by the way, they'll be armed to the teeth again and lethal." Crowe's eyes flickered away from Templestone's and settled on the window high in the wall to the right of where Templestone was sitting on the floor. Templestone saw his Adam's apple move as he swallowed. Score, two-nil. The rule applied, fear.

Crowe tried to cover it up. "OK, old man, have another few hours on your own to think about whether you've got a future and then maybe you'll start talking. I want to know about the scroll in the Knights' Sanctuary. It may be sooner, or it may be later that one of my men will come and pay you a visit. Big Al, they call him. Oh, by the way, he's barn-door big with a lousy temper . . . and he's got a sadistic streak."

10

Dearden called again. His voice echoed into Wiggerland Wood. He loathed to leave the layby and Templestone's car, but it was almost an hour since they left Dearden Hall.

"He's not here Jem," Harry called, from a path some forty yards away.

"I'll take another look at his car," Jem called back. And then to Rowan, quieter, "We might see something that'll tell us where he's gone."

Dearden unlocked the Morris and got in behind the wheel. Rowan went to the passenger side and got in. She looked round and seeing nothing she opened the glove box. There were a user manual and an envelope with documents in it. She gave them to Dearden to look through. They were receipts for repairs. He remembered that Templestone's Smith and Wesson was missing from the gun cupboard and that he had a gun safe fabricated out of quarter inch steel plate welded to the underneath of the passenger side foot-well of the Morris. A hinged lid to get into it was under the carpet.

"Can you pull the carpet up from under your feet?"

"What are we looking for?"

"Bill's gun safe. It'll be easier if you get out of the car." Dearden leant over her and released the door catch. He was conscious of Rowan's shapely legs and the scent of Dior. She got out, gripped the edge of the carpet and pulled. Under the carpet, there was a steel plate with a lock barrel let into it. Dearden sorted the key out from the bunch and opened the lid. The Smith and Wesson was there. Lying at its side was the metallic object Templestone had taken from Sancerre's hand. Rowan picked it up.

"What's this, Jem?" He took the object and turned it over in his hand. It was heavy for its size. It was intricate and the makers must have used the lost wax process for making it. One end had a bigger diameter, he could see a pattern on the surface comprised of a text he vaguely recognised. The opposite end was smaller and had sturdy looking projections around its diameter.

"It looks like a key, and it's made of gold."

Rowan tested its weight and nodded. "What would it unlock?"

"No idea. It's nothing to do with Bill's car." Dearden put it deep in his pocket.

He had an uneasy feeling that Templestone was in bad trouble because he always played safe with his S&W. If he left the car he always removed the weapon.

There was a call from the front of the car. Harry signalled to them. He was bending down, examining the gravel. There were wide skid marks. Harry stood and followed the marks, walking the length of the layby. There were tyre burns on the tarmac where the vehicle sped onto the road in the direction of Warwick.

"That's someone who didn't want to hang around. I'd lay a pound to a penny Bill was with them—"

"And the vehicle's seriously dropping oil," Dearden said, as he touched a patch of oil soaking into the gravel where the vehicle had been stationary. There were drips of oil every couple of yards as it left the layby. "If there are tyre burns and oil spill here, there may be more in the direction they've gone. We might have a trail to follow."

"Maybe Red Cloud can help us follow the trail," Rowan said.

"Maybe so, and we need to get Templestone's car back to Dearden Hall." Dearden keyed his mobile phone and rang Red Cloud. It was Possum Chaser who answered.

* * *

Harry took Templestone's car back to Dearden Hall and parked it inside the walled courtyard. He called out to Gil Heskin that he was back as he came through the front door and went up to his room. He turned on the television and caught the highlights of the Midlands News. A reporter was in Dark Lane off the road leading to Hockley Heath and he was relating how a woman out walking her dog had come across the body of an elderly man floating face down in the water under a bridge over the Grand Union Canal. Harry took a deep breath and turned cold.

He flew downstairs to the room Gil and Frieda Heskin used during their working day. As he burst into the room Frieda dropped a cup she was drinking from. Gil turned with a fist raised within a split second of hitting Harry, thinking he was an intruder. These days he was prepared for odd things to happen at Dearden Hall. They were watching the news report Harry had seen. Heskin lowered his fist. First reports from the police stated that it appeared the victim had been beaten to death. Because of the nature of his injuries the elderly man's identity was uncertain. They were asking for the assistance of the public.

Harry was pale and jittery. "It may be Bill. We think he's been kidnapped. Now there's a man been found dead near Warwick." He pointed at the television.

"OK, slow down . . . sit down and tell us what's going on." Gil listened as Harry told him about Templestone's disappearance somewhere around Wiggerland Wood.

"Jem's getting Red Cloud to help him follow a trail of oil and rubber from the vehicle we think Bill was kidnapped in. It's on the Banbury to Warwick road. This has got me really worried Gil."

"We're not certain it is Templestone in the canal," Heskin said. "So cool down. In the meantime, let's get Mitch Doughty involved. Leave Jem out of it while he's trying to find Templestone."

*   *   *

Doughty was at his house in Warwick's Mill Street after a strenuous few hours capping off a roof with ridge tiles on a restoration in Fillongley. He and Matt Roberts were enjoying a Thai takeaway and discussing the next day's work when Doughty's mobile phone rang. It was Harry Stanway.

"Look at the news Mitch . . . the local news on ITV, quick, look at it." Harry had launched straight into the conversation without introduction, but Doughty recognised Harry and detected the urgency.

Doughty grabbed the remote. "OK, switching on now." The news report that spooked Harry was still on. "What's the panic?"

"Let the report finish, then I'll tell you," Harry noted the phone number the Chief Inspector from Warwickshire Constabulary gave to ring if anyone had information.

When the report finished Harry told Doughty that Templestone had gone missing, possibly kidnapped and that they had found his car with the keys still in the ignition.

11

The edge of the iron band on the cartwheel sliced through the last fibres of rope. Templestone undid the knots holding the remains of the rope on his wrists. He went over to the wall at the back where the bastard-cut file was lying on the brick shelf. He picked it up and felt its weight. There was some concrete at the base of one of the vertical beams supporting the roof timbers. If he had time, he would use it to sharpen the tang of the file. He stuck the tool into the back of his belt, tang downwards and left the chain on the peg until he needed it as a weapon.

Now he was free Templestone could walk around the stable to see what he could use to help him escape. There was the electric light hanging from the ceiling near the doorway. He looked at the door and smiled. An old chair in a corner at the far end of the stable would help. He carried it so that it was under the plastic trunking which carried wires to the light bulb. He climbed onto the chair, pulled off the capping, and flung it to the back of the room out of the way for when the action started.

The feeble light was enough for him to see the two wires, red and black, powering the bulb. He stepped from the chair and turned the light switch off. The light coming through the windows high up was sufficient for him to see by. He went back to the chair, reached up to the red, positive wire and tugged. The screw holding the bared end of the wire into the terminal was slightly loose and the wire came away easily from the lamp holder. He did the same with the black wire.

Templestone walked to the door holding the wires. He analysed the inside part of the iron lever that someone outside the door would grab hold of and press down to enter the stable. He pulled some of the old rubber insulation off the positive wire and twisted the bared strands tightly around the lever of the door-catch. He tested the result, moving the lever up and down. The wire held fast.

The metal sheeting on the outside of the door to reinforce the weakened timber was held on by bolts. The threaded ends were protruding inside the door. He separated the bared negative strands, placed them each side of the bolt and twisted the ends together tightly.

He turned the light switch back on, backed away from the door and put the chair out of the way so that it wouldn't impede the battleground. He went to the concrete at the base of the beam near to where he had been tied, spat on it and started to hone the tang of the file to make it needle-sharp.

Templestone sat on the floor and leaned against the wooden partition, waiting. There would be warnings. He would hear footsteps approaching over the gravel outside. According to Crowe, it would be Big Al, who had a sadistic streak and liked dishing it out. The chain would rattle and then . . .

Templestone fingered the bastard-cut file and felt its renewed point. It pricked his thumb satisfactorily, but he went over to the concrete and passed the time by honing the tang still further. First one face of the rectangular section, then the next.

He felt the balance of the crude weapon and could tell where to hold it for best effect. He noticed the remnants of horse faeces on the floor, so he dragged the sharp point through the debris to poison it.

*   *   *

"What do you want to find out?" Big Al Innis asked Crowe. Innis' muscles were tight under his sweatshirt. He had recently worked out and stunk of sweat. His biceps were a similar size to Cyrus Crowe's thighs.

"I want you to find out where the scroll is that's mentioned in the research papers I found in the old White Star Line trunk. It's got something to do with the Knights' Sanctuary in Temple Balsall. Get the old man to tell you what he knows about the founding documents of the Knights Templar. Anything about the background of the place will help but frighten him so he talks."

Innis caught his reflection in the full-length window in the side of the house as he walked by it. He turned side-on to admire his physique. With power lifting, he could beat most men. With throwing the hammer, he was almost up to national level. His brain had a tunnel mentality, which focussed on his body and the extra kilos he could add to the bar he was going to lift. He gazed at his shoulders, the packed muscles, and felt invincible as he continued walking to the stable to persuade the prisoner to talk. He heard the four by four starting up, with Crowe in the passenger seat driving away with Dan Blundell at the controls and Bernie Crosher in the back. Innis reached for the chain securing the stable door and shook it.

"Come and get it you old bastard," that was the way Innis liked it. He imagined the man quivering inside, ready to beg for mercy, dreading the opening of the door and the powerhouse of a man coming in who would give him pain in all possible ways.

Templestone heard the footsteps coming toward the stable and the shout outside the door. He stood, muscles relaxed, ready. Innis grasped the handle and thumbed the latch.

The door was old and distorted and it caught on the floor. It needed force to get it open. Innis put his hand on the metal sheeting and two hundred and forty volts from the mains locked his grip onto the door catch. His consciousness numbed and there was a buzzing noise deep in his head. An animal-like roar came from inside the stable, the door shattered and smashed into his leg. There was instant pain and he lost consciousness.

Inside the kitchen, Garth Wilde was preparing some food and a drink, when he heard a crashing noise outside and another noise that made the hairs lift on the back of his neck. He dropped the avocado he had cut in half, held the knife tight and raced to the door leading to the courtyard. The stable door was lying in bits and Innis was amongst the wreckage. Wilde ran to see what happened. The big man was still breathing, so Wilde looked inside the stable.

* * *

Templestone was pleased with the way the booby-trapped door worked. He waited inside the stable for the next move after he dropkicked Innis. He heard footsteps running from the house, and from the shadows, saw Garth Wilde first look at Innis, then come toward the stable.

Templestone thought of his friend, David Sancerre. He waited for the killer to get close to the entrance and then lifted the sharpened file shoulder high. Templestone drew his arm back and flung the bastard-cut file at Wilde's shoulder.

"That's for Sancerre," he said, as the weapon struck. Wilde yelled and clutched at his shoulder before he went into slow motion and collapsed onto his back. The weapon had found the soft area below Wilde's clavicle and was well embedded. The two wires Templestone had attached to the door were still live and they sparked when they touched as they swung back and forth across the dry straw.

A few weeks previously, Bernie Crosher noticed that the bulb in the stable wasn't working. The mains fuse to the circuit had blown. Thinking he was doing the right thing, he repaired the fuse with the thickest wire he could find. When the wires Templestone used to electrify the door touched and arced, Crosher's makeshift fuse failed to blow and the tinder-dry straw caught fire.

The breeze through the door fanned the flames and the straw blazed. Templestone hated the idea of dying in a fire, so he dragged the two injured men clear of the burning building and made off over the courtyard.

12

Templestone saw woodland on the other side of the approach road to Alderhanger. He looked back at the stable, which was well ablaze, bent down to tie a loose bootlace and headed off across a lawn toward the trees that would give him good cover. He glanced at the sky, which looked ominous and had the colour of coming snow and as he walked away from the fire he felt the penetrating cold. The conditions were far from ideal. He couldn't risk walking on the open road because of the threat of Crowe and the others returning. They could be cruising the nearby roads and may be back anytime, so he decided to walk through the woodland and the fields for a while in the direction toward Hampton in Arden, and then maybe he could hitch a lift.

A thought occurred to him and he fished around in his pocket, stopped momentarily at the Alderhanger boundary hedge where he affixed a piece of card, and then he pushed his way through a narrow gap in the hedge. He checked all was clear, crossed the narrow lane and a ditch and then entered the woodland.

He stopped and listened from the shelter of the trees, He could hear the sound of heavy traffic in the distance and recalled that the traffic would be on the M40, about a mile away over the fields behind him.

Templestone planned his route as he walked, noting the position of the Sun through the gathering cloud. He shivered and walked faster to keep his circulation going. Compensating for the Sun's westerly movement, he could maintain a straight course heading north. He visualised the map and checked the time, eleven forty-eight. North would bring him to the Baddesley Clinton estate, and a large wood.

Just beyond the wood at Baddesley Clinton, he would encounter the main road from Warwick to Knowle. If he crossed that and maintained a northerly direction over the fields he would come to Temple Balsall. Hampton in Arden and his apartment at Dearden Hall would be just a few miles further on. Once there he would acquaint Jem with the developments to do with Sancerre and Temple Balsall and then snatch some sleep. He was feeling tired and there were a good few miles to go, so he strode on through the growing cold.

With the chill in the air starting to bite, he made quick progress to keep warm. The problem was that the pace he set, which he would have found easy twenty years ago, was sapping his energy.

After a while, the sound of the motorway faded into the distance and Templestone came out of the trees. He checked his direction by the Sun's position, now a dull patch of light in the yellowing sky. He made for a gap in the hedge at the far side of a field where there were some ponds, and a flock of sheep huddled together for warmth.

*   *   *

Templestone came to Chadwick End. A stile with three steps set into a hedge led to a pavement along the main road through the village. The only vehicle on the road was a bicycle. To the left there was an inn with a sign saying it was The Wayfarer's Arms. Templestone had been walking over three hours, some of it over rough ground. He was tired and the pub beckoned. He could rest there and get out of the cold for a while.

He sensed people were looking at him as he crossed the room to the bar. He felt for his change, ordered a double whisky and downed it in one. It did its work and warmed him inside. He asked for another double and a pint of bitter. His eye caught his reflection in a mirror behind the bar and he made a half-hearted attempt at straightening his hair.

His face was filthy from what happened at Alderhanger. He hadn't realised how rough he looked. A tear in the knee had ruined his trousers. His shoes and trousers were caked with mud. He thought it best not to sit on one of the cloth-covered bench seats and went to one of the hard chairs by a table, well away from the door. He felt tiredness creeping over him, leant back in the chair and relaxed as much as he could after the recent events.

After a while, two youths, one with greasy slicked back hair, and the other, wearing a studded black leather jacket and large boots, came and sat at the table next to him. He felt their eyes scanning him but took no notice; he was enjoying his drink and the warmth.

The larger of the youths started making a noise, "Pss," and a few seconds later it came again, longer. "Psssss," and then the other youth did the same, "Pss," and they both began doing it in a staccato rhythm.

"Pss."

"PSS."

"Pss."

"PSS."

Templestone looked up. They were grinning at him. "Pss," the big one repeated.

"It's over there," Templestone said. The big one looked puzzled. "You want a piss, it's over there." The big guy stood up, came over to Templestone and stood uncomfortably close. His companion followed.

"Got any money?" the kid asked.

"May have . . . why?"

"I want it."

"Do you?" Templestone looked over at the bar. The barman was washing glasses, taking no notice. Templestone made a show of searching his pockets. He made out he had found what the youth wanted. He stood quickly and turning sideways kneed him in the groin. The kid gasped, doubled up, bumped onto the floor and his companion backed off.

"Want some more where that came from?"

A middle-aged plump woman behind the bar looked up, saw the youth on the floor and smiled.

"He'll be alright, he tripped up; probably smelt the barmaid's breath," Templestone called. He held his hand out to the youth, who flinched, stood shakily and limped through to the toilet, followed sheepishly by his colleague.

Templestone finished his drink and stood to leave. He noticed that one of the other customers who eyed him up suspiciously when he came into the pub, kept his eyes to himself. Templestone opened the door and walked out into a gusting wind. During the time he had been in the pub, snow had been falling in swirling eddies. It had settled and was deep in places. He turned his collar up against the biting cold and put his hands in his pockets.

There was a phone booth further down the road. He went into it to phone Dearden. It smelt of urine and there was no dialling tone. The receiver clattered and swung on the cable when he flung it down. He pressed on along the pavement until he saw a gap in the hedge that led into some fields in the direction he wanted to go.

He looked at his watch. Two fifty-six. All being well he would be in the vicinity of Hampton in Arden just after dark. He pushed through the gap in the hedge and saw that snow had settled in drifts. His legs were already aching, but he struck off again, as fast as he could, in a northerly direction.

13

Dearden was keeping his eye on the state of the weather, hoping the snow would hold off until they found Templestone. He and Rowan were in the range rover with the engine ticking over and the heater blasting hot air. Rowan turned toward the sound of an approaching motorcycle. Dearden looked in the rear-view mirror as Red Cloud, with Possum chaser riding pillion, pulled up in the layby on his Harley Davidson Screamin' Eagle.

"Am I glad to see you . . . didn't take you long," Dearden said, as Red propped the motorcycle on its stand, leaving the engine ticking over. He checked the big machine was steady on the gravel.

"I opened her up on the Fosse Way," Red Cloud said. "Things sound serious, what's happened, my friend?"

* * *

They travelled at a steady pace as Red Cloud and Possum Chaser followed the trail of oil and the occasional rubber burn until they reached Warwick. Red signalled he was pulling in and they dismounted in a layby at a three-way junction. Red waited for a gap in the traffic and went to the centre of the road. He bent down quickly, found what he was looking for on the tarmac and pointed straight ahead to the road leading to Birmingham.

Three miles further on there was a junction with two minor roads, one to the left and one to the right. As they passed the junction, there was no indication that, past a bend in the road to the left, there were police cars and an ambulance with blue lights flashing, and intense activity below a bridge over the Grand Union Canal. Drawn up in fields each side of the road were outside-broadcast wagons with large dish aerials. Access to the towpath at the side of the canal was out of limits to the public. Below the bridge, forensics had a body on the bank under a tent. Officers wearing latex gloves were probing the area for evidence.

A detective inspector was questioning a woman. She was sitting on a camping chair that her husband brought from their canal boat, moored half a mile away. The shock of the moment was still with her and she was pale and distraught. She was pushing her dog away with her foot. It whined and tried to get close. The dog, Jess, a border terrier, had leapt into the canal and swum to the object that looked like a miniature island floating in midstream. Jess clambered onto it, sniffed at what he was standing on, and tried to dig into it like he was looking for a bone. The island was rocking with a gentle motion that looked pleasant until a bloated face floated into view. The woman screamed, which brought her husband running the fastest half mile he had done in years. He put his arm around her shoulders whispering soft words to stop her awful nightmare.

* * *

The trail of oil and burnt rubber continued toward Shrewley, a small village on a crossroad. Red Cloud and Possum Chaser slowed as they came to where there were a few spread out houses to left and right. They had gone a few hundred yards past the village boundary when Possum Chaser gestured to the right. She glanced back to see if Dearden and Rowan had noticed the thick black smoke and tongues of flame rising a few fields away, where a building was on fire.

Red slowed down at the right turn into a narrow lane leading off at a shallow angle toward the burning building. He saw the slight rubber burn and more spots of oil where the vehicle had turned into the lane.

The fire brigade was there with three tenders. Red Cloud and Dearden pulled up at the top of the drive to a square three-storied Georgian house. Rowan spoke the syllables of the name, Alderhanger that she read on a panel in the wall by a pair of open gates. Despite the situation, Dearden was impressed with how she was picking up modern English.

"We're going in," he said. "When we get down the drive, you stay in the car. I'll make some enquiries." He looked at her to make sure she understood.

"Be careful Jem." He was getting used to her concern. He rather liked it.

He spoke to Red Cloud and Possum Chaser and they followed as Dearden motored down the drive. He stopped well away from the activity and walked to a sweating firefighter, who was directing operations. Hoses snaked across the Staffordshire-blue paved courtyard and a crew were pumping water onto the burning outbuildings. Although Dearden was on the opposite side of the yard from the fire, he could feel the intense heat. The warmth was welcome because of the biting wind. He saw ice was forming at the outer edges of where the water was pooling. He looked at the sky, which was closing in and heavy, as the first large flakes of snow began to fall.

Dearden heard footsteps behind him on the gravel. It was Rowan. She didn't intend letting anyone tell her what to do, that included Jem. He shrugged as she stood close by.

"We saw what was going on and wondered if we could help," Dearden said to the fire officer, who had a who-the-hell-are-you look on his face. A Harley Davidson pulled up and the two red-skinned individuals dismounted. Then he took a longer look at the tall blonde-haired woman. He forced himself to turn away.

"We're rather busy here sir. I must ask you to back off and leave us to do our job."

Dearden pulled an identity wallet out of his pocket and flashed it in the fire fighter's face. It was very official and had the signature of a well-known cabinet minister. The firefighter was impressed and began an explanation.

"We don't know what happened at this point. There was a lot of straw in the place. We might find out more when the investigators arrive."

"Anyone hurt?"

"There was a guy who had a broken leg and burns on his hands. Another had an engineer's file sticking out of his shoulder. They didn't say anything about what happened but it looks as if they had a set-to and during the argument, the stable was set on fire. The ambulance took them away."

"Anything we can do?"

"It's all in hand . . . unless you know where the owner of this place is. Cyrus Crowe, do you know him?"

"Never heard of him."

"Antique dealer according to the brass plate by the front door."

Rowan shook her head, that she didn't know the owner. She flicked some snow away from her eyelashes.

"One more thing sir, can you leave your contact details in case we need to get in touch with you . . . and your companion?" the fire officer looked at Rowan with lingering interest. Dearden gave him the information he wanted and a look that suggested he should keep his eyes off.

"Any idea when the fire started?" Dearden asked.

"We had the call at eleven forty-five. At that stage, it could have been going twenty or thirty minutes. We got here at twelve."

Dearden nodded, then he and Rowan made their way back to the Range Rover. On the way, Rowan spotted something on the ground near a flower border. She picked it up, looked at it, turned it over and passed it to Dearden. He recognised it from the times he had seen Templestone using it. He always had it with him. It was Templestone's ballpoint pen with the initials W. H. T. where he had it personalised. It was an expensive pen, a Mont Blanc, which was a present from his wife a year before she died and Templestone treasured it.

"What is it?" she whispered.

"Templestone's pen. OK, come on, let's go," he whispered.

Rowan picked up the urgency. "What's wrong?" she asked, close to his ear. Dearden said nothing but put his finger to his lips. He grasped her hand and they walked quickly to the Range Rover. He signalled for Red and Possum Chaser to follow. They overtook Dearden and waited by the gate.

"What did you find?" Red asked. He had seen Rowan pick up something.

"Bill's pen, it's got his initials."

Rowan mentally compared it to the plastic Biro she used the other day.

Dearden turned it over. "Here's his initials, W. H. T. His wife bought it and he takes it everywhere with him."

"Must be very special to him." Rowan looked back at the burning building. She had grown fond of Templestone. "I hope he is safe."

"I'm pretty sure he's safe. I think he may have dropped his pen when he went on the run, maybe even left it for us to find. And there's something else."

"What?" Possum Chaser asked.

"The scene over there, the burning building . . . the casualties, they've got the hallmarks of Templestone. He's vicious when he's cornered."

"I wouldn't like to cross him," Red Cloud said. He walked a few yards ahead to the boundary hedge where he had spotted something else. A piece of card caught in the hedge. He plucked it off the thorn and showed it to Dearden. It was the size of a business card, orange in colour. It had the name Artemis Computer Fairs in bold print across the top. In the space for the cardholder's name was the signature, W. H. Templestone.

"He left this for us to find. This is the direction he's going." Red pointed across the lane to the woodland beyond.

"We must follow him." Rowan made out she was going to cross the lane.

"Wait, there is a better way," Red Cloud said. "We must cruise the lanes to see if we can head him off." Red looked up at the sky and the steadily falling snowflakes. "It will be snowing hard later on. Snow will help us with tracking, but it is cold and we need to find Bill before nightfall."

"I think he's heading straight for home."

"Yes. He's going north. Hampton in Arden is due north. From here the next place he'd head for would be Mousley End, then he would make for Baddesley Clinton and Chadwick End."

"Temple Balsall comes after that, then Hampton in Arden," Dearden said. Red looked at the sky again and sniffed the air.

"Then let's go. We mustn't waste time." Red sat astride the Screamin' Eagle and keyed the ignition. Possum Chaser climbed on behind and they roared off down the lane.

14

Templestone looked at the border of the field up ahead. The hedge, with the gap he was heading for by a large elm, was appearing and disappearing as the wind blew the snow in gusting eddies.

He began to think that it had been folly to start on the cross-country trek when all the signs were telling him that bad weather was setting in and there was a long walk ahead. He reasoned that it was a better option than keeping to the roads with the risk of running into Crowe and his thugs. A taxi had crossed his mind when he was in the Wayfarer's Arms, but that wasn't his way. With men about who had his murder in mind, he would be safer off road. He looked at the sky. The snow was closing in sooner than he expected. A whiteout would present serious navigation challenges but he felt confident. He had faced worse in the past and he was good with navigation.

After another hour, the temperature had dropped still further and Templestone was glad of his coat. It was thick and woollen, with deep pockets for his hands and a hood with drawstrings that he pulled up tight. His nose felt numb and he dug his face deep into the protection of his coat. He felt light-headed and tired. Thoughts of a warming mug of hot chocolate came to mind and he imagined himself sitting in his favourite winged armchair by the fire in the great hall of Jem's house.

He was in the chair and it was warm by the fire. Tomahawk was there. The wolf liked lying by his feet, warming them in unusual companionship between the wild and the civilised. He wondered about being civilised, maybe he was. On occasions he had been far from it, but he had always tried to make sure justice was done. That was why he was part of SHaFT. Whatever the judgment on his past, wild or civilised, he liked Tomahawk. They had got used to each other and looked one another in the eye. Sometimes without suspicion.

Templestone was glad with how things had worked out. He saw Becky, his daughter, occasionally and he had put her current man, Tobias Flint in his place with no lasting recrimination on Templestone's part. Tobias, who Templestone thought was an arrogant sod, had thrust his face too close at one time thinking Rebeca's old dad was a pushover. When Tobias got off the floor he changed his tone, realising he couldn't get the better of Templestone. Becky had looked at her dad's knuckles and asked if he was all right.

Templestone felt in the corner of his pocket. He remembered the thing he had taken out of Sancerre's hand and left in the gun safe under the floor in the Morris. It had a curious shape. Broad at one end, smaller and more complex at the other end. It was the first he had thought of it since the incident. There was fluff in the corner of the pocket and he dug it out to clear it. He would have to get the coat cleaned. His hands were cold, so he bunched his fingers and pushed them deep into the pockets as he walked on and came to another field boundary.

His feet were cold but he could do nothing about them so he kept walking. *If you're going through hell, keep going*, old man Churchill had said in the darkest of times. They did keep going and they won out in the end. Team spirit, that's what it was,

Templestone thought as he trudged on. Team spirit won out in the end.

Templestone thought of the time at Alderhanger and laughed to himself. "Come and get it, you old bastard," Big Al had said, when he was outside the door after it had been electrified from the inside. It must have been uncomfortable when he pushed open the door and got drop kicked. Templestone had the rusty old file sharpened up, ready for use and the murderer got it. Probably got blood poisoning too, from the old horseshit he made sure was on the end. Templestone grinned, he hadn't lost his touch for the macabre in his way of dishing things out.

The snow was gathering on his eyelashes. He took his hands out of the warmth of his pockets and brushed it away. He wondered how the dog walker was, the one he had met near the moated manor house, who said that the weather was closing in. Too right, it was closing in. He shivered again. The moat at Baddesley Clinton would be cold now, maybe iced over . . . better not fall in . . . he stopped to check how close he was to the moat, but it wasn't there . . . he was in the middle of a field heading north . . . and it was cold enough to be dangerous.

The snow was relentless and the afternoon sky looked ominous, but it didn't matter. It was strange, he was so desperately tired and yet he felt at ease with himself and with the world. It was quiet with the blanket of snow. A blanket. If only he could go to sleep . . . just for a little while.

15

When they came to Chadwick End, the snow was on the ground in wind-blown drifts. It was hazardous and twice Red Cloud nearly dropped the bike. There was a garage where Red asked if he could leave the Harley inside for the duration of the bad weather. A postman, whose bicycle was leaning against a wall in the workshop, was sitting near a ramp drinking tea and chatting with the mechanic. Dearden described Templestone and asked if either of them had seen him.

"I saw a guy who could be your man." The postman glanced at his watch, "About an hour ago." He described Templestone's jacket and said he saw him coming out of the Wayfarer's Arms. He pointed in the direction of the pub and said it was fifty yards down the road, on the right.

"We can assume Bill's OK and that he's heading toward Hampton in Arden," said Dearden, as they left the garage in the Range Rover, heading to the Wayfarer's Arms.

"Must have a good reason to be trekking overland in this weather," Red Cloud said.

"He was in danger, going by the damage he caused when he was escaping. Templestone only dishes it out like that when he's in a corner."

They walked into the pub, looked around for Templestone and went to the bar. The barman told Dearden a man answering his description had been in the pub for a while. He pointed to where Templestone had been sitting and told how the old guy brought a young menace down to size.

"It was impressive," the barman said. "I saw the thug go up to the old guy and was ready to call the law. All of a sudden, the young bloke was on the deck. Made my day, he's being causing trouble around here lately. The old guy looked a bit rough, clothes were torn and grubby. He left soon after the event."

"Which way did he go, do you know?"

"Out the door to the right . . . is he a friend of yours?"

"Yeah, a dear friend," Dearden said, "Where are the thugs?"

"Out the back worse for wear, playing pool."

Satisfied they weren't on Templestone's tail, Dearden turned to go. The Barman studied the tall blond as the group walked out into the snowstorm.

The snow was cutting vision down to a few yards. "Are you game for a search, Red? It'll be tough going."

"Just you try and stop me."

"Good . . . Rowan, it's pointless you and Possum Chaser being out in this weather. Go back into the pub. Stay inside until we get back." Dearden expected complaints. Most times Rowan wanted to be involved, but with the bad weather and the welcome fire inside she didn't argue. She tried to look into the driving snow and flicked some from her eyelashes with the back of her hand.

"OK, we go inside," she said to Possum Chaser. "We have money." She felt in her pocket to make sure and nodded at Dearden. He and Red turned to face the weather and made their way up the road in the direction Templestone had walked.

Red had his eyes to the ground and walked quickly until he came to the gap in the hedge. He stopped and crouched down, saw indentations in the snow the other side of the hedge through the gap.

"He went this way, in a hurry. Come, his tracks are easy to follow at present." They walked fast, and it kept them warm. "Why did they capture Bill, any idea?"

"Haven't a clue. All I know is that Bill went to Temple Balsall. He goes there sometimes to catch up with the folks he knows. Something took place while he was there. He was away all night at Will Pierpoint's place in Radway. Earlier today he phoned to say that he would be back within the hour and had something urgent to tell us. He didn't get back, and we found his car abandoned, you know the rest."

"Anything happen recently that made him go to Temple Balsall?"

"Not that I'm aware of."

Red grimaced and was silent as they trudged on through the snow.

In the Wayfarer's Arms, Possum Chaser ordered a Gin and Tonic.

"OK, and your lovely friend, what does she want?"

"What do you want to drink Rowan?"

"I want the Meduwyrt." She tried to make it easy for him, telling him the name of the herb used in making the drink.

"What was that?" he didn't know if he heard right with the girl's accent. He tilted his head to hear through his better ear.

"Meduwyrt!" Rowan said louder. She sounded exasperated. "Give me pen, and to write on."

The barman passed pen and paper over and Rowan wrote out *Mead*. She passed the sheet of paper back and didn't like the way the man the other side of the counter was leering at her.

"Why don't you try sweet sherry," Possum Chaser suggested.

Things were getting complicated and she wanted to get away from the barman's eyes.

"Alright, give me the sweet sherry, I try." The barman poured one and put it in front of her, hoping she'd drink it quickly and have another. He would like to see her drunk.

"Is that all you give me?" Rowan looked derisively at the small glass on the bar. "Give me more." She was used to mostly drinking alcohol and was hardened to it. The barman got a schooner and poured, thinking the session was going to be fun with the ditzy blonde.

* * *

"He's come quite a distance," said Dearden, as Red cloud pointed out more footprints, just slight indentations that fresh snow had almost covered.

"He has good stamina for an old un," Red cloud said; but he had noticed Templestone was getting tired and probably confused. The stride was getting shorter and irregular. Red stepped up the pace.

The snow was deep in places where it had drifted and it muted sound. There was no echo of birdsong, no distant noise. The wind and driving snow had abated but Dearden was sweating with exertion. On the other extreme, his feet were numbing with the cold seeping through his boots. There was an old brick building with the roof partially caved in two fields away in the direction they were going. As they got close to it they heard the door creaking as it moved.

They knew Templestone was in there because the trail of footprints circled the building and didn't continue over the field. There was compressed snow outside the swinging door.

Templestone had been through a lot in his life. He was a fighter and he had been a survivor through the worst of circumstances. Dearden didn't speak his thoughts to Red Cloud, but he prepared himself for the worst. As they entered the ruin they could see Templestone huddled in a corner on the earthen floor. Dearden rushed to his side.

"Bill . . . thank God we've found you." He placed a hand on his cheek. He was stone-cold.

Dearden felt the chill of the place sink in. He placed his fingers on the side of Templestone's neck, searching for a pulse. His skin was warm under the jacket and there was a flicker of a pulse. Dearden took his own coat off, placed it around Templestone and shivered. He began rubbing his limbs to get the circulation going. There was slight movement in Templestone's hands.

Dearden went outside and paced the ground, checking that it would be level enough for a landing. He shivered again as he fumbled with the keys on his mobile phone and dialled the emergency number for Jack Green and Bob Mallett, the SHaFT medics. They would be on standby ready to fly the Eurocopter anytime to aid whoever of the SHaFT team were in difficulties. Dearden described their position; it was clear of obstructions, no trees, no fences. A hedge to avoid near to the old brick building where Templestone found shelter. The snow was a foot deep in places, no more.

"I'll mark the landing area," Dearden said to Mallett, and then he gave him their co-ordinates.

Twenty minutes later they heard the twin Turbomeca Arriel turboshafts of the helicopter as it approached at speed. Leaving Red rubbing Templestone's limbs, Dearden went outside and waved his arms. His blue jumper stood out against the white backdrop of snow and Mallett could see the area Dearden and

Red Cloud had marked out with branches they dragged from the hedge. The anaesthetist-pilot guided the machine in, and the engines spooled down.

16

On the way back from quoting for the clearance of a large house, Crowe, Blundell and Crosher called in at the Wayfarers Arms at Chadwick End and stayed there a while to warm up over whisky. Crowe had no idea how close he had been to the man he thought was tied up in the old stable at Alderhanger. Maybe, with the mood Templestone had on him, it was a good job they didn't meet up.

After they had passed through Shrewley, Dan Blundell, at the wheel of the four by four, noticed a glow in the sky from a large fire. He pointed it out and as they covered the last couple of miles Crowe's suspicions grew and his mouth became dry. They pulled up in the drive before they got to the car park. Crowe gazed nonplussed at the scene. The outbuildings were a burnt-out shell, and the paintwork of the previously glossy back door of Alderhanger, painted just over a week ago, was scorched and blistered. Crowe's face was ashen as he stepped from the vehicle.

After the initial shock, he felt the rage coming from within and targeted the officer in charge who was standing by two men operating a high-pressure hose. Other fire officers were working around the site, examining what was left of the buildings. As he approached the chief, his fists were opening and closing in a threatening manner. The officer told him to calm down.

"I presume you're the owner of the house, sir?" Crowe nodded he was. "Two men were injured here, we think they had a go at each other and started the blaze by accident. They ended up in hospital."

"Anyone else involved?" Crowe stepped nearer to the old stable and craned his neck to see where the old man had been tied to the ring in the wall. He hoped the firemen hadn't found a blackened corpse in the old stable.

"There was just the two, why, do you think there was someone else here, sir?" the fire chief hoped they hadn't missed someone. Crowe shook his head and peered past the shattered door into the stable again.

"What happened to the men?" he asked.

"We don't know the details. One had a broken leg and burns to his hands. The other had an engineer's file sticking out of his shoulder. It was a nasty wound, dirty, according to the medics. They said he would need antibiotics and sedation. He was in a state of shock."

Crowe said nothing and walked away with his hands in his pockets wondering what had happened. Surely it couldn't have been the old man . . . but he did seem weird, as if there was more to him than was on the surface.

"We need to inform the police sir," the fire officer called after Crowe. "There was foul play here and we're duty bound to involve the police." Crowe stopped in his tracks and took his hands out of his pockets. He clenched his fists again. He could smell his burned-out buildings. This was *all* he needed.

"Danny, come here a minute will you." Crowe had his back to the fire chief. His voice sounded clipped when he spoke. "And bring the case, the metal one with the monogram on the lid." He turned to face the fire officer. "Will you come here a minute." The man followed him. When they were on their own Crowe spoke quietly. "What do they call you?" the man looked puzzled.

The men called him Gee-gee. He gambled on the horses, but he sure as hell wasn't going to tell this man they called him Gee-gee.

"What do you mean?"

"Mean . . . mean . . . your name, your bloody name, what do you think I mean?" with everything that had happened over the past hours, Crowe was very short on patience.

"Des Pooley . . . why?" there was a hint of nervousness in the fire chief's voice, a slight tremor Crowe picked up. Dan brought the case and gave it to Crowe. He went off and stood by the four by four. He was used to the procedure. The case he took over was the brushed aluminium one with the shiny chrome clasps. Crowe opened the case so the lid stayed open on some catches. His mobile rang and he feigned surprise.

"Hold the case while I take the call will you Des . . . is that short for Desmond?" Pooley nodded it was. He took the case off Crowe and gasped at the bundles of Bank of England notes, Queen's head uppermost. The case had that smell, the one peculiar to a bunch of paper money, that was addictive when there was a lot of it close by, particularly to a gambler who often lost.

Crowe spoke into the phone . . . it was Blundell and he whispered a bad-taste joke, to Crowe. Crowe sniggered and looked at Pooley. He saw the dazed look on the fire chief's face. The reactions were always the same with this method of entrapment. The open mouth, a lick of the lips, a reaction like salivation over a favourite food. The phone call ended and Crowe took back the case and snapped the lid shut. He smiled and briefly looked at Pooley who nodded imperceptibly.

"Alright lads, time to go," Pooley called out. "We can't do any more here, wrap it up now." The man on the pump shut it down and started to reel in the hoses. Others began to stow the equipment.

"Come in the house a minute Des." Crowe went in through the door that was blistered. Pooley followed and shut the door behind him. "I think you have a need Des," Crowe said, giving the case a slight shake.

"Sort of," Pooley said, catching the drift of things.

"What do you mean, sort of? You've either got a need or not." Crowe was not going to make an offer and incriminate himself.

"The case," Pooley said.

"What about the case?"

"I . . . I have a need."

"Oh yeah, what sort of need?"

"Two grand."

"Are you telling me you need some cash?" a fast nod from the chief, as if he wanted to get the deal over and done with.

Crowe laid the case on a nearby table, snapped the catches and lifted the lid. He took out two grand in fifties and laid the pile at the side of the case then shut it again. He turned his back on the fire chief.

"Get your deed done and get out . . . oh, and Desmond, I may have some work for you. Think about it . . . here's my number." Without turning, Crowe tossed a business card with a phone number onto the floor behind him. He heard movement as the man scrabbled for the card and the wad of notes. There were footsteps. The door opened and then closed gently. Crowe waited until he heard engines firing up and vehicles moving out of the yard.

He moved quickly to the door and called Blundell and Crosher. "I want that interfering old bastard back here. Find him."

17

The medics diagnosed severe hypothermia and wrapped Templestone in a self-heating thermal blanket. After a few minutes, he was showing signs of recovery and Green and Mallett stretchered him onto the Eurocopter. Dearden and Red Cloud shielded their eyes from the spicules of driven snow as the helicopter made a rising turn toward Dump 4 at Kineton Base.

Dearden and Red Cloud arrived back at the Wayfarers Arms. They went straight to the fire where Rowan and Possum Chaser were sitting, one each side.

"We found Bill," Dearden said, "We were only just in time according to Green and Mallett. Another fifteen minutes and he'd have been dead. They picked him up in the Eurocopter and took him to the hospital unit at Kineton Base. I am going to find who it was that took him." Rowan was getting to understand Jem's sense of justice. She had grown attached to Templestone and wanted to be part of the justice.

"The temperature's still falling out there," Red Cloud said.

"Come closer to fire," Rowan said. She moved along the bench seat so that Jem was nearer the warmth. Possum Chaser shivered with the cold that radiated from Red when he sat near her. He reached to the heat and rubbed his hands to get some warmth into them.

Dearden stood. "I know it would be good to stay here, but we have to go. As soon as Bill can answer questions we'll make progress with what happened to him."

Rowan nodded and drained the second schooner of sherry. She slipped her jacket on. Dearden saw the barman looking in her direction. He was pleased other men found her attractive. He understood they would, but God help them if they overstepped the mark.

The snow had stopped as they left the Wayfarers but the sky was ominous and probably still loaded with snow. Dearden headed straight to Kineton Base. Fifteen minutes into the journey his mobile rang. Red Cloud answered. It was Harry. Red told him Bill was OK, that they were on their way to see him at Kineton Base.

"Harry has been watching the local TV news. There's been a report that a man's body has been found in the canal near Hatton village. He was worried sick that it was Bill."

"Harry and Bill are close," Dearden said. He thought of how he felt himself when he saw Templestone on the ground in the ruined building.

Dearden had visitor's passes in the glove box. He stopped in a lay-by near Kineton and gave one each to Rowan, Red and Possum Chaser and they wrote their signature in the space provided. Rowan had perfected her signature, Rowan de Arden. She signed and passed the pen to the others. They signed Anders Wiseman and Shauna Wiseman.

Dearden was sufficiently high in the chain of command to authorise entry. The heavily armed guards at the gate did the usual checks, mirror under the vehicle, boot and hood up. They checked the passes, then lifted the barrier and let them through. Dearden drove around the perimeter road to Dump 4 and pulled up a few yards away from the massive steel sliding doors. He told the others to stay in the vehicle and went to an upright girder painted a dull brown with an intercom at the top.

"Captain Dearden, on official business." Two seconds later, a personnel door set into one of the large doors opened. The two men in full combat gear had taken a call from the security blockhouse about the arrivals. They came out to escort them into the building, one of them stood to one side with an Uzi MP-2, his eyes roving about for unexpected movement. The other man indicated to follow him. SHaFT never took any chances of infiltration when the doors were open.

Dearden signalled for the others to get out of the truck, and they followed him through the personnel door. He told them to wait inside and he went back for the Range Rover. The large doors rumbled open and he drove down the ramp into the building.

Red Cloud was used to modern technology, but what he saw inside Dump 4 for the first time surprised him by its complexity and size. The size of the outside of the building visibly belied the enormous capacity of the interior. The entry ramp, with a barricade each side and a security blockhouse at the bottom, sloped down by fifteen feet over its seventy-foot length. Steps led down from the personnel door into the cavernous underground interior. There were vehicles parked side by side in neat rows. And further on there was a line of six fighter aircraft. In a cordoned-off workshop area mechanics were servicing vehicles that Red could see looked civilian on the outside but with armoured steel and Kevlar panels removed, were hi-spec military underneath.

Rowan was at Dearden's side, looking at the equipment they were walking past. She was used to seeing objects that, to her, had no apparent use. She usually challenged Jem about such puzzling things when they were alone in the evening. She held on to the images of what she was seeing in Dump 4. Later on, she would ask, and he would explain their purpose. Dearden sometimes had to enlist the help of Julia Linden-Barthorpe to explain the finer points to Rowan in Anglo-Saxon.

As they drew level with the aircraft, Red recognised one as a Gulfstream.

"What are they?" he asked Dearden, indicating six fighter aircraft. Red had no idea SHaFT could pack such a punch.

"F16 Fighting Falcons, made by General Dynamics; they were delivered three months ago. They've already seen action." All of the aircraft were painted midnight blue with SFT, and a different numeral for identity on each of the tail fins. No other markings were visible.

Dearden led them to the right, toward double doors at the side of the building with the sign *Hospital Bay* above them. They went through into the small brightly lit interior where a charge nurse Dearden recognised as Chris Marriott got up from his desk and approached them.

"Good to see you Jem."

"Likewise, Chris . . . how's Bill?"

"He's making progress, tough as old boots. He's sitting up in bed and wants to go home, but we've persuaded him to stay for another few hours while we do some tests. Sir Will was with him for a while and he came out with a bunch of papers they were discussing."

"Can we see him?"

"Sure, through there, first door on the left."

They went through a set of doors and into a side ward. Bill was sitting up in bed reading the Racing News. He took off some borrowed glasses when he heard the door to the ward open.

"Am I glad to see you, Priest." Dearden went to Templestone and clasped his hand. "When I first saw you a while back I thought you were dead."

"I was completely out of it. Glad you stopped by. Anyway, how d'you find me?"

"You've got Red Cloud to thank for that. Spots of oil and burnt rubber on the road led us to Alderhanger. Your pen and the computer fair card gave us your direction. Then tracks in the snow led us to you. You left your trademark at the house with the fire and the injuries."

"I'm glad you found the evidence. I thought you might stop by."

Rowan reached in her jacket top-pocket, handed Bill his pen, then kissed him on the forehead. He looked at her and smiled, then bent to the Racing News again.

"What are you doing?" Rowan asked as Templestone clicked his own pen open, the Mont Banc, and put a mark on the page.

"He's sorting form," Possum Chaser said. She moved closer to Templestone and saw the list for Warwick races. "I think Charley's Lad will do well in the two o'clock and Top Money in the three thirty," she said. Templestone nodded and put a mark by each.

"It's horse racing and Possy's a mean tipster," Templestone said. "You get them right four out of five times, don't you Possy?"

She nodded, and her smile had a bit of pride. "Heaven Can Wait is odds-on favourite in the two o'clock, but Charley's Lad, who's a forty to one outsider, will romp home," she said.

Templestone reached for his wallet on the top of a side table and took a ten-pound note from it. He handed it to Possum Chaser and she nodded that she would place the bet.

Chris Marriott came in with medical equipment in his hand and a large hypodermic syringe.

"I'm afraid I'll have to ask you to leave now, people. These tests will take a while to do and we need to get them done now. Need to make sure the ticker's OK Bill," he said, brightly. Templestone eyed up the oversize syringe and abruptly sat very upright in bed.

"If you think you're going to stick that thing in me you've got another think coming," he said to Marriott.

"Don't worry, it's not for you, it's for refilling the ink cartridges in the printer."

18

Templestone spent the night in the hospital bay. He was weary after the events of the day and the tests the medical staff carried out. His mind ran through his kidnap and escape. He wondered what the aftermath of the escape was. The buildings were collateral damage and he brought his combat expertise to Big Al and Garth Wilde in full measure. He pictured Wilde with the engineering file embedded in his shoulder a good four inches. He wondered if the remorseless process of septicaemia was claiming Wilde's body. Templestone didn't give a damn, it would be retribution for what he had done to Sancerre.

Templestone phoned Dearden next day to say that he was feeling fitter than ever, and that Sir Willoughby Pierpoint was going to bring him back to Dearden Hall in the early evening.

"Lay on a council of war for when we get back Jem. We need to sort out what we're going to do about a warning Pierpoint and I have uncovered. That's what I wanted to speak to you and Harry about before those bastards got hold of me. We need a good team with us, including those who were closely involved with the Manhattan mission." Templestone wasn't usually so demanding, which told Dearden that what he was going to reveal was serious.

It was the second time Rowan hosted an evening at Dearden Hall and there were Anglo-Saxon plates of food and sweetmeats on the table. As well as white and red wine, there was also a passable Mead. The sense of urgency was palpable and Rowan knew they were gathering to discuss vital things. Since her introduction to 2008 some months back she enjoyed the fast pace of life, and the sense of justice Jem and the others were motivated by appealed to her own desire for fair play. She wanted to be part of the action and was dressed for it in jeans and a maroon leather jacket she ordered for herself on-line.

In the great hall, Mitch Doughty was chatting to Julia Linden-Barthorpe. Mitch and Matt Roberts had come from a grade one listed restoration in Monk's Kirby. They had showered off the building dust and changed. Harry Stanway and Esma were sitting together, and on another sofa, were Red Cloud and Possum Chaser. Lee Wynter arrived, as usual, loudly; this time in an Austin Healy 3000. He liked Austins. A few minutes later, as a clock in the entrance hall chimed seven, they heard Will Pierpoint's Bentley pull into the courtyard.

"I'm sure Pierpoint and Bill had their reasons for keeping us in suspense about what's going on," Dearden said, as he went to let Pierpoint and Templestone in. They came into the great hall with Arthur Doughty.

Templestone waved off questions about his health, saying he was none-the-worse for his ordeal, but he looked pale and drawn. He got straight into a brief explanation about what happened at the Knights' Sanctuary, and how he found David Sancerre dead at Keeper's Cottage.

"How come you got kidnapped . . . what happened?" Mitch Doughty asked.

"That'll do later. First, hear Will out."

"When Bill phoned me about Sancerre's murder, and that he was phoning from Keeper's Cottage in Temple Balsall, the name reminded me of an incident that happened a number of years ago. At the time, it created quite a stir in SHaFT. When Bill phoned I knew the old threat had re-surfaced and couldn't be ignored this time. I'll explain about that shortly. That we had a murder on our hands notched things up a gear and we had to involve SHaFT. I went with some of the lads to put Keeper's Cottage and the Knights' Sanctuary under lock-down."

Pierpoint explained about the folder in his inherited records stamped Most Secret, that its theme was a coming catastrophe, and that there was a link to the Knights' Sanctuary. Pierpoint put the Temple Balsall folder on the table.

Templestone took it up from there.

"David Sancerre was a great friend of mine. He was the Keeper of the Knight's Sanctuary. The position goes back into antiquity. No one knows the function's real origin, but as far as I know, the role of the custodian is both traditional and functional. David looked after the building as a caretaker, but once he mentioned to me that he was the Keeper of an artefact, a scroll that contains a warning, although he didn't tell me where it is within the Sanctuary."

"Presumably Keeper's Cottage goes with the position of Keeper?" Roberts asked.

"It does. But let's get to the folder Will had in his records. We analysed it a couple of days back and found that it's full of research data. We spent hours working on the notes and we only scratched the surface. In one of the sections of research, its author, a Professor Charles Villiers, writes about an artefact brought to England from the Holy Land after the siege of Acre. It looks as though he didn't want to be too specific about his source of information. Maybe he was protective of it, but he didn't describe it in detail. He does say that images and information, supposedly derived from the relic, are carved into the stonework of the Knights' Sanctuary."

Templestone sat down and asked for a drink. He looked done in.

Arthur Doughty took up where Templestone left off. His accent was distinctly County Durham, pure Geordie.

"A major detail in the research notes is something Villiers calls Nibiru, which he describes as a large planetary body, and there are some A4 sheets of complex math appended to the Nibiru paragraphs, which is why we wanted to get you involved, Harry, to help us see if there's any truth in all this stuff."

It took a couple of seconds for the word Nibiru to sink in. When it did, Harry Stanway stood bolt-upright, knocking his chair over. It clattered onto the stone slabs of the floor and startled the others.

"Let me see!" Harry darted to where Pierpoint had the folder. He pushed his hand away and thumbed the pages over. "This is serious stuff." He took the folder back to where the chair was that he tipped over, righted it, sat and immediately concentrated on the contents of the folder.

"Harry, I appreciate your enthusiasm," Pierpoint said, "It's what we need right now, but there's one matter we need to attend to before you read any more of that." Pierpoint crossed over to Harry, removed the folder from his grip, and turned it over so its blank rear cover was uppermost. He took some printed sheets of A4 out of an envelope and pulled up a seat next to Harry.

"Read this and sign it," he said, handing him a pen.

"What is it?"

"The Official Secrets Act."

Harry signed and handed the document back as Arthur Doughty continued from where he was interrupted. "The upshot of all this is that Bill stumbled into a situation that's caused an old case to be re-opened. Originally, the case came to the attention of the forerunner of the SHaFT organisation. It was before my time and Will Pierpoint's, shortly before the Second World War. With the trauma of the war, the authorities shelved the case. In the seventies, something happened that caused it to be re-opened. We think it could have been a diligent secretary, but whatever the reason, the authorities swept it under the carpet yet again. With some force, I might add."

Pierpoint took up the explanation.

"Maybe Nibiru was too hot to handle back then and no one knew how to deal with what was being revealed. Maybe they didn't believe what they were being told. Whatever the reason, this folder and what it contains has lain dormant since the government forced SHaFT to close the case. A few bits of information about Nibiru have leaked out over the years and they've circulated amongst conspiracy theorists, creating some excitement amongst them."

"What is the catastrophe Villiers said was going to occur?" Julia asked. She wasn't sure she wanted to know.

"Villiers claimed that Nibiru will cause an end of life situation for Earth."

"What?"

Other than Julia's loud, *What*, there was stunned silence. After a minute Matt Roberts spoke up, cautiously.

"If the information in those documents is true what will happen?"

Pierpoint said, "We don't know if Nibiru will miss Earth or hit it. What we are trying to establish first of all is whether Nibiru exists or not. If it does exist and Villiers is right with his research, it will hit Earth and the destruction will be absolute.

There is another thing that by comparison might seem a minor issue. Powerful forces have tried to hush this whole thing up. Because of that, whoever hushed it up lost us a chance of a fix years ago, however slight that chance might have been. I want to know who they are and why the silence. Believe me, they are going to face retribution."

"It's a bit late for justice don't you think, if Nibiru's on its way?" Julia was a realist.

"That may be so, but I'll tell you what has changed. SHaFT isn't the organisation it was in the seventies. We now have some real influence and we're opening up the case again. This time, we will not be silenced. If the human race has reached the zenith of its existence, I would like to think that, at the end, a full measure of justice would prevail. That is what I have fought for all my life."

Pierpoint pulled the notebook out of his pocket. The one he was using to devise the plan he conceived after he first showed Charles Villiers' research to Templestone. "I have a plan that involves two pieces of technology coming together. One of them is taking place on an island called Turaroa. The other shall remain nameless for the time being."

He called Rowan over.

"Jem tells me you know how to write your name now, dear girl. Write it here, will you?" He placed a copy of the Official Secrets Act in front of her and showed her where to sign.

19

" **I** 've got something to tell you," Harry said as he came to the second page of hand written math. The smile, usually a permanent feature, had gone. He dug into his memory, to a television program that captured his interest a few years back.

* * *

At the time of the broadcast Harry Stanway was one of the youngest ever students to gain BSc Honours in both Computational Quantum Mechanics of Molecular and Extended Systems, Electrical Engineering and Computer Science, both from the Open University.

A month after the award ceremony, he had been stretched out on a settee, relaxing after all of the concentrated work. He was watching one of his favourite satellite television channels, 'Conspiracy TV'. You had to be a particular type of person to watch that particular program because most of it was bullshit. The directors of Conspiracy TV planned it that way because the gullible viewers believed everything and bought the spin-offs, tee shirts, baseball caps, jeans and books. The revenue generated from the sales kept the income stream healthy and the bosses pay high.

Of the many programs Conspiracy TV put out, five percent were not bullshit and zero point two five percent of the programs were extremely credible, capable of the most rigorous scientific scrutiny. Sometimes, a few nerd types, the zero point two five percent who had a fixation on the program, dug deep and struck pay dirt. Within hours, the information they found would be all over the internet. The ones spreading that information were usually young men in their mid-teens to early twenties who liked a challenge. They were the sort who could break national security encryption and Harry Stanway was in that category

One of the programs on Conspiracy TV was to be *Planet X, The Great Cover-up.* The producers had set out to gather evidence about Nibiru. Was the heavenly body a myth, or did it really exist in the far-flung reaches of the solar system, or beyond? The presenter of the program, Dick Mansfield, went on to discuss a story that existed in different cultures worldwide about the appearance of a giant heavenly body. He presented plausible information, some of it culled from previously unpublished sources, historical and modern. The conclusion he drew was that the stories were too similar and widespread to be a coincidence. Because of that, he said, they must have a common basis of truth.

Toward the end of the program, Mansfield presented information which implied that Nibiru could present a threat to Earth, the like of which had never occurred before. He encouraged viewers to make up their own minds and to send feedback via text or email. However, five minutes before the credits rolled, what clinched the reality of Nibiru to Harry Stanway and fired his enthusiasm to do further research, were some photographs taken from the Hubble Space Telescope, that the program's researchers downloaded.

The photographs originated from one of the managers of the Hubble Space Telescope program, who streamed them live to Conspiracy TV and television news programs across Europe, America and Asia. Fifteen minutes later, after a phone call in the strongest terms from the Pentagon, he was walking down the road, nervously looking over his shoulder, with everything from his desk in a plastic carrier bag.

The photographs had been on-screen for a scant four and a half minutes and then TV screens across the continents went blank. Dick Mansfield was in mid-sentence, talking about a *Threat from the heavens* when the program was pulled. There were puzzled faces and apologies for the technical hitch by presenters. Afterwards, it proved impossible to get the photographs back, and the poor explanations given on screen smelt of excuses.

The photographs disappeared from the Hubble website too. No amount of searching could find *Hubble's Disappearing Photographs*, as the newspapers put it. *This Page Does Not Exist*, and *You Do Not Have Authority to go to This Page*, were regular 404 error messages resulting from searches on the Hubble website for the Nibiru Photographs.

The hiding of information fuelled conspiracy theories and did not sit well with Harry Stanway. The subject had gripped his interest and he had researched it whenever he had time to spare. The fleeting glimpse of the Hubble photographs, coupled with an animation, had shown what could only be a planet-sized body, on an immensely elongated elliptical orbit, that had appeared briefly on the far side of the Sun and slightly to its right.

At the time Hubble photographed Nibiru, it had also become visible for a few minutes to a group of amateur astronomers high up on a mountain. They were doing some spectrographic research into the Sun's corona and had blanked out the fiery disc. The team were wildly excited when they observed the tiny disc of light to the right of the Sun, which they immediately concluded was a previously unrecorded celestial object. They took photographs. That evening, they consulted catalogues; Messier, Caldwell, NGC and others, trying to hunt down the elusive heavenly body. What they also did that evening was to publish the photographs on their website, exploretheskies.com.

Exploretheskies.com was a popular website. It had thousands of hits on a monthly basis. After the photographs became available for the database of fans, it was soon linked to the *Planet X, The Great Cover-up* program. Theories crisscrossed the internet about the discovery. Sixty-eight percent of those who responded to a poll suggested the heavenly body was Nibiru, and the subject grew hot.

There was anger, disappointment and feelings bordering on rebellion when the interest started to go viral and the exploretheskies website disappeared. Searches produced a variety of 404's and there were even death threats aimed at government officials thought to be responsible for the disappearance of the website. It was *an assault on freedom of information*, was the thought amongst the interested public. This was particularly so in view of the suggestion from Conspiracy TV's Dick Mansfield when he was cut off, that Nibiru posed a *Threat from the heavens*.

However, the Hubble and the exploretheskies.com photographs did still exist in obscure regions of cyberspace. They were accessible to a handful of geeks who were heavily into computer science and had the knowledge to infiltrate the obscure places. At the time of the furore, Harry Stanway trawled the internet in his search for further information. With his expertise and a certain amount of cunning, he got into some shrouded corners of national security where he found information about Nibiru that was banned to the public. He reasoned that if the information was under ban there must be some truth in it. Following that reasoning, he concluded that the fleeting Hubble pictures and the evidence assembled by Conspiracy TV, coupled with the exploretheskies.com information, brought Nibiru out of legend, into reality.

In his research, Harry found references to a legendary cataclysm involving a rogue heavenly body that crossed cultures in ancient mythologies as diverse as Celtic, Egyptian, Hebrew, Mayan and Sumerian. What surprised him at the time was that there was a very efficient cover-up about Nibiru, worldwide. Research hardly pulled up any solid information and that was statistically false. The need for secrecy didn't make sense at all.

At the time of the *Planet X, The Great Cover-up* program, Conspiracy TV's researchers had worked on estimates about Nibiru's passage. They had used mathematics and information derived from a stone tablet found in the site of the ancient city of Carchemish. The researchers concluded that the heavenly object was on a cyclic path that took it in the order of four thousand years to complete its orbit. They peered through their telescopes trying to spot Nibiru and they got a glimpse of it by using the ancient mathematics. They had their instruments trained on it long enough to calculate its speed before it disappeared. By Doppler Shift, they found it was covering 6.8 miles per second.

Conspiracy TV's theoreticians, with the scant information they had from the ancient tablet, calculated that the object could well be of planetary size. Its immense orbit was rogue in nature compared to the other planets of the solar system. They conjectured that it could be an immense comet originating in the Oort cloud, halfway to the nearest star, because it wasn't anywhere near the plane of the ecliptic where the planets of the solar system lie.

The program's researchers had been concerned about the very real possibility of a gravitational slingshot effect that would increase the speed of the heavenly body as it drew close to the Sun. Calculations indicated that it would come too close to Earth for comfort. Due to the length of the program to be broadcast, the mathematical proof, or the Carchemish Effect, as the program's theoreticians called it, was not included in the broadcast.

Not wanting to be silenced after the program was pulled, however, and in the true tradition of conspiracy theorists, the program's team created an independent website with an encrypted address that they emailed to their database of die-hard adherents. In this way, they managed to publish their findings. After he decrypted the web address, Harry Stanway was one of the recipients of the information.

Harry remembered how opinions differed sharply amongst the groups of people who acknowledged the planet's presence. Astronomers who received the information wanted Nibiru's presence and orbital parameters revealed so that they could begin a study of it.

Conspiracy theorists, the second category who watched the program, discovered that highly placed government officials had attempted to ban the *Planet X, The Great Cover-up* program from its scheduled broadcast on television. They were outraged because their right to freedom of speech had been defiled. A leaked memo about *Planet X, The Great Cover-up*, which originated from a Member of Parliament in the UK, found its way to the conspiracy theorists and the memo fanned their flames of anger.

Panic brings disorder, and in this situation where a rogue planet could be in a near miss state with Earth, there would be major panic. If that happens, the population will be difficult to control and anarchy will be the likely outcome. This broadcast must not, repeat, MUST NOT take place because it will greatly undermine our authority.

The glow of anger remained in the minds of the conspiracy theorists, ready for re-ignition with the revelation of the next batch of lies.

A well-known hacker, who ranked high amongst the conspiracy theory set, went by the epithet of King Hack. He had opened up links to a number of sources at the centre of government whose emails he trawled for useable information.

King Hack had, for a number of months, been engaged in posting information onto the internet that was close to the truth about the untrustworthiness of government. The posts had been noticed and the truths stung certain highly placed individuals where it really hurt. As a consequence, the hacker was being tracked by GCHQ. When he started posting about the Nibiru cover up, a man visited him from a building on the north bank of the Thames. The visitor came at night wearing black clothing. A black balaclava covered his face. He had a silenced Browning Hi-Power in his right hand, a skeleton key in his left and he was an excellent shot.

Harry explored the conspiracy theories that the *One World Order* and the *Illuminati* organisations were behind the cover-up. There was no conclusive evidence, just a few shady hints in out of the way places that the silence about Nibiru had powerful backing. Harry was sensible and skirted around the detail because he didn't want to attract attention from the wrong people. He went along with the bare facts that there could be something of planetary dimensions on its way to Earth. It would either hit it or pass it close by.

At the time of the conspiracy program, back in 2003, Harry dragged his astronomical telescope out of storage. It was a simple twelve-inch Dobsonian point and go. It was all he could afford at the time, but it was efficient. A few days after the *Planet X, The Great Cover-up* was broadcast, Harry fitted a solar filter that had come through the post and observed the area close to the Sun's disc to see if he could observe the rogue planet. He had viewed the orb of the Sun for a while and could see the coruscations on its surface, and then there was the faintest glimmer to the right, just a pinprick of light. He rubbed his eyes and looked again but it had gone.

Harry became busy with a new job with the Moreton brothers at Electronic Services. He enjoyed the challenges of the gear they asked him to prototype and he gained good qualifications in his field of study. He regularly used his telescope, trained on the Sun, but had no further encounter with the elusive pinprick of light.

Five years passed and then Bill Templestone rang about the strange building he called the Hub, hidden deep in the forest called Leofwin's Hundred on the Dearden estate. Harry moved in with Jem Dearden to try to get the technology inside the Hub working, and then the Manhattan affair took precedence. Nibiru was in his mind for future reference and he had saved all of the information on his hard drive and on each of three memory sticks.

*   *   *

Harry put the research papers back in the folder and stood up.

"I'd like to borrow this Sir Will. There's complex information here and I need silence while I work through it. At this stage, all I can say is that I agree with you, it looks as though Villiers' research might be desperately important."

He told the others gathered around the great hall about the *Planet X, The Great Cover-up* program and the conspiracy theories described by the program's presenter. Harry said that the information was still accessible in cyberspace and that, in obscure places hidden from the public domain, there was information about a catastrophe, attested to by an ancient scribe. He also told them how the presenters of *Planet X, The Great Cover-up* claimed that the cause of the catastrophe, Nibiru, was heading toward Earth.

"They put the information over exactly like you have from the Villiers papers Sir Will, and they claimed that there's a worldwide cover-up about it."

Steadily and as remorselessly in their lives as are the planets in their orbits, circumstances to do with the ancient threat were drawing Pierpoint, Dearden and the others in the great hall, into events of galactic proportions.

20

Salāḥ al-Dīn Yūsuf ibn Ayyūb, Saladin, a dark-haired, dark-eyed warrior with a ferocious temperament, was encamped with a multitude of his warriors as far as the eye could see along the shoreline. They were cutting off the Crusaders, who were besieging the City of Acre from the sea. It was a siege upon a siege.

Guy de Lusignan, the commander of the besieging Crusaders, had received word that over one hundred of Cœur de Lion's ships had set sail from Marseille. Some months later, when word of the Lionheart's impending arrival spread, the mood of the Crusader troops lifted from despair to that of impending victory. The siege had consumed far too much time and energy, too many men had died. News of the Lionheart's coming with a fleet of ships had put fear into the Saracens and hope into the ranks of the Crusaders, who had been stalled for over eighteen months in gaining victory for Christ. The regaining of the Kingdom of Jerusalem had been within their grasp until the arrival of Saladin. Now Richard was on his way, but they still had to survive until he arrived.

*   *   *

Ramon Tailleur de Pierre explained his idea to the men under his command. Ramon's grandfather had been with the Conqueror when he invaded England and had been close to the Saxon King, Harold Godwinson when he had died bravely in the thickest press of battle at Senlac Hill.

Ramon had inherited the skills of his father and grandfather, that of mining and stone masonry and it was sometimes useful on the battlefield. His forebears had settled in the middle shires of England, where they continued to use the skills learned near Saumur, in cliffs near the banks of the Loire. There, they had learned how to carve caves into the rock in which wine was fermented.

Ramon's father owned a quarry for the extraction of building stone, where agate and carnelian were sometimes found amongst the gravel close to the nearby river at Warrewyk. His father had taught him how to look at an outcrop of rock and gauge the strength of its internal structure and where best to split it to avoid wastage.

"Let me show you how to drive a tunnel into the rock," his father said one day, "It may be useful to you if you join the King on a crusade like I did when I was a little older than you. A competent sapeur is always useful if a building or a wall has to be undermined."

In time, Ramon learned how to work the rock with confidence and to carve it into the intricate shapes of gargoyles and saints. He could also drive a tunnel, knowing that the roof would remain firm above as he worked deeper into the rock.

*   *   *

"Tell no one else about this," said Ramon Tailleur de Pierre to the twelve sapeurs he led who were gathered closely around him. "I have heard that there is a holy object lying within the city and that the food stores there are bulging." Ramon had to speak in a raised voice above the tumult of battle. They were Knights of the Temple and took their belief of caring for their pilgrim warriors from the Samaritan who cared for the man at the wayside after he had fallen amongst thieves. Now Cœur de Lion was close, the military engagement would soon be over and the chance to plunder the holy relic would turn into a half-remembered dream unless they acted swiftly.

"We will drive a tunnel into the city and when we have found the relic we will take it with us to England, where it will bring us good fortune. It is supposed to lie somewhere within the Temple of the Sepulchre, at the edge of the eastern market square over there where the fire is brightest." He pointed to the place where a projectile from one of the mangonels had landed. They had heard the fierce whoosh through the air and then screams of the dying as the fiery ball landed amongst them. "We will raid one of the Saracen's food stores while we are there." The bellies of the Crusaders were empty and the Saracen's bellies were full after Saladin had driven a path through Guy de Lusignan's battle lines and replenished the food stores in the city with supplies from his vessels.

"That is where we will dig," Ramon said and he led the eleven comrades behind the shelter of an outcrop of large boulders, where they would take shelter and hack and hammer their way through the soft rock into the city. He had surveyed the wall and the place below it from a distance, shielding his eyes from the glare of the Sun. At times when the Sun was hot and high, he thought of the cool glades of Warwickshire and an especially pleasant wooded valley with a stream where he had vowed to his wife they would make their home. If he managed to get away from this cursed place, he would build a home there for the holy relic too.

Another volley of projectiles hissed over their heads and crashed into the city. They did not even bother to lower their heads now as the missiles raced close by on their deadly work. The place where he had decided to dig pulled him to it like iron to a lodestone. In the shade of the rocks where there was shelter from the pell-mell of battle, the men set up a small encampment and prepared for their work to take the holy relic from the Saracens.

After planning the tunnel, Ramon climbed to the top of one of the siege towers. Fifty men had dragged it to the city wall where one of the commanders said the stonework was weak. The mighty ram, swinging under the siege tower, had been at work, but the attack failed when the Saracens catapulted Greek Fire over the tower. The dry timber had spit and crackled as it burned. The men trapped inside it screamed and cried for mercy as they died, but Ramon escaped with singed brows. Before the burning, he had seen enough to determine the direction and length of his tunnel.

They set to with strength gained from the hope of God's grace, that he would give them in abundance for saving the relic from the Saracens. Once they were below their destination under the city, they chose night-time for the final breakthrough. Ramon mounted a siege tower once again. From its high level he finally checked the direction and length of his tunnel. He was satisfied it was correct.

Using cloth-bound mallets they struck their chisels when the battle noises were loudest and when night finally fell they hammered their way through the final barrier and fresh air came into the tunnel. They had broken through exactly where Ramon had planned. Earthenware floor tiles with intricate Moorish designs had fallen through as the tools of the men clawed at the earth close to the surface. They were by the side of the wall in the courtyard of a deserted house Ramon had spied from the siege tower. It was a place well sheltered from Saracen eyes.

They took clothing off the bodies of some of the dead Saracens lying nearby and then coloured their skin with juice from berries they had gathered previously. In this disguise, they cautiously looked over the wall of the courtyard.

All was clear because most of the men were at the city wall in its defence, so they clambered over the courtyard wall and split up, five toward the Temple of the Sepulchre, led by Ramon and the others hunting for stores of food.

The Temple was unguarded but locked. One of the men twisted his dagger in the lock, manoeuvred it and the door grated open. They entered the tall building, which was windowless and impossible to search because it was so dark. Ramon sent two of the men to get torches and when they returned the search began for the relic.

The Temple was a store for timber during the siege and logs were resting in a criss-cross fashion on one another and piled high. The building had been disused for a long while because a pall of dust covered everything and they left footprints in the dust as they searched.

They found what they were looking for in a small side chapel behind a stout door that they had to break through. They were filled with reverence and awe as they felt their way into the room, for, beyond the door, paintings of saints adorned the wall. The place was truly holy.

The relic they sought was in the centre of the room resting on a stone plinth. It was a box made from a reddish timber. There was an intricate key placed in the lock on one of its sides. The Templars knew it was holy because of its setting and the decoration of the room. In particular, the carving on the ends of the box, depicting cherubs who were there to protect it, suggested how holy it was. Ramon crossed himself before he turned the key. Then fearfully he opened the lid, looked inside and saw a scroll.

The journey back from Acre had been perilous. They had to put in for repairs at Messina in the Kingdom of Sicily after a violent storm dismasted three of their four vessels. Eventually, after a journey of five months, that had many privations, they arrived back in England and moored up in the port of Dartmouth.

* * *

Three years had passed. Ramon awoke to the sound of a thrush outside his horn-filled leaded window in a quiet corner of England called Belesal. Roger de Mowbray had gifted the buildings and surrounding lands to the Knights' Templars for their services in the Holy Land. Ramon kissed his wife and arose from his cot in the room attached to the Sanctuary.

He stretched and looked from his window at the pleasant land that was lush and vibrant. He saw the beautiful valley which was close to heaven-on-earth. He had culverted the stream deep underground to make the sloping field surrounded by oak and elm undivided to the eye. His haven, and his life now, possessed gentleness. Truly, he had done with war. The building of the Sanctuary had been difficult work. Particularly hard was the excavation of the room deep underground that he intended for his final resting place and the resting place of the scroll.

He befriended an abbot in the Abbey of Saint Mary, in nearby Coufaentree and this man was able to translate some of the simpler words of the scroll. It described a catastrophe that befell mankind and gave a stern warning of things to come.

Ramon Tailleur de Pierre had his likeness sculpted in marble by the most skilful of his eleven companions and he was pleased with the result when he saw it lying on the tomb. His sword was there too, the one with battle scars that he used in the Holy Land. With all of the preparation in the tomb, he did not want his demise to be sooner than necessary, but it was a well-prepared resting place.

The lush land at Belesal where the Templar brothers lived was good for the soul. They had great material wealth from Saracen spoils to pass to their descendants, but the Templars had jealous enemies. Even here in England, people were baying for their blood. Ramon Tailleur de Pierre and his eleven brothers had to preserve the sacred scroll and the Saracen wealth for their descendants at all costs.

21

2009 AD.

During the late evening, after the discussion about Nibiru in the great hall, Templestone had a visitor to his apartment over the stained-glass studio. It was Ellis Hayes, the representative of a group of men involved with the Sanctuary. The understanding amongst the public locally was that the Knights' Sanctuary was a building of historical importance and that the Custodian, who would traditionally live at Keepers Cottage, tended the building and its grounds. Apart from an occasional beneficent gift in time of crisis, given on the condition that the gift was not advertised, that is where public knowledge of the Sanctuary ended.

The individuals who met at the Sanctuary were resourceful and determinedly independent. Their meeting at regular intervals was traditional and functional. Templestone was aware that membership was passed on by bloodline, male or female, generation to generation.

Being a long-time colleague of Sancerre, Templestone was on the periphery of the group, a trusted confidante. It broke the rules, allowing him in at all and Sancerre had sworn him to secrecy, although what Templestone had learnt about the place didn't amount to much. Nevertheless, because he was allowed to learn a certain amount about the inner workings of the Sanctuary, he thought there was a purpose behind what he was allowed to learn. Maybe he was being put to the test.

*   *   *

"An important issue has arisen because of David Sancerre's death," Hayes said. Templestone was on his guard about where the conversation was heading. "The role of Keeper has continued in an unbroken line from when the records were first written."

"What's that got to do with me?"

"Actually, it has quite a lot to do with you. Please bear with me, Bill. The importance of the Knights' Sanctuary can't be overstated. Apart from the fraternal work that was assigned to us upon our foundation, there is a tradition that within the Sanctuary there is some sort of warning written in a scroll that we also guard. News has reached us from a contact in scientific circles that critical times are coming. It may be connected to the warning. The trouble is that we have no idea where the scroll is."

"You have strong connections to the Knights' Templar, don't you? David told me as much, but he was tight with his information."

"We are the Old Order of the Knights Templar. No connection to the modern order formed in 1804. Did David tell you there are twelve of us . . . well, eleven now since his death?" Templestone shook his head. Hayes took a deep breath. "We are guardians, protectors if you like, of an oral tradition to ensure the building and the message it contains stays intact, ready for when it can help mankind in a time of crisis."

Templestone said nothing when Hayes' mentioned a crisis. At least Hayes had explained the reason for the existence of the Knights' Sanctuary. He went to his sideboard, took out two glasses, showed Hayes a bottle of Jack Daniels and poured when Hayes' eyes lit up. They took it neat.

"Get to the point Ellis. Why have you come here?" Templestone looked expectantly at Hayes.

"We have a need for a Keeper to look after the building and safeguard the message it contains."

"I had a suspicion you were coming to that."

"We have taken the liberty to research your family history, Bill." Templestone frowned. "Bear with me and please forgive the intrusion. There are clues that tell us your name has a particular traceability through both your mother's and your father's lineage. Your family has the oldest traceable ancestry in this area. We can trace its roots back to the Knights' Templars at the time of the fall of Acre. Your Ancestor's name at the time was Ramon Tailleur de Pierre, Ramon the Stone Mason, and he was in charge of building the Sanctuary at Temple Balsall. Your name has evolved to Templestone over the years," Hayes hesitated. "Bill, we need you to be the next Keeper, you are the most qualified of us to fulfil the role."

Templestone was silent for a minute or so, until Hayes prodded him for an answer.

"I'll need to know a lot more about it than I do now before I even consider it, Ellis. Another thing, there are some bastards who are targeting what the Keeper's protecting, maybe targeting the Keeper as well. Tell me what's involved and I'll think about it."

"OK." Hayes rested his head in his hands. "But don't tell a soul about what I am going to say."

"Carry on." Templestone didn't let on about developments with the Temple Balsall file in Pierpoint's records.

"Ramon Tailleur de Pierre brought the scroll back from the Holy Land after he went on one of the Crusades."

"Where is this scroll?"

"We have no idea . . . now. Ramon hid it in a secure place for its protection. In later years, probably in the seventeen hundreds, it was examined and a conclusion was drawn that the crisis would be repeated, this information was carved into the stonework in the Sanctuary."

"Who examined the scroll?"

"We don't know now, but each Keeper, if he survives to the age of eighty, retires and passes on the location of the scroll to his successor, which is OK if the older Keeper survives to give the incoming one the information. Back in the nineteen sixties, Dick Martel was the Keeper and one day he disappeared so the scroll's location wasn't passed on to his young successor, who was David Sancerre. Now, its whereabouts is unknown." Hayes looked troubled. "When an incumbent accepts the position of Keeper of the Sanctuary, he inherits a small metallic object, a badge of office traditionally thought of as being connected in some way to the scroll. We have a problem . . . it's gone missing."

*   *   *

The stress of the exposure to the weather when he was on his trek had caught up with Templestone and after Hayes left, he turned in early. His mind was working overtime and he found it difficult to settle. He tried reading for a while; that usually brought on sleep, but read as he may, sleep was evasive. From what Ellis Hayes said about the badge of office, Templestone realised that it was the object lying on his dressing table. He picked it up and examined it. It was an innocent looking object, not very big, but it had a complicated shape and no doubt, a complicated history.

It was a hunch, but in the light of Templestone's recent experience, it seemed that Crowe and his mob had got hold of privileged information about the Knights' Sanctuary and the presence within it of the scroll. He rotated the badge of office between his fingers. Templestone's experience as an engineer told him that the object in his hand was a key. From what he had learned over the past few hours, he guessed that the scroll would have great antique value, which must be why Crowe, the antique dealer, was desperate to get his hands on it.

Templestone put his book down and switched off the light, but the image of David Sancerre kept returning. He dropped off into a restless sleep and had a disturbing dream. He was in the Knights' Sanctuary, the door slammed shut and it was dark inside. He heard a noise outside, a rushing noise that grew into a tornado. He could see a bright light through a gap around the door. He rushed to the door and opened it to see what was going on, ready to fight what was outside. Going past the yew trees surrounding the Sanctuary, he looked up and saw a great rushing globe approaching out of the darkness. The globe disappeared. In its place was a patchwork of clouds, their base picked out by light from the city of Birmingham in the distance against the black velvet of night.

He was startled awake by a scream. His heart was hammering and he was bathed in sweat. He tried to penetrate the darkness and fumbled for the switch on his bedside light, and the owl hooted again, close to his window.

22

Templestone fought through the tiredness and swung himself out of bed in the morning. He was eager to get to the Knights' Sanctuary. In the light of the previous evening's discussion, it was crucial to give the interior a thorough examination to locate the information referring to Nibiru. He picked up the badge of office and zipped it in one of the pockets of his combats. When Dearden gave it to him yesterday from the gun safe in the Morris, he also gave him his Smith and Wesson, which went in the other pocket. It was bulky but had a reassuring feel.

Harry was in his apartment upstairs at Dearden Hall. He was in front of his laptop and had the folder open where he had saved his research after the Conspiracy TV program.

There was a knock on the door and Templestone came in. He saw the open folder and the sheets of foolscap spread across Harry's Desk. They had arranged to go to the Sanctuary.

"Hope you've had your maths head on. That's the math we need you to confirm." Harry shrugged and stood up.

"Doesn't look too bad. Lead on Bill, let's get to it." He slung a coat on, picked up his backpack and followed Templestone out the door.

Dearden, with Rowan up front, was driving the Range Rover. Templestone, Harry and Julia were in the back. The windscreen wipers were on rapid to clear the heavy rain. When they reached the Sanctuary, it had steadied to an uncomfortable drizzle and they ran into the shelter of the porch. Templestone turned the key in the lock and walked ahead into the dark interior. They heard a movement down at the far end of the Sanctuary, just a slight pattering noise like someone putting down something soft.

"Out," Dearden got in front of the others. Templestone's S&W was out in a second and he stood with Dearden, while Julia pushed Rowan and Harry out the door. Templestone and Dearden got behind one of the stone columns built into the wall to support roof trusses. The light switch was nearby. Templestone flicked it on and peered round the column. He could see nothing suspicious.

"Two rooms at the far end, left and right." Templestone moved forward.

"Got it," Dearden breathed. "You take the left, I'll take the right. Dearden had no weapon but could handle himself without. He trod carefully and kept his footfall silent.

They moved down the side of the building, hugging the wall, sheltering behind the columns built into the wall every six paces down its length. As they approached the rooms at the end, they could see each of the doors were slightly ajar.

Outside the doors, Dearden held up three fingers. Templestone nodded and Dearden counted down. They each kicked their doors, left and right and rushed the rooms, Templestone, Smith and Wesson sweeping right and left, Dearden with a forward roll to keep small.

A black cat with a white patch on its face and chest dashed by Dearden's side out of the room, heading toward the door at the far end of the building. Dearden stood quickly and looked at Templestone to see if he had seen the performance with the cat. Templestone burst out laughing.

"Good recovery from the forward roll there, Jem," his older colleague said, the S and W now at his side facing the floor. He wiped tears of mirth from his eyes.

"Bet you couldn't do it as quick," Dearden replied.

They walked back up the centre aisle and told the others it was clear inside.

*　*　*

They took their time on the way back into the Sanctuary, studying detail as they progressed. Templestone saw sculpted heraldic beasts and gargoyles protruding from the stone at the head of the fluted columns and by the window abutments. Ranged along the walls were a great many plaques with incised names and dates of birth and death below colourfully painted armorial shields. The deeper into the Sanctuary they ventured, the older the information on the plaques became.

Rowan, walking down the left-hand aisle, drew level with one of the semi-circular columns supporting roof timbers. She went up close to a flat panel chiselled into the curved surface. There were marks on the face of the panel and she tried to make out the meaning. It was different to the other carvings and plaques, more detailed and finely executed, which was what made her call out.

"Come, look at this," she shouted, pointing to the mason's work.

Harry had brought the cat in with him and it was purring loudly in his arms. It jumped down when he got close to Rowan and the column she stood by. He looked at the circles and lines, trying to figure out their meaning. He traced along some of the lines with his finger.

"I think this is what we're looking for." Harry's voice echoed around the building. The cat had come back to him and was rubbing against his leg. The others gathered around. "See how small the minor axis of this ellipse is? By comparison, the major axis is extremely elongated. I think this dot represents the Sun. It's very close to the end of the ellipse called the perihelion. The ellipse represents the orbit of Nibiru and this dot on the ellipse is the planet itself. This small circular orbit, that intersects the orbit of Nibiru at its perihelion, is the orbit of Earth. The figures and symbols, further along, are orbital mathematics." Harry touched the section of characters chiselled into the stone.

"This symbol represents distance, this one speed." He paused sufficiently for the others to get impatient for what was to follow.

"Those two elements are modified by this expression here, which is time." He stood and surveyed the work of the mason. "This is complex stuff," he said, almost to himself. "Reminds me of some of Newton's orbital work."

"What is this?" Rowan pointed to four words and a date.

Ad gloriam Dei
Anno. 1666

"It's when this information was chiselled into the stone. Whoever was responsible for this work dedicated the information to God's glory, in the year 1666. Isaac Newton was 24 at the time." Harry stooped to pick the cat up. It was purring and paddling its paws on his shoes. "The math on the panel is incomplete. I think it was Newton who saw the scroll and arranged to have the information recorded in the stonework. Probably the stonemason had instructions about what to include and a drawing to copy. But see here, where he made a mess of this part, the detail was too complex for his tools, and the stone's chipped away. I think, if we can find the scroll, it will infer the rest of the equation and shed light on the threat."

Harry stood and stepped back. He took a picture of the carving. Zoomed to macro and took another shot but the first one was better. It had more light and shade, which picked out the detail.

"I want to come back and do a rubbing of this," he said, as he took out a reporter's pad and made some notes.

Templestone walked up the centre aisle and some drops of water landed on his shoulder. He stopped and looked up at the roof, to the discoloured area where the tiles were leaking. The droplets were constant, maybe five or six in the air at a time. Good job they were missing the misericords. He hadn't made a decision about Ellis Hayes' proposition that he take on the position of Keeper. If he accepted he would get the roof repaired.

Considering the constant dripping of water coming from the leak in the roof there was surprisingly little gathering on the floor. Templestone went to a control on the wall and switched on the heating. He would let Hayes know the heating was on and that the roof was in need of attention.

"I have enough to work on for the time being," Harry called across to Dearden.

"OK, let's call it a day. We'll get back home and try to make sense of what we've got."

23

Templestone was silent when they got to Dearden Hall. He was sitting in his usual winged armchair with his chin resting on his clasped hands. Dearden knew him well enough to leave him alone. The signs were that he was deep in thought. At times like that he got annoyed if he was disturbed.

"Can I borrow your notebook, Harry," Templestone asked. Harry brought it over.

"Thought of something?"

"May have done." He picked up the newspaper from the floor where it had fallen and turned to the second to last page. He slid his forefinger down the list, the 3:30 at Warwick. He settled on Gorgeous Water, at 35 to 1. He made a note of it in Harry's notepad. Then he glanced at Cheltenham, the 2.45, Dashing Tootsie was in good form and another outsider, this time at 50 to 1. What the hell, it was worth a tenner apiece.

Harry asked, "What's your idea, Bill?"

"Gorgeous Water in the 3.30 at Warwick and Dashing Tootsie in the 2.45 at Cheltenham.

"Mmm?" Harry looked blank. "I thought it was something to do with the Sanctuary."

"No, it wasn't, but there's something at the back of my mind about that place that I can't quite put my finger on."

* * *

Templestone found it difficult to settle down. He couldn't work it out. Something that had gone on during the day just didn't stack up, so he read for a while, got through a chapter and looked at the clock. Twenty past two. He put his bookmark in place and got up to make a drink. Heavy rain was hammering on the window. Back in bed, he read another chapter and felt himself drifting off to sleep. He switched off the light.

He awoke to a clap of thunder close by. He kept the light off, got out of bed and drew back the curtains. A light was shining from the entrance hall window in Dearden Hall, the other side of the courtyard to his apartment above the studio. In the dim light, the first thing he noticed when he looked down into the courtyard was the torrential rain pooling and eddying into one of the drains.

In his peripheral vision, he caught the lights rising from the Hub in Leofwin's Hundred; active again, he thought. There was always more activity during thunderstorms. He wondered who was passing through this time. The lights faded, and once more he looked down to the courtyard. The water was forming a small whirlpool around the drain and suddenly he knew what had been puzzling him. The water coming from the leak in the roof of the Knights' Sanctuary wasn't collecting on the floor, it was draining away through a joint between two of the stone slabs.

Templestone looked at the time, just after five o'clock. With what was at stake the early hour didn't matter. He quickly dressed, put on some weather gear and ran across the yard. The door to the hall was locked. He hammered the knocker. A minute later a bolt was drawn inside. The door opened, it was Julia, in night gear. Templestone stepped in and took off his jacket, shook it and hung it on a coat rack. The water from it pooled onto the floor.

"What the hell's going on Bill, couldn't you sleep either?"

"Got to see Harry and Jem. You as well. It's all to do with water." Julia's first thought was that Templestone was drunk. He went straight through into the great hall walking a straight line and she knew he was deadly serious.

"The Knights' Sanctuary, Jules, there's a chamber below it. He went upstairs and hammered on the doors to wake the others."

*   *   *

They were at the Sanctuary, those who were there the previous day. It was early in the morning. Templestone knelt on the floor to work out what was happening. It was still raining, although it has eased slightly, but the drips were still steadily falling from the damaged roof tiles, drip . . . drip . . . drip. The water was disappearing down the joint between two of the floor slabs and it shouldn't be doing that. Over all of their years in position, the gaps between the slabs would be filled with stone-dust and debris and it should have gone solid, like cement. The joints should be impervious to water unless the debris and water were falling into a void underneath.

"This is it," Templestone's voice echoed around the large space. He could see his thinking was on the money. The others were close, kneeling, standing, trying to see. "It's hollow under here." Templestone stood and tapped the slab with his foot. "See how the water's draining away?"

"You're right. Let's lift it," Harry said. He had the cat with him again. He suddenly sneezed and it leapt out of his arms and sat a few feet away with its tail twitching.

"I'll get the crowbar," Julia said, walking quickly down the centre aisle, and outside to the toolkit in the Range Rover.

There was only a small gap between the slabs and Templestone was unable to get a purchase to lever the slab.

"Here, let me try," Dearden said. He used his weight to get a purchase on the slab near where the water was draining. He levered and it moved slightly. Levered again and the edge lifted an inch.

"Quick, get something under the edge." The slab was heavy and it dropped. They looked for something to use as a wedge. Dearden levered again. Rowan saw some books on a window ledge. She grabbed some and put them on the floor by Dearden. He used the crowbar again and the slab lifted. Harry forced a thin book, spine outwards into the gap by the lifted edge. Dearden let the slab fall onto the book and sat back, sweating. They did the same again with another book placed on top of the first. Dearden glanced at the spine of the book, at the letters in gold . . . The Epic of Gilgamesh.

Dearden, Harry and Templestone got their fingers under the slab and Julia and Rowan got in close, ready to help. Between them, they dragged the slab out of the way and leant it against one of the misericords.

An earthy smell came out of the hole. The cat went up to it and sauntered down some steps. Harry bent down and saw a flight of stone steps fading into the darkness below. Templestone knelt and peered into the void.

"I'll get the torch," Dearden said, already on the move to the Range Rover.

*   *   *

Templestone shone the torch down and counted twenty steps, fifteen against the wall leading off to his left and the remaining five at the bottom at right angles against the adjacent wall. He thought the room looked about thirty feet square.

"OK, after me," Templestone said, stepping down cautiously with the others following. He shone the torch back up the steps for them. Rowan descended, holding onto Dearden's jacket. When they were off the steps, Templestone shone the torch around. It shone on a pool of water from the leak in the roof, and the Epic of Gilgamesh, where it had fallen onto the second step from the bottom.

A stone tomb with its top waist high and a carved warrior lying on top dressed in the chain mail armour of one of the Knights' Templar dominated the centre of the vault. A cross, still with red colouring, was plainly visible on the tunic and shield. The Knight was grasping a two-handed sword.

There was a name on the end of the tomb. Templestone bent to read it and shone the torch on the lettering, which was still sharp, just as the mason had left it.

"Ramon Tailleur de Pierre, would you believe it . . . meet my ancestor," Templestone stood erect and peered at the granite helm of the knight, wishing he could lift it away to see the features it was hiding.

"Take a look at this," Julia called. She had gone to a stone column, difficult to see in the semi-darkness. It was about two feet square, with its top standing waist high. A red coloured wooden box on top, roughly a foot and a half high, matched the dimensions of the column.

The cat leapt up and sat on top of the box, purring loudly. Its eyes were shining yellow in the torchlight. Harry went to it and picked it up. He could see markings on the lid of the box and at each end there was a carved cherub. They had their wings outstretched as if protecting the box. The carving was exquisite in its detail and Julia gently touched the find. She tried lifting the lid, but it was locked.

"This looks like Hebrew lettering. Bill, bring the torch closer." He came away from his ancestor and shone the torch on the box. Julia got close and examined it in the torchlight. It smelt like cedar wood. There was a cedar wood greenhouse in her garden at Moat Field Cottage in Kenilworth and she recognised the distinctive smell of the wood. "I don't know the Hebrew language, but in view of the warnings of catastrophe, we need to get this translated, and quick."

"We may face opposition if we do that, Jules, judging by the enforced silence from the government," Harry said.

"There may be opposition," Dearden's voice had a sharp edge, "But don't you forget, Harry, SHaFT is on the case. When SHaFT gets onto a case it doesn't give up."

"Nos Successio Procul Totus Sumptus, *we succeed at all costs*," Rowan said. Her eyes flashed in the torchlight and Dearden thrilled at the fire in her voice.

Templestone got close to the box and attempted to focus his eyes on a hole in its side. He had forgotten his glasses, and at times like this he wished he had the clear eyesight he used to have. He passed the torch to Rowan. She trained the light onto the box and the beam wavered slightly and then settled. The area around the hole looked blurred to Templestone, but inside he could see metal glinting brightly. He reached into his pocket for the metallic object he found in Sancerre's hand and inserted it into the hole. He gently twisted clockwise, no movement. There was rotation anti-clockwise to the point where he felt engagement. He turned the key and the mechanism grated open.

24

Templestone carefully lifted out the scroll. Some tools, a stone-mason's mallet, a set square and some dividers, all of which had seen some use, were lying below it. A thin length of a raffia type material bound the outside of the scroll to stop it unrolling.

"This is up your street Jules," Templestone said. She took the scroll from him.

"It may be up my street as an archaeologist, but it's way out of my time zone." She saw writing on the outside of the scroll. Visible although faded were the symbols הַמַּבּוּל. According to Professor Villiers, the scroll was written in ancient Hebrew, it was so early that Julia realised it would likely be written in Paleo-Hebrew. She was familiar with the biblical and modern Hebrew alphabets, but had no knowledge of the language itself. Her speciality was the period from Anglo-Saxon to Saxe-Coburg-Gotha. She pointed to the letters one by one reading from right to left and transliterated the letters, mentally adding vowels as an ancient Hebrew reader would have done. She said the word quietly.

"HaMabuwl, the word is HaMabuwl, Harry."

He nodded his head. "I think this scroll will contain the information that helps us complete the calculations on the column upstairs, we have to get it translated to see where we go from here."

"A job for Trent Jackson," Dearden said.

"And ASAP in view of the urgency," Templestone said, as he took the scroll and placed it back in the box. He closed the lid and locked it. "This box is my responsibility now. The post of Keeper of the Sanctuary has been offered to me. I'm going to accept it."

"Keep looking over your shoulder then, Bill," Dearden warned.

"Don't you worry about that. There's more in this old dog than meets the eye."

"I'll give Trent Jackson a call," Julia said, taking her mobile from her pocket. She looked at the information bar. "No signal. I guess that's not surprising, considering we're surrounded by rock. I'll see if there's a signal up top." She went to the stairs and climbed, concentrating on the screen of her phone when she reached the top.

"That's far enough," a voice barked. It took her by surprise and she dropped the phone, which clattered to the foot of the stairs.

"What's up, Jules?" Dearden's muted voice came from below.

"There's company," she shouted. She was weighing up the person holding an auto assault shotgun a few feet away from her. She didn't recognise him. He was one of three, the other two each held a pistol and their aim was steady.

"Is the old guy down there?" the one with the shotgun asked.

"What old guy?"

"Don't mess me around, the old guy who was in the cottage the other night."

"Jules, what's up?" Dearden's voice was more insistent. He was coming up the steps. Crowe, at the top with the shotgun, saw a well-muscled man of average height appear from the hole.

Dearden reached the top and his eyes narrowed. "Who the hell are you?" he asked.

"We're the ones asking the questions," Crowe said, waving the gun and thinking of his burnt-out stable. He was going to have it converted into an orangery, now the plan was dead. He had people here to blame. A plan occurred to him.

"Back down the steps," he shouted. Julia made a slight move toward him. The fire in her belly was coiling up and Shotokan was unmerciful to those on the receiving end. Down below, in the darkness, Templestone heard everything and felt for the handle of the Smith and Wesson. He eased it from his pocket. In the light coming from above, Harry saw what he was doing. He whispered into Templestone's ear and put a hand on his arm.

"It'll be like a turkey-shoot if you aggravate them. Leave it." The cat was purring gently in Harry's arms and then its tail twitched as if sensing aggravation.

"But that's Crowe and his thugs," Templestone said. His finger felt for the trigger. He could probably get a bead on one of them. But there were others, how many was uncertain. Templestone nodded imperceptibly. Harry was getting some good sense he thought, as he pocketed the gun.

There was a loud explosion that deafened Julia and echoed discordantly inside the old building. The cat's claws dug into Harry's arm and it leapt to the floor. The bullet whined as it ricocheted off the walls below. Dearden saw the violence in the eyes of the guy with the auto assault. At that moment Dearden recalled Arthur Doughty's words during the training in his early days with SHaFT. He who retreats undefeated lives to fight another day.

"Come back down Jules," Dearden said, taking hold of her arm. He was calm but firm. She was prepared to take the three on. She could have won out on two, but time may have run out on the third because of his gun. She turned and went back down the steps with Dearden into the darkness below.

"Turn the torch off," she said. The ones above didn't have a torch and she didn't intend giving them an easy target.

There was a grating noise from above. Rowan knew what was happening and she shouted. Dearden heard the same anger in her voice that he heard when they argued back in Heanton in the Arden, almost a thousand years ago, and yet only months back through the Hub. Rowan shouted again, this time in Anglo-Saxon. The light from above gradually faded as the three above dragged the heavy stone over the entrance. It clunked into place. They heard the far-off sound of laughter that faded as Crowe and his men walked away.

Harry switched the torch back on and the beam penetrated the intense darkness.

Dearden went to the steps. "We'll give them ten minutes to leave the Sanctuary, then we'll lift the slab," he said, as he sat by Rowan.

Templestone went to his ancestor's tomb and sat on the floor, leaning against the end. Julia came over and sat next to him.

"If there's one thing I don't like, it's enclosed spaces, but it's OK if there's an easy way out," she said, looking up at the slab sealing them in. She shivered and leant against Templestone.

"And I don't like your acquaintances up there," she said. He put his arm around her shoulders and drew her close. He thought of how he got out of the stable, how uncomfortable two of Crowe's men must be feeling. Now he was thinking about how to get out of this place and what he would do to Crowe when he caught up with him.

"Tight places don't bother me, in fact, I used to go caving. There was one in Yorkshire; it was newly opened and we were doing the first exploration. We came to a sump and—"

"Oh, shut it, Bill." Julia shivered again.

Templestone grinned in the semi-darkness. "Turn the torch off for ten minutes or so, Harry, while we figure out what to do. You know, Jules," he continued, "I am beginning to hate that man Crowe like I've never hated anyone before."

*   *   *

"That's ten minutes gone," Harry said from the darkness near Rowan, who was holding the cat close and feeling its fur and its warmth. Harry had a habit of mentally counting. Sometimes it got in the way, like an OCD. He didn't know why he did it. It might have begun with learning the multiplication tables when he was a kid. But now it had been useful, ten times sixty, counting each second off, spaced accurately until he reached six hundred. And then he switched the torch on.

Dearden stood up. "OK Harry, let's get our shoulders up to the slab," Dearden went up the steps and examined the slab holding them in. Harry gave the torch to Julia and followed. She shone the torch on the top of the steps and the slab. Dearden slipped his jacket off and bunched it up. He draped it over his shoulders and gave the other end to Harry, to soften the pressure as they pushed. "After three we give it all we've got . . . ready? Harry nodded he was.

They both pitted their strength into it but the slab didn't move, not even a fraction of an inch. "OK, relax." Dearden waited a couple of minutes.

"Let's try again."

Still no movement. Those watching below were putting their effort into it too, willing them to lift the slab.

"It's no good," Harry said, treading onto the next step down, panting for breath. He was in worse condition than Dearden, who was twice his age.

"OK . . . let's rest," Dearden said, going down to the foot of the steps.

"If we shout someone will hear us," Rowan suggested. The church is near.

"No-one would hear us, hardly anyone goes to church these days, not even on Sundays, save your energy,' Julia said."

"Let's give it another shot," Dearden tried to be optimistic and went up the steps again. Harry followed and draped Dearden's jacket back around his shoulders.

"My shoulder sure as hell is hurting," he said, as he prepared to get to the task.

"Forget the pain and put your back to it," Dearden said. They heaved after three. After a few minutes trying they were both breathless. When they were back down, sitting on the floor, Julia switched off the torch.

"This doesn't look good," Harry said, between breaths.

They tried the slab five more times over the next hour, trying to alter their positions for maximum effect. Once, the slab moved a touch, but that was all. Their energy was about spent, so they just waited, sunk in personal thoughts. The only sound was their breathing, the occasional shift of position and less often as time went by, there was a burst of action up the steps.

* * *

"Why is the air still fresh?" Harry said, startling the others when he broke the silence. He snapped on the torch.

"It's a large room," Templestone said, "The air will take a while to go stale."

"Yes, but according to my reckoning, we've been here nearly three hours. In that time, the air should be going stale. There's five of us here, we would be using up the oxygen at a fast rate, but there are no ill effects."

"He's right," Julia said. She stood, suddenly re-energised. "The air's as fresh as it was when we came in. It's being replenished."

"Where's it coming from?" Templestone asked.

"I've got an idea how to find out." Harry had noticed that, with the chilled atmosphere and the hot torch bulb, his breath was condensing into a cloud over the torch as he breathed. He shone the torch at the others and could see their breath in the torchlight. Harry wrapped his jacket around him for warmth, tighter than before.

He stood up and when he breathed into the torchlight he watched his breath floating off to the left. He followed the mist a couple of feet and breathed into the torchlight again. He repeated the process, following the vapour as he exhaled. Rowan suddenly burst out laughing as Harry breathed heavy and followed the mist. Harry grinned as he realised how he must look to the others. He ended up near Templestone, who was shivering, leaning against his ancestor's tomb. With what Crowe had put him through recently he didn't see the funny side at all.

25

Templestone couldn't understand what Harry was doing with his heavy breathing onto the torch and shuffling a bit closer to him after each breath. He thought Harry was eccentric at times.

"Would it be rude to ask what you're playing at," he said, gazing up at Harry.

"I'm finding the way out; will you move out of the way so I can get to the tomb?" Templestone grunted and winced as he got to his feet. His knees were stiff at times these days.

Initially there was minor interest and despite the gravity of the situation there was humour in what Harry was doing. The others drew closer and could see the vapour from Harry's breath drifting to the end of the tomb. It disappeared through a small gap between the end panel and some marble cornerstones that framed it. Julia laughed derisively, but Harry took no notice and breathed once more across the beam of the torch.

"Hold the torch for me . . . someone? Rowan took it. "Shine it here, on the end." At first, the beam floated around and then it settled on the end of the tomb. Harry rapped the stone with his knuckles and took a sharp intake of breath. He rubbed his knuckles and then searched his pockets. He took out a Swiss Army knife with a solid end, which he used to tap the stone panel, starting at the edge and working to the centre. The noise grew from solid at the edge, to hollow in the centre.

"Sounds promising," Templestone said, moving closer to Harry's tapping.

"Try the sides of the tomb, see how they sound," Dearden suggested. The sides sounded solid, as did the opposite end.

"I think the tomb was planned as a way out," Harry said, pushing each of the panels in turn, but without any effect. "See how my breath disappears into it." He pushed harder, took the torch and shone it on the end panel. "See how Ramon's given us a clue? His name's here and this end panel's the only one with any decoration. There's a definite separation between the panel and the frame surrounding it."

"You're right. Normally a tomb like this would be decorated all over." Julia felt the weight of the vault pressing in on her. She hated the enclosed space. She got close to the end of the tomb and kicked it, but it failed to move. Kicked harder and it hurt her foot. "Open damn you," she kicked it again, and then again.

"OK Jules leave it off, that won't do any good, least of all to your foot," Dearden said. She backed off.

Rowan was studying the warrior's helm, which was more utilitarian compared to the ornate Anglo-Saxon mask helms she was used to seeing warriors wearing. The sword was immense, so different to the seaxes the fighting men used in her own time.

The sword, resting sharp edge upwards on the effigy of Templestone's ancestor, was even bigger than Aelfrythsgiefu, the magnificent jewelled sword Countess Aelfryth gave Leofwin on their betrothal. Rowan touched its pommel and its leather-bound handle. It was quite plain, built solely for purpose, different to the rest of the effigy because the sword was real and had battle marks on the blade. She flicked the blade with her finger the same as she had seen the armourer do in Heanton in the Arden.

"That is how you tell good steel from bad," she said. "Can you hear how it rings?" she flicked the sword again and heard the ringing sound travelling down the blade as if it was going to escape from the sharp tip and fly into the room.

* * *

Afterwards, Rowan told Jem that she was not aware why she had done it, but she took the pommel in her hand. She felt an upward movement, so she lifted the handle further and as she did so, the tip dipped into a slot in the effigy, pivoting about where it was fixed in the middle.

The balance was good, so she carried on lifting and there was a shout from Harry who was kneeling close to the end panel. The others drew back quickly as the panel pivoted out of the way, revealing a flight of steps picked out in the torchlight.

Rowan lowered the sword and the panel pivoted back down.

"No, keep it up," Harry shouted, "Find something to keep it lifted." Rowan lifted the weapon again. Julia was near the plinth behind the image of Ramon Tailleur de Pierre. The box with the scroll inside was lying by the steps up into the Sanctuary.

"The box . . . get the box," Templestone called. Harry grabbed it and took it to where Rowan and Dearden were holding the sword up. He put the box under the handle and Rowan and Dearden let the sword go. The panel stayed open.

"That's our cue . . . let's get out of here," Dearden said.

"You've forgotten something," Harry shouted.

"What,"

"The scroll . . . do I have to think of everything? The rest of the equation . . . remember?" Harry got the box and put the scroll into the poacher's pocket in his coat. Dearden pivoted the sword and Harry placed the box under the handle.

*   *   *

"I'll lead," Julia said. "You lot can't be trusted to get anything right. Give me the torch" She grabbed it from Harry, squeezed into the tomb and onto the steps below. The cat, back in Harry's arms, struggled as they descended into the darkness.

The inside of the tunnel was cold and damp. Julia shone the torch back on the steps to light the way for the others coming down and they gathered at the bottom. Just then, the cedar wood box fell to the floor in the vault above and the stone panel in the tomb hinged back into place.

"Bill, I've got a question," Julia could barely see his face in the fading light from the torch.

"Well?"

"Your ancestor,"

"What about him?"

"He isn't in the tomb, where is he?"

"Your guess is as good as mine . . . I don't know."

They moved forward in the tunnel, making sure their footing was sound and as they rounded a bend, they could see dim daylight reflected further on and there was the faint sound of running water. After walking fifty paces or so on a downward slope, they came to where the tunnel joined a large culvert. There was a stream running through the culvert and daylight many yards away in both directions.

26

The water was thigh deep and cold and Harry lifted his coat to save the scroll from getting soaked. The cat struggled in his other arm as they sloshed along the stream. They came to the end of the culvert and scrambled up the bank outside. Templestone lay on his back, exhausted. The efforts of the past days had caught up with him. Whatever the threat was with Nibiru he was too exhausted to do much about it and he felt himself drifting off to sleep.

"Is Bill alright?" Harry asked. He had grown close to Templestone over the past couple of years. He thought the body in the canal in the news report had been Templestone and although he felt concern for the ones grieving over the dead man in the canal, he was relieved more than he could describe that the corpse was not Bill.

"He has been through many bad things; he is a tired man, that is all," Rowan said, kneeling down by Templestone. She knew Harry was close to Bill and explained what she saw to the younger man to reassure him. Harry was still holding the cat. Now it was away from the water it seemed content to stay with him.

"You keeping cat?" Rowan asked, stroking its head. He nodded.

"Have you given him the name?"

Harry looked down at the cat and fondled its ears. "I've called him Calculus," he said, looking back at Templestone.

"Oh . . . what does Calculus name mean?"

"Small stone. That's what Calculus actually means; and it is the study of continuous change. But I just like the sound of the word, without what it means."

Rowan accepted the explanation.

Templestone was wiry and tough. Harry looked at him sleeping, exhausted on the bank of the stream. Bill was a friend who reached deep into his heart.

"Bill," Harry shook his arm, willing him to wake up.

"Mmm?"

"We need to go." Templestone looked at the sky and thought back through the years to Jennie, Becky's mother, the love of his life so cruelly taken from him with cancer. We've had some lovely times, she had said, as she lay pale and riddled with pain in the last days they had together. He longed for their young years again.

"Bill, we need to go," Harry said, more insistently.

"OK . . . OK." Templestone raised himself on his elbow and looked at the surroundings. It was peaceful. "Not a bad place to end your days," he said quietly.

Harry was close enough to catch his words. "Come on Bill, none of that, there's work to do." He said it so the others didn't hear, but with some force in Templestone's ear.

"Yeah . . . I heard." He shook off Harry's arm when he tried to help him stand up.

"What now?" Julia asked Dearden, looking around, thinking of the men she heard laughing after they dropped the slab in place to imprison them in the Sanctuary.

"We'll head back to Dearden Hall. Then Harry can put his considerable talent into completing the equation that tells us about Nibiru's approach."

Daylight was fading. They were chilled. Their clothes were soaking as they made their way to the car park outside the Knights' Sanctuary. Rowan felt the water sloshing in her trainers as she walked. Dearden, by her side, was quiet, still smarting from the way the three in the Sanctuary got the better of him and forced him and Julia back down the steps at gunpoint.

He stepped on the gas on the way back to Dearden Hall. Rowan, sitting up front, had never travelled at the speed he hit. On some of the bends, she clutched at his arm. On a particularly tight bend, the tyres squealed on the tarmac and Dearden grinned as he heard an Anglo-Saxon expletive still currently in use.

Dearden was aware that the information carved into the stonework of the Sanctuary and the additional text in the scroll was of desperate importance and needed translating. As Julia suggested in the burial vault, Trent Jackson would be the man for that.

If Nibiru was heading for Earth, as separate sources of information implied, those with influence in government and science needed to be involved in a concerted strategy to attack the problem. Dearden, as he drove, was working the facts though, trying to develop a strategy. From what Harry said, and he seemed to be already clued up on Nibiru, powerful forces worldwide had known about the threat for years, but for some perverse reason, they hushed it up.

They arrived back at Dearden Hall after dark and pulled into the car park. They were almost dry from the heater up full in the Range Rover. A number of vehicles were parked up that hadn't been there when they left earlier in the day. It looked to Dearden that the call had gone out that help was needed. Sir Willoughby Pierpoint was pro-active that way. Mitch Doughty's Land Rover in Desert Storm camo was there alongside Matt Roberts' Austin Healey and Pierpoint's Bentley Mulsanne.

"Looks as though we're here in force," Templestone said. The presence of more of his SHaFT colleagues reassured him, particularly after the train of events since he found the Keeper dead.

"If SHaFT were to get fully involved do you expect them to be able to do something about the problem?" Julia challenged.

"Not really," Templestone said. "More to the point, can anyone address the threat? But I'll tell you what, it might at least bring governments together amicably while they work the problem through—"

"And then, after that, how long before they restart with the killing and the corruption?"

"Not long, if past performance is anything to go by."

Dearden opened the door and climbed out. "It's a grim old world at times. If nothing can be done it'll get a lot grimmer before too long. Let's see if Harry can iron out any of the uncertainties." He went to the front passenger door and helped Rowan out.

The rear door just behind him opened rapidly and almost hit him. Julia stepped down. She was finding it difficult to keep her hidden demons inside, particularly her jealousy. Dearden had helped the Anglo-Saxon woman out of the truck. *He's even held the sodding door open for her*, she muttered under her breath.

She disregarded the fact that Rowan was Jem's wife. Julia had her chances with Dearden in the past but had dismissed them. Now she was paying the penalty. She tried to marshal her thoughts, set them in order and hold them tight. She did the same with Shotokan to keep her bristling temper controlled within the lethal power she could summon up.

Julia pushed the jealousy aside and keyed her mobile. She found Trent Jackson's number, not the one he used for GOELD, his Guild of Extinct Language Decoding, in London, but his private landline, where he lived near Bletchley Park.

27

"Trent Jackson." The cultured voice of the linguist answered. The calmness of his voice quietened Julia's angst. She got straight into the conversation without preamble.

"It's Jules. We've got a big problem here." Her manner put Jackson on guard.

"Really. Another problem in your neck of the woods?" Jackson's involvement translating the manual Julia found in the Hub had cost him some sleepless nights; and he knew from his translation of the manual, that part of the small English forest called Leofwin's Hundred was alien.

"We need you to come up to Dearden Hall, it's desperately urgent."

"What makes it so urgent that I have to drop what I'm doing?"

"An ancient scroll in Hebrew with a very modern twist."

"Tell me more, Jules."

"Afraid I can't over the phone, you'll understand when we meet. What I can tell you is that there's something going on that has global implications. We need you here to help us get to grips with it."

Jackson was dedicated to his work and Julia knew it needed a good reason to lever him away from London. But an ancient Hebrew scroll hooked him.

"When exactly do you need me there?"

"Tomorrow. Please, Trent, do this for us ... do it for all of us." It was unusual for Professor Julia Linden-Barthorpe to plead, but it cemented the arrangement.

"I'll see what I can do, I'll ring back later." An ancient scroll in Hebrew with global implications made Jackson rethink his schedule while they were speaking. He was working on a complex language structure on a tablet from Byzantium. After he put the phone down, he talked the Byzantium tablet's detail through with his deputy. He could carry on working on it while Jackson was away.

"Trent Jackson says he'll call later about when he can get here," Julia said. In the great hall the scroll was unrolled and a book was lying on each corner to save it curling back. It went against the grain for Julia to see the way they were treating the ancient manuscript; it should be in an air-conditioned environment, but the urgency of the situation made her push aside thoughts of preservation.

She put on cotton gloves and told the others to handle it as little as possible.

"We'll leave you to it," Pierpoint said. They went over to the fire and sat. Templestone was already there, asleep. In subdued tones, so as not to wake him, Dearden brought Pierpoint, Mitch Doughty and Matt Roberts up to date with the events of the day. Julia could see concentrated looks, serious conversation and gestures. The whisky was out. At the moment, they were on singles. Julia knocked some of hers back and wondered how in hell's name she had got into another tight spot with Jem Dearden.

Julia turned her attention to the scroll. The discoloured parchment was a light tone of Van Dyke Brown. The lettering was a deeper tone of the same colour. Its length rolled out was just short of the length of the table, which was about eight feet. The scroll didn't consist solely of text. There were appended drawings, lines drawn using a straight edge for a guide and there was a circle, crudely drawn by hand, touching the lines.

"Surprising how good the ancients were with maths," Pierpoint said. He had come to stand next to Julia, she nodded.

"And construction, they pulled off some amazing building work."

"They did," she said. She walked slowly along the scroll and passed drawings littered with Hebrew text. There were footnotes and black-ink marginal annotations in Greek and some in Latin. A later academic had obviously worked on the data.

Harry came down from his room upstairs. He was carrying Calculus he was unusually attached to the creature, as if it supplied something previously missing. Tomahawk was in his usual spot on the rug by the Norman fireplace, which was big enough to walk into while the fire was blazing.

The action in the room was immediate and full of feral madness when Calculus leapt out of Harry's arms and headed for the window, which looked like an escape route, but he bounced off the glass and stood dazed for a moment.

Tomahawk moved quicker than Dearden thought possible, but Calculus was quicker still and clawed up the heavy curtain. He perched on the rail at the top, spitting furiously. The wolf sat at the foot of the curtain, snarling at the invader.

Dearden had shouted at the same time as Harry and he dashed for the wolf's leash. He crept up behind Tomahawk, whose gaze was fixed on Calculus and attached the leash. A harsh word of command and a strong tug on the leash caused a stand-down and Dearden, laughing at the unbridled anger, tugged Tomahawk down the great hall and out the door, past the outbuildings, to his outside run. Inside the great hall, there was a round of applause and laughter as Calculus leapt down and hid under a sofa. The antipathy between the two creatures had given welcome relief to the tension.

*   *   *

Julia had recognised mathematical symbols in the Greek marginal references, which was what Harry was concentrating on as he took notes.

Sir Willoughby Pierpoint was in conversation with Dearden and Templestone. Matt Roberts, his hair longer than when she last saw him, was talking animatedly to Mitch Doughty and Red Cloud, who had arrived with Possum Chaser.

Rowan and Possum Chaser, with Freda Heskin, were arranging food and drink on the sideboard. There were cold snacks, cooked meats and canapés, made with precision by Freda. Her husband, Gil, brought more wine from the cellar and Rowan instructed him to put the drink and glasses on Leofwin's table. She indicated to put the wine near where Leofwin used to sit. Occasionally she missed her life in Anglo-Saxon times. It was far slower than her life now, but she had grown used to the fast pace and she liked it. She particularly enjoyed being mistress of Dearden Hall.

Rowan sensed Julia's gaze on her. Julia had changed in recent days. Rowan thought she was harder. Whereas previously Jules had been willing to help her, translating into Anglo-Saxon the meaning of difficult words that Jem spoke, now she sensed reluctance with Jules and an animosity that was difficult to understand. She wished Esma was here, her companion from her own time, but she was staying with the Romanies named Hicks, who lived on the land owned by Red Cloud.

Dearden joined Julia and Will Pierpoint. Templestone was there too, telling Pierpoint and Dearden that he heard Crowe telling his cronies about a seagoing trunk he found, which was full of research to do with the Sanctuary.

"So, it seems to be conclusive that they're after the scroll we found," said Dearden.

"Looks that way. Crowe's found copies of Charles Villiers' research. It has to be the same information you've got in your records Will. Crowe and us ending up in the Knight's Sanctuary at the same time shows we were looking for the same thing."

Julia's mobile rang and she went aside to answer it. It was Trent Jackson. She was only a minute on the phone and when she rang off she came over and interrupted Templestone.

"Trent Jackson says he will be here in the morning to help with the scroll. He's catching an early train." She stood at Dearden's side, got close. They acknowledged what she said and then continued the conversation as if she wasn't in the room.

Harry had his laptop booted up near the scroll and found an online Hebrew-to-English translation program. He converted his keyboard to Hebrew and typed in the characters, יַצֹןְ, written on the outside of the parchment, that Jules transliterated as HaMabuwl. He pressed the translate button and read the result.

"Hey, look at this," he called. "I've just translated the text on the outside of the scroll. It says The Deluge."

*   *   *

They had an early start next morning and the sense of anticipation was acute as they waited for Jackson to arrive. It was still dark when they heard over the intercom that a taxi had pulled up to the gate. Gil Heskin pressed the button and the taxi pulled through into the courtyard.

Trent Jackson's pedigree in the field of language was illustrious. It was helpful that he had dug deep into the early Paleo-Hebrew script with a translation of some very early fragments found in an isolated jar in the Qumran caves.

"This scroll is the work of a man named Sho'mer," Jackson said to the others over a black coffee. They were standing close, to take in what he was saying. "Sho'mer wasn't only a name; it was also a word describing the position that the man who wrote the scroll held in his community. In that context, Sho'mer means to guard. He was a guardian of records.

Jackson read on for a short while and then suddenly pulled up a chair and sat quickly. The colour had drained from his face.

"Are you OK Trent?" Rowan asked. He responded with considerable effort. He was normally very in-control, all bow-tie-and-brogues suave. When he responded there was a tremor in his voice.

"This word." He pointed to נה with the tip of a pencil. "Do you know what it says?"

Julia got close to the scroll to see it better. Pierpoint put his glasses on.

"Reading from right to left, the first symbol is Nun, the N sound, the next is a He, the symbol for H," Julia said.

"No, it isn't. It is easy to mistake it. With the symbol for the H sound," Jackson pointed further along the line of text to the symbol h, "See here, there's a break between the left-hand leg of the letter and the bar at the top? That is H. Now look at the other letter I pointed out."

"It is slightly different, there is no gap," Pierpoint said. "The fact that there is no gap makes a monumental difference to the sound of the letter *and* the meaning of the word. The last letter, pronounced a*ch*, is spoken at the back of the pallet."

"So, what does the word mean?"

"It is a word that means 'to rest', as in settling down. Any idea what it could be in English?"

Julia didn't have patience for psychological games,

"You're the linguist, just tell us will you."

"OK. The letter sounds are N, followed by ach, anyone reading it in Hebrew would have known to add a vowel in between the letters. The vowel added would have been an *o*. In English, the word becomes Noah."

There was silence, then incredulity as the name sunk in.

"In this scroll, Sho'mer gives a contemporary account of the global flood that we read about in the book of Genesis. He claims to have been on the Ark with Noah and his family and to have survived the flood. He is also giving us information about the cause of the deluge, which he says was *a second moon from the heavenly firmament*. He attributes the appearance of the second moon to a divine cause responding to the evil widespread on Earth at the time . . . do you realise the importance of this scroll?"

Harry came into the room. He had been working half through the night on notes he made from the scroll and looked dead-beat. He wasn't too dead-beat to miss Jackson's words about a second moon. A frown replaced his usual smile.

"You're describing the first pass of Nibiru," he said, coming to Jackson's side.

"Nibiru?" Jackson's eyebrows lifted.

"Look, here's the evidence." Harry slapped some A4 sheets in front of Jackson and the others. He had bypassed the need for Jackson's translation. Through the Greek annotations in pure mathematics, he had derived the fulfilment of the equation.

"Nibiru is on a collision course with planet Earth."

"What are you on about?" Jackson sounded uncertain. He sat back in his chair. In a way, the youth, who Jackson thought was probably around twenty, had saved his face. Although he had a powerful intellect and earned great respect, Jackson suffered from an inferiority complex. On the odd occasion, when he was under pressure, he stammered. The problem came from one of his very early tutors who said he was a failure. The words stuck. Jackson, against all the odds, had proved his mettle and gained a professorship and the coveted prize of his own well-respected business in London's you've-made-it territory.

He was thankful for Harry's intervention.

"Are you H . . . Harry Stanway," he asked. Julia had told him about the intellect of the young man and recognised this was him.

"I am . . . and you are Professor Jackson, I do believe," Harry held out his hand for a shake. Thus, began a long and fruitful friendship.

"What do you know about this?" Jackson asked him. Harry looked worried.

"I know that Nibiru is the worst possible danger Earth has ever faced. It makes the Doomsday Clock pale into insignificance. Nibiru is coming on a second pass and we are powerless to prevent it blasting us to kingdom come."

28

"I've got more information to back up what Harry and Trent are saying," Pierpoint said. "I've been poking around in various murky places under the radar, and I've located the photographs of Nibiru taken through Hubble that were shown on the Conspiracy TV program. I concur with you that it is real and the threat is on its way." Harry shrugged, as if to say tell me something new, but he listened attentively for what was coming next.

"I have it first-hand from an elder statesman who was twenty in 1945, that there has been a conspiracy of silence about Nibiru since those times. Sit down, all of you . . . I want to tell you a story."

*   *   *

"One night in July 1940, after Winston Churchill had become Prime Minister, he had a visitor to number 10 Downing Street; it was a Professor Charles Villiers. A short time before the war Villiers tried to alert the authorities to some information he discovered about Nibiru," Pierpoint nodded at Harry, "Yes it was known in government circles back then. The military told Villiers to get lost because they thought he was a crank. They thought they had a bigger fish to fry with German militarism and Adolf Hitler.

"In the room that night sharing whisky and cigars with Winston were one or two of his close associates and a young up and coming politician. He was the man who is now our eighty-two-year-old elder statesman, who shall remain nameless. I have talked to him and he told me that he heard everything there was to know about Charles Villiers' research into Nibiru. He said Winston took it equally as seriously as the need for breaking the Enigma codes, but the pressing need, first of all, had to be the defeat of Germany. That result had to come before everything else.

"Churchill dealt with Hitler and then in 1945 he was voted out of office. When he left office, he passed on some important unfinished business to his successor, Clement Atlee. One of those items was Professor Villiers' research. In June 1947, Atlee remembered Winston's words.

"He sent for his foreign secretary Ernest Bevin and along with our elder statesman as a young man, they went to America armed with Villiers research papers. Bevin argued the case for addressing the Nibiru situation, *in camera*, in front of a select committee of eight representatives of the newly formed United Nations. He put the case eloquently and the council voted on it. A day later, Bevin and his colleague were given the decision that everything about Nibiru should remain secret. The reason given by the council was the wish not to load more stress onto the war-traumatised public.

"What Bevin did not know, that our elder statesman learned about some years later, was that, behind the scenes, a powerful group had put pressure on the council and forced the no vote. He didn't know why at the time, but the pressure on the select committee to keep silent about Nibiru was lethal, wives and family had been threatened. Our elder statesman said that there were death threats to every one of the select committee of the United Nations. Some of them disappeared under mysterious circumstances that have not been explained to this day."

Pierpoint cleared his throat and asked for some water. Rowan came over with the carafe and a glass with ice cubes. She poured. Pierpoint drank and carried on. "As we now know, death threats aside, the decision to enforce secrecy was definitely not in the public's interest. Another element comes into the equation here. A powerful group were holding sway over the decision-making, not only of the United Nations, but of governments as well and this information is important because that threat is still with us today.

Matt Roberts, a man of the outdoors with an acute sense of justice, wild looking with his long hair and a bandana, wanted more answers.

"So, you're telling us that the biggest threat humanity has faced was hushed up by some bastards at the highest level."

"Apparently so."

"How did they get away with it?"

"Believe me, that is what I intend to find out and I'm going to the top to do it."

"If you want some help, count me in," Julia said. Her Shotokan and fiery personality came in useful at times. She was incensed at what Pierpoint had revealed, and she, like the others in the room, wanted something done about it.

"I might take up your offer of help some time, Jules, but this is something I have to do alone." With that, Pierpoint went for his coat. Dearden joined him to see him out the door.

They relaxed. The smell of cooking had been coming from the kitchen for the past hour. Dearden had asked Frieda to prepare a meal from a recipe often cooked on Thursdays which Rowan described from the time Leofwin owned the manor house.

Rowan involved herself in the kitchen and ensured the right level of herbs and salt flavoured the dish. She found it difficult to come to terms with how abundant the valuable commodity of salt was and she had filled a shelf with containers of it in the larder.

The food was brought in and they sat around the big table and began to eat. The atmosphere lightened and Matt Roberts told of an incident when he and Lee Wynter, who was expected to arrive, had been in La Réunion. The mission was complete and they were sitting with the families they had protected. The children were there too, three of them, two boys and a girl who had the cutest eyes and dark hair. The kids were laughing at the strangely dressed pair, who were still in full combats. The meal was a hurriedly got together affair, but they were all hungry and the food was good. The point of Roberts' tale was how a meal, even when times are tough, can add a touch of normality to a situation.

"We need to do this every day," Rowan said. Red Cloud disagreed. "To do this every day implies that times will always be tough. We should have a meal together like this only when we have finished with tough times. That is what our ancestors on the Great Plains did." He looked at Possum Chaser, who nodded her agreement.

She said, "I was told that after Little Big Horn there was a great hunt for Tatanka and a meal followed that lasted two days." There was general laughter.

Dearden often brought Tomahawk into the great hall at meal times and Harry suggested that he bring Calculus down from his room. Hopefully, there would be no territorial challenge this time from the wolf. The two creatures had reached a state of angry tolerance.

Dearden went along with Harry's request. He was impressed with the young man and wanted to give him the freedom of most of Dearden Hall so he would treat it as his home. Harry seemed at ease in his new surroundings. He went up for Calculus and when he came back down with the cat, it was unsettled and spitting. Its twitching tail expressed the gravitas of re-entering the room of the beast and it leapt out of Harry's arms to hide behind a sofa.

* * *

The sound of a powerful engine approached outside. Leon Wynter always arrived with the speakers of his vehicle playing at full blast. He always used an open-top, even in the depths of winter. The noise stopped and a minute later Wynter breezed into the great hall.

He stopped for a second inside the door and looked around to see who was there, then sauntered in. His dreadlocks were longer than when they had seen him last.

"Howdy to y'all, he said in his Bronx drawl as Dearden stood and grasped his hand. They all greeted him. His presence always brought the atmosphere upbeat. Dearden made room for him so that Wynter would be sitting the other side of him from Rowan.

Wynter had responded quickly when Sir Will Pierpoint rang to say an issue had arisen that would need his input.

"What's goin' on my man," he had asked on the phone. Pierpoint wouldn't elaborate. All he did say was that if he was interested in helping out with something that was the worst threat there could be, he should turn up at Dearden Hall, quickly.

It was unusual to get a phone call directly from Pierpoint. Whatever the issue was, it had to be real big, and worth turning up for.

29

Pierpoint was determined to get governmental authorities on-side to present a united front in the face of the coming danger. Even if powerless to avert catastrophe in the nineteen forties, an attempt at a fightback, rather than enforced silence, should have been organised.

As commander of SHaFT, with its raison d'être the pursuit of justice, Pierpoint had contacts in high places of government across continents. The contacts, sworn to secrecy as part of the deal, were each unaware the others knew him. He was a shadowy figure in a shadowy organisation that appeared in their time of need to take on threat and eliminate it. Afterwards, when payment had been made into the Swiss account, he disappeared again into the background.

* * *

The premier was expecting Sir Willoughby Pierpoint, who had contacted him on the scrambled phone line behind a small sliding door in the corner of the room in 10 Downing Street. The Prime Minister had never met Pierpoint before, so he made enquiries on the side about the man who was on the edge of anonymity and somewhat legendary. Apart from Pierpoint's early career in the Special Forces, there was no more information, only things that had been related over the years by word of mouth. This unsettled the PM because he always wanted to be one step ahead of anyone he met and right now he felt disadvantaged.

If Prime Minister Fenton Bull had been able to find information when he researched Sir Willoughby Pierpoint, he would have read how Pierpoint was a gentleman on the outside, but a ruthless hunter on the inside. Bull would have seen that Pierpoint was a peculiar hunter, in that his target was justice for the oppressed. As Bull read on he would have seen that Pierpoint had built up SHaFT as an extension of himself, a mechanism for the attainment of the justice he craved.

The Right Honourable Fenton Bull rose from the seat behind his ministerial desk and advanced across the room with his hand outstretched. He held on fractionally too long for Pierpoint's liking. The PM led him to the desk and invited him to sit. Bull saw a tall man with greying hair, probably in his early seventies. Pierpoint was wiry, still well-muscled and fit. Military, by his bearing. Bull set a Newton's cradle in motion. Tic . . . tic . . . tic . . . tic, it annoyed Pierpoint.

"To what do I owe this privilege Sir Willoughby?" Fenton Bull indicated a chair on the opposite side of the desk. When he got the phone message from Pierpoint, it sounded urgent. Pierpoint had said *there is a threat to all life, as we know it* and Bull wondered what on earth Pierpoint would deliver next.

Pierpoint said nothing. He didn't sit and he slapped one of the sheets of paper with MOST SECRET in red stamped across it in front of the PM. Bull glanced down at the sheet and read the words WITHHOLD FROM PUBLIC KNOWLEDGE, also stamped in red. The PM froze at the words he saw. The subject matter of the typewritten paper in front of him was always one of the items on the agenda for discussion at the meetings convened every few months under the label, *Eisenburg*.

He attended the meetings held under the tightest security, usually at some exclusive isolated country house and usually somewhere in Europe or the Americas. No records were made of what went on at these meetings; consequently, conspiracy theories built up around them.

Bull picked up the top sheet from those Pierpoint put on his desk. His heartbeat lifted a notch as he recalled the last Eisenburg. There were 182 leaders of industry and government in attendance. Not one of those present had a fortune less than multi-millionaire, most had billions in assets and cash.

"How did you get hold of this?" Bull asked, in a not-too-friendly way. His eyes puckered and his mouth worked nervously. He loosened his tie and looked down at the wording on the MOST SECRET sheet of foolscap. The paper size was old fashioned foolscap. The writing was readable but faded.

"I want answers Fenton, this has been muted far too long, what do you know?"

Bull was silent for a long moment. Then he cleared his throat.

"What I know about the contents of that document is highly privileged information. I insist you tell me where you got it from."

"Come on, Fenton, you don't expect me to disclose my sources with a thing this big, do you? We need to get people onside. Seriously, we're running out of time."

Bull stood up and went to the window. He looked out at the garden behind Number 10, wondering how to avoid getting into a discussion that was dangerous. He decided on being direct.

"We do not talk about this. End of matter." His hand swept downwards in a forget-it gesture. Bull had his back to Pierpoint. There was a tremor in his voice.

"Where does the fear come from, Fenton?"

The premier turned abruptly, which caused Pierpoint to notice his face was florid, disturbed.

"Fear?" Bull laughed briefly but there was no humour in his eyes. He went to his chair and sat down heavily. The Newton's Cradle was still ticking.

"Are you alright Fenton?" Pierpoint asked. He remained standing on the other side of the desk, with his hands resting on it.

"I knew this would catch up with us at some point," Bull said. He looked around at the daylight through the window and then back to Pierpoint. He placed a finger inside his collar, which was suddenly tight, and undid the top button of his shirt.

"What exactly is catching up with you?" Pierpoint asked.

"The silence."

"Tell me more."

Bull stabbed the foolscap paper with his finger. "This issue has continually spooked Eisenburg over the years and they won't give way on it. I think they were hoping it would just disappear." Bull went to a side cupboard and took out a bottle of brandy and two glasses. "Want one?" he asked Pierpoint. Pierpoint shook his head. The PM poured a stiff measure. "Did you know Eisenburg even holds sway over the UN?"

The mention of Eisenburg had surprised Pierpoint. "Are you involved with Eisenburg?" he asked.

"Personally involved? Of course I am. Most heads of state and government are. The majority of billionaires and industrialists have their finger in the Eisenburg pie. It calls the tune on the economy worldwide and has the ultimate say on keeping things stable."

"Why would Nibiru trouble Eisenburg?"

"Can't a man of your stature work it out, Sir Willoughby? Let me explain. Eisenburg operates on keeping the population where they want them. It ensures a working measure of social order in which the leaders come to the fore and the rich get richer. Acquisition is how it works and even warfare bolsters up the edifice. Politics at party level let the population think they've got some say in governmental matters, but they haven't really. While they're working out who to vote for and fiddling around in their own little lives, it keeps their noses to the grindstone. While they keep working they shore up the platform for Eisenburg's plan of world domination.

Bull didn't see Pierpoint's brow darken.

"World dom—"

"If we'd told them about Nibiru, it would have altered the focus. Panic amongst the masses would have made the Eisenburg edifice start to crumble, Sir Willoughby. We couldn't allow that. Over the years, we have built our plans on order and obedience from those down there. They're like lemmings, you know." He stabbed a finger in the direction of the floor. The Prime Minister realised he had charisma, almost idol status to some. It was his personality and a certain amount of cunning along with political nous that brought Fenton Bull to high office. He thought he had Pierpoint in his aura. "It is fun at times, you know, Sir Willoughby. We politicians are the actors on the main stage."

"That's what you think, you bloody hypocrite. I'm about to take you to drama school." Pierpoint lifted his fist but then thought better of it. He swiped the Newton's cradle off the desk and it clattered to the floor. Bull's complexion paled. He eyed up

Newton's balls, rolling away on the floor. He had said too much. Sometimes he was too damn honest. Sometimes, he had thought he ought to have gone against Eisenburg, spoken up against the threat, but he hadn't and now the secret was out.

"What I've told you, Sir Willoughby, it is in strictest confidence of course." All of a sudden, Fenton Bull felt he was teetering on the edge of a precipice.

Pierpoint said nothing. He picked up Villiers' paperwork, walked out the door and slammed it shut behind him. The Prime Minister looked at the door, thought for a minute and made his decision. He reached for the phone on his desk and dialled a three-figure internal number, intended for use if there was a breach of security or a direct threat to the safety of the premier. Bull felt threatened because he had opened up things that should have remained private and he suddenly became frightened of reprisals from Eisenburg. The internal number responded quickly.

"The man who just left my office, don't let him out of your sight. He's dangerous, probably armed and he is ruthless. He needs to be stopped. Do it." Two men on standby from MI5 responded and ran down a passageway to the rear of the building. They saw Pierpoint heading to a Bentley. They stepped up their pace to a BMW series 5 and followed Pierpoint's Bentley at a discrete distance.

30

When Pierpoint got into the Bentley he told his driver, Harvey Proctor, to step on the gas and put the blue light on. Proctor opened the window and put the magnetic unit on the roof. He liked these times when Pierpoint used his influence and effectively raised two fingers to the law. In reality, it was all within the law, because shortly after a phone call from Pierpoint, four official looking military motorcycle outriders with flashing blue lights joined them from a side road. They made good time through the suburbs and hit the M1.

Since the night Pierpoint realised the Nibiru threat could be real, he had been busy working on a plan. He did behind the scenes research. Spoke to people, but never divulged why he was speaking to them. His plan was theoretically in place. Now it was time to put it into action.

* * *

Dearden picked up his mobile, the ringtone was the one he had assigned to Pierpoint.

"Jem, I've had a meeting with Prime Minister Bull. I confronted him about the silence surrounding Nibiru. He admitted there's been a cover-up on a monumental scale that goes as high as the UN. I intend to blow this thing wide open. It is criminal on an obscene scale."

"You watch your step, Will. I detect strong motive and desperation behind the silence. You might easily step on the toes of those who want it kept quiet."

"I know that, but Arthur and I are going to give it a shot. I'm calling in a favour. There is something I've heard on the grapevine that the UN possesses. I know someone with a great deal of influence in the States. I'm going to see him and get him to action its use. It just might save the day."

"What is it?"

"I can't say . . . yet. No-one outside a select few is supposed to know about it. We'll have to keep it that way for now."

Dearden let that sink in. "OK. While you pursue that in the States, we'll concentrate on observing the region of the heavens nearest the Sun. Harry's ordered some astronomical gear that'll be with us tomorrow."

"OK, keep me posted." Pierpoint rang off, which left Dearden wondering what idea the commander of SHaFT had up his sleeve and what it was that the UN possessed.

After finishing the call to Dearden, Pierpoint rang the flight crew of SHaFT's Special Missions Gulfstream G550 and told them to prepare for a flight to JFK. Not too long before, at the time of the Manhattan Mission, he developed a SHaFT contact who lived in a Carnegie Hill condo on East 96th Street. He phoned the contact and arranged to be picked up from JFK.

On the M1, still with blue lights and sirens, they were pushing ninety. Pierpoint rang Arthur Doughty. He told him the Nibiru situation was ramping up and that he was going on an eleventh-hour attempt to jerk people who mattered into action to address the threat. Pierpoint wouldn't give any more detail in case they were being eavesdropped, but Arthur Doughty could tell by Will's tone of voice that the action was about to start.

Art Doughty was silent on the other end of the phone waiting for more, and Pierpoint asked him if he was still there.

"I am. What can you tell me . . .? I've got to explain this to Caro."

"Only that we can be quite persuasive together, and we need to challenge a particular man who may have enough influence to swing the machinery of governments into action. The trip will take four days. Can you come along?"

Pierpoint heard muttering in the background as Doughty put his hand over the mouthpiece and muted the phone. He caught a few of the words Doughty spoke to his wife.

Caro knew that her husband, who was officially retired, still had active links to the military. She sometimes resigned herself to a few days of being on her own. Over the years, Caro had never truly found out about her husband's role and she had never heard of SHaFT. There was one occasion, however, when she became aware of the nature of his other work, and it had nothing to do with the stained-glass studio he owned in Leamington Spa.

It was some years back. Arthur had come back after five days away and was sitting relaxed in his chair, watching the television news. It was something he commented on about a news report. He had been half-asleep and had added to the news, saying that the number of terrorist's holding prisoners at the embassy had been eight, not five as reported.

Caro knew Arthur almost as much as he knew himself and she could tell his accidental response to the news program must have been from first-hand knowledge of the situation. She was aware he had a military past, but he never wanted to talk about it. She caught him looking at her in a questioning sort of way afterwards when he realised he had said too much; she smiled and passed it off.

The times he went away these days was far less than it used to be and she was thankful for that. He always called her by her full name, Caroline, before he went away and he did so after he told her Sir Willoughby Pierpoint was on the phone.

"It'll be four days, sweetie," he reassured her in his Northumberland accent, "I'll bring you something back."

"I know Art. Just take care and hurry up back. I love you."

"I know you do and I love you too." He took his hand off the mouthpiece of the phone."

"OK Will, it's on."

"I'll pick you up in a couple of hours. The crew are preparing the Gulfstream. Oh, and you'd better bring a suit and tie."

Arthur went upstairs and chucked a few things into a holdall. He chose a suit and tie and wondered who it was they were going to see.

Pierpoint rang to say he was five minutes away. Doughty gathered his holdall, said a hurried goodbye to Caro and walked down the path to wait at the end of the drive. He was committed to SHaFT. Its motto went through his mind, *Nos Successio Procul Totus Sumptus*, We Succeed At All Costs. Over the years, they had succeeded in their missions and had made a difference for the better to the lives of a good many people.

Doughty looked down the road at some approaching headlights. They passed by, and then more came in view, wider apart than the average car. Pierpoint's Bentley drew to a halt and Harvey Proctor opened the rear door for Doughty and put his holdall into the trunk.

"I hope Caro isn't too annoyed, but this business is as serious as it can get, old boy," Pierpoint said, as Doughty climbed in.

"She's OK with it, but I think these days she puts up with it on sufferance."

"I promise not to take advantage of her good nature too often but let me explain about the problem." It took just ten minutes to bring Doughty up to speed.

"So why the suit and tie Will?"

"We're going to the United Nations."

"What?"

"The United Nations. The gathering of nations, whose building is in New York with Isaiah chapter two verse four on the wall, *They shall beat their swords into plowshares.*"

"And you think we can make representation to the UN?"

Pierpoint tapped the side of his nose. "We'll see."

* * *

The Bentley passed through the outer gate of MoD Kineton. Security, as usual, was tight and the armed guards checked Pierpoint's car over with mirrors and spotlights to make sure it wasn't carrying anything terrorist into the largest ammunition dump in Europe.

Proctor eased the car past the guards and drove to Dump 4. Pierpoint spoke into the intercom outside the steel sliding doors covering half the side of the building and within seconds two armed men in combat gear came out through a personnel door and checked that the arrivals were who they said they were.

The motors on the big sliding doors engaged and when they rolled open sufficiently, Proctor drove the Bentley down the slope into the brightly lit interior. The doors rumbled shut on their bearings.

Pierpoint led the way into his office, which was next to Arthur Doughty's. He put a sheaf of papers into a briefcase.

"I want you to read this on the flight Art. It'll make sense of what I've told you so far. The Gulfstream's on the runway with the engines rotating. There's just two of us on the flight. Grab your luggage, let's go stateside."

They walked to the classic Maudslay Marathon coach parked outside that they used for transport from Dump 4 to the aircraft and climbed aboard.

31

Lee Wynter was catching up with details about the threat. Pierpoint had told him over the phone that there was a planet-sized problem, but he hadn't elaborated. He told Wynter to ask the others about it when he got to Dearden Hall. Julia had a good way of explaining things, she always filtered out what was irrelevant. In the space of twenty minutes, Wynter had hold of the major facts. The enormity of the situation was difficult to take in. Wynter, Dearden and the others could normally fight their way out of trouble, but this was different.

Further along the table Calculus, his tail moving restlessly, was perched on Harry's knee, staring unblinkingly in Tomahawk's direction. If the wolf moved slightly the cat did, their relationship had progressed away from tooth and claw violence, to an uneasy truce.

With Pierpoint and Arthur Doughty away at the UN on their mission to meet with the person of influence, the conversation around the table turned to another strategy. It had been on Dearden's mind as a possibility since it became obvious Nibiru was a reality.

"If Pierpoint doesn't get anywhere, we'll attempt to communicate with the aliens to see if they can offer some help. They left us the means to link up with them." The statement was a bolt out of the blue to all but Harry Stanway. Harry was enthusiastic, but what Dearden had suggested brought silence to the rest of the room. Harry's enthusiasm for contacting the aliens hadn't abated since they returned to their own world.

"They gave us the means to contact them. I suggest we do so as soon as possible."

The way the conversation was developing caught Trent Jackson by surprise. Dearden had intimated about the out-of-this-world goings-on in Leofwin's Hundred and Jackson had researched the manual found in the Hub, but the conversation brought the words off the page, into reality.

"What can the aliens do to help?" Mitch Doughty asked.

"Think it through Mitch. The Wasiri-Chanchiya are light-years ahead of us in technology. They've discovered the grid, found materials that resonate with it to create an infinite-speed form of transport. We can communicate with them by means of the grid. They may have methods to help us that we couldn't even dream about. I'd say they're our best shot at survival."

Templestone was cautious, "If we contact them, we need to be aware that we might open up things we can't handle."

Dearden nodded. Lan-Si-Nu's words of warning were still clear in Dearden's mind. *You will need to be sure you can cope with the great changes.* Lan-Si-Nu hadn't revealed what the great changes would be. Dearden speculated that they could be more than the people of Earth could handle, or even bear, psychologically. As a counterpoint, he thought of the change Nibiru would make, which was obliteration and there was no choice about which way to go.

"Lan-Si-Nu spoke of great changes that would occur, not just for us, but for the whole world. Have we got the right to impose those changes?" Dearden asked. He knew they had to make contact, but he was challenging the others, playing devil's advocate.

It produced a reaction from Matt Roberts, "I agree there's no choice. Nibiru is forcing changes onto the whole world, like boom and then the big sleep. We have to contact Lan-Si-Nu to see if he can help us."

Julia and Rowan were just as adamant that they go to the Hub and activate the contact sequence.

Rowan stood from where she was sitting by Jem. She looked serious and what she said next floored any doubt remaining in the room. "Matt is saying correct words. If I can make big change coming to you from Myrce, you can make big change with your lives. Bill, Jem, all of you, stand up, be men."

What Rowan said sharpened the focus.

Dearden summarised, "OK. Let's see what Pierpoint comes up with in the States and then make a final choice. We'll call Pierpoint's option, Plan A, contacting the aliens, Plan B. We can't leave it long before we attempt to make contact so we'll organise it in the background. Keep the alien contact plan under your hat . . . it is a very long shot and we don't want to create false hopes."

*   *   *

Templestone came over from the winged chair by the fire and sat next to Dearden and Rowan. Mitch Doughty and the others drew close. Templestone was a good counsellor.

"Rowan has swayed the argument for us to stand up and be counted. But Pierpoint has to have a chance to figure things out. He knows the right people. If anyone can rattle the cage to activate the beast inside, Sir Willoughby Pierpoint can. Jem, you say he has something up his sleeve. When Pierpoint has a plan it's best to give him space to try it, but I think alien contact has to be attempted as soon as we can to give us two options."

"OK, I hear what you say." Dearden was worried. "I just hope he doesn't rattle the cage too hard and get himself a bad reaction. I'm concerned about the conspiracy of silence to do with Nibiru. It could be very dangerous if Will oversteps the mark."

"I've known Pierpoint a lot longer than you have, Jem. He was the founder of SHaFT, along with Art Doughty and you don't get an organisation like that under way if you pussyfoot around. I can hold my own with most men, but I wouldn't like to face up to Pierpoint when he's in a bad mood."

Dearden smiled at Bill's candour and wondered if Pierpoint would say the same in reverse. He had a feeling he would.

Trent Jackson came into the great hall from his room upstairs. He had translated another section of the scroll. Enthusiasm had replaced his nervousness at handling the precious document.

"It's a vivid account," Jackson smoothed out the scroll and put books on the corners to save it curling. "It is very detailed and Sho'mer has written it in prose rather than poetry. I've started to write out the translation." He held up the notepad with the title, יצנך written on the front cover.

"Of course, it will never be included in the canon of inspired scripture. Scholars agree that the Holy Bible is complete, but HaMabuwl could probably be included in the Apocrypha. Sho'mer's use of Hebrew is a lighter tone than we find in the book of Genesis, supposedly written by Moses. Sho'mer writes as an outsider, but what he tells us is invaluable because he gives us a time period from when Nibiru was first seen in the heavens until it passed close to Earth and caused worldwide tidal surges."

"The Great Flood?"

"So it seems, Jules."

"How long did it take for Nibiru to get to Earth back then?" Doughty asked.

"Sho'mer says it was one hundred and fifty-eight days—"

"That is from when it first became visible to the naked eye against the glare of the Sun," Harry interrupted.

Dearden asked Harry, "How come Villiers was able to confirm Nibiru's presence in the late thirties when we've only just found the scroll?"

"He must have had access to the information in the scroll."

Templestone said, "Traditionally the Keeper is the only one of those associated with the Sanctuary who is privy to the scroll's location."

"That might be so, but to produce such quality information and math, Villiers must have been in collusion with a Keeper, who gave him access to the source document.

"That would have been Dick Martel," Templestone said. "My guess is that Martel contacted Villiers because he recognised the importance of the carving on the pillar and was worried about what he'd heard about its link with a coming catastrophe. It's in Pierpoint's records that Villiers lived in Temple Balsall from the thirties through to the fifties. It was common knowledge that he was a physicist at Cambridge, so in Martel's eyes he was the right person to contact."

Harry booted up his laptop. He opened a folder called Nibiru and located a file labelled speeds and distances. "At the time of his research, Villiers couldn't have seen the planet itself, it was too early in its orbital cycle to show up, so his work was purely theoretical. It was clever stuff and most of it based on the ancient math. This is some information I noted when the Controversial TV program went out." Harry angled the laptop for the others to see. "Nibiru was still way beyond the Sun in relation to Earth. There were brief sightings by the program's researchers and they postulated the speed of the planet at 6.8 miles per second."

"So how long have we got until it arrives?" Julia asked Harry.

"Until we have a positive sighting that's an open-ended question. At present, it has to be in excess of Sho'mer's one hundred and fifty-eight days because it hasn't yet been seen with the naked eye. I suggest we organise our own regime of observations so we pick up Nibiru as soon as it becomes visible without instruments. When the program's researchers observed it, it was on the far side of the Sun and they reported that perturbations in Nibiru's orbit allowed them to see it. It will be hidden by the Sun's disc most of the time until it's distance is the same as the Sun is from Earth. Then it should be in plain view for all to see."

"Will it be drawn into the Sun?" Possum Chaser asked.

"I don't think so. Its orbit won't have varied much. It wasn't drawn into the Sun during Sho'mer's experience so it shouldn't be this time, but it did get too close to Earth for comfort on its first pass. We can't rule out a collision."

Red Cloud had been deep in thought, trying to make sense of the bizarre situation. All he wanted was a quiet life with Possum Chaser and the wolf pack. "When would we time our observations to find it?" he asked.

"During the time around sunrise and sunset, while the other planets and stars are still around to give us accurate relative positioning. I'll get a rota organised. Shall I include you, Red?"

"Yes, and Possum Chaser too."

Dearden stood and went to the fireplace, leant on it, the usual thing he did when he was working things out. It saved him pacing, which was too theatrical.

"OK, set up a rota Harry, I've got a Meade ETX 125 astro scope we can use, I'll get it out of storage."

"The Meade will do for a start, but we need a scope with a far larger aperture than that to pick up all the light we can from the area. The Sun will be bright and Nibiru will be small so we need the best instrument we can get hold of to spot it as soon as it shows."

"How about your own reflector?"

"I had to sell it to go toward course fees."

"Then you'd better tell me what you need."

"A 12-inch Astro-Royal E22b reflector with premier coated lenses and an E23 tripod. It's also essential to get a metal-on-glass solar filter and a good CCD camera, I suggest a Huygens 6 Mklll. My laptop will be fine for image storage and analysis; I've already got the software downloaded that I need."

"Sort out where to get the kit and give me the information."

"Already done." Harry took a crumpled printed sheet with prices and contact details from his pocket and handed it to Dearden.

"All the information's there. They have everything in stock. It can be with us tomorrow p.m. by courier if it's ordered—" He checked his watch, "Within the next hour. What we also need is a buddy situated a long distance away to take part in an identical operation to ours.

"Why," Wynter asked.

"When Nibiru appears the buddy and I will photograph it at the same time. It will appear to be in different positions on each image. We'll measure the differences of position of Nibiru from other known objects on both images. Knowing the length of the baseline between our two observation points, we'll be able to roughly calculate the planet's distance from Earth. With that information, and a few days' observation giving us changes in position relative to other objects, we'll work out a rough measurement of its speed and time of arrival."

Dearden was impressed. "And let me guess, Harry. You already have the buddy—"

Matt Roberts interrupted. "It would be better if you could give us an accurate measurement, rather than a rough one, Harry."

"I'm coming to that. I do have a buddy in Chile, Carlos Mendulas. He has his own astronomy equipment at Coquimbo, where he lives, but he's also the site manager at the Gemini South Observatory. Once we patch Carlos in on the urgency of the situation we should get some time on the Gemini South scope. It's got an eight point one-metre primary mirror and with the Doppler shift equipment they've got we'll be able to calculate Nibiru's orbital velocity and arrival time very accurately. Another thing, when we pick it up, others will and then the silence will definitely be broken." Harry nodded in Matt Roberts' direction as if to say up yours, for his challenge about accuracy.

32

The Maudslay carrying Pierpoint and Arthur Doughty was half way to the Gulfstream, which was in the holding position on the runway. Pierpoint was on the phone to Dearden, who could hear the Maudslay's engine in the background.

"We're on the Maudslay heading for the Gulfstream. We'll be airborne and heading for New York within minutes . . . hold on, what's happening?"

Dearden heard a sudden screech of tyres and the steady background drone of the Maudslay's engine slowed down. Arthur Doughty's voice shouted, "Will watch out . . ." and then the phone went dead.

It took a couple of seconds for Dearden to catch on. He shouted, "Will what's up?" but there was no reply. Again, "Will, come on!" He waited. Still nothing.

Mitch, something's going on at Kineton Base, your dad was shouting, now the phone's dead. We need to get there, quick."

* * *

Arthur Doughty saw the laser-pointer through the front window of the coach. It had wavered slightly and then found its target, the coach driver's eyes. Proctor jammed his foot on the brake and as the coach skidded to a halt Doughty shouted a warning.

Pierpoint and Doughty dived for cover as two men in combat gear were picked out in the coach's headlights. Each of the men had an Uzi SMG and were moving around to the door with the guns aimed very seriously. One of the gunmen stayed by the outside of the door, while the other took a walk around the outside of the coach and looked through the windows to see if he could spot the target he was sent to eliminate. He could see neither the target nor the target's companion.

The first one through the door, gun forward, said nothing, but saw Pierpoint and Doughty on the floor and with a flick of the gun motioned for them to get to the back of the coach. They stood, but didn't go to the back, they just stood, separated from each other by the width of the aisle. The second gunman went to the driver's seat. Again, saying nothing, he indicated with the gun for Proctor to vacate the seat and get off the coach. When he began to protest the gunman aimed the gun slightly right and loosed a single shot into the front seat behind the driver's position. Proctor sped up and reached the steps. He looked back at Pierpoint and mouthed sorry, and as he was stepping off the coach, the gunman hit him on the back of the head with the Uzi to speed him up some more. Proctor fell to the ground and didn't move.

During the distraction, Art Doughty whispered to Pierpoint that he was going to take the man nearest to them. "I'll take the other," Pierpoint whispered back. "Got to get nearer my target. Need a ruse." The gunman that hit Proctor got into the driver's seat and leant his Uzi in a corner. Pierpoint suddenly staggered and lurched against a nearby seatback.

"Heart attack, help . . . help me," he sounded convincing and looked convincing as he sagged against the next seat toward the front of the vehicle. The Maudslay's engine started and the driver looked back and grated the gears.

Doughty shouted, "Mind what you're doing with those gears you bloody idiot, this vehicle's valuable." The gears grated again and the driver swore. He didn't know how to double de-clutch

"Heart . . . heart attack," Pierpoint croaked and lurched again as the Maudslay jerked forward. He gained another three feet nearer the driver.

Doughty shouted again. "I told you to watch those gears," The gunman nearest him frowned as he got sick of the noise from both of the men behind him and told Doughty to shut his mouth or he'd shut it for him. Pierpoint groaned again and staggered another two feet. He sounded as if he was about to die and then said, in a wavering voice, "This is it Art," and they both leapt forward.

Shots rang out as the action started.

The first burst of rapid fire from the Uzi spread wide and ripped into seats and body panelling. The coach swerved as the driver turned to see what was happening. Pierpoint had almost reached the front of the coach when a second burst of shots spread around the coach. Art Doughty cried out and fell to the floor. Pierpoint stopped his headlong flight to the driver and spun round. Oblivious to safety, he brushed past the Uzi, taking the gunman by surprise. He could have taken the chance with the gun, grabbed and swung it in an upward arc, floored the assailant and stamped on his throat, but Arthur needed him.

Pierpoint knelt at his side and saw it was bad.

"Move away from him," the gunman ordered.

"I can't, he's losing blood. We need medical help; I'm going to use my phone." Pierpoint reached for where it had fallen.

The gunman kicked it away. His attention was distracted as the phone clattered against the side of the coach and it was enough for Pierpoint to make a move. He lunged for the gunman's legs and took him down; the Uzi scattered a burst into the ceiling and shattered one of the windows of the Maudslay. Pierpoint was strong and wiry, deceptive for his age. As the gunman went down he hit his head on one of the seat supports with a metallic clang. The man lay dazed for a couple of seconds. Pierpoint stood and saw the driver trying to concentrate on driving, and at the same time trying to turn to see if what he could do for his downed colleague.

The stunned gunman yelled when Pierpoint stamped on his arm and the bone snapped. The Uzi dropped from his hand and Pierpoint grabbed it. He crashed the butt end into the gunman's temple where it was soft and the man lay still.

The driver in the cab of the Maudslay glanced in the mirror facing back to the passenger compartment and saw Pierpoint looming up behind him fast. He accelerated, cut across the grass and took runway 16-34 southeast at speed. It lay at one hundred and twenty degrees to the main airstrip and headed toward an area near the perimeter of MoD Kineton, where thick woodland grew close to the security fence.

33

"Security,"

"This is Dearden . . . there's been a security breach." The man on the Kineton Dump 4 phone became attentive.

"Give me the code, sir." he commanded. Every day SHaFT security generated a new code for its operatives.

Dearden spoke the code.

"You're in, what can we do?"

"We've had a call from Pierpoint; he's in the Maudslay with Arthur Doughty, heading for the Gulfstream. Get to it and see what's going on"

Dearden rang off. "Mitch, Matt, get field kits together, we're heading to Kineton base." Dearden chucked Mitch Doughty the key to the storeroom down the steps at the side of the great hall.

Dearden rang Bob Mallett and gave him a thirty-second outline of the situation. The anaesthetist pilot of the medic team was on permanent standby where he lived with his family in Hill Wootton. In another apartment of the large house, Jack Green, the surgeon, was relaxing with his wife. He picked up the live-op phone on its first ring. It was Mallett.

"We're on the move. Rapid transport to Dearden Hall to pick up Dearden, Doughty and Roberts. Onward to Kineton base where there's trouble."

"With you in two." Green leapt up from the settee. He lived for the adrenaline of these times and his wife went along with it. Always after a sudden call to action there followed a time of comparative peace and an item of ceramics by Clarice Cliff to add to her collection.

Green grabbed his backpack off the hook and headed to where Mallett was finishing his pre-flight checks on the helipad aided by the two engineers who lived on site. The twin Turbomeca Arriel turboshafts were up to temperature. Green looked at his colleague and wondered what this mission would bring.

Mallett lifted the machine and swung it, nose down in a fast climb toward Hampton in Arden.

It never failed to impress Rowan when she heard the sound of a powerful engine. Her introduction to twenty-first-century life in the past months had been a relatively passive transition after the time shift from Anglo-Saxon times, but she loved the sound of a powerful engine. She came into the hall with Possum Chaser and saw Dearden in animated conversation with the others around him. She had heard the sound of rotors in the distance. He looked at her and gave her a brief smile.

"I was going to come and tell you, there are problems at Kineton Base."

"Bad problems?"

"Will Pierpoint and Arthur Doughty, things don't seem right." Rowan looked around. There was tension in the great hall. Mitch Doughty and Roberts ran up from below. They had large bags slung on their shoulders and were dressed in black combat gear. What conversation there was going on was crisp and focussed. Dearden called to Heskin to get the spotlights on in the car park ready for the helicopter, went to get his field kit and change into combat gear.

Rowan recalled similar activity during her time with Aelfryth and Leofwin at Heanton in the Arden. The alarm bell near the entrance gate sometimes rang and the men at arms would rush about with a clash of chain mail and steel, ready to defend the manor house.

"What's happened?" Templestone asked. Dearden had called him over from his apartment above the studio. He was still suffering from the hypothermia, although he wouldn't admit it.

"Pierpoint was on the phone from Kineton Base, they're on the way to the States."

"Already? He's moving quick."

"I hope he is; Arthur's with him and I heard Art shout a warning over the phone. The call was cut off . . . listen up all." The sound of the Eurocopter circling above forced him to shout.

"I don't know how long Mitch, Matt and I will be at Kineton Base, but in case we're not back soon, you others need to work along with Harry when the astronomy gear arrives tomorrow."

Harry nodded, "OK, we'll try to contact Lan-Si-Nu as well."

Dearden said, "No, do the astronomy first, that's important and it'll be enough to cope with. Just set up shifts so that it's not too taxing. We'll attempt to contact the aliens when we've located Nibiru so we have something concrete to talk to them about."

"We're in between the devil and the deep blue sea with this Nibiru thing," Wynter said. "We've got the planet comin' that ev'ryone's wishin' was still a legend, and we're goin' to ask a bunch of oversized woojies to give us a hand. Some damn choice."

"Just shut the negative crap, Lee." Wynter's comment had irritated Harry. It was rare Harry got wound up, "We've got a threat coming that happened once before. The book of Genesis and Sho'mer's scroll tell us there were survivors from that incident."

"Yeah, man, but we ain't got an ark."

Dearden turned to Templestone. "Bill – you've got your old job back again."

"Let me guess, does it include a shot-gun?"

"Yep, you're rear-guard and my second in command while I'm away. I have no idea how long that'll be."

The sound of the turbines spooling down outside brought the room to readiness and Dearden pulled up his combat hood and kissed Rowan. Julia saw it and felt a surge of anger as the jealousy slid back in again. She wondered what was going on in her mind. As Dearden was about to go out the door he turned back to Julia.

"Jules, make sure Rowan's OK while I'm away will you?" he followed Mitch and Matt out to the waiting helicopter. Five minutes later, after a gale of wind-blown debris, the navigation lights had become a speck in the night sky.

They trailed back inside. Rowan thought it was bad that Julia had stayed in the great hall, while everyone else saw the men off as they went into action.

34

"We'll land in five minutes," Mallett said as he surveyed the instruments and the lights dotted around the landscape below. "We've just passed over Barford on the right and Bishops Tachbrook to the left." He started the descent, "over to the left you can see Lighthorne and there's Moreton Morrell Agricultural College. "That's Dump 4 up ahead; the helipad's lit up for us."

"Overfly the area with the landing spots on Bob, we need to locate the Maudslay." Dearden reached into his backpack and pulled out his Beretta. He breached a round and slipped the safety off as Mallet contacted the control tower, gave them his security code and told them what was going on.

Mallett began to circle the Eurocopter around the MoD site and floodlights came on all over the place. Armoured personnel carriers were rushing to the entrances and two were churning the grass as they raced in opposite directions around the inside of the perimeter fence. Mallett took the Eurocopter low and fast at thirty feet southwest along 04-22, the main runway. The landing spots picked out all the detail. Dearden could almost pick out the grain in the tarmac.

"Nothing here Jem," Mallett said, settling to a hover at the end of the runway. "We have two runways running off this one, 16-34 and 10-28, let's take a look." He brought the Eurocopter up one hundred feet and backtracked the main runway to 10-28 and veered along it up to the end where a barrier lay that was marked for aborted take-off and landing. There was no sign of the Maudslay.

"Let's try runway 16-34." Dearden was impressed at the way Mallett handled the helicopter. It was tight and precise. He executed a G-inducing turn over the grass and sped southeast along 16-34. Dearden took a quick glance at the map and saw there was a wood coming up the other side of the perimeter fence. The trees were ahead in the glare of the landing spots and there was something else, beyond the reach of the lights.

"The coach is over there Jem, getting near the boundary fence, see it?" Mallett pointed. Putting the power on, he got to the coach in seconds and brought the helicopter to a hover over it, looking for a landing place.

Below, in the coach, Pierpoint had slipped the belt out of his trousers as he ran down the centre aisle to the driver, who was struggling to maintain control of the coach and get to the pistol in his shoulder holster at the same time. The coach was moving at nearly forty miles an hour, bouncing over the grass when the driver tried to drop it a couple of gears. The gearbox grated as he forced them to engage.

Pierpoint reached the cab and with a single movement hooked his belt under the driver's chin, drew it tight around his neck and pulled with all his force. The driver's feet left the pedals, kicked in the air and his hands left the steering wheel. The coach snaked from side to side and drifted to a stop on the grass near the runway a few yards away from the perimeter fence. Pierpoint had heard a helicopter nearby as he tightened the belt around the driver's neck he buckled it, leaving the man losing consciousness.

"More fool you for taking me on," he said to the man as he left him with the belt buckled. He rushed to Arthur, who was lying on the floor, pale and gasping for breath.

"I'm cold Will . . . so cold . . . the light's going." Arthur was shaking and Pierpoint took his coat off and placed it over his friend to keep him warm He grabbed his mobile phone and dialled the medics. Jack Green answered. He said they were landing close by with Dearden and two others.

"Get here quick Jack, Arthur Doughty's been shot, he's in a bad way." As Pierpoint rang off a vehicle pulled up outside the coach, its headlights glaring through the windows.

The door crashed open and two SHaFT men in combat gear rushed in, shouting, "Get down, get down, guns, guns." They saw Pierpoint kneeling over Arthur Doughty and two hostiles incapacitated.

Outside the sound of the helicopter's turbines were cycling down. Arthur was trying to say something. Pierpoint bent low to hear what he said in a whisper.

"It's . . . it's been good Will, we've made a difference you know." He gasped again as the pain came in another wave.

"Make way . . . move," Green and Mallett rushed in and the two SHaFT security guards moved along the coach to give the medics room to work. Green ripped Doughty's shirt open. He looked at the position of the wound, which was close to the heart. He took his stethoscope and listened to Doughty's heartbeat. It was weak and erratic. Breathing was abnormal. He looked at Mallet and shook his head slightly.

"I think there may be internal ricochet damage to the lungs. OK, topical Lidocaine, oxygen and immediate surgery. There isn't time to fly him to the hospital bay. Let's get to it." During Jack Green's rapid assessment, Mallett had been preparing Doughty for Ketamine general anaesthesia and was introducing it when Dearden and Roberts came through the door. Mitch Doughty came in last and saw the bullet holes and the smashed window. Someone was on the floor, with Green and Mallett working urgently on him, triage equipment close-by, blood on the floor and Pierpoint looking pensive, which was unusual.

Mitch went up close, saw it was his father, unconscious and deathly pale on the floor. Dearden held him back.

"No Mitch, back off," he said, taking his arm firmly, forcing him to the entrance of the coach by the driver's cab.

Mitch could hear Green saying, "He has tension pneumothorax, give me a 14 gauge TPAK chest decompression needle and a Heimlich valve." Green found the access point and inserted the needle. The pressure inside Arthur's chest cavity escaped through the valve.

Mitch looked at his father on the floor and felt a storm of anger welling up inside. He turned to the driver of the coach who was gasping for breath with Pierpoint's belt still around his neck. Doughty got to the man in a second and put his hands on the belt. Both Dearden and Pierpoint didn't move a muscle to stop him.

"You bloody bastard," Mitch Doughty spoke low and quiet. He grasped the belt in both hands, one hand on the buckle and the other hand on the free end. Contrary to what the others thought was going to happen, he slipped the prong from the hole and freed the belt. He put his hands up to his head, ran them through his hair and roared his anger out. The driver put his hand to his throat. There were two ugly welts where the leather had dug in. He gasped for some seconds and then breathed easy and thanked Mitch Doughty.

Pierpoint held his hand out for his belt and put it back around the driver's neck. "I thought you were going to finish the job then Mitch, it's best you didn't, we may get some information out of him. Get to your father, see if Green and Mallett need assistance." Pierpoint turned to the man gripping the steering wheel, whose knuckles were white.

"If you've hurt Harvey Proctor as well as Arthur I'll put you through all sorts of things that will make you wish you were dead," Pierpoint threatened.

"He'll be OK," the driver said.

"You have hurt Arthur badly . . . I don't think I can forgive you for that." Pierpoint's voice was cold and harsh. Dearden had never heard him like that.

The driver was gasping again. "Loosen the belt, will you?"

"No . . . I want more answers, then I might loosen the belt. Who are you working for?" the driver flinched at the question, his clandestine training forgotten.

"The man at the top," he said.

"Which man? Name him." The driver reached up, trying to get to Pierpoint, but his hands flailed about. "The name," Pierpoint said.

"Bull . . . Fenton Bull."

"Mmm . . . you should never trust a politician . . . now tell me your name."

"They call me Rickshaw, I was an asset in China."

"What instructions did Fenton Bull give you?" Pierpoint toyed with the end of the belt strap.

"To follow you."

"And then what?" the driver went quiet. Pierpoint called Dearden over.

"Jem, hold this ape's arms, persuasion's needed."

"Pleasure's mine," Dearden said, he grabbed the man's arms and pinned them back. The man panicked.

"Alright . . . alright, I'll tell you. Our instructions were to stop you."

"Stop me in what way?"

"Permanently."

"Why?"

"How would I know? I'm just a grunt on the lower level."

"Lower level of what?" the agent hesitated. Pierpoint grasped the belt again. The driver didn't want to open himself up to comeback from his controllers, so he hinted to Pierpoint who it was he worked for,

"Vauxhall Cross."

"Oh . . . you're from across the river? So, Bull didn't want the local boys to deal with me, did he? Thing is, you don't realise what a nest of vipers you've crawled into . . . do you?"

"We've got the bullet," Green called. He was tidying the wound area. "Let's move him quick, the internal damage is bad." He told Mitch Doughty they were keeping his dad anaesthetised to lessen the shock. They said something about doing their best and an induced coma.

Mitch cut himself off from the situation. He and his dad had the best of times together and they were close, like best of friends. If things went badly it was too soon to lose him. To lose him to old age was one thing, but not like this. But Mitch couldn't allow the anger, revenge and sadness to come. He needed his mind clear, to work with his colleagues on the impending threat. Mitch saw Pierpoint slipping the prong out of the hole in the belt, but he didn't undo it. To the flailing of arms and desperate gasping from the driver, he saw Pierpoint tighten the belt and pull it as far as it would go.

35

The Eurocopter landed on the helipad yards away from Dump 4 and a medical crew on standby transferred Art Doughty to the hospital bay. Pierpoint headed to his office with Dearden. He took out his mobile and made an urgent call to Templestone at Dearden Hall.

"There's bad news. Arthur's been shot. The injury's near his heart."

It was a body-blow.

"Will he be all right?"

"We don't know. It's too early to say. Green and Mallett are doing their best with him."

"How did it happen?"

"Two MI5 operatives infiltrated the Maudslay on our way to the Gulfstream. It happened by order of Fenton Bull. He wanted to take me out because of what he told me about Eisenburg when I met him at number ten."

"Eisenburg are involved?"

"Very much so. They're at the back of the conspiracy of silence. More to the point, Fenton Bull is in deep with them. He opened up and what has become obvious is that he's frightened to death about reprisals because he's told me too much."

"What now?"

"I need your help."

"Tell me how."

"Come to New York with me. Pick up where Arthur was taken down."

"When?"

"Pack your bag. We'll be with you in the Eurocopter within the hour to bring you to Kineton Base. I'll talk to Mitch Doughty and get him along as well."

"What's going to happen in New York?"

"I have a favour to call in. We're going to the United Nations to see if we can get concerted action to address the threat, Lord knows, we need it. If the UN has what I have heard they've got tucked away we'll try to avert a disaster by using it. It's a bit of a long shot, old man, but worth a try. Apart from that, Eisenburg is not going to take SHaFT down. If it's the last thing I do, I will destroy Eisenburg and their criminal wall of silence."

"There's another long shot to add to yours Will. Jem's going to try something he has in mind to do with the Hub. He calls it Plan B."

"I'll talk to him about it. In the meantime, speak to Matt Roberts. See if you can drag him along as well. He can be usefully persuasive at times." Pierpoint rang off, sat at his desk and indicated the seat opposite for Dearden.

"Priest said you have a Plan B, Jem. Tell me about it."

* * *

Templestone got some essential travelling gear together and called Julia and Matt over to his apartment. He explained the mission and Roberts agreed to go. Julia would ride shotgun while Templestone was away. Being part of SHaFT had made her resilient to change. She was used to fast action and quick decisions, but she was concerned about what had happened to Arthur Doughty and told Templestone to take care. She didn't want Templestone to jeopardise himself.

* * *

The engines spooled up to full throttle and the Gulfstream surged forward. There were four passengers and the jet had the usual four crew.

When they reached cruising altitude Tez Macaulay, the mission pilot came aft, leaving the controls with Len Sexton, the co-pilot.

"Anything you need sir?" Tez asked. It wasn't often the chief rode with them and he wanted to give Pierpoint his personal attention.

"Jim Beam, if you will, with Canada Dry and a touch of Angostura bitters. That would go down well," Sir Willoughby said. "But don't drown it with the dry."

"And for the rest of you gentlemen?" They ordered and Macaulay brought the drinks on a silver tray.

Pierpoint outlined his strategy. "We'll be flying into JFK. Lola Petrel will pick us up; by the way, she hates the name Lola so everyone knows her as Storm. She has influence via her father's bank and she has helped SHaFT a number of times in the States. Storm will take us to the UN buildings. Two of us, you and me, Bill, will go in to see the man in charge. Mitch and Matt, you hang around close by and try to look casual, but cover our backs, Fenton Bull may have a long reach. The big man at the UN has given us thirty minutes. He and I have met several times on SHaFT business. He owes me some favours, hence this meeting."

Pierpoint leant forward over the table and indicated for the others to get close. He spoke in low tones so that the flight crew wouldn't hear. Not that they couldn't be trusted, but the fewer that knew, the better. "I have heard from a reliable source that the UN ensured something no one could handle safely was locked away. It could well help us out of the coming catastrophe. I intend to convince the chief to use it."

"What is it they have in the cupboard?" Matt Roberts asked. The three reacted in different ways when they heard what Pierpoint said. Raised eyebrows, a surprised look, a disbelieving shake of the head.

"You do get into the right places for information," Roberts said. Roberts was unconventional. He was honing the Bowie knife he called Mavis to a fine edge on the corner of the expensive marble topped table that separated the four men, two each side.

"It's surprising what you get to know heading up SHaFT." Pierpoint, who was unconventional himself, looked at Roberts in his bandana in the way a father might look at an errant child, but he said nothing. His way of leading was from the front. He was easy with it too. Tolerance of his team members' individuality helped cement them into a cohesive achieving force. SHaFT respected him for his tolerance.

Mitch Doughty's thoughts returned to his father, how he had seen him lying in a pool of blood. He forced the image from his mind to prevent it jeopardising the high stakes they would be playing for in New York.

"Mitch and Matt, I'll be specific about why you're here. When I was with Fenton Bull, he told me about Eisenburg's role in the United Nations, how it was them who, with a very heavy hand, ensured the widespread silence about Nibiru. Bull admitted he's part of Eisenburg. The conversation got heated up and I told him what a hypocritical bastard he is. He must have regretted his candour because he sent those two MI5 goons to kill me, and injured Arthur in the process. Bull may have worked out I would go to the UN, so you two are here to cover our backs because Bull may have a long reach." Mitch Doughty nodded and felt the Colt in his right coat pocket. He jiggled the boxes of shells in the other pocket. Roberts instinctively moved his coat and thumbed the honed edge of the Bowie he called Mavis. He had his throwing knives with him too.

*　*　*

The Gulfstream touched down at JFK and was guided to a holding area. Doughty and Roberts looked out the window in the door and could see an officious looking individual ready to receive them. By his side was a tall brunette woman in a trouser suit. She had shoulder length hair and a tan.

"That's Storm Petrel," Pierpoint said from behind the group. "She can be a bit headstrong, watch your step." Mitch saw Matt Roberts looking with more than casual interest at the woman on the tarmac.

"She's all there," Roberts said, out of the side of his mouth to Doughty as the cabin door opened and the internal stairs extended to the ground. Doughty and Roberts descended and stood each side of the stairs on the tarmac checking for unexpected movement. Pierpoint and Templestone came next and walked forward toward Storm and the man by her side, who stood a good six inches lower.

"You made good time," the brunette said. "Follow me Sir Willoughby, there are just a few formalities to get you through

U.S. Customs." Storm Petrel spoke with a Southern States accent that Matt Roberts thought was the sweetest thing. He analysed the style of her walk.

Doughty nudged his arm. "You're looking for interlopers, not the scenery."

Roberts sniggered and Storm turned around; she gave him the hint of a smile.

The official who met them with Storm Petrel was a representative of Milt Herschel, Secretary of U.S. Homeland Security. Pierpoint had rung him with an urgent request for quick entry into the States, telling him it was an urgent mission of the highest priority.

"Milt, I can't stress enough how important this is. No doubt you will hear about it before much longer."

"OK Sir Willoughby, you're as good as through the gate. I know when you say somethin's urgent, it sure damn well is urgent."

The official left them as soon as they were through customs and Storm led the way to a Cadillac Escalade. Roberts was quick to get to the front driver door, which he opened for her. She flashed him a smile, "Thank you, sir I'm sure," she said, in pure Missouri, "But I can quite well see to my own door."

He shrugged his shoulders. "OK, maybe next time." He sounded disappointed. Storm Petrel opened the front passenger door and indicated for Pierpoint to get in and then she opened the doors in turn for Templestone and the others. She made sure Roberts came last.

36

When Cyrus Crowe and his two men dropped the stone in place over the vault in the Knights' Sanctuary, he was right in thinking that the old man who had caused him trouble was amongst those trapped in the space below. He had heard his voice. The man gave him the creeps with his attitude. The way he said his name was Death had been un-nerving. The best way to deal with him was to seal him in the stone tomb in case he had seen Garth Wilde at Keeper's Cottage. It had been the best way to deal with the others too. They had been getting close to the scroll supposedly hidden in the sanctuary and Crowe wanted it himself.

Crowe reasoned that the old man and his compatriots must have picked up the same information about the Knights' Sanctuary that Villiers had accumulated in the White Star Line trunk. On top of that, they had deduced that there was a vault in the sanctuary where the artefact might be hidden.

It was a simple way to deal with the situation. By now, they would all be dead, probably of starvation, or by running out of oxygen. They would be lying around the artefact, or on the stone steps, with their nails scraped to the quick from trying to claw their way through the stone to get to the air and light outside.

It was time to go back to lift the slab and lay claim to what was his. He chose to go to the Sanctuary at three o'clock in the morning. That was the time when people in the village would be in their deepest sleep and any noise they made would be masked by slumber. With how the police were kept busy with town-crime there would be no patrol in Temple Balsall.

Crowe left Big Al lying full length with his leg in plaster on the settee in the lounge at Alderhanger. Garth Wilde was slipping in and out of consciousness in hospital. Doctors had conversed in serious tones around his bed discussing test results. They decided to administer strong antibiotics intravenously to rid him of the septicaemia taking over his body from the festering wound in his shoulder.

The four by four slowly pulled up on a narrow road near the Knights' Sanctuary. A thick mist had fallen and Dan Blundell had to lean near to the windscreen to pick out the edge of the road. He was looking for the car park.

"There it is, just ahead to the left," Crowe said from the passenger seat. He had the window open and his head was out the window as he tried to gaze through the mist in the glare of the headlights. Blundell drove on a few more yards and spotted a gap in the tall yew hedge. All the crime scene tape had gone, but he still eased the vehicle through slowly. He parked at the far end of the car park and switched off the lights and the engine. Crowe notched the door open a touch and listened. The heavy mist enveloped their sounds. It was better that way for what they had to do, but Crowe didn't relish opening the tomb up and sorting through the corpses for the artefact. It was an appropriate night for that sort of work with all the mist. Crowe had the auto assault shotgun gripped tightly as he walked through the gap in the yew hedge.

"Use your tools on the door, Bernie," Crowe said, shining a torch on the latch. Crosher got a small jemmy and a thin three inches by six sheet of steel from his pocket and got to work on the door. Five minutes later, they were in and the door was shut behind them. The torch in Crosher's hand lit the way down the centre aisle.

"That's where the entrance is," Crowe pointed to a large, expensive rug on the floor. He grabbed one of the ends and threw it to one side, exposing the slab sealing the burial chamber.

"Jemmy it open," Crowe said to Crosher. "You'd better wear one of these." He handed Crosher and Blundell a mask each that, according to the hardware shop where he bought them, would filter out chemical and toxic odours. He assumed that would include the smell of rotting flesh. Bernie Crosher put the crowbar into the gap and forced the slab upwards.

"Stick the wood under it," Crosher said to Blundell. Blundell tried putting the wood offcut he had with him in the gap.

"Lift it some more," Blundell said.

"I can't, it's bloody heavy. Give us a hand Crowe, don't just stand there. Crowe didn't like the tone of voice, but he came and leant on the metal bar. The slab lifted sufficiently for Blundell to force the wood in the gap. They eased the pressure off the crowbar and the slab settled down onto the wood.

They grappled with the slab and lifted until it was standing on its edge, then dragged it clear of the dark entrance. Crosher stepped back a few paces.

"Shine the torch down there . . . come on, don't arse about." Crosher was holding the torch and didn't like the surroundings in the Sanctuary. The darkness added to the earthy smell from the ancient woodwork and stone. He took a deep breath, then shone the beam of light down the steps, then froze.

"What's the matter, something waiting for you down there?" Crowe asked, playing on Crosher's nerves. He craned his neck to see past Blundell's shoulder, to see into the void.

No one on the steps, that's odd . . . they should be there.

"Give me the damn torch, I'll go first." Crowe had steeled himself against the harrowing sight of the bodies on the steps of those he buried alive clawing for air. He forced himself past Crosher and went down the steps with an outward show of bravado, but he slowed down as his head ducked below ground level. Crosher's nervousness was catching.

He got to the last step and shone the torch around. Blundell came next and then Crosher, whose breathing was fast and shallow.

"They should be here." Crowe missed his footing. Blundell caught the back of his jacket and stopped him falling. Crowe steadied himself, allowed his heartbeat to settle and then shone the torch around. All he could see was red sandstone walls, an effigy and a stone plinth.

"We shut them in here, didn't we? You saw it." He was uncertain about there being no bodies.

"It was solid as a rock when we shut them in, there is no way they could have disappeared. Shine the torch around again," Blundell suggested.

The light cut through the darkness into the far corners of the vault. Crowe had an uneasy feeling about it. A cold feeling down his back. He ventured further into the room and shone the torch into all the corners, onto the marble effigy of a knight in the middle of the room, and a plinth about waist high behind it. The torchlight picked out an ornate box on the floor at the base of the tomb. It was empty.

"According to the records, there should be an ancient artefact in the sanctuary. We've covered everywhere upstairs, so it has to be down here. My betting is that it was in that box. Crowe picked up the box and examined it. He smelt it.

"Cedar," and then he turned it over, examining the carpentry. He could tell it was ancient, could see the tool marks of the carpenter. The box itself would be worth a lot, apart from what used to be in it. "They've got the scroll, and they've escaped."

When Crowe faced Blundell and Crosher his face was twisted with anger and his hatred surfaced. "This is what we'll do. One, I want that old bastard who saw Wilde, and wrecked my outbuildings, dead. Two, I want the artefact that was in that box." The other two knew not to cross Crowe at the best of times, but in this mood, he was dangerous. They nodded they would get it done.

As Crowe looked around the vault, he was mystified about how they lifted the slab and got out. It was heavy for the three of them above ground to manage, let alone trying to lift it from below in the confined space at the top of the steps. Despite his anger he felt very uneasy about the old man who had escaped. The chill of the vault seeped into his bones and fear shivered down his back.

37

Storm Petrel had negotiated the exit from JFK and as she picked up Grand Central Parkway heading to Flushing Meadows, Pierpoint's mobile phone rang.

"There's been a change of venue. We are going to his private townhouse, number 3 Sutton Place."

"I know it. Parking could be a problem. We shall see. I can wait nearby until you call me that you're finished."

"Why the change of venue?" Templestone asked Pierpoint.

"The man says he's changed his schedule to give us more time. I think it was a little something I said to him when I rang to say we were on our way."

* * *

They passed the United Nations Plaza with the sculptures.

"Damn hypocrites," Storm said, with attitude, giving the sculpture of a pistol with its barrel tied in a knot, the finger.

"They talk peace and then a bunch of them go in with the damn gun. Damn hypocrites."

"They do their best like we do, sometimes there's no option," Matt Roberts said from the back seat."

"Mmm, I'm sure as hell you think you're right about that, Mister Roberts, but I have my doubts."

"What does your daddy do Storm? Is he in the arms business?" Roberts asked. Sometimes he couldn't resist a wind-up, the cut and thrust of words. The Cadillac swerved slightly from its straight course. Storm looked in the rear-view mirror and saw Roberts' grin. Another half mile of banter and Storm pulled up at the side of the road outside a double fronted five-storey building with grey doors and shutters. Number 3, Sutton Place.

There were two military guards outside the door. One of them advanced with his HK 416 aimed at the car. He opened the driver's door.

"Yes, ma'am what is your business?" he glanced into the car and saw the four men. He kept the gun in a prepared position.

"Sir Willoughby Pierpoint is expected." Pierpoint handed over his passport and those of the other men. The guard looked at the photographs. Scrutinised the men.

He was expecting them to arrive. Internal security had emailed their photographs. The information had come from the very top of the Department of Homeland Security. He looked at the four men when they got out the car. One of them was a mean looking individual with a bandana.

He asked them to follow.

"You too ma'am." He signalled to the other guard by the door, who called inside and a man came out to the Cadillac. "Sergeant Markland will drive your car into the side street . . . it will be perfectly safe.

"I'm sure it will," Storm said, looking at the gun. She handed over her keys.

The guard led them into an entrance hall with French doors and an Art Deco marble floor. A burly individual in a dark suit with a bulge near the shoulder looked them over and spent longer eyeing up Matt Roberts than the other men and longer still looking at Storm Petrel.

Roberts knew the type, ex-military judging by the close-cropped hair. Like a bull in a scrap, but with no finesse, down on the floor in five seconds. "Please follow me, the ex-mil said, in a voice too high for his body.

He led them up a wide oak staircase with a thick pile carpet and at the top, he went straight ahead past a series of side doors to one that lay straight ahead. He opened it and went straight in. It was a sumptuous room with furnishings and pictures in the Scandinavian style.

"Please sit," he said, and knocked on an inner door. They sat, apart from Roberts. There was a call from within. The voice sounded cultured north European. The escort went in and there was a muttered conversation and then he came out again. He looked at Matt Roberts first then Mitch Doughty, and then again looked at Storm for longer.

"Sir Willoughby Pierpoint and William Templestone will be called shortly. You others are requested to wait here." The man made for the door. Roberts moved so he stood in front of it. Mitch was sitting in a chair at the side. Everyone who came across Roberts could tell he was a maverick. The bandana and the long hair was a giveaway and some thought the intensity of his eyes was disturbing.

"Excuse me, sir," the large man said. His voice, although a touch high, was demanding, imperious, even. His size always made other men accede to his demands. Roberts moved slowly to the side, not enough for the large man to get out without asking again. He motioned with his finger for the man to come near because he had something to tell him. He whispered in his ear that he wanted his name.

"Cohlin."

"What?"

"Cohlin."

"Colin will do me, it's simpler. Colin, keep your dirty eyes and hands off the girl." The man gave him a vicious look. Roberts got close to his ear again. "If you so much as lay a finger on her I'll break your fat neck." Roberts stepped to one side and, without another look at him, indicated Cohlin could walk out the door.

Roberts walked further into the room and sat down on a double seat next to Storm Petrel. There was a call for Sir Willoughby to come in. It was then that Roberts noticed the polished brass plaque on the door. Lars Knudsen, Secretary-General of the United Nations.

Sir Willoughby Pierpoint opened the door and stood aside for Templestone to walk in and he shut the door behind them.

* * *

Lars Knudsen stood and welcomed them.

"Sir Willoughby, to what do I owe this pleasure?" he indicated seats but remained standing himself. Pierpoint looked at the Norwegian Secretary-General and could see by his eyes that the meeting was anything but pleasurable.

"You know why I've come, Lars, I intimated it was about Eisenburg. For a start, I might add that when they asked me years ago if I wanted to become part of the club, as they put it, I refused on moral grounds. I prefer to be guided by my conscience, rather than by what's expedient or popular, it works out better in the long run."

"Eisenburg works as a collective conscience."

"So why has the collective conscience maintained silence about the Nibiru issue over the years?" the words were unexpected and hit home. Pierpoint and Templestone could see Knudsen was caught out by the question and he sat down hard in the seat behind his desk. He thought for a moment how to frame his answer.

"We couldn't risk a breakdown in World-order. There would be chaos if news of that thing got out. Anyway, so we are told, there is a good chance it will veer off its course when it comes into the proximity of the Sun."

"I can assure you it won't, it's headed straight for us and I have that information on the authority of the best mathematician there is around these days. Here's documentation to prove it." Pierpoint slapped some of Harry Stanway and Professor Villiers' calculations down on the desk in front of him. He looked at the sheets of information, flicking through them quickly.

"The silence was an effort to buy time until we found the best way to deal with the problem without overreaction from the public," Knudsen said, as he pushed the papers away. "I know Nibiru is supposed to be there Sir Willoughby."

"Supposed to be there? Come on," Pierpoint pounded his fist on the desk. "It bloody well *is* there. I detect hypocrisy again. Why didn't you at least consider giving the population a fighting chance? There's a collective of brainpower out there," Pierpoint pointed out the window, "And necessity has always been the mother of invention. If the knowledge of Nibiru had been in the public domain, ideas would have come forward to deal with it, even if the chances of success had been minimal. As it is, the silence, including yours as head of the United Nations, has been criminal."

"What are you suggesting we do? If you are correct, we are on borrowed time and all the other problems the United Nations are trying to solve are insignificant by comparison."

"Which brings me to the other reason I'm here. Let's get to the point. I understand you have something that was an offshoot of the Manhattan Project that has been hidden from prying eyes. As far as I am aware it was never even tested because it was considered too lethal."

Lars Knudsen's eyes narrowed. His voice had become cold "Who told you that?"

"Never mind who told me, is it true?"

Knudsen fiddled with a Newton's Cradle and set the balls in motion. Tap, tap, tap, tap, tap, tap. Pierpoint hated Newton's Cradles. What was it with men of power and Newton's Cradles? He smiled inwardly about knocking Fenton Bull's off his desk. It would be counter-productive to do that to Knudsen's.

Knudsen fixed Pierpoint's gaze and answered, "It is true, it does exist, and there was a test. Professor Charles Villiers and his team separated themselves from the Manhattan project on moral grounds and returned to England. They made a discovery that dug far deeper into the nature of matter than the atomic bomb. No doubt you have heard of Robert Oppenheimer's comment after the Trinity test?"

"I have. I believe it was a few words out of the Bhagavad Gita, 'Now I am become Death, the destroyer of worlds.' The latter part of the statement would be useful if we were able to do it at this point in time."

"You remember well, Sir Willoughby. And there was a small-scale test of the weapon. There was fear about what the result would have been if there had been a full-scale test. Villiers informed Oppenheimer about the theory of his idea and convinced him that even the hydrogen bomb would have been like a firecracker by comparison to the super-weapon he had devised. After that, Oppenheimer distanced himself from Villiers. There was some sort of rift. We shall probably never know what was really behind it. It could have been jealousy. Sometimes scientists are rather precious about their brainchild.

"After the separation of Villiers and Oppenheimer, Villiers carried on with his own research. A mole in Villiers' team notified the UN about how disruptive to world order Villiers' project would be and a security council of trusted individuals was charged with the job of wrapping the project up. They had to ensure no one got their hands on it. The weapon is far too powerful to contemplate any of the rogue nations getting hold of it and holding the rest of us to ransom. Sir Willoughby, Charles Villiers created Pandora's Box and it had to remain secret."

"Are you confirming that the weapon is still in existence?" Pierpoint asked.

"Oh yes, it is."

"Where is it?"

"I'm afraid I can't tell you. That information is highly classified."

38

Lan-Si-Nu's warning, that there would be great changes for the people of Earth if contact was established had been at the back of Dearden's mind. His imagination toyed with what the changes might be. What would be opened up for Earth and its people in its future.

After Dearden became aware of the presence of Nibiru, he rationalised that any change, however great, if the aliens could help avert disaster, would not matter one iota. Discussing the matter with Pierpoint cleared the path.

"Do it Jem," Pierpoint had said, before he left for the States. "You have my blessing; there's nothing to lose." Dearden thought there could be a lot to lose because the plan was so radical. But what the hell, six months down the line radical things would occur. Anything would be worth a shot to save getting wiped out by the rogue planet.

"OK, I guess the worst they can do is say no," Dearden concluded, "And the sooner we find that out, the more prepared we'll be for our fightback."

* * *

Red Cloud and Possum Chaser were at Offchurch, where Esma was staying to help with the wolves. With Pierpoint still away in the States, Dearden gathered the depleted team into the great hall. Rowan, Harry Stanway, Julia Linden-Barthorpe and Lee Wynter were there.

"At this point, it's a trial," he said, holding the box Lan-Si-Nu had given him. It was how holding the primed bomb had been on the mission to Venice a few years back. A false move would have spelled disaster. His cool nerve had saved the hostages when he had walked out of the room in his black combats and lobbed the bomb into the canal. He got a soaking and a steel splinter penetrated his shoulder.

Back then he had been on his own. This time he was glad of his companions. Certainly, Harry's brilliant mind and Julia's academic thinking would be useful. Dearden had sensed recently that Julia was backing away from the team and he wanted to bring her back.

He passed her the box.

"Jules, you open it," he said. As she held it, an image of a pantomime she went to with her parents when she was a child came back to her. Picked out in the coloured floodlights, Aladdin had rubbed the golden lamp and by a wonder of stagecraft, a genie who began to weave magic had appeared. Julia hesitated and looked at the others gathered around. They were eager for her to carry on and she lifted the lid cautiously.

She looked at the object in the box. It was complex and beautifully engineered. Lan-Si-Nu had shown them where it fitted into the control panel in the Hub. He had given them the warnings, but he hadn't demonstrated its operation.

When the key is used it opens up an altogether different type of circuitry in the Node, he had told them.

With the galactic distances involved, when we need to communicate, a concept of science with which you are not familiar comes into play, and the communication is instant. He had held up the key. *This key is the interface between you and us, and to your travelling the Grid. You must use it wisely.*

The words rang in Julia's mind. She closed the lid and looked the others in the eye. "No time like the present," she said. "Let's go and see how the key works in the Hub."

*   *   *

Apart from Harry Stanway, they hadn't been in the Hub for some months. When he undid the secure padlock on the outer door and they entered, Julia had a sense of walking into a forbidden place. She tried to shrug off the uneasiness and followed Harry up to the Control Room. They gathered around the control panels with their alien symbols and lettering.

It was a momentous time and Julia took a few seconds to assess the team. Harry, with his winning smile and his brilliant mind, was very likeable. And Lee Wynter, showing caution because of the superstitions of his early upbringing, was courageous and dependable.

Rowan was with Dearden at the front of the group of friends. Julia, maybe in a time of honest appraisal, would admit to being jealous of Rowan's closeness to Dearden. But she would always admit that Rowan had courage. Making the decision to let go her life in Anglo-Saxon England and travel up the stream of time with Jem took guts. And there was Jem, with his arm around Rowan's shoulder, showing the love they had for one another. It had bypassed time itself.

Strange existence we are sharing, Julia thought. *What's going to happen now?* She shivered and took a deep breath.

Julia inserted the key into the position Lan-Si-Nu had shown them. It slipped in with three distinct differences in pressure and reached a stop at the end of its downward movement. Julia hesitated. She looked at Dearden for reassurance and caught Harry's eye. He nodded, as if to say do it, and she turned the key. Nothing happened other than that the large central screen built into the wall lit up for the first time. It was brighter than the others each side of it. There was a series of the alien symbols they were becoming familiar with on the large screen. These then morphed into a visual of a double sun seen in an azure blue sky that blended into carmine red at the base. An animation of a planetary system followed and a scene with many buildings . . . a parklike city unlike any that the viewers had seen before. They stood transfixed as the vision unfolded before them. A building larger and more imposing than any of the others reached way up into the sky. The introduction closed and an alien that was different to Lan-Si-Nu in stature, being squat, with an olive-green skin, appeared centre screen. Taking short, shuffling steps, it beckoned them to follow.

He or she, it was difficult to tell the sex, opened a door and walked ahead into a tall and spacious interior with great green grass-like plants which were moving, touching each other and then immediately separating. They were growing in profusion in artistically chosen positions.

"Hey man, it looks as though photosynthesis is universal and humanoid isn't," Wynter observed. He was enthralled by the whole scene which exuded tranquillity. The alien they were following came to another door, which it opened, allowing the viewers to proceed before it into an immense, cathedral-like space with many ranks of seats overlooking a vast open floor area. There was one of Lan-Si-Nu's race sitting at the centre of the space at an ergonomically shaped desk and he was preparing to speak.

The words came in the musical language of the Wasiri-Chanchiya that Dearden remembered and then there was a voiceover translation into English.

"The key that you have used in Node 4902385 has told us your planet of origin is the one you call Earth, which we know as The Second One. We bid you welcome. When any race first makes contact with us over the Grid, we show them this room. It is the Great Chamber of the Hnioss. The Hnioss is the council of planetary races. Our voyages of exploration are continuing. Most of the races we meet work with us to develop peace and unity throughout the galaxies of our dimension. Whenever there is contact with a new civilisation we need to assess their determination to follow those principles."

Dearden began to speak, but the alien spoke over him. He frowned and looked round at the others, then spoke again, but the alien didn't hesitate.

"It's a recording," Wynter said.

"That's no bloody good to us," Dearden said. "Let's hope we don't get the music." He had psyched himself up for what was going to be a planetary plea for help and got a pre-recorded message.

"Take it easy," Harry whispered. 'They're giving us an easy introduction, they know this contact you're making is a momentous thing, Jem, bear with it," Harry was useful to have around. Dearden got short on patience when stress was ramped up and the younger man's voice of reason re-focussed him. He nodded his thanks.

The screen went blank for a second, then became live and they saw a figure they recognised. There was relief amongst those from planet Earth watching the screens.

"You have contacted us sooner than we expected, Jem Dearden."

"Sooner than *we* expected, Lan-Si-Nu. It is good to see you again. The reason for contacting you is that we have a dangerous problem here on Earth. We are trying to address it in our own way, but we are asking for your help in case our attempt fails."

"What is your problem?"

"There is a rogue planet on a Trans Plutonian orbit that, according to Harry Stanway's calculations has progressed from somewhere our astronomers call the Oort Cloud. The planet, which we have named Nibiru, is on a collision course with Earth." Lan-Si-Nu's brow puckered at Dearden's description. "Harry's here, he can give you more information."

Harry sounded nervous when he began to speak. He was in awe of the intellect of the alien and sometimes forgot his own prodigious abilities.

"Hi, Lan . . . good to talk again." Harry gave a half-wave and cleared his throat a couple of times. "I have the approximate orbital parameters of Nibiru for you. It ranges from one hundred and fifty to nine hundred and seventy- five astronomical units about our sun. Nibiru has shown up recently from a position beyond the Sun due to perturbation in its orbit. We have calculated the speed theoretically to be six point-eight miles per second and it's on a collision course with us." At this point, Harry dried up. Dearden took over.

"There have been a group of people called Eisenburg, who exert great power on our planet. The majority of people were unaware of this. For many years Eisenburg has taken strong measures to ensure that the Nibiru crisis remained secret. Now it has come to our knowledge and we have little time to prepare countermeasures to protect planet Earth. We have a weapon that we intend to use to destroy or deflect Nibiru, but we are using technology that was only tested in miniature. We are uncertain about the outcome." There was a moment's silence that made those in the Hub uneasy, and then,

"What do you want us to do?"

Dearden answered, "You have an understanding of technology that is far in advance of ours. If our method fails, we need you to intervene to help us, that is, if you can." Dearden looked at the others gathered around him. There it was, the plea for help and he could see nods of approval about what he had said.

Lan-Si-Nu answered.

"You have just been shown an introduction to the way we organise our affairs . . . these planetary matters that you have a problem with must be presented before the Hnioss."

"How do we do that?"

"You must come here yourselves and present your case to the Hnioss, but there are two things you must do. First, you must think seriously about whether you should use the weapon you have described against the world that you call Nibiru, and second, you have to bring Harry Stanway with you."

39

In New York, Pierpoint told Knudsen that three of the team in the anteroom needed to get involved. Knudsen was exasperated with the way the meeting was going, with the breach of strict secrecy about the weapon. He was also aware of the weightiness of the events being discussed, and indicated it was OK for those waiting outside to be included. Templestone went to the door and signalled them in.

Lars Knudsen was surprised. "Hello Storm, what brings you here?" She came through the door followed by Mitch Doughty and Roberts. Knudsen had sometimes met Storm on social occasions and they had mutual respect.

"These gentlemen needed a chauffeuse and I happened to be free," Storm said nothing about her connection with SHaFT.

"OK . . . please sit . . . all of you." Knudsen indicated chairs and they dragged them up to his desk.

Pierpoint got straight to business after he introduced Doughty and Roberts. "Right now, we must address the Nibiru situation as best we can while we still have time. You three are coming in partway through this conversation, so listen in. What you need to be aware of is that Villiers had the foresight to develop a weapon specifically to counter the Nibiru problem. Listen in and pick up the thread as we talk."

Templestone questioned what Knudsen had told them. "When Oppenheimer implied he had become the destroyer of worlds, are you suggesting that a planet could literally be destroyed with what Villiers devised?"

"I was told that it could happen. A highly placed military man told me that was the reason Oppenheimer and his team backed out of getting involved with it. They also thought Villiers was a madman, going on about Nibiru like he did."

"Can you tell us more about the weapon?" Roberts asked Knudsen, who sank into silence.

Pierpoint notched up the pressure. "I'm sure Lars can tell us more. The question remaining is whether he wants to. The time for silence is over Lars. The world faces the worst time in its history, and we only have a few months to address the problem. What are you going to do?"

Knudsen knotted his fingers together and placed his thumbs on his temples, trying to massage away the tension of reneging on his vow of silence to Eisenburg. He straightened up in his chair.

"Very well. I will tell you what I know. It will take a while, so I beg you to be patient." He rang through to his secretary to bring coffee.

*   *   *

"In the immediate years following the Manhattan Project and Trinity, there was feverish competition between the Western and the Eastern Blocs. Each was trying to outdo the other with diabolical weaponry. The Cambridge spies, including Burgess and Maclean, actually did the world a favour. By giving the Soviets the West's atomic secrets, a balance occurred. It might have been an uneasy balance, but at least West and East were on an even footing. MAD was an appropriate acronym, Mutually Assured

Destruction. The race became fiendish, with one nuclear test after another, picked up on each side by seismograph recorders.

"The research on the weapon we are talking about was called The End Time Project and it caused many of the original Manhattan project team to capitulate. They wanted nothing more to do with weapons of war. They were appalled by the results of the device they had made when it was unleashed on Hiroshima and Nagasaki. A great many of them wanted out. Villiers and a small, elite team of scientists pressed on with their research to develop a super weapon that would have one purpose only, to combat the threat of the rogue planet. All this took place about ten years after the McCarthy witch-hunt era when patriotism had reached a new high.

"In nineteen sixty-two the results of the research, and news that such a weapon had been built came to the knowledge of President John F. Kennedy and the UN Secretary-General at the time, U Thant. They held serious discussions in camera and the result was that the End Time weapon was officially denied and put into storage." Knudsen went quiet as he considered the possible consequences of breaking the oath of silence. Thinking six months down the line it wouldn't matter. "It is in your area of England, Sir Willoughby."

"My area?"

"Where else? The research and building of the weapon took place in England and MoD Kineton is the largest and most secure ammunition storage facility in Europe."

"Can you be specific?" Pierpoint needed accuracy.

"It lies deep in one of the bunkers at MoD Kineton, but I don't know which one."

"Well, at least we have the End Time weapon to get rid of the threat, thanks to Professor Villiers' foresight," Roberts said.

"We need to find it and organise a delivery system to get the weapon to target."

"You are jumping the gun, Mr Roberts. You have forgotten Eisenburg. You have no idea of the hold they have over governments worldwide. I will have to arrange a meeting to consult them."

"I have never heard such crass bullshit," Roberts stood and rounded the desk to Knudsen, looked him straight in the eye, close-up. Pierpoint stood quickly, ready to step in. He thought Roberts, often a wild-card in SHaFT, was going to hit Knudsen. Pierpoint caught Templestone's gesture, to let Roberts have his say.

"Things just don't stack up with you Knudsen," Roberts said. He sat sideways on the desk. "What have they got on you that makes you so damn scared to make the decision to fight the threat with this weapon you know about?"

"I will not have you talk to me like that Mr Roberts; don't you know who I am?"

"I know exactly who you are and before I heard what you just said I had a lot of respect for you. You've just lost that, Mr Knudsen." Roberts flicked some hair off his face that had come adrift from his bandana. Storm Petrel was impressed with the way he levelled with Knudsen. Templestone took up where Roberts left off.

"Is Eisenburg your paymaster Lars? How much money's involved?" Knudsen stood up quickly. He faced the others. He was looking rough around the edges, more so than when they first saw him half an hour back.

"I will have you know that I have always acted honourably, but at times it's like walking on hot coals. The demands of others sometimes supersede what we want ourselves. In retrospect, we may have regrets, but we have to stick by our decisions."

"You made the decision to go along with the secrecy, you've got to live with that. You made your bed, you've got to lie on it. Tough." Roberts took his chair to the back of the room and Storm Petrel followed suit.

"Damn hypocrite," she said it loud enough for all to hear.

"Is your bed comfortable, Lars?" Pierpoint knew Storm could be incisive, sometimes a loose cannon, but what she had said was useful. He took advantage of the personal thrust.

"Listen up Lars. What we are suggesting about using the End Time weapon we are calling Plan A. At best, we could say it's a long shot. There hasn't been a need for anything like this before, but it's better than going down without a fight. We do have another option which we're calling Plan B. I'm not giving you any details yet, but it is deadly serious and it may work. If it does and the threat passes us over, you will have a lot of explaining to do to a pissed-off population that will want answers about non-action and dereliction of duty. Take my advice, give permission to let Project End Time do the job Villiers designed it for."

"You are asking a lot, Willoughby. You don't know the power Eisenburg have got."

"We certainly know that Eisenburg has got Premier Fenton Bull where they want him and that he put some of his operatives onto us with guns. My old colleague is lying desperately injured as a result. I am very angry about that and you really do not want to know me when I am angry. Do us a favour, Lars. For a start, get onto your fellow Eisenburger, Fenton Bull and tell him to reign in his goons, otherwise it will be open warfare between him and SHaFT and I guarantee that neither he nor anyone else who takes on SHaFT will win. Next, make your decision based on what we've discussed and present needs. If you release End Time you will be respected for it for generations to come."

Knudsen stood and turned his back on the room. He looked down at the heavy traffic passing along Sutton Place. From four storeys up there wasn't much noise. He thought that between them, the men and woman of SHaFT had reasoned well. He went back to his desk and slumped into his chair. He thought for a minute and then sat upright, decision made. "As Mr Roberts said, we would need a delivery system. We would also need a team to put the delivery system together. If I authorise the release of Project End Time, we will need to get NASA involved to deliver the weapon."

"There is a better choice," Pierpoint said. "NASA are contracting missions out to the commercial sector. One of them stands way above all the others with their hundred percent launch success rate and their entrepreneurial approach to space flight. A chap called Evan Blake heads up the organisation. It's called Frontier Spaceflight and they have been developing a heavy launch vehicle for a manned mission to Mars and beyond. They have also been buying up expendables, hardware past its sell-by date. Much of it is still quite serviceable and they can raid it for parts, or send it on non-return missions. I have heard that they have acquired three Saturn V rockets that were to be Apollo 18, 19 and 20. We may be able to persuade them to use one of those."

"With End Time as the payload it would certainly be non-return," said Templestone.

*   *   *

Having made his decision, Knudsen became enlivened.

"Very well, you people of SHaFT have put forward an eloquent case. Although I am persuaded, there is one proviso."

"And what is that?" Pierpoint asked.

"That you keep me acquainted with every step of the action. I am going to get tough with Eisenburg about their policy of silence. A challenge is long overdue."

"Do you want SHaFT backup?"

"Not at present, I have my own security, they are trustworthy, but I'll bear your offer in mind."

"If you need reinforcements get straight onto me and we'll get a cell flown straight out to where it's needed. In the meantime, we will get back to the UK to find Project End Time at MoD Kineton."

* * *

Mitch Doughty was in Matt Roberts' hotel room. They were planning the best approach to MoD Kineton's commanding officer about bringing Project End Time out of storage.

Storm Petrel had knocked on Pierpoint's door a few minutes earlier to discuss the return to JFK, for the flight back to the UK. Bill Templestone was sitting by a window overlooking Roosevelt Island. He was half listening to the conversation between Pierpoint and Storm.

"But why do you want to come to the UK, Storm. You're useful as a contact over here and we pay you well."

"I'm sick of being used as a lackey Sir Willoughby, that's the point. As you said, I am useful as a contact. I have contacts on all five continents, and whoever it is I don't know, I can get to know."

"I don't doubt that at all." Pierpoint, the epitome of an English gentleman, was aware of the force of Storm's femininity and maintained his distance from it. He thought about her request to go to the UK objectively. She would be closer to the heart of SHaFT and because of her femininity, she could be a femme fatale and have men eating out of her hand, she could get into places the men of SHaFT would be unable to get into.

"We'll give it a try for three months and see how you shape up. You will have to do some tough training. It will involve live-fire exercises and hand to hand combat."

"Yes," her fist punched the air and she crossed the two feet between them and hugged Pierpoint hard.

"You won't regret this one little bit, Sir Willoughby."

At that point, Matt Roberts came into the room. Pierpoint didn't see the wink Storm gave Roberts. Templestone, still looking out the window and passing no comment, saw Storm's wink behind him reflected in the glass and smiled. He could understand both sides of the situation. He recognised how useful Storm could be to prise information out of criminality SHaFT sometimes needed to infiltrate and he knew about the item that Storm Petrel and Matt Roberts were becoming. If he were younger himself Roberts may have had a challenge on his hands, Storm certainly had a special sort of beauty. He stood up and stretched and turned to face the centre of the room.

"So now we have a new recruit. Let's get to it Will. The sooner we get to MoD Kineton the sooner we can start to do something about Nibiru."

Pierpoint's mobile phone rang and he listened for a minute. When he answered he was subdued, then he ended the call. He turned to Templestone.

"It's bad news Bill."

"What is it?"

"It's Arthur . . . he died a little over an hour ago."

"Oh no . . . no. Not Art." Templestone sat down heavily and looked back out the window. It was sunny out there. Cold maybe, but the Sun made it a bad day to lose a dear friend. Arthur should be sharing the sunshine. Pierpoint interrupted the thoughts.

"Green and Mallett did all they could but Arthur's internal injuries were too severe and he died of heart failure." Templestone's throat was tight and he found it hard to speak. His friendship with Arthur Doughty went back to when he was a young man. Arthur was slightly older. He had originally approached Templestone about SHaFT during a game of cricket. Templestone joined the organisation because of its high ideals.

"Does Mitch know about Arthur yet?" he managed to ask Pierpoint.

"Jack Green phoned him first."

"What will Caro do, she and Art were very close?"

"Jules is on her way to see her to make sure she's OK. Caro has a sister who's coming down from Newcastle on Tyne."

"Arthur will leave a big space to fill," Matt Roberts said.

"Bigger than most know about," Pierpoint said. He sounded sombre . . . "We have to carry on Bill."

Pierpoint drew himself up to his full height. He was still an imposing figure although he was in his seventies. "Is the Cadillac outside, Storm?" he asked.

"It is, and for the time being I'm still your chauffeuse."

"Then let's go. We have important work to do. Thanks to Eisenburg's interference we have little time to do it in."

* * *

Mitch Doughty took the death of his father hard and vowed revenge on those responsible.

"Don't go down that route Mitch, not yet," Templestone said, after taking him to one side. "We'll get to the bottom of what went on when we get back to the UK. Fenton Bull's behind the ambush on your dad and Pierpoint. Sir Willoughby intends to confront Bull about it. It's best to leave him to do that." Mitch Doughty was unconvinced.

Storm Petrel drove the Cadillac into the short stay parking area and waved to her cousin who was waiting by the ticket booth. He came over and she gave him the keys.

"Look after the condo Jake; I may be gone some time."

"But—"

"Never mind the but. I don't know when I'll be back, but I'll keep you posted." They had grown up together and Storm had always been wilful, played soccer when she was a kid, rather than netball.

"Take care Storm, send me a postcard," Jake said. She gave him a playful punch on the shoulder and led the others off toward the waiting Gulfstream.

40

I t was a quiet funeral. A large event would have drawn too much attention to Arthur's involvement with SHaFT. Each of those who attended had their own memories of Arthur Doughty. The forthright North Countryman had earned a lot of respect amongst the men and women of SHaFT. There were many who would have liked to attend, but because of the need for secrecy, they did not. Instead, they thought of him and some said prayers at the time the curtain would be closing and he was being consigned to the flames.

In Dearden Hall that evening conversation was subdued. Arthur's son, Mitch was away with his mother in Leamington. He would stay with her for a few days.

* * *

"Pierpoint." Sir Willoughby, back at Ireton Grange, was expecting the phone call.

"This is Evan Blake," the man on the other end said. The accent was Missouri, he came from the same town as Storm Petrel, but he said his name, Evan the Welsh way, like Eevan.

"My P.A. told me you need to speak, that it's urgent."

"It is desperate rather than urgent," Pierpoint stressed. He was impressed Blake returned his call within minutes of getting the message.

"What's it to do with?" Blake asked.

"Have you heard of Nibiru?"

"I've heard whispers, why?"

"It is imperative we meet. I can't say too much over the phone in case there are listeners. I will explain everything when we meet. I have some documents that I think will interest you. All I can say at present is that we need to talk about space flight. I will have three trusted colleagues with me. Oh, as a precaution, Evan, I advise you to increase your personal security."

* * *

While Evan Blake was waiting for Sir Willoughby Pierpoint's flight to arrive he did some homework. He had heard the name Pierpoint before, but couldn't remember where. It was something someone said to him once, a rumour, but that was all he could remember. He did some searching, asked questions of people who ordinarily would know about these things, but all he came up with were uncertain answers. Pierpoint was an enigma.

"Sir Willoughby Pierpoint and his colleagues are here, sir," Blake's PA said into the phone on her desk in the plush office outside his room.

"Send them in Donna." Donna looked the four people over, the wild looking man with the bandana Sir Willoughby said was Matt Roberts, and the elegant trouser-suited woman he said was Storm Petrel, who stood by Roberts, and an older man by the name of Templestone.

"Evan Blake will see you now," Donna purred, getting up and leading them to a pair of burr walnut doors.

She knocked, waited for an answer and opened one of the doors into a room with a large Persian rug in the centre of maple parquet flooring. The wide-open space oozed money. Donna introduced Pierpoint and the others. She had never met an English Knight of the Realm before. She was impressed. He had a noble bearing, just as a knight should be, but without the armour.

"Did you have a good flight?" Blake asked Pierpoint when all four were in the room and the door was shut. Blake spent slightly longer looking at Storm Petrel than the others, which was what Pierpoint was hoping for. He had brought Storm along as leverage to help get Blake onside.

"It wasn't bad, apart from the turbulence when we were landing," Pierpoint said to the man who looked in his early fifties, who obviously worked out, but had prematurely grey hair.

"The turbulence is a permanent feature of our airfield," Blake said. "It's the only drawback."

"The approach is precarious over the mountains. You are rather isolated in Polynesia; do you get many visitors to Turaroa?"

"We don't and that is the main reason we chose this place. It is far enough away from the beaten track to deter the press and unwanted visitors, but large enough to suit our purposes."

"And you have a protected harbour."

Pierpoint looked over Evan Blake's shoulder. Out of the picture window at the top of the high building, he could see an atoll with anchorage for cargo ships. A very tall rectangular building lay to the right of the harbour. There was a cluster of other industrial style buildings. Pierpoint could see the gantries of two mobile launch towers in the distance. Adjacent to one of the launch towers was a large rocket, with what looked like six external boosters clustered around the body. He could see the diminutive figures of personnel working around the rocket at the top of a gantry.

Blake saw where Pierpoint was looking. "Interested Sir Willoughby?"

"Very."

"I'll take you on the tour after you explain the reason for your visit. Why have you come here?"

Pierpoint had taken an immediate liking to Evan Blake. His manner was forthright, as if he could be trusted. He had to be.

"Have you heard of Nibiru?"

"Isn't that the mythical Planet X?"

"It is what is called Planet X, by some, but I assure you, it is not a myth."

Pierpoint laid some of the TOP SECRET documents and a page of Harry Stanway's calculations, with accompanying geometric drawings, on Evan Blake's desk. He explained the HaMabuwl prophecy and the mathematics backing it up.

* * *

Blake looked over the detail without saying anything for some ten minutes. He looked grave when he spoke to Pierpoint.

"This is the very worst kind of news. Tell me, why have you come to me, rather than other organisations, Sir Willoughby?"

"We need a reliable delivery system to take a solution out to Nibiru. We feel you can provide that."

"You say you have a solution to the problem?"

We have two possible solutions. With the first one, the delivery system would involve you and your rocketry. The other solution is theoretical at present."

"If this information turns out to be true, how long do we have before Nibiru impacts?"

"The old records infer that from first sighting until the worst part of the event, the count was one hundred and fifty-eight days. The modern event is slightly in excess of that at present."

"Not long for an operation of this magnitude." Blake went to the picture window and gazed upwards. "Come here please, all of you."

They went and stood at his side.

"We first made our money out of oil years ago. Henry Ford needed oil and we had it. Now I build big fireworks for playthings and I have dreams. My dreams lie out there, Sir Willoughby." He pointed upwards.

"You do have an impeccable launch record to reach your dreams."

"Ah . . . that is due to my team. I want to bring two of my team in on this. We'll see what they make of these things you're telling me. We'll also see if they recommend me spending my money on it; but if what you've told me is true, I might as well spend it." He picked up the phone on his desk and asked Donna to put a call out for Brett Morgan and Mart Schlesinger.

"Brett is my chief engineer and Martin Schlesinger heads up research. Between them, they will understand the implications of this data."

"Do you have manned flights planned Mr Blake?" Storm Petrel asked. She was looking at the rocket.

"We do Storm, why, are you volunteering?"

Pierpoint spoke before Storm had a chance to answer. "There is something else you ought to be aware of."

"And what is that, Sir Willoughby?"

"What do you know about Eisenburg?"

"I hate them like the plague. Why do you ask?"

Pierpoint confided how the Eisenburg group used their influence to have information about Nibiru withheld from the public domain. Filters set up on the internet, extreme sanctions for any in the know who went against Eisenburg's ruling of silence about the threat.

"How have they acquired that sort of influence?" Blake asked.

"I had to dig deep to find that out." Pierpoint didn't tell him that it was Harry Stanway who had infiltrated the software.

"Eisenburg was innocent enough when it started back in the 1870's. If you were an industrialist and you wanted to get on, you joined the club, but Eisenburg's modus operandi changed at the turn of the twentieth century. Certain government ministers were invited to join so that they would be with the in crowd—"

"And power corrupts," Blake interrupted.

"As do riches in the wrong hands. Certain rich men who were prepared to forget moral values became richer by devious means. Billions of dollars were made as the arms trade geared up for the First World War. Those with influence did nothing to stop the process because they were with the in crowd. They learned to be silent so they wouldn't be held to account. It's all to do with control. Eisenburg appears to be passive on the surface but peel away the layers and their influence is there, working like a virus."

The phone on Evan Blake's desk rang.

"Yes Donna, send them in."

There was a knock on the door and a tall lanky individual came in, followed by a man of medium height and build. Blake introduced the tall man as Mart Schlesinger, head of research and the other as his chief engineer, Brett Morgan. They spent a while looking through the data and discussed it among themselves. Blake had coffee brought in and asked their opinion.

"If Nibiru exists, as this information suggests it does, we will soon to be facing the very worst kind of threat," Research Chief Schlesinger said. What we have to establish with absolute certainty is, does it exist?

Pierpoint added more detail, "Its approach is all but hidden from us because of its approach from behind the Sun. There was a minor perturbation in its orbit which made it visible for a short while. That is documented, although denied at the highest levels of government. So yes, it does exist and it did make a previous appearance, with disastrous consequences, that a Hebrew named Sho'mer wrote about in a scroll which is parallel to part of the Genesis account."

"You are requesting one of my vehicles as a delivery system. What exactly is it you intend to deliver, Sir Willoughby?"

"A device known as the End Time weapon, which has been hidden away under wraps for many years. My informant told me it uses anti-matter, and I have heard you have Saturn V's in your warehouse for its delivery."

"Judging by its name it would pack one hell of a punch. I have heard nothing whatsoever about the End Time weapon, which is surprising because I have sources in many places."

"You won't have heard about it. Knowledge of its existence had to be kept quiet because if it got into corrupt hands, like those of Eisenburg, it would cause a desperate situation in the balance of world power."

Blake pictured sitting the End Time bomb atop a Saturn V rocket.

"What distance are we talking about?"

"When Harry Stanway picks up Nibiru and does the math we will be able to give you a precise distance. Assume that when it is seen, it will be the approximate distance that we are from the Sun."

"At that point, you say we would have one hundred and fifty-eight days, so any amount of time we have before it is sighted will be a bonus. Sir Willoughby, had the distance to the target not crossed your mind? It is rather more than the Saturn V was designed for."

"I know, but you have three of them. Strapped together that would be a lot of static thrust to punch the payload on its way."

"You have a point. Fifteen Rocketdyne F-1 engines would produce 22.5 million pounds of thrust to be precise; but such a mission would be difficult, if not impossible to achieve, particularly with the time strictures involved."

"Why?"

"Because each separate stage would have to be clamped to its neighbour and separate effectively. It would be complex, to say the least. The planning and build would take more time than we have available. What do you say, Brett?"

"We could do a feasibility study on it and give you a definite answer in a day and a half, complete with computer models. Personally, I think the idea is impractical. Nevertheless, I'll do the study so we have the information to hand. It could be useful at some point. How heavy is the payload?"

Pierpoint said, "I am told it is in the region of 30,000 pounds."

"It would be preferable to have a more precise figure than in the region of, Sir Willoughby; do you know its overall dimensions?"

"The same informant told me that the outside diameter is six feet, but it is long, ten feet or so."

"I will use those figures to set up the study. But considering the importance of this proposed mission, I would suggest we consider a more practical delivery method."

"OK Brett, I propose that you initiate the feasibility study aided by Mart. Work on it with all speed and you, Sir Willoughby, get back to the UK and acquire End Time. Bring it here and we will take it for a ride. We will find a way. But before you go I'll take you on a tour of Frontier Spaceflight."

Evan Blake accompanied Pierpoint and the others on the tour of the Turaroa launch facility. He took them into the massive storage bay where the three Saturn V rockets lay, horizontally, side by side, with their stages separate.

"Of course, if we were to strap the three of them together we would need a different mobile launch platform. I am thinking we would have to use three of the original Saturn V mobile launch platforms together rather than produce a new one, but there would be a lot of prototype engineering with that concept. We don't have the time to accomplish that. I have a better idea, Sir Willoughby and friends. Let's go visit the Condor VI heavy Lift. Unlike Saturn V with the antiquated Apollo system, the Condor VI Heavy is brimming with the very latest in spacecraft technology."

*   *   *

At the time Pierpoint, Templestone and the others were on a tour of the launch facility housing the Condor VI Heavy Lift, Harry Stanway finished setting up the Astro-Royal telescope. Harry and Lee Wynter had assembled an observation dome between the boundary of the courtyard at Dearden Hall and the densely forested Leofwin's Hundred. The dome was equipped with gear for serious astronomy. Harry had explained the procedure for operating the computerised telescope to Wynter and Rowan. The night was approaching and the first stars shone.

"Early tomorrow before sunrise, we'll begin the hunt for Nibiru. It will be tedious because we will only be observing a small portion of the heavens. I suggest we divide the observations into shifts of twenty minutes each."

"Should be OK, but what are you going to show us now?" Wynter asked.

"We'll take a look at the Andromeda Galaxy."

Using the handset, Harry scrolled through the list of Messier objects until he came to M31. He selected it. The telescope slewed to the galaxy that he said to the others was 2.5 million light years away. Harry looked through the eyepiece. Although he had observed it many times before, he couldn't help the wow he vocalised when he sighted the Andromeda galaxy through the Astro-Royal.

He stood aside for the others to look. The result was always the same for those new to astronomy. The exclamation because of the overwhelming beauty and then hogging the eyepiece as if no one else was there who wanted a turn.

"Let's look at the lunar surface," Harry suggested after Wynter and Rowan spent a while observing M31. He took the handset and selected the Moon, focussed on it and began tracking. He stood aside for the others to have a turn.

After a while the cold began to bite, Harry shivered. A frost was forming and he and Lee Wynter had been working since dawn. They were tired. Harry switched off the supply to the telescope and slid the shutter of the dome closed.

* * *

The daylight observations continued over six days with no result and then there was a breakthrough. It was during Rowan's shift with the telescope. She had settled into what promised to be another uneventful session, looking at the right-hand side of the Sun. She could see the ceaseless movement on the surface of the great orb, its intensity shielded by the screen Harry fixed to the front of the instrument at the start of each day.

Rowan realised there was something very different about what she was observing. About a quarter of the width of the Sun's disc, to the right of it, there was a small circular object reflecting light. She didn't react at first. Then she yelled aloud in Anglo-Saxon. Dearden was sitting on a chair by her side in the observatory.

"It is here . . . Jem . . . Nibiru." Her shout startled him out of the novel he was reading. Dearden leapt out of the chair. Harry had primed the observers with what to expect when the target came into view. He had stressed, when they first started a few days ago, that the work would be tedious but to stick at it. Rowan got the reward. Dearden looked through the eyepiece.

"Looks as though you've found it."

Harry heard the commotion and came running from the workshop. Dearden backed off for Harry to look.

"That's it," his shout was loud for those close by. "Start recording. Quick." Dearden turned to the workbench and pressed the remote start for the astrophotography video-cam. Harry changed to a higher-powered eyepiece, re-centred the image and corrected the tracking. He whipped his mobile phone out of his pocket and rang Carlos Mendulas in Coquimbo, Chile, putting the phone onto speaker mode so that all could hear the conversation.

A voice in well-educated English, with Spanish overtones, answered. "Harry . . . is this the call we're preparing for?"

"Sure is, Carlos, when's sunrise at your end?"

"Three hours after yours."

Harry looked at his watch, "OK . . . Nibiru is in plain view here. Its presence will be out in the open soon, on the net, the news, everywhere. How long do you need to get set up?"

"An hour should be enough. I will ring when we have sunrise and we are tracking."

"OK. Then all being well we'll derive the triangulation we need. Carlos, it's looking positive, good visibility here, how is it your end?" Harry looked out of the window and saw the sun above the horizon and the last vestige of stars above.

"The heavens are magnificent tonight. Harry, there is a bonus. In fact, we have two bonuses. How do you say it in English, we have bonii?"

"Maybe, but what bonuses do we have?"

"The first, I'm on Gemini South."

"The big one?"

"None other and I have it for the whole day after I arrive at six."

"Brilliant. What's the second bonus?"

"I have a colleague, Rob Fisher, who owes me a big favour. Like you and me, he has followed the Nibiru situation from the time of the Conspiracy TV program. Apart from our triangulation and Doppler Shift, we need radar verification of the planet's distance, speed and direction and Rob is telescope manager of some useful equipment. Guess what it is."

"This is not the time for guesswork. Tell me."

"He manages the Lovell Radio Telescope at Jodrell Bank."

41

Sir Willoughby Pierpoint had met the Station Commander, MoD Kineton, Lieutenant Colonel Michael Ramsay, several times. He asked Jem Dearden, Harry Stanway and Bill Templestone over to Ireton Grange. They were formulating the best approach to Ramsay about getting Project End Time out of Mothballs.

"I am hoping he'll react favourably to the evidence we have. Villiers' research and Harry's calculations can stand up to the most serious scrutiny, but I think we will have to break it to Ramsay slowly. He's an intensely bureaucratic man and likes a form for everything, so it could prove difficult."

"Who do you want with you?" Templestone asked.

"I want you to come, Bill and I want Jem and Harry along as well. We four have all the details in mind. There is a little matter of information gathering that I want Jules to involve herself with; she's the best for that because she knows her way around academia. I'll talk to her about that now."

Sir Willoughby keyed Julia's number on his mobile phone.

In her role as owner of L-BarX, Linden-Barthorpe Archaeological Explorations, Julia was back on a long-term dig at Burton Dassett. She wiped the mud off her hands onto her jeans and answered her mobile after four rings. They spoke minor pleasantries and then Pierpoint got down to business.

"Can you get yourself to Cambridge Jules? I need you to poke around in the archives for the time Professor Ernest

Rutherford was Director of the Cavendish Laboratory. I think we will find that our Professor Charles Villiers was there for some time during Rutherford's tenure. We need you to try to find out about something called Project End Time. After his spell at the Cavendish, it was something Villiers and others were working on as an offshoot of the Manhattan Project. We are trying to confirm what its destructive capability would be. Look for any mention of it, however slight or tangential. You must be absolutely discrete with this," Pierpoint said.

"We're just about to open up another Iron-Age grave."

"Jules, the grave can wait . . . Nibiru can't. This is the start of the fight-back." Julia was briefly silent, then, "OK, Sir Will, of course you're right. I'll hand the dig over to Wilf Sheldon."

* * *

Sir Willoughby Pierpoint's Bentley pulled up outside Lieutenant Colonel Michael Ramsay's headquarters at MoD Kineton. Pierpoint had spoken to him on the phone. He told him it was a matter of the utmost urgency. The sentry outside the entrance to the building stood to attention as Sir Willoughby approached the door with Dearden, Harry Stanway and Templestone.

They were shown into an office on the upper of two storeys, which was devoid of personal touches. The room had good natural daylight from a steel-framed multi-paned window of the nineteen forties. It was strictly military. There were maps on the wall, a plan of the layout of the many bunkers comprising MoD Kineton and photographs of tanks in combat at El Alamein, with dates, from the 23rd October to the 11th November 1942. At the centre of the line of battle photographs, there was a picture of Viscount Bernard Montgomery of Alamein in Field Marshal's regalia and an equally large photograph of the Queen on the opposite wall.

Ramsay stood and indicated seats in a semi-circle in front of his desk for the four men to sit, but they chose not to. Ramsay was a slightly built man with a sharp-featured face, sporting a clipped moustache.

"Sir Willoughby, how are things in Dump 4?" he asked, sensing tension because the four men kept standing.

"Things are smooth and resilient at present, but along with the wider world, that is shortly going to change."

"And why is that?" there was a slight frown.

Pierpoint took the sheaf of data out of his folder and spread it out for Ramsay to see. He had an addition to his folder. It was a dated photograph of the portion of the heavens including the Sun with mercury in transit. To the right of the Sun, there was another disk, which was larger than Mercury. Pierpoint took out the photograph and laid it on top of the other data.

"What is this?"

"This is Nibiru," Pierpoint said, tapping the dot to the right of the Sun.

"Means nothing to me."

"Give it a few months, then it will," Harry said. "It's approaching Earth on a collision course and we might have less than six months to do something about it,"

The plan was to give Ramsay the bare bones of the facts quickly. They would gauge his reaction and then explain the hard data about the coming destruction. Finally, they would offer the escape route, Project End Time.

"How are you with math," Pierpoint asked Ramsay.

"Where is all this taking us, Sir Willoughby? If it were someone else standing there instead of you, I would get you thrown out for your impertinence. By the way, when I knew you were coming, I dipped into the file we have on you. I have only been able to find information about a shadowy career and my searches go deep, believe me. I look on with great interest at the comings and goings at Dump 4. Then damn me, when I enquire higher up the chain of command for permission to come and look inside your big steel doors I get a *don't go down that route* shouted at me."

Pierpoint's eyes narrowed, he was in no mood for games, but Harry interjected before he got the words out. "Sir Willoughby asked how you are with math, Lieutenant Colonel. He asked for a very good reason. I need to know your capability with math for me to explain why we are desperate for your help."

Something in the way the young man spoke made Ramsay listen to him, so he told Harry, "I was a university entrant into the army and came in with an Oxford first in Mathematics and Engineering Science. What is it you want from me?"

Pierpoint spoke just three words. "Project End Time."

Ramsay was obviously startled by what Pierpoint said. He avoided Sir Will's gaze and fiddled with his tie, which was straight, but he made it go askew. They all saw his reaction and waited for Pierpoint's three words to sink in.

Harry spent the next twenty minutes explaining about the coming threat from the far reaches of the solar system, backing it up with hard facts. He included the data he and Carlos Mendulas linked from their separate observations and the input from Jodrell Bank, from which they had computed the exact distance, speed and orbit of Nibiru.

* * *

Ramsay looked at his watch. It was nearly lunchtime.

"OK Harry, I have seen your figures. They look good. Sir Willoughby, you have explained that there has been a conspiracy of silence leading to non-action at the very top. Off the record, I have had my suspicions about the power Eisenburg hold for a very long while. Bill and Jem, you have shown me the translated record of an ancient cataclysm. What the three of you are saying sounds far-fetched, to say the least." Ramsay clasped his hand to his chin and shuffled through the evidence on his desk. He looked deep in thought.

"Sir Willoughby, I must ask what on earth you think I can do about it?" Pierpoint came to the end of his patience.

"You just don't get it, do you, Ramsay? I made the suggestion before we began our explanation and it was quite obvious by your reaction that we struck a nerve. You know about End Time, don't you? Release the End Time Project and help us stave off annihilation. If you look for a form to authorise that, believe me, I will break you and your damn career into the tiniest pieces. I'll give you twelve hours to sort your mind out."

42

Julia anticipated a long and intense day of research and arrived early at the Cambridge University Library. The receptionist directed her to the Manuscripts Reading Room on the third floor.

She had browsed the catalogue of archives online the previous evening. Nuclear physics would be the main search category, with the subcategory of nuclear weapons. Julia reasoned that experimental notebooks written up by the academics involved with those subjects between the dates 1920 to 1960 should produce results. She filled in the request slip for the first five of the series and after a twenty-minute wait, the bundle arrived in a cardboard box.

During the wait, she filled in a request slip for the following five notebooks in order of date. She handed it to the archivist and was told that when she returned the notebooks she was reading she could order more.

"If you knew how important this is you would put the whole bloody shelf on my table for me to read," she said.

"I am sorry, miss –" he looked at her name on the request slip, "Sorry . . . Professor Linden-Barthorpe. I'm afraid I can't change the rules." She gave him the look that had melted a number of hearts. "Well, I'll see what I can do, but keep quiet about it," he whispered and she flashed him a smile.

The procedure continued until lunchtime. There had been no result by the time the archivist on duty called the approach of the hour shutdown. Julia had a sense of history in what she was handling, notes by physicists that were household names, John Cockcroft and Ernest Walton, who first split the atom under the directorship of Ernest Rutherford. There was a reference to Rutherford's notes and letters, which would have been fascinating, but there was no time to be side-tracked by those records.

The final call for lunch came and Julia acted on a hunch that had come during the morning. She went to the desk and spoke to the archivist, who was probably three or four years younger than she was.

"Can you recommend anywhere for lunch?"

He thought for a few seconds.

"The Eagle is good. It's a pub on Bene't Street, near to the Old Cavendish Laboratory. The food's good and it's academically famous. So the tale goes, in 1953 James Watson and Bernard Crick went into the Eagle to announce they had discovered the structure of human DNA."

"Do you feel like a meal there? I'll buy." Julia stepped a bit closer.

"Yeah, that would be good. I was leaving now anyway. My shift's over for the day. Hold on, I'll get my coat." He stepped into a room at the back and came out a minute later with his coat on and a college scarf draped loosely around his neck.

* * *

The meal was just as good as Clive – that was his name – Clive Fraser, said it was going to be and the conversation soon loosened up into what they both did. He, a senior archivist, Julia a Forensic Archaeologist. She told him about her latest dig, where bronze brooches and pins were being unearthed. He was interested and said to Julia how he was leading a team of archivists in the restoration and preservation of a sixth-century manuscript found recently in a cellar in the old part of town. Then she told him she would prefer him calling her Jules, rather than Professor Linden-Barthorpe.

"What are you looking for in the archives Jules?"

The critical time had come. She had his confidence, but she really started to like him as well, which complicated matters.

"I am looking into some research that was done between the late nineteen-thirties and probably the mid-fifties by a Professor Charles Villiers. He is dead now, or rather, presumed dead and I've drawn a blank with the search so far today." She looked him in the eye. "Don't suppose you've heard of him, have you?"

"Villiers . . . the name does sound familiar, but I come across so many names in my line of work that I can't place where I've seen it. What was he involved with?"

"The atom. I have heard that he may have been associated with Rutherford in the Cavendish. Charles Villiers may have been one of Rutherford's students."

"You've started off in the right direction, looking at the experimental notebooks."

"Yes, but I've looked through them all now."

Clive was cautious: he looked around before he answered quietly.

"You may not have come to the end."

"What do you mean?"

Clive drew up close. "There's a vast underground section of the library that isn't open to the public; it's where all the research and restoration goes on. A lot of records are archived there too. There are more of the experimental notebooks from the Cavendish down there. They are slowly being categorised, but some of them will never get into the public eye."

"Why won't they?"

"They are too sensitive."

"Can you get me in to see them?"

"Yes, but there is another avenue that may help as well." Clive seemed uncertain about continuing.

"Come on, don't hold out on me, what avenue may help?" Clive took a sip of his beer, bolstering himself up to reveal a confidence.

"There is a man who is a mine of information. His name is Anthony Shaw. He used to be the porter who was involved with the Cavendish in the years immediately after the war until the late sixties. It was his job to know everything about everyone. It kept things running smoothly. He may recall if there was a Professor Villiers, and he would know who was working with him."

"Can I get to see Mister Shaw?"

"Possibly . . . It'll involve a phone call." Clive took out his mobile and scrolled down the numbers. "Tony Shaw has helped me out a few times, Jules. He's given me a lead when research has drawn a blank – damn, there's no signal – I'll see if I can get one outside, bear with me a minute."

Julia went to the bar and ordered another Pinot Grigio for herself and another Bass for Clive. He came back in and the drinks were on the table.

"I've set a meeting up. He isn't expecting any visitors this afternoon."

"How far is it?"

"On the outskirts of town. He's in a care home, won't take long to get there."

"How about the archives under the library?"

"There's not enough time for that now. Maybe we won't need them. We'll see what Tony Shaw's got to say. Thanks for the drink." Clive took a sip of the Bass. Then he noticed how people had gathered in front of the television set on the wall at the side of the bar. The room had gone unusually quiet, music was turned off and then a girl's voice said *Oh no* in a strange sort of voice, rather . . . falsetto. A man responded *It'll be alright, it's probably nothing to worry about.* He slipped his arm around her shoulder. *What are we going to do?* She asked him in a scared sort of voice.

Julia caught sight of the screen. It was showing a shot of the Sun and to the right of it there was a small disc. She knew exactly what was being reported, although from where she was sitting she couldn't hear the commentary, but the urgency crowded in on her.

"Drink up Clive, we've got to go."

"But —"

"No buts Clive, we have to go. There's no time to lose."

43

Outside the Eagle, in Oxford, Julia checked her mobile phone. A text had arrived from Harry.

Check the TV news, ASAP. Rowan spotted Nibiru early this morning. Amateur astronomers worldwide have seen it. They are flooding the internet with the news. Professionals are following suit. There's a guy in Hungary who calls himself The Breaker who's found a way to knock out the filters on Nibiru that Eisenburg has put in place. Information is pouring out. There's no holding it back now. What's happening your end?

She texted back to update him and then checked the time. It was three-thirty, close to the shortest day and the light was fading.

"Read this text, Clive." She handed him the mobile and he read it through.

"What does it mean?"

"You saw the news flash when we were in The Eagle and how people had gathered around the television, didn't you?"

She told him about the threat as they walked rapidly through the town to where she left her Jeep Grand Cherokee. When she first mentioned the threat, he stopped and looked at her to see if she was serious. By the look on her face, he could see she was.

"Oh hell . . . now what happens?" he asked, as they walked past a branch of Comet where televisions were displayed in the window and a crowd was silent as they stood watching. A shop assistant had put a television in the doorway and jammed the door open with a wedge. He had turned up the volume, thinking it would pull in more sales, but no-one was in a buying mood; they just wanted to watch the news inside the shop. Further on, an independent television retailer had drawn a similar crowd. People walking by were looking serious. A man middle-aged man had his arm around a woman's shoulders; both were openly crying.

"Who was the guy who texted you, Jules?"

"Harry Stanway, he's an electronics specialist and a brilliant mathematician—"

"And you're going to tell me that he knew, and you knew about this Nibiru problem before it was on the television?"

"You've got it."

"Why do you want to find Professor Villiers' research? Tell me more."

It was a calculated risk telling Clive Fraser about End Time and the plan to place it on a rocket in an attempt to destroy Nibiru, but she felt she could trust him; so she told him.

"Destroy it? You surely don't think that's possible, do you?"

"I have it on the best authority that it is possible, but we need to verify the energy released by the End Time weapon to ensure it's a viable option. It could need modifying."

* * *

They had not been waiting long in the room at the St. Francis Rest-home for the Collegiate Elderly when a man with a cherubic face and a jolly smile came in. He was using a walking stick to help his progress and was walking unsteadily.

Clive stood and went to help him but Tony Shaw waved him away.

"Hello, Clive . . . and Julia, isn't it? Give me a hand if I fall, will you? Until then I'll try to manage myself, thank you." He made his way slowly to an easy chair, sat down and sighed.

"Now, how can I help you?"

"Do you remember a Professor Charles Villiers who worked in the Cavendish?" Clive asked him.

"Charles Villiers . . . I remember him alright. At times, he was a real tearaway. He faced any challenge head-on. Do you know, once he was dared to free-climb the outside of four Cambridge college towers, Trinity, Jesus, Kings and St John's? He had to light a Roman candle at the top of each one to show he was there, then free-climb back down. He had courage, did Charlie Villiers."

"Do you know anything about his research?" Julia asked Shaw.

"I never knew anything about what went on inside the Old Cavendish, but what I do know, is that it was in that building that they first split the atom. Did you know that when Ernest Rutherford died in 1937, the authorities sealed up his room for nearly forty years? It was finally certified as decontaminated in 1977."

"I had no idea. Do you know of anyone who would have known about Villiers research?"

"Why do you want to know?" Anthony Shaw asked sharply.

Julia fancied the old man became suspicious of where the conversation was leading. She couldn't risk that, so she appealed to what she thought would have been his sense of fighting against a common enemy, forged in his youthful years in the late nineteen thirties. She told him about Nibiru, how she and her colleagues had a desperate fight on their hands.

"We need your help, Tony. Anything you can remember about the team working with Villiers will be useful."

Shaw seemed to withdraw into himself. His eyes began to close with tiredness after the concentrated effort of the conversation.

"Tony," Julia urged him to wake up, then louder. "Tony."

"Mmm? Oh, yes . . . you asked about Charlie Villiers' team. They all seemed to fade away after Charlie disappeared; it was in the nineteen sixties. I remember there was a bit of mystery about it, as if things were being hushed up . . . he just vanished from the face of the earth, but it's so long ago now that I can't tell you anything more . . . the memory fades you know. There's only one of them alive now, Professor Robert Cranford, Robbie Styles Cranford."

"Where does he live?" Clive asked.

"He's got a nice place in Green End, has Robbie, out at Comberton. I've got his number somewhere."

∗   ∗   ∗

Professor Robert S. Cranford looked as though he still enjoyed outdoor life despite his years and the onset of winter weather. He had a tanned look and was short and stocky. He had a grey beard and walked surprisingly quickly despite his ninety-four years. He welcomed Julia Linden-Barthorpe, a fellow professor who he had heard of, and Clive Fraser who he remembered vaguely. Drinks were offered. Whisky was refused but coffee was accepted and Cranford got straight to business.

"First of all, why do you want to know about Charles Villiers? I would rather his memory remains unsoiled. These days, people are often vilified after they pass from this mortal coil." His voice was firm. Julia recognised the type, an academician of the old school whose rule had been law. If his career had been in public schooling, rather than a university, he would have enforced his rule with a birch rod. Julia showed him her SHaFT identity.

Cranford seemed satisfied. The signature impressed him, but he was persistently evasive about giving them any information. It was as if he was playing a game. Julia took a different tack and suggested that he turn on the television.

"Why on earth are you suggesting that I turn on the television?"

"You'll soon see. The reason we have come to see you is more serious than you realise and I'm sick of the bloody game you're playing." Julia didn't suffer fools gladly.

Cranford at first looked offended and then his eyes sparkled and he burst out laughing. He wiped his eyes with a tissue.

"You have caught me out, young woman. Let us see what's on. What program do you suggest, BBC one, ITV?"

"Sky News." Julia took out a pen and notebook as Cranford switched on the television and located Sky news. The grin disappeared as he heard a newsreader doing a voice over across visuals of the Sun and the small orb to its right. The newsreader was talking in subdued tones about a grave emergency that would affect everybody.

There was a sharp intake of breath from Robert Cranford and then – "Holy mother of God – the time comes at last, just like Charlie said it would."

"I thought that would stop you laughing. Now, tell us what you know about Villiers and the End Time Project."

* * *

With the sighting of the rogue planet, information was being gathered at a speed akin to panic by amateur and professional

astronomers the world over. Speed and direction was confirmed and the information collated into usable data. There
was a clamour of voices from high government and the man on
the street about what was being done to address the problem.
Foreign ministers, prime ministers and presidents were talking
and the phone lines of their communication were busy as they
tried to devise a solution to address the threat of doom.

NASA, the European Space Agency and the Russian Federal
Space Agency were in constant contact, and then a name filtered
through to them, Evan Blake.

44

"The Old Cavendish . . . so much went on there. People don't know the half of it. We were on the frontier of the research into the nature of energy and matter. We academics were so full of enthusiasm. The atmosphere in the Old Cavendish was vibrant. Charles went over to the USA with two other members of the team to correlate Cambridge research with that of the University of Chicago where Enrico Fermi was trying to achieve a controlled nuclear chain reaction.

"They worked together on this until Charles became acquainted with J. Robert Oppenheimer when he was visiting Fermi in Chicago. Charles was invited to a summer school at Oppenheimer's building in Berkeley. The theme of the summer school was to be bomb theory."

Clive butted in. "Tony Shaw said that Professor Villiers was a pacifist, how come he was involved with a discussion about bomb theory?" Clive was also a pacifist.

"I thought you might ask that. When we saw him later Charles said that he was under the impression that only part of the summer school was to be bomb theory and he thought that he would be able to absent himself from the discussions he disagreed with."

"What has this got to do with Project End Time?" Julia asked. Cranford's countenance became more serious.

"Initially Charles was involved in the Manhattan Project research, but right at the start, he could see that the direction

Oppenheimer and his team were taking was the potential release of energy from the atom aimed at weaponry for use against their fellow man. Trinity, which led to the first detonation of the atomic bomb, was in its planning stage and there was a determination to use the product in combat, remember, this was during the Second World War. Charles made rather a fuss about it in military places and his voice became unwelcome in the States."

"So he came back to England," Clive said. Cranford wanted to move the discussion on and looked at his watch.

"He did come back to England, but not before he gained invaluable knowledge in the States that would spur him on with his own project. The purpose of Villiers' project was peaceful in concept. The next turn of events was when Charles came back to the Cavendish from a stay in Warwickshire. I remember the morning when he came back into the lab. He had such an intense look on his face. I can picture it as if it were yesterday. He gathered us around and told us that a few years previously he began to be associated with an old building in Temple Balsall to do with the Knights Templars. Inside it, carved into the stonework, was a prophetic message about a coming destruction. Charles had taken what he found in the building very seriously and it was the underlying element of his research."

"I know the building . . . look, I'm sorry to rush you but can you just get to the point," Julia persisted. She was waiting for the information that was specific to End Time and was poised with a notebook.

Cranford took the hint.

"Charles focussed the destructive potential of his research onto something he called Nibiru, but only a few of the academics in his team believed him. Most of them thought he had been overworking and was reacting badly to being unwanted in the States and in England, so one by one they transferred to other work. It was difficult at the time because it was right when England and the Commonwealth were having to dig deep for survival. After the war, with having to pay off lease-lend to the States it was no better, we had our backs to the wall.

"Charles became very unpopular. He openly defied the morality of building atomic weapons. People construed his defiance as unpatriotic, but he had the greater threat in mind, the one about Nibiru chiselled into the wall of the Knights' Sanctuary. He was so unpopular that the authorities outwardly dismissed what they called his ravings about the rogue planet."

"Outwardly dismissed?"

"Yes. You see, Charles Villiers was well known as an original thinker and because of that, certain ones in authority had taken note of him."

"Including Winston Churchill," Julia said.

"You've heard about that?"

"I have . . . carry on."

"Eventually the war ended with the use of two bombs that were the product of the Manhattan Project at Los Alamos. It was just as Charles Villiers predicted, Hiroshima and Nagasaki felt the wrath of the Destroyer of Worlds.

"Villiers left the Cavendish with a few of his closest colleagues, including me . . . who were disillusioned with the way our branch of science was going. We were also convinced he was right about the Nibiru threat. We wanted to try to do something about it and we managed to set up a laboratory at a place called Kineton, in Warwickshire." Julia sat bolt upright, startling Clive and Professor Cranford.

"You had a lab at Kineton?"

"A lab, and a machine shop to produce the hardware. It was very secure, and there was a lot of space there so that we could keep well away from prying eyes with what we had in mind. Do you know Kineton?"

"I know it well, it's near where I live." Julia remained quiet about exactly how well she knew MoD Kineton.

Cranford continued.

"We had done the math on the Nibiru threat. We worked on it individually and all five of us came up with the same result, that there definitely was a threat. It would be well into the future, maybe beyond our lifetime, but a threat there definitely was."

"What did you attempt to do about it?" Clive asked.

"Patience Clive, I am sure you can grant me another half an hour to explain what happened."

"I hope it's worth the wait," Julia said.

"Oh, it will be worth it Jules, have no doubt about that. Charles Villiers managed to get funding by devious means. There was a lot of worry about atomic weaponry in the immediate years after the Second World War. It was a time of nuclear proliferation. Nations were clamouring for the bomb, with mutually assured annihilation as a defence against aggression.

"Charlie Villiers devised a great cover for his Nibiru research. He set up a project to investigate the harmful effects of radioactive fallout and how best to protect first the government and the royals and lastly, the people, with shelter and atmospheric filter design. The government funded it and Charles channelled some of the funding sideways into End Time. We had the very best equipment at Kineton for our research and development."

"Was there a finished product?" Julia asked him.

"There most certainly was."

"Did you test it?"

"Well, if we had tested the full-blown weapon we wouldn't be here talking today. You are no doubt aware of $E = mc^2$?" Julia felt they were getting close to the reason for the visit to Professor Cranford.

"In very simple terms it is an expression of energy. We can see the colossal amount of destructive energy it does express in the detonation of a nuclear bomb. That fiendish apparatus Oppenheimer and the Los Alamos team started, Villiers and his team at Kineton, continued, but in, how can I describe it . . . in a tangential way compared to the known physics of the time. Remember, Villiers' work and his motive was specifically to address the threat from afar in the solar system and the work took us in an entirely different direction to Oppenheimer's Trinity Project. We did not intend the end result to get into military hands because that was against our code of ethics. We were experimenting with a particular type of particle physics . . . it was unique at the time and it hasn't been pursued in that particular form since. All of Charlie Villiers' work has been shelved and forgotten."

"You were in deep," Julia said.

"That, my girl, is an understatement."

"How destructive is it?"

"It would make a Hydrogen Bomb appear like a firecracker, which is all I could say. It is postulated that all matter in contact with ground zero would be altered into a minus state."

"Was it ever tested?" Julia asked the question again because when she asked it previously she noted that Cranford shifted his gaze to the side and down, the classic body language of a lie.

Cranford's eyes took on a far-away look as he remembered what happened years ago.

"OK, I'll tell you. I'm ninety-four now, so what does it matter. We were all sworn to secrecy, but as things seem to have taken a different turn of late I'll tell you what happened. Remember that what Villiers headed up was in a different league of physics to anything else that had taken place. We theorised about the possible results and were convinced that our experiment wouldn't get out of hand, but we didn't know exactly how it would shape up. In the early sixties, we took our experimental device minus a detail that would take it to criticality, to an uninhabited island in Polynesia called Paka'Piu. It was ten miles by three and a half, and five hundred miles away from anything else inhabited. We cruised two hundred miles away from the island and detonated the weapon. We knew it was going to be spectacular, but we were totally unprepared for what happened. Afterwards, we all agreed that for an instant of time we saw a darkness that one observer said was blacker than the blackest night, I can hear him saying it now after all the years. I digress. The darkness spread around and above the area of the island. It was a darkness like none of us had experienced before. Another of the scientists described it as a total absence of anything.

"At the core of the darkness we saw a circular luminous void. I can still picture it. It was spinning; I can only describe it as a vortex that had its entry at the place where the island was and it was moving like a whirlpool in reverse, with the narrower part of the cone upwards. It was trying to seek a target, maybe a weak point, lord knows where or what, but what it sought lay somewhere beyond Earth, up there in the heavens." Cranford energetically pointed upwards.

"Was it a physical phenomenon?"

"Are you asking if we had disturbed some dark force?"

"Well, had you?"

"Of course not, it was purely physical . . . but it was unique."

"What are your thoughts now?"

"Regarding what?"

"Regarding what you had created, in the light of current research."

"Current research hasn't touched what we made back then. We were in a very different league to the rest of science."

"You must have some thoughts about it." Julia looked at Cranford's bookshelf. It had titles relating to the latest research. Cranford saw where she was looking.

"I do keep up to date Jules. The body may be wearing out but the mind is still active."

"So?"

"Think of Black Holes."

"Mmm . . . it had crossed my mind."

There was a pause in conversation, then,

"What was the result of the test?" Julia asked.

"The Island had disappeared and the disturbed sea remained. By the time we got to where the island had been it was as if it had never existed. The device imploded and at the time of detonation, we felt the atmosphere around us being sucked into the vortex. It was frightening. It was then that we realised that what we had created, in its unrestrained mode, would probably do the job for which it had been created . . . to destroy a world. The problem was that we couldn't deliver the bloody thing back then. Rocket science was in its infancy and there was the enforced silence of that damn organisation that was re—"

"Eisenburg . . . they have a lot to answer for." Cranford glanced quickly at Julia. He nodded.

"Professor Cranford, did you know that the United Nations Secretary-General is aware of End Time, Eisenburg and Nibiru?"

"I am not surprised. There was a secretive arrangement, unofficial, man to man. Charlie Villiers spoke to the Secretary-General at the time and an arrangement was made for each Secretary-General to inform his successor about the weapon until there was a possibility it could be used.

"There was always the spectre of Eisenburg hovering in the background. They run counter to all moral sense. The End Time Project had to be kept out of their hands. Imagine the power that possession of the End Time weapon would give them. With that they would be able to call the tune to every government on Earth. For that reason, a select committee of eight representatives from the UN was formed to take responsibility for the weapon. It was all very secretive because the project had to be kept from Eisenburg at all costs."

"So at least some back then had the guts to try to do what was right."

"They most certainly did, Clive. The pressure on them was intense, but that's not relevant to what we're talking about. In 1957, the select committee visited Villiers' laboratory at MoD Kineton along with Anthony Eden. Eden had been involved in negotiating for a British atomic bomb. During that meeting, Project End Time was discussed in the context of Nibiru, with a view to using it at some point in time in an attempt to annihilate the problem."

"And like you said, at the time there was no way of getting the End Time weapon to the target, apart from which, the planet's course and velocity was theoretical. We have the proof now and we most likely have the delivery system."

"Have you really Jules? Then now all you want is Project End Time and permission to use it."

"Permission be damned. Just tell us where we can find it."

"You will find it in one of the bunkers at MoD Kineton. They were always changing the numbers of the buildings back then. Security, you know."

45

SHaFT forensics had finished their investigations at Keeper's Cottage and Templestone went to straighten the place up. He felt like an interloper in his old friend's house. Lee Wynter and Matt Roberts were there too, with Storm Petrel, who was intrigued with the fifteenth-century cottage.

Templestone was coming out of the local grocery store when a four by four that was passing screeched to a halt a number of yards further on. The driver's door opened and Dan Blundell stepped out. Bernie Crosher came around from the passenger side and they confronted Templestone.

"This is where I'm supposed to warn pussies like you that if you try anything on you may end up dead," Templestone said. The two looked Templestone up and down and found it difficult to believe the man in front of them caused so much damage at Alderhanger. To add to that Big Al Innis's leg was broken in multiple places, and the bacteria in Garth Wilde's shoulder was having a field-day. It was full of pus and doctors were saying he was losing the fight.

"We want you, old man," Blundell said, inching closer to Templestone. Crosher, at Blundell's side, nudged him hard on the arm as a warning to go easy out on the street, just before Wynter came out of the shop and saw what was going on.

"Friends of yours Bill?" Wynter called.

"What? I wouldn't have Neanderthals like these as friends. They were part of the team who killed Sancerre."

"Wanna hand?" Wynter stepped forward a couple of paces.

"No, keep back Lee, don't spoil the excitement."

Blundell nodded. He thought the two of them against Templestone would have stood a chance, but the addition of the Afro-Caribbean with an American accent on the old man's side made a difference.

"Another time old man, we've got a score to settle." Templestone went to move forward, but at that time a column of schoolchildren with two teachers, one at the front and one at the back, filed around the corner and came between Templestone and the two men.

The duo climbed back into the four by four and drove off with the turbo blowing black smoke. Wynter stood by Templestone and they watched the vehicle disappear around a bend in the road.

Roberts put the vacuum cleaner away under the stairs and they both looked around the room, the last one that needed tidying.

"Bill's moving in to this place in a few weeks," Roberts said to Storm Petrel as he put a match to the fire, "He's something to do with the building near the church, the Knights' Sanctuary; Keeper's Cottage goes with it."

"What's the Knight's Sanctuary for?" Storm asked.

"I'm not sure,"

They heard Templestone's Morris Minor Traveller skid to a halt outside. It was unusual because Templestone usually handled the classic vehicle with kid gloves.

Roberts had looked out the window. "There's a problem, I can tell by his face," They went to the door and stood aside for Templestone and Wynter to come through. Templestone looked in a foul mood.

"We've just encountered Crowe's men," he said. "They're not giving up easy."

"They've got to be stopped before they cause us some serious damage," Matt Roberts said, as he fingered the hilt of Mavis the Bowie, in a sheath on his belt.

"It nearly was permanent until Harry got us out of the vault. They are deadly serious," Templestone reflected on the cold and the darkness when they were in the vault.

"I suggest we pay them a visit," Roberts always came up with the revenge ideas.

"And I say we do it on the quiet, man, not a word to Jem," Wynter said.

Templestone had been thinking it had been a job unfinished. "We need the upper hand, when shall we go?"

"Tonight," Roberts said.

Storm Petrel wondered what she had walked into. Back at Dearden Hall she looked out the window and saw the lights of the Morris Minor pull out of the car park with the three of them inside. She checked the time. It was after dark, eight fifteen. Matt said they would be back within two hours.

Storm was developing a fierce loyalty to Matt. She hadn't known him long but felt she had known him half a lifetime.

"Don't say anything to anyone about what we're doing," Matt had said, and she assured him she wouldn't. The way he looked and dressed, the bandana that kept his long hair back, and the knife at his belt, kept hidden by his jacket until he needed it, made her think he was like a buccaneer. He told her he had once been in the British Navy, with the rank of commander until he couldn't stand the rigours of discipline any longer, so he punched his captain on the jaw and got a dishonourable discharge.

"At least I was in control of my life again," he told her. She liked his honesty and his loose-cannon bravado.

She waved at Templestone's car from her window as it sped off, and she fancied she saw an answering wave from the back seat where Matt was sitting.

* * *

Templestone pulled up in a layby which was three hundred yards down the narrow lane approaching Alderhanger. The grounds of the house were in darkness, but lights were on in three windows downstairs. Templestone switched on a torch and led the way to the curved walls at the top of the drive. The gates were locked.

"There's a gap in the hedge further on," Templestone said. He strode to the gap where he made his way from the grounds after his escape and forced his way through. He shone the torch back for Roberts and Wynter.

They were cautious as they walked down the drive. No security light came on right up to the doorstep. They planned for Templestone to knock the door on his own.

He shone his torch around the yard and picked up the ruins of the stable and the other outbuildings. He shone the torch on the door. The paintwork was satisfactorily blistered from the heat of the fire.

There were a bell and a heavy brass knocker, and Templestone chose the knocker for effect. He thrashed it heavily six times. There was a sudden, startled movement inside the house, and rapid footsteps to the door, which opened a few inches.

"Your two bastards I saw earlier today said you want to see me. Well, here I am. Going to let me in?"

"Uh . . . n—"

"No? Why did you want to see me Crowe, is it because you want your door painting? Have you had a fire . . . Mmm?" Templestone stuck his foot in the gap between the door and the frame. Crowe opened the door a foot and tried shutting it sharply on Templestone's foot but he was wearing steel-capped boots.

Crowe visualised Garth Wilde in his hospital bed with his distorted shoulder. He visited him two days ago and when he got near to the bed, he smelled the corruption. Crowe hit Templestone's foot with the door again and all the man with his foot in the door did was laugh. He was inhuman – cold. Crowe's confidence had waned with all of the opposition he had faced recently, and he had developed the habit of checking there was no one following him.

"Dan . . . Bernie, come here."

Dan Blundell and Bernie Crosher were watching the television. Blundell had practised his shooting without ear defenders, so his hearing was damaged and the sound on the television news special about Nibiru was up loud to compensate. Crosher had drifted off to sleep, so neither of them heard either the door bumping onto Templestone's steel toecap or Crowe's call for help.

The first they knew something was wrong was when Templestone stood in front of the television and turned it off. Blundell made to stand up but Templestone delivered a straight right to his chin. The sound of the connect on Blundell's chin jerked Crosher into wakefulness. He looked with unfocused eyes on the vision of the man they saw earlier in the day. That was the last thing Crosher remembered until he woke up covered in hoar frost, tied to his two companions on the ground outside the burning Alderhanger.

46

Lars Knudsen was a first-class fighter pilot. Evan Blake was surprised to get his call. It was strictly 'off the record' and scrambled, and it had to do with Nibiru.

"When will you arrive?" Blake asked him, expecting at least a week's grace to make preparations.

"Tomorrow at noon," Knudsen said.

The Secretary-General had an ex-US Air Force colleague who came into inherited railroad money and set up a 'fighter jet experience' business. The private arrangement to do with an aircraft would be ideal and untraceable.

Knudsen's colleague had a selection of high-performance jets. The fastest was a MiG-29 Fulcrum, which had a maximum speed of Mach 2.25 and could reach sub-orbital height.

"No-one must know about the flight," Knudsen said to Colonel Ryan Lindhoff. "We have to start before dawn and go sub-orbital. All trace of the flight must be obliterated after the event. There is another matter. At some point before long, we may have a need for a large transport aircraft to carry an object from the UK to Turaroa. Sir Willoughby Pierpoint is going to give you a call."

*   *   *

Blake was surprised to see the MiG-29 with American markings touch down on the airstrip. The pilot was marshalled to a hangar with open doors, which shut behind the aircraft as soon as it was inside.

"Good to meet you, Evan," called the Secretary-General when Blake approached the steps down from the cockpit. Knudsen had researched the progress of the entrepreneur.

"Mr Secretary-General, it is good to meet you too, although it would be better if it were under less trying circumstances." Blake led the way out of the hangar and through narrow corridors until they came to some lifts, one of which led directly to Evan Blake's penthouse suite.

"Sir Willoughby Pierpoint has acquainted you fully with the problem?" Knudsen said.

"He has and my team have been working on the situation around the clock. Sir Willoughby also told me that the problem has two strands. The major one is Nibiru. The other is Eisenburg and its regime of silence. It seems Eisenburg have held ministers of governments to ransom with the threat of retribution if they revealed the presence of Nibiru."

"Eisenburg is no longer a problem. Observatories worldwide have observed the planet. It's all over the news and the internet. The filters have been lifted. There is anger out there because of government duplicity and people feel they have been cheated."

"And so they have, Lars."

"A problem that has arisen. A group called Conspiracy Alive are coordinating widespread demonstrations. In London, Fenton Bull and some others are under siege inside the Palace of Westminster. Vienna, Paris and Berlin are seeing action. It seems that people want a scapegoat. They are gunning for Eisenburg and its adherents."

"Can you blame them? It is about time there was honesty in government."

"Yes, but we have to live by the rule of law. The alternative is anarchy and it's already taking place. One of Eisenburg has been strung up on a lamp-post in Montmartre. Conspiracy Alive are saying that those responsible for the cover-up will pay for their crimes, so it's turning nasty."

"With what the future holds I'm not surprised; folks have lost hope. They need hope, a focus."

"Hence my visit, Evan. Let's talk about our fight back against Nibiru."

"I take it you want to pursue the plan I have agreed with Sir Willoughby Pierpoint about using one of my rockets. I took Sir Willoughby on a tour of our launch facility. It was quite informative for both of us, but I told him to go away and find the End Time weapon. When he does, I will assign a vehicle to the task."

"One of your Saturn V's?"

"One of those would never do. The Saturn V is a short excursion vehicle, meant for a trip around the block. No – if he finds the weapon, I will give Sir Willoughby a Condor VI Heavy Lift."

It was all Knudsen needed. He was relieved. He had a personal guarantee that he had Evan Blake onside and that he was not part of Eisenburg. Now he had to get back to New York before there was a need to account for his time. Apart from that, he rather enjoyed having control of a high-powered fighter jet again. But first, just a few hours rest.

* * *

Back in Sutton Place, Knudsen turned on US TV News 24. There were scenes from across the globe where demonstrations and running street battles were taking place against governments who had conspired to be silent about Nibiru. Water cannon and rubber bullets were in widespread use across Europe to quell the riots. Demonstrations were getting out of hand in African nations and in Asia. The scene was turning ugly with armies and police confronting the angry crowds on the streets in place after place.

The scene on the news channel changed to a floodlit market square in Koblenz, where a middle-aged industrialist named Bruno Geisler, who, it was revealed, was an Eisenburger, had taken the law into his own hands. Standing on his balcony, he opened fire with a shotgun above the heads of a crowd of protesters.

"You will do as we say. We know what is best for you," he shouted through a loudspeaker before a police marksman shot him. The rest of the crowd rushed his house where his family were in hiding and they set fire to it. There were no survivors and then the police moved into the square and shot into the surging crowd.

The disturbing report went on. A great mass of humanity in African countries were on the streets. Fires illuminated Red Square, in Moscow. In parts of Asia where there were repressive regimes, the crowds became a seething mass of disorder after they heard the news of impending cataclysm. Either by the bullet or Nibiru, oblivion was in sight. It didn't matter which way it came, it had the same result. So they looted and pillaged while they still had a chance to do it.

Lars Knudsen turned off the television and sat heavily in his seat, feeling the full weight of responsibility as leader of the World's organisation for peace. With the widespread mistrust of governments by the people, he grasped his role as Secretary-General of the UN and made a unilateral decision to bypass the corruption of government. He had sometimes questioned his role when his operatives went in to a situation as peacemaker armed and battle-ready. With the breakdown of law and order on such a wide scale, the time for urgent action and transparency of motive had come. The people needed an answer to the threat. To drive that forward Knudsen needed to arrange a meeting of the Security Council to discuss the deteriorating situation, and inform them about the possible solution.

When he spoke into the phone, his PA sounded unsettled, but Knudsen rode that out.

"Abe, I need you to set up a meeting of the Security Council for two pm today. It will be held in camera." He gave the PA some precise instructions for the meeting that, he stressed, had to be carried out to the letter. Knudsen picked up a notepad. He wrote the names of the fifteen representatives of the Security Council. He studied them for a few minutes and went to a steel filing cabinet where he located six files and spent the next forty-five minutes studying them. He looked at the fifteen names on the pad again and put a heavy line through the six of them that he thought couldn't be trusted.

47

It was after dark in Radway. They needed the shelter of night. Dearden and Doughty pulled into the drive at Ireton Grange and Sir Willoughby met them on the doorstep. They immediately went down to Pierpoint's offices in the vaulted cellar to discuss the plans for the search at MoD Kineton.

"We are meeting Ramsay in his office in forty minutes. I have his confidence in our actions after young Harry's fine reasoning about the presence of Nibiru and my persuasion about Ramsay's career. Gentlemen, when all is said and done, Michael Ramsay is a man of great moral courage because he has elected to help us search for Project End Time and release it without the authority of his superiors. He understands that without it probably none of us will survive, and that to obtain an official release for it would be well-nigh impossible. The officials he would have to approach can't be trusted. Ramsay suspects that at least five of them are in with Eisenburg."

Pierpoint cocked his head on one side, he had heard a noise from above, a motorcycle with an offbeat tone to its engine.

"Someone else has arrived who's helping with the search."

The doorbell rang. They heard subdued conversation and after a minute there was a knock on Pierpoint's office door.

"Come in, don't stand on ceremony," Pierpoint called. Harry Stanway came in, still in his motorcycle leathers.

* * *

They passed through security at the main gate of MoD Kineton in Dearden's Range Rover. There were the usual stringent security checks. Lieutenant Colonel Ramsay was waiting for them outside the administration block and he led them up to his office, explaining his progress in the search for End Time as he climbed the stairs.

"I've searched through all the records to do with the deposits of the ordinance here in Kineton over the past seventy years and there is no mention of End Time. I am at my wits end about where to look for it." The louvre blinds were down over the windows of his office. The lights were dim and two trusted men with automatic weapons stood at the entrance to the building and two outside his office door.

"Are all of the ammunition dumps accounted for in the records?" Pierpoint asked.

"All of them have clearly recorded deposit information. They are meticulously itemised. You must remember that there is some extremely nasty ordinance here and due to the nature of the weaponry, all movement must be well documented."

"All the historical hearsay tells us Project End Time is here, so if it doesn't appear in the records, where might it be?" Dearden asked Ramsay.

"I can assure you it isn't in any of the ammunition dumps in Kineton. I have spent hours looking at the records and I've drawn a blank." Harry was looking at a plan of MoD Kineton that was hanging on the wall. It was based on an aerial photograph which was showing forty large grass-covered mounds, each of which had the letter D followed by a figure printed over it, D1 to D39.

"Why is Dump 40 missing?" Harry asked, looking over the plan of the site. He traced each mound with his finger and came across a raised mound that was larger than the others, with R1 printed over it. "What is R1?" Harry asked Ramsay.

"Repository One. It is a store for things like cookers and fridges, timber for repairs, old bikes and vehicles, old armaments and things like that. Equipment is there that's used to keep the site running.

"How long has it been used?" Harry asked

"Well over a hundred years. It may go back to Napoleonic times. It's like a museum. Pity it belongs to the MoD."

As he mentioned the MoD, Ramsay's eyes began flitting from one to the other of the men present.

"Oh, the military mind," Pierpoint said. "Sometimes it is so blinkered."

"Shall we go?" Harry said. "That's where it is guys. It's amongst the museum stuff."

* * *

Two vehicles pulled up outside R1. Four armed men in special services gear disembarked and spread out, two each side of the large steel doors. Ramsay went to the small personnel door and after trying a number of keys on a bunch chained to his belt, he found the one that unlocked it. It was a bigger key than the others.

Ramsay pushed open the door. Leading with a torch he turned to the right and found a light switch. A feeble glow came from rows of light bulbs in green metal shades. Pierpoint, followed by the others, came through the door. Two of the special services men came in last, latched the door behind them and stood with automatic weapons at the ready.

A musty smell pervaded the air. It was a mixture of wood, oil, military grease and age. Harry scanned the interior. From where he was standing, he could see that five aisles stretched the length of the building. Racks piled with all manner of items, were nearly touching the curved ceiling.

Pierpoint gathered the team around him.

"What we are looking for will be large. Professor Cranford told Jules that the weapon was crated and ready for transport. The box would have been about fifteen feet long by seven feet square, so it should be obvious. OK, let's make a start, one of us to each aisle."

Harry took the centre aisle. Objects were stacked high and it was impossible to see what was lying behind the objects at the front of the top shelf of the rack. There was a rolling ladder at the beginning of each aisle and Harry wheeled one along to see what lay behind a number of office desks on the top shelf of the racking.

There was a gap between each of the desks and Harry stepped off the ladder and walked through the gap to the centre of the rack. In front of him, going away from the entrance to R1, he could see a number of Second World War type fur-lined flying jackets hanging on a rack. He found one that fitted him and kept it on.

Further on were some Sten Guns in a rack and then four Norton 16H motorcycles in desert camouflage colour. He passed box after box with stencilled serial numbers and military sounding descriptions. Belts: Khaki Webbing, Brass. Next was a group of Vickers Machine Guns, interlocked together on tripod stands and shiny with grease. He continued past the guns and came to objects belonging to older eras. Tee handled trench shovels, racked and greased with a tie label dated 1915 were next to trench boots. Harry picked one up, the still pliable leather had been protected with a waxy substance that smelled of animal fat. What became obvious as Harry walked on, was that the deeper into Repository One he went, the older were the objects.

Harry, from his high vantage point, took note of the shelving on the racks each side of the one he was standing on, but there was nothing of a size that fitted Pierpoint's description. He got to the end of the rack and looked over the edge at the five levels of racking below. He reckoned each one was spaced about ten feet vertically from its neighbour. The area was busy with stored equipment. It was difficult to take it all in and the end wall of the repository was in semi-darkness. Harry looked back at the overhead lighting, the last dim bulb was a number of yards behind him, but he was attracted to a shape in the end wall. It was an area of deeper darkness. He made a mental note to look at it later.

Harry walked back along the top tier to where he left the rolling ladder and stepped down to the ground. He quickly paced down the aisle, looking to left and right. He rounded the corner of the centre rack and in front he saw the dark area that had interested him. He walked up to it and saw that it was a semicircular tunnel. It was about fifteen feet at its highest point and had been constructed out of blue engineering bricks that gave it an eighteen hundreds' look.

The opening had tall, iron-barred gates with a heavy chain and padlock. Harry grasped a bar on each of the gates and tugged. The chain rattled and an echo of the noise came back out of the tunnel.

"Are you OK?" came a call from somewhere behind and to his right. It was Dearden's voice, he had heard Harry rattling the iron gates.

"Yeah . . . I'm OK, have you had any luck?" His voice echoed back to him from the depths of the tunnel.

"No luck so far," Dearden called.

"Then maybe you should come and look at this," Harry called, as his eyes tried to penetrate the darkness of the tunnel.

*   *   *

They gathered around Harry, who had his flashlight shining on the chain.

"It's got to be in there," he said, giving the iron gates another shake. The noise echoed back at them from the tunnel.

"How far does this go back?" Pierpoint asked Ramsay.

"I don't know. I had no idea it even existed."

"So, you don't have a key?"

"Not that I am aware of." Ramsay took the bunch of keys out of his pocket and chose the biggest to try. A large key was needed judging by the size of the padlock, but none of the keys on the bunch fitted.

"There was some oxy-acetylene welding gear on the racks further back," Mitch Doughty said. He rattled the chain. "We'll burn through this in no time."

48

When Evan Blake and Knudsen had met and talked on Turaroa, Blake reeled off the benefits accomplished over the years by the desire to shed the bonds of Earth.

"With each generation, there have been many advancements from space exploration. Micro-miniaturisation has brought great improvements in medical treatment, it is often far less invasive now than it used to be for major surgery. Technology and construction have been given a host of new materials and adhesives. The Condor program is the culmination of all that and more. It is far ahead of its time. We have developed an innovative engine to power the third stage. On staging, it boosts the payload capsule in a continuous controlled acceleration to a speed in excess of 800,000 miles per hour. It could reach our target in the region of the Sun in five days."

"Has it been tested?

"Both in the lab and interplanetary space. Condor VI is how we are going to showpiece the new drive as the next generation of deep space transport and exploration. You would be surprised at what we have accomplished, Lars."

"Then let's hope Will Pierpoint and his friends find the End Time weapon without being jumped on by Eisenburg, or governments under their influence. I have information from a reliable source that Eisenburg would dearly like to get hold of End Time. I think their greed for power is about to kick them in the teeth because they are facing the same fate as we are now."

"Too right they are. But let's concentrate on the positives. With End Time on board my Condor VI Heavy Lift, we should have a chance of survival."

*   *   *

In the United Nations building, there was an intense argument at the door of a small room where the Security Council were due to meet. Knudsen anticipated there would be problems, and had armed guards posted at the door with instructions to bar entry to six men who Knudsen knew were associated with Eisenburg. The excluded six were not pleased when the guards stopped their entry and one of them, who threatened violence was led away at gunpoint.

In the Security Council meeting, which lasted barely two hours, Knudsen revealed the existence of the End Time weapon and a viable transport system for it. One of the older members of the meeting, an Englishman, had heard rumours of the existence of such a weapon but had dismissed it as fanciful hearsay. The meeting was much heartened by Knudsen's revelation. They agreed that a way to defuse a worldwide slide into anarchy would be to publicise the hope of a solution immediately.

The member for the UK suggested, "Publicise the fight back using the Condor VI Heavy Lift with the End Time weapon as the payload. OK, so End Time's precise location has yet to be confirmed but publicise Condor everywhere. If we give people a future to aim for, it will pull the situation back from anarchy."

Knudsen gave the United Nations PR team directions from the Security Council to compile a short video for general release. The Security Council had brainstormed a list of scenes to present the reality of the threat, and to conclude the presentation, information about a hopeful solution.

The video, with a voice-over in the world's major languages describing the danger, would begin with Nibiru shown in its Earthbound orbit near the Sun. The next scene would be snow-capped mountains, a rain forest with waterfalls and birds in song with gorgeous plumage. Following this, there would be sunlight playing on a stream where there were children of different races playing together in childish innocence showing what would be in danger of being lost. There would be the sound of the children's laughter, which would fade to nothing.

Switch to an approaching maelstrom of waves. Looking skywards, Nibiru would be large in the sky, the children would be looking at it fearfully, their clothing whipped by a fierce wind.

Toward the end of the ten-minute video, change the scene to Turaroa and a close-up of the Condor VI Heavy Lift on the launch pad, a bright symbol of hope. The voice-over would describe the Condor's payload as a weapon designed to destroy the threat. An animation of the countdown to launch the mightiest rocket the world had ever known would commence, and the Condor VI Heavy Lift would rise on white-hot fire on its mission to destroy the threat. Within eight hours of its inception, the video went live on news channels world-wide.

*　*　*

After the broadcast finished, Lars Knudsen switched over to the Norris Parnell program special, *Nibiru, the Truth*. It was designed as a follow-up to the UN broadcast. Parnell, the fearsome anchor-man, famous for eliciting truth out of squirming politicians, introduced a leading astronomer from Great Britain, Chris

Howard, the Director of the European Space Agency, Greet van Dorsten, the Administrator of NASA, Dale Perry, and from Korolyov, Moscow, via satellite, Pavel Ivashin, Deputy Head of Rosaviakosmos, the Russian equivalent of NASA.

Norris Parnell was dead against inviting along any government representative because of possible affiliations to Eisenburg, who he described in his preamble as the worst kind of political cancer. He launched straight into the questions, firing from the hip, as was his style. He aimed the first salvo at the astronomer.

"Why has this thing called Nibiru been hushed up for years by people like you?"

Chris Howard came in with a succinct answer. "There have been rumours about Nibiru for years, Planet X is another name for it. The problem is that its orbital path, which was directly behind the Sun until very recently, kept it hidden. Its presence was unproven."

"But a man named Villiers found out about it years ago, before the Second World War in fact, but he was shut up . . . why?"

The interview went on in this fashion for a full half hour and during his turn at the receiving end of Parnell's mouth, Ivashin, in bullish mood, came on the attack, claiming that it was only the Western democratic governments which laid themselves open to being courted by Eisenburg because of their inherent greed. Parnell countered this by one word, a name, Lukashenko, and he raised his eyebrows. Ivashin was immediately quietened because he had connections with the Lukashenko Ordinance works, which had connections with Eisenburg.

Ivashin was used to lying through his teeth and quickly regained his composure by saying that his organisation,

Rosaviakosmos, was ready to discuss plans and share technology to ward off the impending danger from the skies. Parnell looked at Ivashin with a smirk, and a one brow up and one brow down expression that said you're a damn liar.

He directed his final question at Dale Perry. "Why have you, as the Administrator of NASA, not been able to come up with a viable transport system for this End Time weapon, also a brain-child of Professor Villiers, I might add? After all, NASA has pulled off some spectacular stunts."

"We have been pulling out all the stops to implement an asteroid impact defence plan and using our current technology we may stand a chance to divert a small-scale threat, but I fear to say, we could deflect nothing the size of Nibiru. All credit must go to Evan Blake. His entrepreneurial spirit and his determination to succeed with state-of-the-art rocketry have put him ahead of us and any other organisation in the military or the commercial sector. We have committed all of the resources of NASA to back him up."

"Is NASA working with Blake?"

"We are standing by to do so should he request our help."

"As are we," came the voice from Moscow.

In conclusion, Norris Parnell praised Evan Blake and those working with him. He also said how indebted we all are to the late Professor Charles Villiers, who was one of the few people of his calling who had the moral courage and the foresight to try to ward off disaster. Parnell then made a pact with his audience, which was claimed to be in the billions. He said that he would not rest until he saw justice done regarding Eisenburg. The audience was hooked. They were elated. Someone was working on their side. Parnell had some clout and he knew the right people. Retribution would be meted out on behalf of the common man, woman and child worldwide who had been duped by Eisenburg and government for far too long.

*   *   *

Mitch Doughty opened the acetylene valve slightly, lit it with a lighter he always carried and gently added the oxygen. He adjusted the valves and the flame changed from yellow with black smoke to an incandescent white. Doughty tipped the darkened glass welding mask down and played the torch on the chain holding the gates together. Within seconds white-hot metal was dripping to the floor, sparks flew in all directions and then the chain fell apart.

Harry pulled the gates open and in the beam from his flashlight he tried to see the detail in the tunnel beyond. Doughty flicked on his torch too and held it high. On the wall, he saw a double switch. The first he switched on produced a noise from the ceiling above them and the second turned on a line of dim light bulbs, some of which were not working. Interspersed at various points were extraction fans that were creating the whirring noise. The semi-circular tunnel continued into the distance. It was faced with cream coloured glazed tiles and had a dark-green tiled dado rail about shoulder height.

"This must have been built with some purpose in mind, although what it was I do not know," Ramsay said. "The tunnel is definitely not on the plans."

"So let's walk on and find out what lies ahead," Dearden said, striding out with Pierpoint by his side.

After a quarter of an hour, the iron gates at the entrance had dwindled to nothing in the distance. Dearden took out a pocket compass.

"You can never tell when one of these will be useful," he said, flipping it open. "We're heading south-west."

"Directly towards Edge Hill," Harry said. He had noted the direction of the layout of R1 on the plan in Ramsay's office.

"This area is honeycombed with tunnels, there's one from Ireton Grange to the Church and I know of at least three others that come from religious persecution at the time of the civil war. There are parts of MoD Kineton that originated in the late sixteen-hundreds," Pierpoint informed them.

Another ten minutes and they came to the end of the tiled surface on the walls of the tunnel. It gave way to rock, with the marks of the tools used to cut it still evident.

"According to my reckoning we have passed under Radway and we are nearing Edge Hill," Harry said. His habit of counting told him he had paced nearly one point eight kilometres. He gazed into the poorly lit distance. "What's that up ahead?" he asked, speeding up his pace.

A hundred paces further the tunnel ended in a room cut out of the solid Hornton Ironstone of the Edge Hill escarpment. The room appeared to be about three quarters the size of a tennis court and the same height as the tunnel leading into it. Machine tools, both large and small were dotted systematically about the room. Around the perimeter, there were racks where items of tooling were stored and over in the left corner Harry could see steps leading up to a heavy looking studded door set in a Gothic arch.

In an open space in front of the door, there was a large wooden packing crate on a low six-wheeled trailer painted in military khaki, hitched to a heavy haulage six-wheeled road tractor with a long hood. The light was dim from the few light bulbs in enamelled metal shades, which were still working. Harry pulled a torch from his pocket and shone it onto some faded lettering stencilled on the side of the crate. Dearden stepped onto the trailer and with his hand, brushed away the dust from the lettering, P. E. T. Mk Ω.

49

"P.E.T., Project End Time. Now we can move ahead, as long as this thing works," Dearden said, as he stepped off the low loader and brushed the dust off his jacket.

Harry shone his torch on the Greek Omega symbol. "And he had a sense of humour too."

"What makes you say that?"

"The Omega symbol."

"What of it?"

"The beginning and the end. In the Book of Revelation, the Alpha and the Omega refers to God being the beginning and the end of all things. Villiers has used the omega symbol to denote the end of all things with the potential of his End Time weapon."

"It is to be hoped he was right when his weapon reaches the target," Doughty said.

Pierpoint was at the front of the truck, shining his torch onto the radiator at the front of the long hood of the tractor vehicle.

"I thought I recognised the shape of this rig. It's a Diamond T980 Tank transporter." Pierpoint undid the clips, lifted one side of the hood and looked at the engine. "This is the diesel version. When I heard that the bomb weighed in at 30,000 pounds I wondered how we were going to move it, but this is the ideal vehicle for the job."

Harry climbed into the cab on the passenger side and Doughty slid behind the steering wheel. Dearden stepped onto the running board on Doughty's side. "The key's still in the ignition," he said.

"They must have kept the weapon ready for transport," Doughty tried turning the key. "The cells will have degraded. Battery's bound to be dead."

Harry's heels touched something that moved under the seat. He reached down and felt a handle. He took hold of it and pulled up a brown leather briefcase, worn with use. His torch picked out the initials C.V., Charles Villiers, in faded gold leaf.

Dearden and Doughty were discussing the fuel, that it could be OK. Doughty said that he had heard of diesel fuel being used after thirty years in storage. Harry tucked the briefcase under his arm and climbed out of the cab. The others didn't notice him slipping away, as he went past the machine-tools to the stone steps leading to the door in the corner of the room.

At the top of the steps, he pressed the door catch with his thumb and pushed. The hinges grated slightly and he looked behind, but the others hadn't heard. Harry's mental calculation of the distance and direction from R1 told him that he was probably under the old Castle Inn, which lay on the top of Edge Hill, which would account for the Gothic shape of the door. Maybe, he thought, the door was part of an escape route used at the time of the Civil War. He entered the space on the other side of the door and shone his torch on some spiral stairs which were worn with use. There was a light switch on the wall. He flicked it down and light bulbs in metal shades flickered on. Harry switched off his torch and climbed to the top of the stairs, where there was another door, which he pushed open and went on through.

"Well I'll be damned," he said, as he gazed at the equipment of a well-stocked laboratory. There was electronic gear, dials and gauges, Cambridge chart recorders, autoclaves and furnaces.

There was so much equipment that it was impossible to take it all in with a cursory examination. He noticed, in a corner where the lighting was dim, that there was a flight of six stone steps leading upwards. He climbed them and stood in front of a door at the top, which was positioned between two large square metal pillars that felt warm to the touch and had turnbuckles on panels on the sides facing each other. He opened the door cautiously. Immediately the other side, a wall made of the locally quarried Hornton stone blocked the way forward. Harry fancied he heard a noise, filtering through the stonework. It was a hollow sound as if there were a great distance beyond and he could hear an occasional movement the other side of the wall, that was faint and insistent.

Harry hazarded a guess that the way beyond the door led to the Castle Inn at the top of Edge Hill. If that was so, the stairway had probably been blocked to save unauthorised entry when Villiers and his team moved in to the laboratory. The owner of the inn at the time would have been complicit in the closure of the passageway. Harry wondered what Villiers said to him. Oh, by the way, we're fitting out a laboratory under your property and we'll be building an experimental weapon that could annihilate the planet.

The problem was that the faint noises the other side of the wall didn't fit with sounds to be expected from an inn. There was no music or laughter, no chink of glasses, or buzz of conversation. No roll of casks in a cellar. The sound was unrecognisable and not only did it make Harry curious, but he felt uneasy about what lay beyond the wall.

He turned back to the laboratory. It was a large rectangular room carved out of the rock. A desk was by one of the walls, with a leather upholstered chair drawn out as if it had been recently vacated. The desk would have been Villiers' centre of operations and there was a blackboard, with equations chalked on it, fixed to a wall nearby. The most noticeable object on the desk was a plasma globe, albeit a crude one. Harry flicked on an in-line switch in the braided cotton cable and the globe lit up. He touched it, and streams of plasma followed his fingers as they traced the curve of the glass sphere. The light from the plasma reflected off the glass protecting a photograph. Harry picked it up. It was a full-length photograph of a man, maybe in his mid-fifties. He had hair that was greying at the edges, a handsome man with film star looks. The chin strong, the eyes kindly. Harry turned the photo frame over and saw the signature on the back, *Charles Villiers*, and below it the location, *Outside the Cavendish Laboratory*.

So this was Charles Villiers. Harry gently returned the photo to the desk and sat on Villiers' chair. He tried to work out why everything seemed in a state of suspended animation. A cigar over four inches long was still resting in the groove of an ashtray. It had been lit and had burnt out. The ash still lay below it. Two and a half sandwiches, one partly eaten and now in the last stages of decomposition, lay on a discoloured piece of greaseproof paper. On his way from the cab of the Diamond T through to the lab, Harry noticed that one of the lathes in the machine shop still had swarf in the trough below the bed. Harry knew from Bill Templestone that any self-respecting engineer kept his machinery clean. All the evidence implied that Villiers and his team left the machine shop area and the laboratory in a hurry.

Harry surveyed the other items Villiers left on the desk after his exodus. There were some coloured pencils and a set of graphite pencils for sketching, 4B through to H. By the side of them were a pencil sharpener and a putty rubber. Nearby there was a slide rule and a book of logarithmic tables. They were lying on top of two notepads, which Harry flipped open. One of them was foolscap, narrow-ruled, which had the imprint of writing on the top sheet. A remnant of jagged edges showed where some of the sheets were torn out without much thought for tidiness; more evidence of a hurried departure.

The other pad contained graph paper, with an incomplete graph directly below the cover. Harry looked at the legends written against the axes of the graph. The vertical y-axis represented Mega Electron Volts Applied, with a magnitude from zero to 500. The horizontal x-axis was labelled Captured Particle: antihydrogen and the magnitude of the captured particles were marked off in parts of a gram, from zero up to 5 grams. There was no resultant curve rising from the zero position, but there was a label where a curve would rise after calculation. The words within the label were, Equivalent Yield, Decillion Tons of TNT

Harry analysed the writing. It was in a firm hand, in the Copper Plate style of a time gone by, written in blue-black ink. It was headed with a single Greek Ω, symbolising the end. Harry considered the implications of the yield being measured as decillion tons, one, followed by thirty-three zeros, and he began to understand the workings of Villiers' mind. If the professor had his computation right, the device on the trailer in the room down the stone steps was truly a destroyer of worlds. Its yield, in tons, would be greater that the weight of the Earth. *Little wonder he did not want to test the full-blown weapon*, Harry reasoned..

There was another item on the desk, insignificant in one way, but poignant. It was a brass plate deeply engraved with the text, Prof. Charles Villiers. Harry picked it up and looked around the laboratory, considering how Villiers worked tirelessly behind the scenes in this corner of Warwickshire to try to avert the coming disaster.

Harry looked at the name in brass he was holding, trying to get the measure of the man. He felt saddened by the fact that, even when agents of both the government and Eisenburg were tracking him down, Villiers wanted the dignity of recognition and had his name engraved in brass. He managed to establish his laboratory against all the odds and had the foresight to begin the fight back against the coming catastrophe.

Harry used the camera on his mobile phone to photograph the laboratory and he put the two notepads into Villiers' brief-case. He wished he had more time to investigate the door which opened onto a stone wall, and then he descended the stairs back into the machine shop. The lab door closed behind him loudly.

"Where the hell have you been?" Dearden looked worried.

"In Villiers' lab." Harry pointed. "Up those steps and through the door." He felt the brass plate with Villiers' name, in his pocket.

"You've found his lab?"

"Yeah, and I've found some of his reasoning on End Time."

50

"The tyres have deteriorated on the tractor, we won't get far unless we change them," Pierpoint dug his nail into the rubber and pulled a piece off to demonstrate his point.

"I can do better than that," Ramsay said. "We use another Diamond T to transport heavy stuff around the MoD site, it's got good tyres. I'll get the lads to bring it to R1, we can swap the tractors over." Ramsay got out his mobile and checked the signal. It was only partial, but good enough because he got through to someone he called Archie. It was a brief conversation, about the Diamond T.

Ramsay went to the trailer and kicked one of the tyres. He bent down and examined it, tried digging his nail in like Pierpoint had. He looked up. "There shouldn't be any problem with the trailer. These are solid tyres and they should be good enough to get the load from here into R1."

He and Pierpoint went to the other side of the trailer where Harry was speaking to Dearden and Doughty about Villiers' laboratory. Harry was saying that he had a suspicion about what happened to Villiers. "It was a formula he left on the blackboard in his lab, along with a diagram, but at the moment the outcome is conjecture until I spend more time on it—"

"I was speaking to my elder statesman friend yesterday," Pierpoint interrupted, "He remembers the time Villiers got into the public gallery in the Houses of Parliament. The outburst between him and Peter Thorneycroft, the Secretary of State for Defence, was fiery. Apparently, after the public gallery incident, things got too hot for Villiers, he was threatening to go public with everything he knew about Eisenburg. He found out that suits with guns were looking for an opportunity to quench his excitement. After that he disappeared. No trace left whatsoever."

Harry nodded. "That ties up," he said quietly. The others didn't hear. And then louder, "He was doing his damnedest to do something about the threat by constructing the End Time weapon and he was vilified for it."

"He was, poor chap," Pierpoint was a hater of injustice, like Harry. "Back then his effort failed, but we're the inheritors and in a few hours, it will be on its way to Turaroa and Villiers' project will see some action."

They were walking up the centre aisle near to the entrance of R1 when they heard the brakes of a vehicle and the tick-over with a powerful engine pulling up outside.

"That's Wilson and the lads with the Diamond T," Ramsay said. He stepped up the pace to the front of the building and signalled to the armed guards inside to open the doors.

They opened ponderously on rollers and revealed the vertical bars of a large, steel radiator grille picked out in the meagre light shining out of R1. The front of the tractor vehicle, bearing the logo of a diamond with the letter 'T' in the centre, vibrated with the torque of the fourteen and a half litre engine as Wilson drove it into R1.

The outer doors were shut and Pierpoint hoisted himself up into the cab, followed by Ramsay, and the others stepped up into the loading area behind, with Wilson's men. Pierpoint pointed the way forward and the vehicle moved slowly down the centre aisle with just eighteen inches to spare each side of the vehicle.

There was more room for manoeuvrability when they entered the tunnel. Wilson stepped on the gas, and very shortly they came to the end of the tunnel. With a few grating gear changes, he turned the T980 and within thirty minutes, the substitute tractor was hitched to the trailer carrying the weapon. Wilson gunned the engine. The gears engaged noisily, and the T980 moved forward, easily pulling the weight of the cargo.

There was a desk where a clerk used to sit, nestled into the right-hand corner of R1 between the right hand and the front walls. Harry pulled a chair out for Pierpoint and emptied the contents of the briefcase out onto the desk. Dearden, Doughty and Ramsay came alongside. There were a burgundy coloured fountain pen and twelve sheets of foolscap paper covered with notations and calculations, and the two notepads from the laboratory. Harry opened the notepad and offered the loose sheets up to where the stubs of the pages remained. They fitted perfectly.

Pierpoint switched on a desk light and Harry tapped his finger on the first sheet of paper. "This is important," he said.

"What is it?" Doughty asked.

"Detonation information."

"It does help to have that, given the present circumstances," Pierpoint said. He looked up as the sound of turboprops grew loud and pulsed the air when an aircraft passed low overhead. "This is organisation at its best, Colonel Lindhoff's on time. He was Lars Knudsen's recommendation."

"I've heard Ryan Lindhoff's dependable when the schedule's tight," Dearden said.

"And dependable is what we need right now," Doughty added. Pierpoint nodded and stood to one side where it was quiet. He keyed a number on his mobile phone.

*   *   *

On Turaroa Island, Evan Blake's phone rang.

"It's Will Pierpoint. We have the End Time project in our possession and I have a Hercules C130 H transport landing right now at MoD Kineton courtesy of Colonel Ryan Lindhoff's collection. We will be on our way as soon as we have loaded and secured the bomb."

"OK . . . I'll advise the team to be prepared to make modifications to the capsule when we have the weapon on Turaroa. We are planning launch windows as I speak. The next opportunity is 0730 your time one week today."

Pierpoint saw Harry turn to the next sheet of documentation from the briefcase.

"One more thing, Evan, Harry Stanway found the detonation procedure for the bomb. He says it'll take a while to get to grips with it, but when he has I'll get him to tie his findings in with your engineers so they can plan it into the Condor software."

51

The team were watching BBC News 24 in the great hall as they waited for Pierpoint to arrive. Late the previous night, after the Diamond T hauled the crate into Dump 38, Pierpoint spoke on a conference line to Lars Knudsen at the UN and Evan Blake at Frontier Spaceflight. They spoke of how the video produced by the UN Public Relations had gone down well, with an estimated sixty percent cessation in violent protests according to stats provided by international news organisations. To cement public confidence in the outcome of the Condor VI Heavy Lift mission, the three men devised a press release with further details about the plan to counter Nibiru.

"We must be upfront with everything. Give out some hope and leave no room for mistrust. Eisenburg has done more than enough damage with their double-dealing," Pierpoint said. In view of this, Evan Blake, with Knudsen and Will Pierpoint's input, drafted out a detailed report about the rocket being readied on the launchpad and the weapon it was going to deliver. They analysed the completed report, honed it for an hour until it was sharp and then it was broadcast.

After the broadcast, Pierpoint slumped into the easy chair in his office below Ireton Grange. He rubbed his temples to try to ease a headache. *What the hell*, he thought, *Other than Jem succeeding with alien contact, Condor's the best we can come up with. We can do no more.* He turned the television back on.

Nigel Sayers, an outside broadcast news reporter who had the habit of vaguely dancing to emphasise his words, summed up the reactions the threat was causing around the world.

"People are reacting to the situation in different ways. Many are turning to religion. The statistician, Julian Finch, has revealed that, in a poll taken amongst congregations coming out of churches of most denominations on Sunday, eighty-seven percent have never attended a church before. They are doing so now because they're trying to cosy up to God to get him to help them."

The news editor himself had taken charge. He was in studio nine at Broadcasting House. Sayers heard his voice in the earpiece. None of the millions tuned in to the news program saw the slight change in Sayers' eyes, the sideways glance as he listened to the editor's voice.

"Get ready for a big one Nige. It'll be after the tour operator advert. Autocue will roll in four minutes. Get ready, tourism. He did the countdown on his hand, 5 . . .4 . . .3 . . .2 . . .1, cue tourism." Sayers spoke after the advert, following the autocue.

"Tour operators are in great demand for holidays in the West Indies, the Bahamas and Hawaii, and there has been a surge in the housing market. It is now possible to buy a house in London, similar to one in Grimsby for much the same price. There is a great levelling going on."

Sayers found it easy following the autocue, but that was his job. He had reported in war zones. "It is thought that people are selling up on all continents to pay for the last fling before the end comes, but there is that ray of hope to hold onto. The United Nations have released another report explaining the situation we are facing in detail, and the mission they have organised."

The news editor's voice came in the earpiece, "Get ready, description, Condor VI Heavy Lift, in 5 . . .4 . . ." and again Sayers glanced slightly sideways as he took in the autocue. The scene changed to a launch pad with an immense white rocket being readied for launch, gleaming in the Sun. Sayers read from the prompt.

"Currently, as you see on the launch stand, the UN are in the final stages of organising a state-of-the-art rocket ship that you must have heard of by now, known as the Condor VI Heavy Lift. This rocket, which is half as tall again as the Saturn V which took man to the Moon, will carry the super-weapon we are all depending on. A Professor Charles Villiers secretly developed the weapon, appropriately called End Time.

During the nineteen forties and fifties, Villiers and his team broke away from the old Cavendish Laboratory in Cambridge. They worked separately on a new concept, solely, get this . . . on a weapon to address the very problem we are now facing. Yes, Villiers knew about the threat all those years ago, but he was silenced by the organisation who have lately come into the headlines, Eisenburg. They have much to answer for.

"The United Nations have taken responsibility for the mission to transport the weapon to the vicinity of Nibiru to either destroy or deflect it. Professor Villiers tested a miniature version of the weapon years ago. There were worries at the time about the potential size of its destructive capability, so they kept the test small. Apparently, the weapon involves a branch of physics that was lost after Charles Villiers disappeared. All that can be said, is that the experiment back then proved that the End Time weapon was viable.

"Condor VI Heavy lift is the largest and most powerful rocket ever built. It is the brainchild of entrepreneur and philanthropist

Evan Blake. The launch, if all goes according to plan, will take place within the week. We will keep you informed about the project's progress. Nigel Sayers, BBC News 24, London."

The scene changed to the studio, and the female newscaster, Elena Grey, who was conducting the studio presentation at BBC News 24. She picked up a piece of paper handed to her by someone off-screen whose arm appeared on camera. Her eyebrows lifted in surprise, and she looked at Miles Fox, the newscaster sitting at her side. She quickly scanned the report and began reading.

"Just in, and more of this later; it appears that even the world's most repressive regime is making an overture for peace. The Supreme Leader is offering the hand of friendship and the technical expertise of his nation to fight, as he put it, the common enemy of mankind —"

"A short break will follow," Miles Fox cut in. "After which, along with broadcasting organisations worldwide, we will be repeating the documentary released by the United Nations a few days ago."

* * *

After the United Nations documentary, the cameras focussed once again on Miles Fox and Elena Grey. Fox said words to Elena which shouldn't have been broadcast, but millions heard something like, *they're forcing the bastard out*. He shuffled in his seat and spoke straight in the eye to the large audience picking up BBC News 24, which was also being aired on Sky TV, CNN, Russia Today and other media outlets, with the voiceover translated into major languages.

"Events are happening fast. We can hardly keep up with the changes here in the newsroom, but we will keep you informed as events unfold. The secretive Eisenburg organisation, who you heard about in the UN documentary, has been thoroughly discredited. Worldwide, as we speak, those known to have been associated with the group are having to face justice for forcing the presence of Nibiru to be withheld from general knowledge. It has come to light that, since the late eighteen-hundreds, assassinations of some of the leading figures in politics, industry and science who were opposed to Eisenburg have taken place."

Elena Grey broke in on the report. "And now for the sports news . . . back shortly with more on the fight-back against the threat heading our way." She usually had a coquettish smile enhanced with delightful dimples, but now she looked more serious than people had ever seen her look on-camera.

The sports news was well short of its usual ten minutes and then the news desk came on again. Miles Fox began reading off the autocue.

"As we were saying, Eisenburg is being held to account across the continents. It's as if there's a clean-up going on." Fox couldn't understand why his hands shook slightly. He normally found it difficult to be neutral in political affairs where Fenton Bull was concerned. Whereas a short while ago he would have been delighted with the next news report, it didn't seem to matter now.

He cleared his throat. "News just in, Premier Fenton Bull has been forced to resign because of his connections with Eisenburg. Some of the leading figures in politics and industry worldwide are scuttling out of harm's way. However, they will not be able to avoid the same fate as the rest of us if the Condor fails in its mission." It was very sudden that the reality of the newscast caught up with Fox, he had previously felt distance from it, but not now. He stuttered and then fluffed his words.

The camera quickly switched to Elena Grey. When Fox was off camera, he took out a handkerchief and wiped the sweat from his forehead. Elena pursued the story.

"The Houses of Parliament are quiet again. Fenton Bull has been arrested on a charge of endangering human life by neglect of responsibility whilst in public office. Who knows whether it will stick, these people have a habit of wriggling away from justice.

"Next . . . in a superb effort of investigative journalism, Panorama has discovered that there has been cross-party collusion between eight MP's to withhold the truth at all costs about Nibiru from the general public. Scott Schofield, who you all know because of his caustic approach on ITV's *This Week in Focus*, challenged the right honourable UK members now under investigation. Since then they have gone to ground.

"This is not just a UK thing; news reports are pouring in from our sources abroad that in many places there is an overturning of the establishment with no military intervention to prevent it. The eminent social commentator, Professor Emeritus, Julian Graves from London's King's College said, *If we survive this threat we may be on the threshold of a new world order.*

"Today is being called The Day of the Deputies, as politicians and industrialists implicated by association with Eisenburg are being forced out of power, and others are being sworn into office to take their place."

Miles Fox came back on. He looked outwardly calm, but he was churning over inside. He was thinking of the months ahead and the remorseless approach of the threat, but he followed the prompt.

"Parliament has given the green light for Deputy Premier Stephen Marston to take the reins of power under a coalition until the summer when there will be a general election. He will have an audience with the Queen tomorrow. This is a day of great worldwide change. Our hopes lie with the Condor VI Heavy Lift. If it does its job, an old saying will ring around the world. *Out with the old and in with the new.* Don't forget to watch Panorama at eight o'clock tonight. Now for the weather from Giles Munroe."

* * *

Pierpoint was organising a team to go to Turaroa for the launch. Harry Stanway was a necessity with his ability to apply intuitive analysis quickly to a situation and get the answers right. His intuition in restoring the Hub in Leofwin's Hundred to its full capability and using it to prevent the death of Jem Dearden and Mitch Doughty in the storm drain in Manhattan, caused Pierpoint to highly value Harry's contribution to SHaFT.

He wanted Matt Roberts to go to Turaroa, but Matt's growing closeness to Storm Petrel could be a problem. Matt's mind would be elsewhere. It would be better for him to remain with Dearden in Hampton in Arden. He and Storm would be useful helping Dearden in his attempt to communicate with the aliens, and in the follow-up to that process, wherever it may lead.

Of the core group at the heart of SHaFT, Lee Wynter was an obvious choice for Turaroa. Pierpoint trusted his solid reasoning. Dearden had once said Wynter could think in three dimensions and that he might be useful in the fourth dimension, time. So Wynter was in.

Templestone was involved with the Knights' Sanctuary. There had been demands for him to be more involved with the sanctuary by the men who were calling to see him regularly. It was all very secretive and after Templestone's decision to be the new Keeper, which Pierpoint thought was a rather vague position, it would be better for him to stay in the UK. Bill had given invaluable service to SHaFT. But now his loyalties were divided his reasoning could be flawed.

Pierpoint's thoughts turned to Arthur Doughty, his old friend who he missed more than he cared to admit. Arthur had always been objective. His son Mitch had similar reasoning to his father. It would be good for Mitch to be part of the process in Turaroa.

Pierpoint wondered about Julia Linden-Barthorpe. He had noticed the hard look in her eyes when Rowan stood close to Dearden one evening, and he detected her jealousy close to the surface. Julia had changed for the better in the past couple of weeks. She had become more her old self since she met Clive Fraser in Cambridge. For that reason, her incisive mind and her sheer guts could be useful in Turaroa.

* * *

"Will you come to Turaroa with me?" Pierpoint asked Harry.

"For the launch? You bet I will."

"I want you to be on hand with the math as part of Evan Blake's team."

"I have no problem with that."

Harry Stanway was now fully aware of the role of SHaFT in the pursuit of justice, and the role of Jem Dearden and the others in the organisation. Harry wanted to be fully involved.

"Wait another two years Harry," Sir Willoughby Pierpoint said to him a while back, "And then we'll see about it."

Harry was closer to Bill Templestone than he had been to his father. He could talk to him and he told him what Pierpoint said.

"When it comes to it, Harry, I'll help you get into SHaFT if that's what you really want. Don't make your decision lightly, it can be dangerous at times, your life or death hanging on a split-second decision. Jem and I have been there often, believe me."

Harry had avidly followed the launch of the major expeditions to Mars and the missions to the outer reaches of the solar system, but he had never been at a live launch, so Sir Willoughby Pierpoint's invitation fulfilled a dream. He would have a pivotal role to play in ridding Earth of the greatest threat it had ever faced, and that was cool.

52

In the great hall, the atmosphere was a mixture of anti-climax and anticipation about what was to come after the activity of the past few days. There was a need to regroup, to set the forthcoming action into sharp focus.

Templestone was writing in a notepad, setting down facts and events of the past weeks in the order they occurred. He used to do that when he was younger, in the heady days of his early association with SHaFT. He would prepare for a mission that way. That was what he was doing now, testing and probing with his mind. He found it difficult to let it go, but he knew he had to. With the Knight's Sanctuary events, his life had changed.

It occurred to him that his new position as Keeper of the Knights' Sanctuary was connected with it all, pivotal to the whole series of events. It might become obvious at some point. He wouldn't speak his thoughts to the others; he just needed to write them down privately, for the record, as generations of Keepers had done before him.

Julia was sitting in a chair drawn up to the ancient table in the great hall. A couple of weeks ago she had been sitting in the same place and anger had knotted up her insides. The anger had made her hot, physically, although at the time a cold draught had chilled the expanse of the great hall. At times in the winter months, it could be a cold room unless logs were stacked on the fire. Dearden usually made sure the fire kept the chill at bay. Julia had been sitting one side of Dearden, Rowan had been sitting the other side and it took a lot to harness the anger.

Since she met Clive Fraser in Cambridge she felt easier with herself. He had been so helpful, particularly when they stayed the night in a room with a four-poster bed at The Eagle, after they met with Professor Robbie Cranford. That was the time her jealousy with Rowan had faded back to friendship. Julia had arranged to meet up with Clive a couple of days later in The Eagle. She was being cautious, but she couldn't wait to see him again, and when Sir Will asked her to be in the team to go to Turaroa, she refused point blank.

Pierpoint finalised the plan for transporting the End Time bomb to the launch facility on Turaroa Island. Evan Blake had instructed his team of mathematicians and engineers to work round the clock on the information Pierpoint had given him about Nibiru. They had worked day and night to verify the figures Harry Stanway had provided and couldn't fault them. Now all they were waiting for was the detonation procedure for the weapon, and the hardware itself.

* * *

The Lockheed Hercules C130 H's four Rolls-Royce Allison turboprops were rotating steadily. The End Time bomb had been winched on board the aircraft and then anchored with wire hawsers to the heavy-duty cleats in the fuselage. The wooden sides, end and top of the packing case had been stripped off. Pierpoint was on the flight deck, talking the forthcoming flight through with Colonel Ryan Lindhoff and his co-pilot Si Decker, and the rest of the four-man crew.

"That's a nasty looking beast Harry, my man," said Wynter, who was in the cargo bay with Harry and Doughty. He was suspicious of the awesome force in the black metallic chamber.

Harry said nothing. He just nodded and with one of Villiers' sheets of notes, he went to a rectangular panel on the side of the bomb. There were catches to release the panel. Doughty analysed the shape of the weapon. It was ellipsoidal, about six feet in diameter at its minor axis, by roughly twice that length at its major axis.

"Take a seat and fasten your seat belts, gentlemen," Lindhoff's voice came over the intercom as the loading bay door hydraulics actuated, slowly closing out the daylight.

The fuselage lights were sufficient for Harry to read Villiers' explanation of the detonation procedure, and as the turboprops spooled up and the brakes were released, he settled down to continue analysing the professor's words.

* * *

The Hercules reached its cruising altitude of 28,000 feet and levelled off. Wynter and Doughty settled into conversation, discussing Manchester United's game the previous Saturday. A recent convert to soccer, Wynter was extolling the virtues of the latest striker who gave United a three goals to one lead at full time.

Harry detested most forms of sport. His activity was more cerebral than physical and the conversation from the two sitting close by him was intruding on his concentration. With Villiers' briefcase grasped tightly under his arm, he made his way toward the forward end of the fuselage where there were more seats. On his way past the End Time weapon, he looked once more at the panel, behind which, he had just read on the topmost sheet of the sheaf of detonation papers, lay the arming circuitry.

The bomb had been constructed in two halves, and Harry counted the bolts passing through a flange holding the top half to the bottom. He walked around it. There were fifty bolts in all, and a different type of material was sandwiched between the flanges. He poked it with his finger and managed to mark the surface with his fingernail. It was lead, which explained why the bomb weighed so much for its size.

He continued working on one of the sheets Villiers had headed up *Trigger, Explosive Accelerator, 600 MeV*, followed by explanatory math. Harry's attention was drawn to a subheading lower down on the same page and he pondered its meaning. *Antihydrogen Mass, Alternative Research, a side-issue. After research, this issue was expanded upon in the laboratory. Most interesting! Antimatter! Reaction still persists. I do not know how long the reaction we have created will last, but whatever we have stumbled across, it is now sealed behind the panel of stone and lead in the upper exit from the Laboratory, until we have more understanding. It appears we have created an opening, an entrance.*

Harry knew that Villiers' words had to do with the vague noise he couldn't recognise coming from the blocked off region beyond the door in the laboratory. Intriguing or not, that would have to wait. He carried on with the detonation math.

Pierpoint, who was up some steps on the flight deck, caught sight of Harry. He indicated for him to come up. Harry wondered how long the disturbances would go on and Pierpoint saw his perturbed look.

"It'll only take a minute," Pierpoint called out above the heavy drone of the turboprops. Harry, clutching the briefcase, which was the last thing he wanted to put down right now, went up the ladder. The first room on the flight deck, where Pierpoint was standing, was a confined space, with seating and equipment for the navigator.

Harry looked to where Sir Will was pointing. Out of the windows to port and starboard, two each side, the four delta-winged fighters with the RAF roundel were in a protective role.

"We've got the RAF on side Harry," Pierpoint said. "Deputy PM, now Premier Stephen Marston, has scrambled the Typhoons to escort us safely part way to Turaroa. At least we've got someone in high government on-side now. We'll have an escort at various stages during the flight."

The Typhoons were impressive, but they didn't grab Harry enough to make him want to stay any longer.

"That's some serious backup," he said. Then he showed Pierpoint the sheet of Villiers' detonation notes and then his own page of conversion into C++ coding. He thrust it close to Pierpoint's nose.

Pierpoint backed his head off a few inches. "What is it?" The sheet had sections of complex mathematics as well as computer code.

"The information about detonation."

"I'm glad you're here to sort it out, I wouldn't have a clue where to start."

"I know. And that's the point. It is a challenge and do you know something?"

"What?"

"It is nearly complete, but I need to be undisturbed to finish converting the damn information." Harry turned tail and stomped down the ladder into the cargo bay.

* * *

Harry, sitting in a utilitarian webbing seat at the side of the fuselage, finished the math and the conversion. He learned from the notes that inside the shell of the weapon there was a linear accelerator in miniature. He was stunned when he realised that Villiers was heavily involved in particle physics research.

On the fourth of the series of twelve pages torn from the notepad, there was information explaining Villiers trail of research. It had taken the professor in a very different direction to Rutherford and his team at the Old Cavendish and Oppenheimer and the others at Los Alamos. Villiers, years ahead of his time, took a similar route to particle physics research at CERN, but he had gone Miniature.

A well-executed diagram on page nine pictured the concept and convinced Harry that he understood the procedure. At that point, he opened a conference line to Turaroa, requested an urgent conversation with Brett Morgan and Mart Schlesinger, heading up engineering and research concepts at Frontier Spaceflight. Evan Blake joined in when the call was underway.

Harry gently removed the cover on the side of the weapon and he described to Morgan and Schlesinger what he found inside. He added the detail of how to add a high amperage electronic switch to trigger an electro-mechanical actuator inside the bomb's casing.

"And I take it that this switch will initiate when the final burn of the payload vehicle commences upon approach to the target," suggested Brett Morgan.

"That's right."

"Can you confirm the physical size of the bomb?" asked Schlesinger. Harry had measured the circumference and length at the major axis points. He had also checked the diameters at one-foot lengths along the body of the weapon so that he could define the profile for engineers to work on a cradle for the flight.

He said he would email the Americans the information and sketches, and finished the call. He put the briefcase down at the side of his seat and leant back in its webbing. It was comfortable and he was tired. The mental exertion had sapped his energy and he was soon asleep.

* * *

In the High Andes, Carlos Mendulas had been observing the Sun and its immediate surroundings, waiting for Nibiru to appear. He had been stealing time on the big telescope. With the planet now filling the news he told his boss, a thin Australian by the name of James McCorquadale, what he had been doing. McCorquadale said Carlos should observe the advance of the planet full time using the Gemini South, with one proviso, that Carlos video a regular report, which he would then forward digitally to Reuters for editing and daily broadcast on Channel Nibiru, which was relayed to news broadcasters world-wide. McCorquadale saw dollar signs in the arrangement.

* * *

In the great hall Dearden was discussing with Julia and Templestone, how they should approach the Hnioss.

"OK, so we wait until the others return after the launch of Condor and then we make our move." Dearden concluded.

"I want to go too, you know," Templestone said. "You young-sters need some sensible backup . . . particularly when you face the Grand Council of the Hnioss."

"I know, it but your presence is needed here to ensure things are kept on an even keel. We need some good sense here too."

"Mmm. I guess age is catching up with me, if truth be told," Templestone said.

"Age is definitely not catching up with me so you'll have to include me in the trip, I do not intend to be left out," Julia said. She was startled as Calculus leapt up onto her lap, snuggled into her jumper and started purring. Before long, the claws would start teasing her jeans and then they would get through to her thigh. Tomahawk, disturbed by the purring, looked up from his place in front of the fire. He plodded over to Julia and sat on her feet. He was big now, full-grown, but he was still a pup inside, sometimes jealous with it too. A jealous wolf isn't good to have around, she thought and then she remembered how she had been with Rowan a couple of weeks back. The anger. The jealousy. But now she felt so incredibly light, and it was all down to Clive Fraser.

The operator on a KC-135 Stratotanker separated the flying boom from the refuelling receptacle positioned above the cockpit of the Hercules. Lindhoff tooled the Herc down steadily a couple of hundred feet and the Stratotanker peeled off to starboard to return to base. It was the last refuelling of a wearisome journey.

"It's a good job we know the right people between us, Sir Willoughby," Lindhoff said.

"What do you mean?"

"Where do you think the fuel's come from for this trip?"

"Ah, I take it you mean you have folk who are prepared to stand up and be counted, in view of the current emergency."

"Too right I have and I think you have, too."

53

Doughty was sweating in the tropical heat of Turaroa. He followed Wynter to the door and stepped onto a heavy duty hydraulic service lift platform. It had been intricate work strapping the bulky End Time weapon into its fabricated aluminium and carbon fibre cradle. He flipped his sunglasses down from his forehead to cut out the glare of the Sun. It had become a habit when wearing sunglasses to take a quick glance at the Sun and the planet in silhouette to its right.

Five hundred and seventeen personnel working around the clock had ensured that the cargo was ready for launch with two days to spare. In the final stages of preparation, Harry worked with Blake's technicians in the cargo bay of the Condor, overseeing the upgrade of the electro-mechanical triggers of the accelerator which lay behind service panels of the weapon.

Journalists were getting constant updates for the news-hungry public. Within the space of a day of the first naked-eye sighting, Sky Television assigned a free channel to report updates on the planet's advance and the progress of the Condor VI Heavy Lift at the Turaroa launch site. Evan Blake was interviewed. He explained some of the challenges he and his team were facing to intercept Nibiru in its orbit and guide the lander with the bomb inside it down to the surface.

* * *

Pierpoint and Harry were relaxing in the executive guest suite off Even Blake's penthouse. A luxury after the intense few days.

Wynter and Doughty burst into the room.

"Television –" Wynter shouted.

Pierpoint stood quickly, momentarily thrown.

"Put on the damn television, man."

Harry grabbed the handset and flicked the switch. It was already tuned to the Nibiru channel. A young professor of physics was being interviewed, the well-known handsome man a lot of girls had a crush on, and he mentioned outgassing that could start on Nibiru. A close-up of the Sun came on, with its surface coruscating under the intense heat of nuclear fusion.

The interviewer, Marsha Sefton, a cute brunette, pressed for an explanation. "Can you tell us in simple terms, for the sake of us simple mortals what outgassing is?"

"It's like farting . . . but imagine you are holding a balloon and you put it near a fire, what would happen?" Marsha thought for a minute.

"The heat would make the air inside the balloon expand."

"Exactly. Now, what would happen if the heat were intense?"

"The balloon would burst."

"Which would prove to be the most violent outgassing the balloon could experience. Not much else goes on inside a balloon other that the containment of the air within it when it is inflated. In the case of a planet, there are incredibly complex chemical structures, and active processes going on inside and around it."

The professor, Shaun Latimer, lit a Bunsen burner, and slowly walked toward the flame with an inflated balloon in his hands. He was wearing gloves. There was a loud explosion and a bright flash when he got close to the flame.

Marsha, who was usually calm and collected, ducked and swore.

"Sorry about that, Marsha. I filled the balloon with hydrogen, but it proves the point. Substitute the Sun in place of the Bunsen burner and Nibiru with all of its complex systems, in place of the balloon and what do you get?"

"Farting—"

"Exactly. We sometimes get this on the Earth. With active volcanoes that are driven by the internal forces of pressure and heat, we get violent eruptions."

"I get your point . . . add the Sun into the mix and things would get really violent."

"Which is what might have happened to Nibiru when it passed by the Sun. We are uncertain about this, but it could have started to eject gas and other types of matter violently, which would be unfortunate for the surface of Nibiru."

"Will that be a problem for us?"

"At this point in time, that's anyone's guess. We are uncertain about what's going on because we have picked up a spectrographic oddity. We have evidence of something around the planet that's like a mirage." Shaun Latimer turned the Bunsen burner off with a flourish and smiled at the camera. Without waiting for his exit cue, he walked off-camera theatrically.

Marsha sometimes added a touch of irony to her reports. "What did we learn from that, apart from farting? Precisely nothing about Nibiru's approach to Earth, but there is a mirage around it, I wonder if there are pink deserts and six-legged camels?"

* * *

Wynter and Doughty sat on one of the sofas in Harry's apartment and both started speaking at once. They stopped, and then Doughty said that, apart from waiting for the launch window, the Condor VI was ready for lift off.

"Two days to go and the fight back will start," Wynter said.

"In earnest," Harry answered, as he changed the channel to BBC News 24. It was Elena Grey and Miles Fox. Elena looked her usual feisty self, but Fox looked jaded.

Doughty had seen how, up to a few hours ago, some of the workers on Turaroa had looked the same as Miles Fox. They had become lethargic as if they were losing the will to get basic tasks done. Evan Blake spoke to his team over loudspeakers, and it gave hope to his team as he praised them for their stupendous effort preparing the Condor VI Heavy Lift for flight.

On the television, there were scenes of crowds of people flocking to football grounds and parks in different lands, which were linked via satellite. The crowds were engaged in various activities. Pop groups were strumming insistent beat and singing to the crowds. At other venues, God was being beseeched to intervene in the sincerest tones heard for many a year. No doubt about it, people were forgetting their differences.

Elena Grey commented on the irony of the possible extinction of the human race being the catalyst making folk work together, even in places where they had previously been trying to blow each other apart.

The camera turned to Miles Fox, who fluffed his words yet again. He took a drink of water. His complexion looked unnatural and Elena took over. There was a gurgling noise in the background. Elena glanced quickly sideways before introducing Nigel Sayers, who was standing in Oxford Street.

Off camera, a medical team was at Miles Fox's side within a minute of his collapse. The doctor had a worried look on his face as he listened for a heartbeat. He shook his head and drew his hand across his throat.

Elena Grey, still at her seat as news anchor gulped before she spoke to the editor in harsh, subdued tones.

"Get him moved out of shot."

Fox was slumped over the news desk with one arm close to Elena. She pushed it out of the way and it flopped down with a dull sound and swung. She asked for Ken Travis, a newscaster whose day off it was, to be brought in. "I know he's at home, I called him earlier, he only lives around the corner."

Mayhem was going on behind the scenes in the studios, and mayhem was taking over wherever populations and governments were trying to steer events. Mayhem ruled over most of the Earth. There was a gap in transmission due to Miles Fox. Music and a still photograph of an ancient hill-fort filled some empty transmission time. The editor was left to pick up the flack. "Keep it going out there Nige, say anything to keep the punters happy. There's a problem in the studio. That bastard Miles Fox just died on us."

Nigel Sayers came on screen. His eyes moved quickly, indicating rapid thinking. His words came naturally under pressure, which is what put him in the top rank of news reporters.

"Take a look around Oxford Street. This is the heart of the metropolis, and on a Wednesday, it should be teeming with shoppers. Where have they gone? Selfridges is empty, restaurants are closing, and there's no traffic around Marble Arch. Where are they all? I'll tell you. People are scared, they are hiding, trying to find comfort in the ordinary things of life, not the glitz of the

High Street. But all of us are grateful that Evan Blake's spacecraft will deliver us from the danger we are facing."

Before the scene changed to tropical palm trees and an azure sea with gentle waves lapping a sun-drenched beach, Sayers face changed. He was usually very animated. The camera caught a blank, dead look. He saw himself on a monitor and recovered quickly.

"This place of demi-paradise is Turaroa. It is out of bounds to all but the ones directly involved with the launch of the Condor VI Heavy Lift. You will be seeing a lot of Turaroa over the next few days." The camera panned upwards and to the right. First, it focussed on some tall skeletal towers and then further on into shot on the right the launch complex came into view. The service tower was in place against the spacecraft, clasping it in a steely embrace before lift-off.

"We will now hand over to our team on Turaroa. Edward Geary is our science correspondent, Keith Hayes, who we often see on The Sky at Night assisting Patrick Moore, is there and we have Angie Lester, professor of astrophysics at the University of Michigan. Assisting them will be our own Professor Shaun Latimer, Professor of Physics from Trinity College, Cambridge. We are fortunate to have an illustrious team on site who will be covering the hours up to launch and beyond. Over to you Eddie."

* * *

In a private blockhouse, a mile away from the launch pad, Dearden's voice, speaking through loudspeakers from the Hub in Leofwin's Hundred, updated Pierpoint and the rest of the SHaFT team about the contact with Lan-Si-Nu.

"They've agreed to help us," Dearden said, "But it is conditional. We have to present our case before the Grand Council of the Hnioss and we must think again about destroying Nibiru."

"Think again about destroying the threat?" Pierpoint's voice was raised. "What does he take us for, Jem, does he expect us to give in without a fight?"

"They have a different mentality to us. They renounced violence much further back in the past than we can count and it works for them. They are trying to encourage us to do likewise."

"Very well. If that is so, and we go along with their way of looking at things, what about this Hnioss, where do we present our case?"

"On their world. We're going to get to use the grid."

"Have they told you what to expect?"

"Only that the Hnioss is the way they're organised and that there are many united worlds, but get this; they have stipulated Harry must be present. Once you return to base we can transfer over the Grid, Harry."

"OK. Ok . . . time transfer I have been involved with, but two places at once I cannot do, at least, not yet. I'm with launch control until we are sure Condor is on target."

"How long will that take?"

"Launch is tomorrow at 0803 our time. We're at GMT minus eleven so that's 1903 your time. The injection burn of the third stage to intercept Nibiru's orbit will take place fifty-three minutes into the flight. That's when Evan Blake's experimental drive system will take over and we speed on our way. We'll know all's well and that we're on target by 2005 hours, your time. The crew of the Hercules will be standing by for an immediate flight . . . by my calculation, we'll be back at Dearden Hall by 2100 hours the day after tomorrow."

54

Virgil Wright was at his place amongst the team in Flight Control where screen upon screen displayed information from the multitude of sensors on board the Condor. He glanced out of the window at the giant spacecraft on launch platform one in the distance. Tanked up and ready, clouds of condensation arose into the tropical air from the cryogenic hydrogen cooling the grouped Mustang EB-9 engines.

The configuration boasted sixteen engines powering the central core and four Mustangs powering each of the six boosters: this was the first stage. The second stage engines, eight of them, were the more powerful Mustang EB-12, designed to punch the spacecraft into a high parking orbit around Earth.

With only a partial orbit completed, the Magellan EB 7 Beamed-core Proton-Antiproton engine, would power the third stage into a Hohmann transfer orbit in preparation for the mission to intercept Nibiru. This is where Harry Stanway came into his own. With a show of intellectual brilliance Harry Stanway planned the trajectory to Nibiru from the Hohmann transfer orbit, while the guidance team were still considering the information to upload into the guidance computers.

Evan Blake had a sense of fatherly pride in the Condor. It was clearly seen from the bunker, through an armoured glass window. Blake had spent billions developing the Magellan engine, named after the early explorer and he had it installed on the third stage of Condor. It would be the first mission-use of the engine that would propel a vehicle at a considerable fraction of the speed of light, and Blake was a little short on patience as he eyed the countdown clock, waiting for lift-off.

* * *

"This is Edward Geary speaking for BBC News 24 on Turaroa Island. We are overlooking launch pad one. You can see it over there, about two miles away. On the launch pad, attached to Earth only by umbilicals and explosive bolts, is the state of the art Condor VI Heavy Lift."

One of the cameras focussed on the Spacecraft. Although it was two miles distant, it was still huge.

"Here too we have a gathering of many heads of state. Most nations are represented here by their leaders." Another camera panned the view of three grandstands.

"On the centre stand, we have what must be the largest gathering of nations' representatives ever seen. We can see there, The President of the United States with his wife, sitting by the UK's new premier, Stephen Marston and his fiancée. Countries with serious differences are now sitting next to each other and talking.

"For the time being, it seems to me, the differences these nations had up to a few days ago have become squabbles of the past. Probably they are now discussing the chances of survival. I think they have left theatrical politics, at least for the time being, to join the real world with the rest of us.

"On the stand to the right of centre are members of the scientific community. They are the best logical brains in the world, but again they wait with bated breath for the outcome of the mission where both accuracy and brute force is being called into play. Take another look at the spacecraft over there. Atop its dizzy height sits the End Time bomb. It is a weapon of awesome force and the destiny of humanity lies in its successful deployment to Nibiru."

"In the grandstand to the left of centre we have the newsfeeds and crews, that's us. We're ready to beam every detail of the launch and the subsequent mission to the waiting world." The camera focussed on the crowd in close-up and it showed not one smiling face. A slightly unsteady magnified image of the oncoming planet took its place.

"I will now hand you over to Keith Hayes and Angie Lester who will explain what we are looking at here."

Hayes took up the commentary.

"You see here an image through a specially adapted camera. If you look at the Sun through a telescope or binoculars, always use a special solar filter. If you ignore that advice, you could ruin your eyesight. Angie —"

"Thanks, Keith. The image to the left of the screen is live, compare it to the image on the right, which is from yesterday. You can see that in today's image the planet is larger. Nibiru has come closer to Earth in the intervening hours. Evan Blake and his team are doing their level best to eradicate the threat for us.

"Let's watch the countdown and follow along as Dan Scott, P.R. spokesman for Frontier Spaceflight, talks us through the final stages of the launch of the Condor VI."

The camera shot showing the oblique view of the grandstand gave way to the large mission clock at the front of the grandstands, which displayed T minus sixty minutes and counting.

*   *   *

Things were tense at Dearden Hall. Dearden and the others sat around the television in the great hall. It was quiet in the hall apart from the commentary on Sky News. The tension was palpable as the mission countdown clock slipped the seconds away to launch. Templestone was still writing in his notepad, describing what he saw and what he felt as time drew close to the start of the Condor mission. He looked up and rubbed his eyes. They were tired. It passed through his mind that with this latest passage of Nibiru, humanity had a fighting chance of survival, and if all went well he would record it all.

Templestone looked casually around the room. People he knew and loved were in various attitudes of attention as they viewed the unfolding events on the large television screen. The public voice of Frontier Spaceflight, Dan Scott was explaining the major features of the launch. An animation demonstrated the separation sequence and the onward journey of the third stage of the Condor to its target.

Dearden stood and went to the side of the room where the drinks cabinet stood close to the wall. He took out a bottle of Courvoisier and two bottles of 1938 vintage Amandio's Old Tawny Port. It was a team thing and it often happened before a mission. The tradition harked back to Dearden's first introduction to SHaFT. *Port and Brandy; it makes the heart rejoice and smooths the edges, I'm a great advocate of it, Jem,* Arthur Doughty had said as he poured out a generous measure and told Jem about the organisation that stood for justice, whatever the cost. And now Arthur was dead as a result of injustice. Dearden felt the anger rising, but then Rowan called the Heskin's to join them in the great hall.

With some of the inner group in Turaroa for the launch the room looked empty. Storm Petrel and Matt Roberts were somewhere on the North Cornwall coastal path bivouacking. Matt said he could be reached on his mobile if necessary. They could be back within six hours. Red Cloud and Possum Chaser were at Offchurch with the wolf pack. Esma was with them. They too would return quickly if needed.

Dearden poured the drinks, a measure of brandy and a measure of the port into each glass, ready to hand round after the launch. He sat and looked at the screen. There was an animation showing the release of the End Time bomb, and its slowing as it approached the surface of the planet. This was substituted by an image of the planet from a distance of fifty thousand miles. An area of intense blackness suddenly shrouded Nibiru and a twisting vortex lensing into the background of stars.

Dan Scott gave a running commentary, explaining that the animation portrayed the demise of the threat to the Earth. He said that the animation was constructed from data collected from a small-scale test of the weapon in the nineteen-sixties, which proved its destructive capability.

The Countdown clock showed T minus nine minutes. They were on the last built-in hold of the count to zero. Dan Scott's calm voice described the scene as the camera panned to show blockhouses and the waiting spacecraft.

"We have a built-in hold while systems managers check out their area of responsibility. If their checks are positive, the launch will take place. Let's take a peek inside launch control." The camera, which was placed high up in a gallery, zoomed in on Virgil Wright, Flight Director, Condor, seated in front of his console.

"In four minutes Virgil Wright will be, as they say in Flight Control, *going around the horn*, communicating with his systems controllers in the Mission Operations Control Room, checking status for a go or no-go for launch."

Julia winced as Calculus got well into the comfort zone. His claws dug into her thigh. She eased them out. As she did so the movement woke Tomahawk and he slinked closer to Julia's feet. She slowly put her hand down to his muzzle, still cautious of his wild ancestry. They seemed to have an affinity now, cemented over the past months, and during the wild time of Dearden and Doughty's rescue from the storm drain in the Manhattan Affair. Tomahawk still demanded respect. He was the alpha male dominating his lair, which was Dearden Hall.

Julia turned back to the scene on Turaroa and felt the tension ramping up. So much depended on the next few days. The emotion of the situation took over and she felt tears that she tried to subdue, but they flowed in the quiet place where she was sitting. And with the tears, she felt a great sense of pride at being one of the major players in the mighty events about to take place.

55

"**C**ome out you little turd," Esma commanded from the doorway of Possum Chaser's kitchen at Offchurch.

"You shouldn't say those things to me," said the Native American woman who stood five feet two in moccasins. She looked up from kneading the dough for tomorrow's bread. She was angry and she pummelled the dough a little harder. She hadn't seen Little Titch; the brown and white fox-terrier pup stray that Esma found, who had sneaked in under the kitchen table. She thought Esma was talking to her.

Esma, Rowan of Maldon's handmaid in a long-ago time, spent enjoyable hours with the Romanies who Red Cloud and Possum Chaser allowed to live on their land. The Hicks family had arrived one day in their traditional caravan with the rounded roof. The Lakota Sioux man and woman, being of an ethnic minority themselves, empathised with the Romany family who had been subjected to some cruel abuse.

"Stay on our land, keep it tidy and help out with the wolves and all will be well," Red Cloud said to them. Tobar and Nadya did just that and bought another caravan too. They restored it to its former glory with traditional colours and patterns. That was five years ago and all did go well.

The Hicks children, a twin boy and girl, Pesha and Aishe were at the age of great adventure when they took delight in learning swear words. They passed these on to Esma and, to their great delight and wild laughter, she repeated them until she got the sounds right, which is where the colourful word she used by the kitchen door came from.

Esma had changed. There was freedom in 2009. She had wild looking hair, and she changed its colour every few weeks as the mood took her. She wore skinny ripped jeans and had a stud through her left nostril. As she leant on the kitchen door-frame she was sizing up the cooker that was coming up to temperature. The digital display was climbing one degree at a time and fascinated the young Anglo-Saxon woman.

She was startled when there was a knock on the back door, which led from the kitchen to the back of the property.

"They're standing at an odd angle," Possum Chaser said. She could see the profile of two men through panes of Reamy Slab glass, which distorted everything seen through it, but gave a door some character. Dearden fitted the glass into the door after the original panes were smashed in an attempted burglary.

Fred Gough, the local detective inspector and his sergeant Mervyn McVitie, who was called Biskit by his colleagues, called twice a week at B.W. Breeders for refreshment. Gough had a yen to own a wolf but his wife wouldn't let him, so he made up for it by calling on Red and Possum Chaser occasionally to get close to the wolves.

"'Fraid there's no progress on the burglary front, Possy," Gough said.

"Doesn't matter. They would not have got far if they came in. We had Hiníkčeka Shan of Offchurch sleeping in the kitchen. Hiníkčeka is Lakota Sioux for Black. He has a black heart where strangers are concerned. He would have gone for their throats." Possum Chaser smiled as Gough looked around warily.

"Do not worry, Fred, Black is in the enclosure."

"There's more to worry about than wolves at the moment," said Gough. "We were near your place and heard on the radio that the rocket's ready to launch, can you switch the news on?"

They went through to the open style lounge where they had a fifty-inch Samsung fixed to a wall. The others went into the lounge and sat. Possum Chaser switched on and sat, ready to follow the event on Turaroa.

McVitie sat next to Esma. He liked her punk hairdo and the accent that he couldn't quite place. She shifted along the settee. Harry was never far from her thoughts and she didn't like the Biskit getting close. She looked at the men and women in the busy room they said was Flight Control on the TV, she knew Harry was there and she felt close to him.

Red Cloud came in, nodded at Fred and Mervyn and said that Tobar, Nadya and the kids were coming over to see the launch.

The same thing was going on the world over. Families were grouped together. There were gatherings in village halls and community centres. Congregations in churches had put televisions on altars. Factory canteens were packed with men and women watching big screens. From the sumptuous surroundings of property in Avenue Princesse Grace in Monaco to the desolate town of Pibor on the border of South Sudan's border with Ethiopia, where someone had stolen a television and a generator so that the community could see what was going on, people's eyes were fixed on the small screen.

Despite the inequalities, they were all driven by the same hope. Condor was hope, a gift held out and never had there been a need for such a gift, or such anticipation. Hearts beat fast. Palms were sweating. Throats were constricted and the great audience hung on with white knuckles to what they were watching.

And then Esma saw Harry in Flight Control. He was sitting at a desk in front of one of the screens. He was smiling. Harry smiled most of the time. When he looked back at her briefly when they were riding his motorbike, he smiled.

The voice of Dan Scott came on.

"We are now in the critical five-minute period leading up to launch. We'll listen in to Flight Director, Virgil Wright, as he directs the mission until take-off."

"Condor VI Heavy Lift Flight Controllers. It's time to raise the roof. I want your go, no-go for launch, patch me in on your status.

"BOOSTERS,"

"Go."

"RETRO,"

"Go."

"FIDO,"

"We're go, Flight."

"GUIDANCE,"

"Guidance is go."

"GNC,"

"We are go."

"TELMU,"

"Go."

"CONTROL, END TIME."

"Go, Flight."

"PROCEDURES."

"Go."

"INCO,"

"Go."

"FAO,"

"We are go."

"NETWORK,"

"Go."

"MODCOM,"

"Module Communication is go, Flight."

"Over to Launch Control One . . . this is Flight, we are go for launch."

The voice of Royce Benton came from Launch Control.

"Roger that, Flight . . . Pad Leader, Give me your status."

"We are go for launch. T minus sixty seconds and counting, FD Loop, stand by . . .

"Roger that."

"RUN PUMPS,"

"Pumps go."

"GUIDO,"

"Guidance, we're ready for lift-off."

"LAUNCHCON,"

"We are go for launch. T minus—"

Virgil Wright cut in, "10 . . . 9 . . . 8 . . . 7 . . . 6 . . . ignition sequence starts."

Incandescent flame erupted from the forty Mustang EB-9 engines,

"3 . . . 2 . . . 1 . . . Zero."

The ten explosive bolts holding the giant rocket to the pad detonated, gantry arms and propellant lines separated and the strong-back hinged away.

"We have lift-off!" Virgil Wright's tone of voice took on the enthusiasm built into the launch team by Evan Blake.

In towns and cities, villages and hamlets, palaces and shantytowns the world over, people raised the roof. The cheer ascended in a mighty roar. It arose like a majestic prayer, urging the Condor on its way into the heavens.

*   *   *

In Dearden Hall and the sitting room in Offchurch, there was extra tension in the air with the closeness of some of the participants to the mission now under way . . . At Offchurch Fred Gough, Mervyn McVitie and the Romanies had no idea they were sitting close to some of the major players in the action.

McVitie stole a sly glance at Esma, whose knuckles were white as her hands gripped the arms of her chair. He could see the almost childlike expression of wonder on her face as the Condor VI Heavy Lift roared into the air on the white-hot column of fire as the Mustangs' eight million pounds of thrust punched the rocket on its way.

Rowan's grip on Dearden's hand increased as the commentary continued from Turaroa Flight Control.

"This is Flight, FIDO, report."

Doug Sampson spoke for Flight Dynamics. "Looks good. Course right down the line, Mach 1 . . . NOW."

"MAXIMUM DYNAMIC PRESSURE." A shaky telephoto shot showed the atmosphere coning away aerodynamically.

"BOOSTERS 1, 3 and 5, JETTISON."

"Ouch . . . sod off," Julia's shout as she shoved Calculus off her lap startled the others in the room. "This little sod sharpens his claws just for my thighs." The others took no notice of the outburst. Tomahawk ambled after his small companion as the cat went over to the fire and curled up on the mat in front of it.

"BOOSTERS 2, 4 and 6, JETTISON."

"MECO."

PR man Dan Scott stepped in to the commentary, "We have first stage main engines cut off, MECO. In a few seconds, we will have stage two ignition. This is the kick in the pants that will take Condor's stage three to high Earth orbit ready for the transition to the Nibiru intercept trajectory."

There was a burst of fire from high up. The vehicle was out of sight, but its passage was still heard as a deep rumble, so strong that it was felt in the chest by those in the three grandstands straining to see its upward passage. There was spontaneous applause from those gathered looking skyward as Dan Scott confirmed stage two ignition.

"There will be two burns of the nine stage two Mustang EB-12 engines, the first burn, which is now under way, will last for three hundred and twenty-five seconds. The second burn will fine-tune the altitude and acceleration of the Spacecraft, preparing it to leave Earth orbit using the stage three Magellan EB 7 Beamed-core Proton-Antiproton engine in sixteen minutes from now.

"I can confirm stage two final shutdown and jettison. We now await Magellan. This will occur when the spacecraft has completed a partial orbit of the Earth. This particular type of engine has had thorough, albeit secret testing of its systems. It is entirely new. Magellan doesn't ignite, as does a cryogenically fuelled rocket engine. To begin its operation, it comes on stream as protons meet antiprotons and produce reactive force. It is a controlled process, economical in its operation, but expensive in the production of the antiproton element.

"Here at Frontier Spaceflight, we have a dedicated team involved in the production of the antiproton element. We have reduced production costs considerably." The news session editor spoke in Dan Scott's earpiece and he followed the cue.

"Let's listen in to Flight Control."

"This is Flight, give me MODCOM status."

"MODCOM, stage three Magellan on stream on my mark, minus five seconds . . . 4 . . . 3 . . . 2 . . . 1 . . . MARK . . . Magellan is now on stream."

"FIDO, Mission is on the money. Looks good Flight."

"Roger that, Flight Dynamics, and thank you, Doug . . . trans-Nibiru injection trajectory is confirmed . . . this is it guys, we're on our way."

Fists punched the air worldwide. People shouted and screamed and wept with relief as the Condor VI Heavy left its' trail in the sky, bound on its one-way mission.

56

Rowan took the tray of port and brandy, with double measures in each glass and handed them round. She took an adequate sip herself and felt the liquor releasing the tensions that had built up over the past days. At least Jem was still at Dearden Hall. He was saying that there was an important trip relating to the Condor Mission coming up.

"Where will we be going, London?" She thought they might go to the capital of the shires, London now, rather than Medeshamstede, to see the men of the government. The top one had changed, his name was Stephen Marston and when she had seen him talking on the television, that made him look small, she thought she could trust his eyes more than she could the previous government man, Fenton Bull.

"It won't be London," Jem said. "But I will take you there when we get out of the danger we're in."

"It really is serious, the danger that is coming?"

"Couldn't be more serious."

"We could go back to Leofwin's time, escape from what is coming."

"And buy ourselves some years . . . I know we could. But we're not like that Rowan, you're not, I'm not. We don't run from a problem, we face it head-on and we fight it."

"I know we do." A brooding silence followed. "So where are we going?"

"Up there." He pointed skywards. "I don't know where exactly and it isn't certain we are going just yet. If the Condor diverts Nibiru, or destroys it, we may not need to go . . . but we might be invited anyway. Lan-Si-Nu is anxious to see Harry Stanway."

"Who else is going . . . can I come?"

"You are best to stay here, Rowan. If things do go wrong, get the team together into the Hub and go back to Leofwin's time." He saw a tear fall and drew her close.

"Will you be goin' on the cosmic railroad, man?" Dearden's throat was tight, but he laughed at Rowan's Bronx accent imitation of how Lee Wynter described the Grid. He hurt inside at the thought of leaving her, but there were so many unknowns involved. At least there would be an escape plan for those close to him if all went wrong.

Rowan smoothed her hair back and drew on her inner resolve. "We will not be parted, Jem. We are meant to be together, for all of time."

They clinked glasses and re-joined the others.

*   *   *

Esma and Rowan had secured Elvara, the bay mare and Modig, the stallion, in the stables after a gallop over the fields along the River Blythe. The river hadn't changed much in the years since they were back in Leofwin's time because, in many places, it was coursing over bedrock. Some of the bends had straightened out, but the two women still recognised the general shape of the river. They knew the places to avoid around Bradnock's Marsh, where the clumps of tussock sedge grass marked where the going was soft and sometimes dangerous. They found it natural to read the land and the weather.

Esma heard the sound of Harry's CX500 pulling into the courtyard. She dropped the curry-comb she was using and ran outside. Harry was resting the Honda on its side stand and he turned as Esma called his name.

"Oh hi . . . you look good," Harry smiled. She was allowing her hair to grow longer and it was returning to its natural blonde. He removed his helmet and she kissed him and clung on. His arms around her felt good.

"I am glad you are back. You have been busy, yes?"

"Very . . . it's been full-on, did you see the launch?"

"We are watching the Condor. I saw you in the Flight Control, but we are having too much time inside the great hall and Lady Rowan wanted to get out and ride Modig."

Harry clasped her hand and pulled. "I need to be watching Condor's progress too. Coming?"

"No – I must go to horses and finish with them." She shook loose and Harry headed to the house. He went into to the great hall, where he saw Dearden talking to Templestone and Julia. The television was on in the background, the Nibiru channel.

The power draw on electrical supply in most countries had gone through the roof. Everyone with a television had it on most of the time to watch the mission as it developed. Others watched on-line, those without used a radio. Some, a wind-up radio. The ones without any communication had seen a strange new light in the sky and they became fearful.

*   *   *

Two days had passed since the launch. The news-hungry public received a four-hourly update through some of the world's great optical telescopes as they came, in turn, to bear on Nibiru. In each live video stream, the planet was slightly bigger and large surface detail started to be discernible. Although they were in a difficult position, having the same fears of destruction as the rest of the population, most of the newsreaders remained objective. If a show of nerves was detected by the news channel director, another camera would cut to a different member of the team.

And then a scene was broadcast that created euphoria amongst the audience and presenters alike. The cheers came, the tears came, and the hardest of men, including the leader of the rogue nation, felt a sense of relief as the confirmation of a positive outcome slipped onto the screen. One of the video cameras that was facing the direction of travel on the End Time Module showed Nibiru with crosshairs centred on it.

Many of the viewers had seen similar video shots from fighter-bombers in action in countries where terrorists were plotting carnage. They had seen the crosshairs centred on buildings from high above and then boom, and the target smoked, and sometimes there was questionable *collateral damage*. But Nibiru was like a terrorist with dark threats who came by night with murder in mind. It was a target that would soon go boom, and disappear with no collateral damage when End Time blitzed it to hell and back.

* * *

The close group of friends were sitting around the table in the great hall, back together after the launch. The mission was into its third day and the door to Dearden Hall was locked to the outside world. While Frieda and Gil Heskin, at Rowan's behest, kept them supplied with food, coffee and sometimes stronger liquid, they drew up the details of a case to present before the Hnioss.

It was a difficult situation. Templestone likened it to night-flying with unfamiliar instruments. They all shared input, including Rowan and Esma, who had brought the terrier pup back to Dearden Hall. Esma watched Titch go up to Tomahawk, who studied the creature disdainfully and then made room for him on the rug by the fire.

Harry shut the lid of his laptop.

"According to my calculations, if we didn't have the End Time bomb to stop Nibiru it would come closest to Earth in ninety-seven days." Carlos Mendulas at the Gemini South telescope in Chile had emailed Harry with the results of Doppler shift tests on the advancing planet. That information, coupled with the feedback from Jodrell Bank and the other radio telescopes and Harry's math, confirmed the planet's speed and distance from Earth. Only Julia noticed that Harry had said, *come closest to Earth*, rather than hit it.

"There is a complication," Harry added. The Earth and the other planets in the Solar System proceed around the Sun in a counter-clockwise direction. Nibiru travels clockwise. Its rogue nature indicates that its origin is different to all the other planets. With our eighteen point-five miles per second and Nibiru's six-point eight-six, at the point of closest proximity, there would be a closing speed of twenty-three point five-six miles per second. What Carlos also said was that there has been a large perturbation in Nibiru's orbit, probably due to the influence of the Sun and the major planets combined."

"Have those influences altered its trajectory?" Julia asked.

"Yes. It will miss Earth now for sure, but the effects here will still be catastrophic. The highest tides imaginable, no power, no food, almost complete inundation by water."

"A repeat of the legend of a world-wide flood," Matt Roberts said.

"Legend my arse . . . it did happen, all the evidence is there across cultures if you just take the time to do some research. Unless we can prevent it by either Plan A or Plan B, it'll happen again." There was silence around the table. Harry was unusually serious.

"The story of a great flood is in the Lakota Sioux culture as well," Red Cloud added.

"And in Aboriginal folk law," Storm Petrel said. She had lived amongst the Native Australians for a while.

"But we do have an ark of sorts, in fact, we have two of them, so let's keep optimistic," Dearden said, as he shuffled some papers together and passed them to Pierpoint.

"What's the latest update from Module Communications at Turaroa?" Pierpoint asked Harry.

"MODCOM was too busy to talk, but he told me not to miss an interview with Flight Control at ten o'clock tonight. We'll get all the updates then."

*　　*　　*

Edward Geary was in Flight Control. There was a background of busy screens, systems managers and technical talk. Virgil Wright was at a desk with FLIGHT DIRECTOR on a nametag. His screen summarised the many systems manager's operations. Wright turned to the camera and answered Geary's question about stage three, carrying the End Time module.

"The launch was perfect and our telemetry is telling us that the trajectory is on the nail. The Magellan EB-7 Beamed Core Proton-Antiproton Engine is behaving as designed and the speed of the spacecraft is as expected."

"What is the speed of the Magellan propulsion system, I've heard a lot of rumours about it?"

"Currently it is travelling at two hundred and fifty miles per second, which is zero point one three percent of the speed of light. No other spacecraft has travelled at that speed and we have plenty more in reserve with the Magellan engine. We could get to a serious percentage of C."

"Could the Magellan enable us to reach warp speed?"

"We shall—"

An alarm siren wailed in the background and Launch control came to life. Team members became ultra-attentive. Virgil Wright frowned and turned to his screen.

"What's going on," Geary asked, moving in closer to Flight's screen.

"Not now, Mr Geary, something's come up." Wright looked in the direction of some large screens at the front of the room. Geary saw that he was focussed on the centre one, the screen showing the view out of the front of the End Time module. Nibiru was in glorious colour, seen for the first time through a telephoto lens actuated by MODCOM. Figures at the bottom right of the screen showed information about End Time's approach to Nibiru in time and distance. It was Twelve hours and ten point-eight million miles from impact.

The whole planet filled the large screen. Through a shimmering haze that made detail blurred, the blue of oceans, dark coloured continents, snow-capped mountain ranges and the green of forests could be seen. Geary saw active volcanoes, with plumes of yellow coloured gas exuding from them and floating high above the surface of the planet.

"What's going on?" Geary spoke loudly from his position a few yards away from Virgil Wright. He looked around Flight

Control, the relaxed atmosphere had gone. In its place, there was intense concentration. Serious journalist that he was, Geary pressed Virgil Wright for more information.

"What is that place?"

"That is what I intend to find out. MODCOM, the spectrograph reading of this planet, get it . . . and make that damn quick."

57

In the great hall, Dearden turned up the volume on the television. Ed Geary's raised voice in Flight Control asking what was going on cut through the conversation and Pierpoint held up his hand for silence. Harry got closer to the television to hear the answer, and then the screen was filled with the telephoto image of Nibiru seen from Condor's stage three module, complete with target acquisition crosshairs.

After a minute of background conversation in Flight Control, Edward Geary, in a head and shoulder shot, replaced the image of the approaching planet.

"This latest information is completely unexpected. All the efforts of the scientists involved with this mission have been aimed at destroying the threat to Earth. It appears that the planet that we have sent the End Time bomb to destroy has features that are very similar to those here on Earth. Currently, the team here are pulling all the stops out to investigate the details on the surface. This whole place is buzzing with one question only. Will there be signs of life?"

Almost as one, Harry and Sir Willoughby Pierpoint stood, startling the others. Dearden was next up. Harry Stanway said he had to make some calls urgently. He left the great hall by the side entrance at a run, making for his room along the landing. His first call was to Carlos Mendulas.

"Did you see the latest report from Flight Control at Turaroa?"

"The surface features . . . too right I did and I'm doing a spectrograph right now . . . I'll have the results in forty-five minutes."

"I'll call you back in forty-six."

Harry signed off and thumbed the keypad for his next call. It was to the Very Large Array in New Mexico and Bev Harding, head of system tracking. He had primed her on the possible need for assistance. Harry had been engaged in some tangential thinking about Nibiru. It had crossed his mind that it might even be artificial, but never this . . .

"Harding."

"Beverley, are you watching the newscast?"

"Would I be doing anything else?"

"Comments?"

"We've got the VLA tracking and we're listening in."

"Any results?"

"We're cycling through possible frequencies."

"Yes, but are there any signals yet?"

"Not so far."

"Keep me posted Bev."

"I sure will Harry, and quick. How about Jodrell and SETI?"

"I'm onto them next."

"Good luck, keep me posted."

"I will . . . must go, Bev."

Harry dialled Fletcher Adams at the SETI institute in Mountain View, California. Fletch recognised his number.

"I half expected you'd be calling, Harry. This situation is a complication too far with the bomb only hours away."

"What steps have you taken Fletch?"

"I'll hand you over to Connie. She's been alerting the big dishes." There was a fumbling noise and then the phone muted as Fletcher passed the phone to Constantia Rios, a dark haired, dark eyed Latino with a warm laugh and a delightful accent. Despite her femininity, Connie could cut to the quick, and she used her charm and an astute business brain to get services and funding for SETI, the Search for Extra-terrestrial Intelligence.

"Harry . . . hi, here's who we have on stream as well as the VLA. We have Jodrell Bank standing by, Parkes is up and running, as is Area 31 in Ontario. At present, I have thirty other observatories coming on stream. Do you want me to list them?"

"Not now, but as soon as you get a bite from any of them let me know, will you."

"*If* we do Harry, we've had a lot of false starts here over the years but stay hopeful."

* * *

Harry was back downstairs with the others. They were around the table deep in discussion when Harry's mobile phone rang. He shoved his chair out of the way and stood quickly, indicating he wanted silence. He mouthed that it was Carlos Mendulas on the other end. He put the phone on speaker mode so the others could hear.

"The spectrometer tests were surprising Harry. There is a presence of CFC's and ozone above an oxygen-based atmosphere. There is also a questionable percentage of carbon dioxide in the atmosphere. Nitrogen is on the spectrum too. All of these elements are present in the atmosphere at a level we would expect to see in an industrial society comparable to ours back in the 1940's."

"How the hell does he know that?" Mitch Doughty asked.

Carlos heard the question. "Take my word for it, there is evidence of atmospheric pollutants that could only be caused by the artificial use of fossil fuels."

"Hey man, are you sayin' we're about to destroy a civilisation?" Wynter piped up. Carlos didn't answer him straight away.

"Answer, Carlos, don't shrink from me, man,"

"I'm not . . . but there has to be more evidence before we call an abort to the mission."

"Like what evidence?"

"What Jodrell Bank, Parkes the VLA and the other radio 'scopes are working on, whether they have picked up a radio signature."

Wynter stood quickly.

"You mean, if we hear some alien Marconi type blasting out rap we wouldn't kill 'em off? I'm with that reasonin'. I say we give the suckers a chance. We've got over ninety days before the sonofabitch planet hits . . . *and* we do have a Plan B, which is probably more than those little Nibiru bastards have got if they're like back in the early 1940's. We have to proceed with contacting our friend out there, the Lan-Si-Nu guy." He stabbed a finger skywards. Again, there was silence.

Carlos, in Chile and all in the great hall chewed over what Lee Wynter said for a minute, apart from Rowan and Esma, who were unable to understand New York Bronx at speed. Esma patted her thigh and Titch leapt onto her lap

"There's truth in what the American said." Harry had informed Carlos about Lan-Si-Nu under strict orders of secrecy. "Who is that American Guy?"

"Lee Wynter," Harry said.

Ed Geary came on camera again on Turaroa. There was a news flash from inside Flight Control.

"Here is an update. I am told by Evan Blake himself that the mission has come to the point where the End Time weapon has to be armed. There is a three-hour window in which that process has to be initiated and MODCOM, module communications, are the team managing that event . . ."

Bill Templestone stood slowly and went to the head of the table where everyone could see him. He raised his hand. The general chatter stopped and they waited for him to speak. He usually spoke sensible things even under stress. He reached for the TV remote and turned the sound down.

"We find ourselves on the horns of a moral dilemma. It would take the Wisdom of Solomon to arrive at the right decision here, but this is how I see it at present. Visually, and given what Carlos told us about its atmosphere, there are great similarities between Nibiru and Earth. How that can be I do not know, because to all intents and purposes there should be little atmosphere left on Nibiru after its passage by the Sun."

Pierpoint assessed what Harry had said and then, "You might have some opinions about that Harry, but for the time being we have to go by what we can prove." Pierpoint stood and walked over to the fireplace. Standing in Dearden's favoured place, he leant against the massive stonework and took his phone from his pocket. He fiddled with it until he had set up a party line and pressed connect.

In both Flight Control on Turaroa and the UN Secretary-General's building on Sutton Place, Manhattan, information from scientific institutions worldwide was being analysed. In readiness for nearing Nibiru, both Evan Blake and Lars Knudsen had drafted in mathematical analysts and statisticians to work on the information streaming in. Blake and Knudsen answered the party call from Pierpoint.

"You've both seen the latest visuals of the surface of Nibiru. Any comments?"

"Great surprise, but what do we do now?" Knudsen ventured. Evan Blake was the more astute of the two men who had a finger on the button of End Time.

"I don't like it," he said.

"What don't you like?" asked Pierpoint.

"The implications, if it *is* similar to Earth."

"I thought the same as you . . . and there is more information. Carlos Mendulas, at the Gemini South 'scope in Chile, told Harry that the spectrograph results show that Nibiru has an atmosphere and it's breathable."

"That is impossible, considering its orbit," Evan Blake said.

"I wish it was, but check with your analysts, you'll find they're saying the same."

*   *   *

There was a euphoric atmosphere as the image on the large screen changed from the distant view of Earth to the full-on view of Nibiru superimposed by crosshairs and constantly moving figures at the bottom of the screen. A great cheer arose that echoed over London from Hyde Park. It was similar in Central Park, Manhattan, Le Jardin Du Luxembourg, Red Square, Tiananmen Square, and on a high plateau in Nepal. Worldwide in such places, the crowds were gathered and they cheered until they were hoarse as the tensions released. It was as though the whole world breathed a huge sigh of relief. In a custom started that night, people began to exchange gifts and leave flowers near the large screens in a symbol of unity.

Harry's mobile phone rang again. It was Constantia Rios from SETI and she sounded breathless.

"Stanway."

"Harry, thank God I've been able to reach you, it's a bad line, speak louder."

He spoke up, "What's the problem?"

"The End Time bomb, we have to stop it,"

"Why . . . is it what I suspected?"

"Jodrell Bank and the VLA have picked up a radio signal from Nibiru. It's modulated on a carrier wave and it *is* intelligence based. Nibiru is inhabited."

58

SETI was geared-up to correlate and analyse the masses of information coming in from many different sources. It was what they were set up to do. There had been no primary signal during their whole long run of listening since, first of all Big Ear and then the Allen Telescope Array at the Hat Creek Radio Observatory in California was switched on in 2007. However, they kept on listening and never lost enthusiasm.

Harry plugged his mobile into a speaker dock and called the others to come and listen to what Constantia Rios, at SETI, was saying. She hung on until he told her to speak.

"OK, we're ready, Connie. Anyone else picked up the signals apart from Jodrell Bank and the VLA?"

"Yes . . . a number of dishes are reporting the busy use of radio frequencies and something else has been picked up. There is an anomaly that we weren't certain about at first. It has been analysed by three astrophysicists who are working with us. There is a plasma-like force field surrounding the planet at a distance of eight thousand miles. It is bordering on the visible spectrum, and tests indicate that the force field provides a shield that protects the planet from outside sources of disturbance—"

"Which must be how the planet survives the extremes of temperature in its orbit."

"Yep, including its passage by the Sun. Nibiru has a self-regulated temperature control and protection system. Nothing harmful gets through the shield, but excess temperature from the planet is allowed to bleed off through it and waves in the radio spectrum escape."

"Has anything been learned about the radio signals?"

"We can't make sense of them, but they are definitely coming from the surface. They're intelligence-based, in a spoken language." Hearing this, Julia Linden-Barthorpe got closer to the mobile dock.

"Have you recorded any of it?" she asked.

"We have,"

"Email it to us will you, we have an acquaintance who might make sense of it." She had Trent Jackson in mind.

Pierpoint left Julia and Harry talking to Connie. When he walked away he signalled Dearden and the others to join him.

"Intelligence is a difficulty none of us envisaged," he said.

Dearden nodded, "Too right it is. We cannot destroy a civilisation when we have an alternative. End Time has to be aborted."

"As long as it's not too late for that," Mitch Doughty said.

Harry and Julia rang off from Connie Rios. "That's it then. Decision time," Harry called to Pierpoint."

"It is. We appear to have run out of choices. It's over to you and Lan-Si-Nu now. Jem, just do it," Pierpoint said.

* * *

"FLIGHT."

"This is MODCOM, what are your instructions. We have the point of no return for arming End Time in forty-eight hours on my mark. 5 ... 4 ... 3 ... 2 ... 1 ... Mark."

Flight, Virgil Wright, surveyed the information on the screen in front of him. After MODCOM's countdown, he called his team to gather round. He glanced at the data flooding in from the scientific establishments concentrating on Nibiru. All were indicating activity on its surface.

The Flight Managers drew chairs close to Virgil Wright, Evan Blake came in the door and headed over. Blake usually sauntered around Frontier Spaceflight in a self-assured way, as if nothing would phase him. This time his walk was urgent.

"Virge, things are hotting up. The UN Secretary-General's just come out of a meeting with the Security Council. There's going to be a public announcement . . . they're saying to abort the mission—"

"That's our conclusion, sir . . . with strong evidence of an intelligent life-form on Nibiru, we need time to sort out alternatives. This is not going to go down well with the public. They're counting on the Condor."

"There is an alternative. Sir Willoughby Pierpoint and his team in the UK intend to go ahead with it."

"What are their intentions?"

"Make way; that's what I've come to tell you." The team parted and Blake went to Flight's desk.

He spoke on the PA. "Be prepared to have your minds stretched, folks." Those listening followed every twist of Blake's explanation. Some of them, hearing the talk of a mission abort, were re-visited by the fears of impending destruction they had before the launch of Condor. The future had looked safe with the launch and now there was no future a few months down the line. Blake saw the concern on the faces of his team, the pallor, the sweat. Difficult as it was for himself as well as the team, he had to give encouragement.

"The information Pierpoint gave me is sound, although it is highly unusual." Blake remembered the evening they spent together, Pierpoint, Harry Stanway, Lee Wynter and Mitch

Doughty when Harry put a DVD into the player. Blake had a copy of the DVD. He slipped it into a player and the video began playing on a big screen at the front of the Flight Control room.

Blake told all to watch and listen. What followed on the screen was a conversation between Harry Stanway and a tall, slender creature who Harry said in a voice-over was an alien from a place he called Wasiri-Poya. Two more of the aliens were in the background talking to Lee Wynter and although Wynter was a good six-foot tall, the two beings towered above him. They were in a building that the alien talking to Stanway called the Portal. Evan Blake thought the room they were in resembled a flight deck. But it was different to any flight deck he had seen before and he had seen a good many.

The being, who Harry addressed as Lan-Si-Nu, was describing some of the theory about the transport system he and his colleagues had used to visit Earth. The alien explained that as a by-product of the positional transport system there was also a temporal transfer function. Lan-Si-Nu finished by saying, in perfect English with a slight melodic accent, that if ever Harry and his colleagues needed help, he would provide it.

Blake removed the DVD and looked at his team gathered around him. There was a range of reactions. From downright disbelief portrayed by a smirk, to a look that said tell me more. Someone at the back laughed and didn't stop, the laughter became hysterical. The man was escorted from the room and taken to the sick bay. Flight, Virgil Wright, spoke for all present.

"I mean this with the greatest respect, Evan. How do we know that what we have just seen isn't a sick joke? Special effects are good these days. Just ask Stephen Spielberg.

"Trust me, Virgil. All of you, trust me. I haven't let you down so far. Look at what we've accomplished together." Blake punched his arm toward the vacant launch pad they could see through the armoured glass window. "I haven't led you through that project with deception." There was anger in his voice and agreement all round. "Men, these alien guys are light years ahead of us and I'll tell you this, we could really learn from them. If we get over this Nibiru problem, the future could be very exciting."

"Show us the DVD again," Mills Warner shouted from the back of the room. It was more a demand than a request. Warner came to Frontier Spaceflight from the film industry to head up the animation side of PR. He could tell instinctively if a scene was doctored. He strode to the front of the room and stood critically at the foot of the big screen.

"OK, play it again . . . sir, will you please?" Despite the circumstances Blake recalled Bogart's words to Sam in Casablanca and he smiled.

The DVD cycled again and Warner moved to the right to view the vid at an oblique angle. Then he went left, also oblique, stayed there for some five seconds, analysing.

"Steps . . . get me some bloody steps," he shouted. Someone ran from the room and came back within seconds with some tall aluminium stepladders. He came panting to the front and held them as Warner climbed. He faced centre screen for a few seconds, studied profiles of inanimate objects and then the edges of the forms of both humans and aliens. He held onto the top of the steps and turned to face the room.

"It's real," he called to the team who were willing it to be real. "It's bloody real, guys. This is evidence of first contact and they've offered to help." They all clutched at his words and Frontier Spaceflight burst into wild applause and cheering.

59

The case to put before the Hnioss was complete. Templestone formulated it with input from the others at the heart of SHaFT who were at Dearden Hall. It took five hours to thrash out the detail. Pierpoint reminded them of the legend at the base of the stained-glass window Arthur Doughty fitted in his room in the studio in Clinton Street; *Nos Successio Procul Totus Sumptus, We Succeed At All Costs.*

"I guess we'll never face this sort of threat again," Sir Willoughby said. "Whether we succeed or not we will see in a short space of time, but write down our effort, Bill. It will show that at least we stepped up to the fight."

"It is being written," Templestone said, "Sho'mer the Hebrew recorded Nibiru's first pass at the time of the Great Flood. I'm recording the second pass."

"And if all goes well your record will be on show for all to see," Dearden said.

Will Pierpoint always found the right words at the right time. The choice of words and his attitude made him a superb leader and he always led from the front.

"Write this down, Bill. We tried. Never let it be said that we gave up without a fight. SHaFT is about justice for the op-pressed and this time we fight for justice on a cosmic scale. Let's get to it."

* * *

Over vast millennia, the Wasiri-Chanchiya used the Portal NJA 4902385 as one of the many elements in their space-time transfer system. They named the planet where they built that particular Portal the Second One – it was just as beautiful as their own planet and in some ways, more so.

Initially, when the Wasiri-Chanchiya built the Portal in the primeval forest, there were no Earths. Great lumbering creatures ambled about and flying beasts flapped in an ungainly way through the skies. They ate vegetation, like the Wasiri-Chanchiya.

The Ancestor-travellers in those ancient times wrote in the Great Annals of the day that their instruments detected the energy of the First Cause working in the region that the Earths eventually named Mesopotamia. Four rivers flowed from this area of special beauty. The Wasiri-Chanchiya travelled there to try to see the energy in greater detail. They longed to see the First Cause at work, but they were too late. They were always too late. Not long after that, the Wasiri-Chanchiya saw their first Earths in a clearing. A male and a female.

Many Earth years passed and then the Travellers witnessed a Starship from Chakrakan heading to Earth. With that, anger and brutality came and as if directed to bring order to the chaos, Chakrakan's close passage occurred and caused inundation of Earth's land-masses by water.

* * *

The Portal, hidden deep within Leofwin's Hundred, a small part of the forest called Arden, frightened the local people in medieval times because of the lights in the sky and the activity associated with it.

In their explorations, whenever the Wasiri-Chanchiya arrived on the Second One, they stayed for a while. They were interested in the Earths. As a race, they had a potential for greatness, so the Wasiri-Chanchiya observed them at a discrete distance and recorded what they saw. They never intermingled, but in time the Travellers learnt the Earth languages and followed the population's progress toward wisdom and scientific learning.

They detested the acts of barbarity some of the Earths inflicted upon their own kind and other creatures but were unable to interfere because of the freedom of will to choose their own course possessed by intelligent races. However, the Wasiri-Chanchiya acquired books from Alexandria, written by those of the Earths who were the more learned and they placed the books into a section of the Cosmic Library of Learning attached to the Hnioss.

In the time of Lan-Si-Nu, the crystal in the Portal became unstable and the Travel Leader and his crew became marooned on The Second One. They led a secretive life in the forest and only ventured out of the Portal at night to gather food and observe and learn. They came to recognise the various Earths who lived nearby, including an interesting family that went by the name of Dearden.

* * *

"The Earths have discovered that Chakrakan is inhabited," Lan-Si-Nu said to the Preceptor of the Hnioss.

"How are they reacting?" the illustrious person asked the newly promoted Grid Commander.

"The planetary passage is nearing criticality, but those of the Earths in command of the mission to deal with Chakrakan have concluded that they must not use the weapon they have devised to destroy it. They possess the principles allowing them to ascend to the next level of learning. The group of people known as SHaFT fight evil on their planet, but they lack the insight and the technology to deal with combatting evil with anything but overwhelming force and weaponry."

"They sometimes think there is no other choice. What do they intend to do about Chakrakan?"

"They will contact us again and confirm they need our help."

"And it is then that they must appear before the Hnioss."

Since Jem Dearden had initially contacted him to ask for help, Lan-Si-Nu had been leading the investigation into Chakrakan's approach to Earth. He had been hoping Dearden and the group of Earths involved with what they called the End-Time weapon would renounce its use and take advantage of the offer of help Lan-Si-Nu had left with them. But it had to be their choice. The Wasiri-Chanchiya applied a code of non-interference with alien races and Lan-Si-Nu intended to follow that ingrained principle without deviation.

*   *   *

Harry Stanway was sitting in the commander's seat with Jem Dearden to his left and the others gathered around them. Lan-Si-Nu and his two companions held Harry Stanway in high regard. In a surprising display of intellect, the young Earth had restored the Portal to its full connectivity to the Grid, enabling

Lan-Si-Nu, Fen-Nu and Thal-Nar to return to their home planet. For that the Wasiri-Chanchiya would be forever grateful.

Lan-Si-Nu finished the conversation with Harry Stanway about the threat the Earths were facing and closed his communicator down on the scene in the Portal. An elusive thought whisked around in his mind. It was a thought as obscure as the mist-shrouded landscape on the planet Triadon. Despite mental effort sharp enough to produce sweat on his brow, he was unable to bring the obscure thought about Chakrakan into sharp focus. He knew it was important. The thought had been teasing his mind since Dearden contacted him using the key just a few Earth-weeks back. At the time, Lan-Si-Nu had alerted the Hnioss to the pressing need the Earths had for direct intervention with Chakrakan bearing down upon them on a near-miss course. He had also made a recommendation to the Hnioss about the special one of the Earths, Harry Stanway, who should receive recognition for his remarkable help with the Portal. Lan-Si- Nu awaited the Hnioss' decision.

Whilst Lan-Si-Nu was waiting, he searched, in the Building of the Archives, for an answer to what was on his mind. He sat and entered the neural network by donning the snug fitting helmet and entering his personal code. He allowed his mind to go quiet and prepared himself for communication with the Quantum Processors at the heart of the system. He reached the silent part of his mind and joined the Q-Gate. The memory that had been ill-defined became a shade clearer, like a vision gradually appearing through a mist.

The memory was from one of his transfer-of-information sessions when he was a young student. The information uploading to his mind through the Q-Gate enabled him to lock-on to the neural thread he downloaded into the library back then. He had a suspicion that the planet Chakrakan was not straightforward. The issue had been important physically but had moral implications too. The search for information in Lan-Si-Nu's own dimension produced no result.

Lan-Si-Nu thumbed the buttons on the headset and selected Multi-dimensional mode to deepen the search outside his mind. He thought up the keypad on his viewer and inserted the name, Chakrakan. At first, there was no response, the machines were often slow in the Multi-dimensional mode. The organic probe forced its way down, searching through the layers into the deep dimensions where there was archived information far away in antiquity. The probe did its work, and the result started to lift through the dimensions to his own set, dimension one and it appeared on the external screen.

He removed the helmet and absorbed the archived material. He noticed that there had been a more recent addition that had been appended to the ancient information.

CHAKRAKAN. A Sister Planet of Earth.

(Addition: Chakrakan is Nibiru in the language of the Earths).

Chakrakan is a planet orbiting the Sun, Neross, in an 'E' type spiral Galaxy, known as Phaelon 23057C. Chakrakan also orbits Earth at twice the distance of Earth's Moon. In the one hundred and seventeenth cycle, galactic year twenty-two, day two hundred and five, an event was written into the Great Annals.

A Star Ship left the surface of Chakrakan, the twin third planet orbiting Neross. The drive of the vehicle warped the Grid and our sensors detected this phenomenon.

As its subsequent actions proved, the vehicle's mission was not benign. It entered a trajectory to intercept the orbit of the fourth planet in the Neross solar system, called Merzin, from where it attacked and eliminated every vestige of its life before beginning to extract minerals. All that remains on Merzin are the dry beds of an extensive canal network. We fear that the Chakrakan's lust for violence has reached the Second One, the planet of the Earths, because of the predominance of hatred that has entered amongst them.

ACTION. Cocooning. Using the forces of the Grid and its Nodes, there is to be an attempt to move Chakrakan into an orbit where its influence will no longer be a danger to the other planets of the Neross solar system.

CONCLUSION. In the interests of universal peace, all external activity originating from the planet Chakrakan has now been stopped by cocooning. The planet has been assigned a benign orbit, but it is not the one that our programmers had planned. Whatever forces they applied to Chakrakan from the Grid were over-ridden by the intervention of a far greater external force that locked Chakrakan into an extraordinarily eccentric orbit around Neross. This over-riding of our efforts has the hallmark of action by the First Cause, and we must obey it. At some future time, the reason for this may become obvious because Chakrakan will again pass close to Earth. We will monitor the situation when that occurs.

The population of Chakrakan are now isolated. Their advancement will be restricted. The cocooning will protect the Chakrakans from the temperature extremes of interstellar space whilst in their extreme orbit around Neross. The Neross system itself is now protected from further influence from the Chakrakans.

Lan-Si-Nu stored the information in his personal memory recorder and clipped it to his belt. He forwarded his findings to the Hnioss in the hope it would provoke a quick response, and it did. They responded within the space of sixty-three heartbeats. The body of learned Wasiri-Chanchiya, of whom he was one, agreed to help the Earths in principle, but they said that the representatives of the Earths would have to approach the Hnioss and commit themselves irrevocably to the ways of peace in return for the help they needed.

*   *   *

Dearden and the team were in the control room in the Hub deep in Leofwin's Hundred. The team were tense, seated and standing around Dearden, as he took the key from the box and inserted it into the slot just as Julia had done in the trial a few weeks before when they first asked Lan-Si-Nu if he would help.

Dearden pushed the key downwards, felt three distinct differences in pressure and then turned the key. Instantaneously, the largest screen on the wall at the front of the Control Room became active. After a brief greeting one of the aliens with similar features to Lan-Si-Nu, but this time obviously female, spoke a greeting. That the message was a recording was apparent when Dearden said he needed to talk to Lan-Si-Nu and the alien continued speaking, disregarding him.

"How do you tell these suckers apart, man?" Lee Wynter's exclamation was ignored.

Lan-Si-Nu's voice interrupted. His voice had a regular beat to it, he was walking fast. As he spoke, the view of a tall, pinnacle building replaced the head and shoulders shot of the alien giving the greeting.

"We have been following your situation. I understand it is now critical."

"It is. The End Time weapon is approaching the target. There is a severe problem. We have discovered that there is intelligent life on the planet—"

"We know there is life on Nibiru. That being so, you should not countenance using your weapon against the planet. The code we know as the Life Ethic always takes precedence. The preservation of life, Jem. Life is a gift. It must be honoured as a gift and always preserved."

"We are aware of that. We have prepared our case to put before your Hnioss."

"Good. I have looked into your situation since we last spoke. We have been involved with this type of event involving planetary movement before . . . the process is drastic and difficult. We have used the process five times where there was success and twice where we failed. I regret to say that we are unable to guarantee the outcome. What I can say is that the events in the distant past were entered into the Great Annals for everyone to study. They are held before us to learn from, but there is a margin of uncertainty involved in the outcome for you."

"What do we have to do next?" It was Storm Petrel who spoke up. Julia Linden-Barthorpe tried to weigh-up Storm, the stranger in their midst. The newest recruit who seemed as though she might be tough and opinionated.

"You must deflect your End Time weapon. When that is dealt with you can appear before the Hnioss."

"Why can't we come to the Hnioss now?" Storm asked.

"Because the weapon must be disposed of first. That way you will demonstrate your intentions. Once you grow away from the

ways of violence you people of Earth will live far more meaning-
ful lives than you do at present—"

"OK. Give us a date and time to see the Hnioss . . . we will
work with you," Harry Stanway cut across the conversation.

"We put the situation back to you, people of Earth. Resolve
your End Time weapon that threatens the entities of Nibiru.
When that is done you can travel to Wasiri-Poya with your
request."

* * *

"Flight to all managers, this is an abort with End Time, I say
again, abort. Act immediately, abort." A few seconds passed.

"FLIGHT, this is MODCOM, we have disabled two of the
three actuator servos for triggering the bomb, but we have a
technical problem with the third one."

"What is your problem exactly?"

"It won't disable."

"Damn." Virgil Wright's icy calm cracked. "MODCOM, run
through the procedure again. I repeat, run again."

"FLIGHT, this is MODCOM. we have repeated the disable
sequence four times, but actuator three remains unresponsive."

"OK, team, I want all of you on this. The End Time module
has to be diverted. MODCOM, give us a re-direct. We want a
new trajectory within the hour. Send the bloody bomb somewhere . . . anywhere well out of the way. Let the Magellan engine
give us all it's got. I kid you not, the speed of light would be good
at this time. I want all systems managers and engineers working
on this NOW, with the utmost urgency."

* * *

Before the live broadcast was cut from public networks, people the world over knew there was a problem because they heard Virgil Wright lose his cool and request an abort. Announcers said to stand by for an important announcement and the audience became nervous. Everyone with a television or a radio got a little closer. Volume was turned up. Children were told in no uncertain terms to shut up, listen and look. *This is important Johnnie . . . Jane, come and sit with me and be quiet . . . just for a little while sweetie.*

Elechi, come here and listen and you, Adan sit with your sister and be silent. Shush, stop laughing and be good.

Internet users were so desperate for live streamed information that network congestion was causing outages. *Please try later, we are experiencing an unprecedented amount of network usage at present.*

The draw on electrical power grew to the highest level ever, and cuts began to occur. In cities unprepared for such high activity, generators overloaded and, in some cases, shorted out.

Darkness ruled in nations whose time was after sundown and there was no electricity. Echoes of fearful people penetrated the darkness. Anger grew and took to the streets again because the population did not know what was happening. They needed to know. They were fearful. They wanted answers and were prepared to fight for them as if there was no tomorrow.

A dark haired, dimpled announcer with a honey voice and lustrous hair introduced Lars Knudsen. She first of all gave his credentials, which were impressive. Translations into the world's major languages and many of the minor ones began as he spoke. It was a triumph of broadcasting, considering the time strictures involved.

Knudsen was sitting at his desk in the quiet surroundings of his Sutton Place residence that oozed calm. The setting chosen by the UN-PR team was intentional, an effort to induce calm amongst the billions of viewers before the broadcast began.

"Three, two, one." The director, outside broadcast raised his fingers and counted Knudsen down for when he was on air.

"We have an announcement that affects every man, woman and child on this planet, the Good Earth, as one man once called it." Knudsen's voice was reassuringly calm after his double shot of Aalborg Akvavit. "That man was an astronaut adventurer who viewed Earth from afar and his name was Frank Borman. People of the Good Earth, we must tell you that our effort to deflect or destroy the oncoming planet, Nibiru, has come to nothing. The reason, I must reveal, is that we have discovered that the planet we intended to deflect or destroy is inhabited. Because of that, the mission cannot proceed any further. We have had to make a moral decision."

As they heard the words in their languages, billions of hearts missed a beat. Hopes and aspirations were in the success of the Condor VI mission. It had secured the future. Now this man Knudsen was saying that the mission had been called off because the target was inhabited, of all things. It was unforgivable. And *if it is inhabited*, they thought, *so what, blast it to hell*.

Attitudes polarised into three camps. The ones who had raw anger, the *blast it to hell* group, reacted to the deceit they thought they had been subjected to and they had to unleash their anger.

On the other hand, there were those who had given up. With them, a collective sigh arose because of the coming darkness of death. Their imagination ran riot with thoughts of the violence of their end. Over them, a great silence reigned.

A minority of folks took a centre path of certainty. They had a blind faith in whatever god they worshipped and they were convinced he, she or it would intercede and put things right. They smiled and said, in their certainty, that all would be well in the end, although it looked as though the odds were stacked against that result.

Those at Dearden Hall, with Plan B ready to roll, came into that certain group, with one major difference; Dearden and his colleagues had a proven faith in the Wasiri-Chanchiya's ability to intercede. After all, the Wasiri-Chanchiya had brought Rowan back from the brink of death.

60

The riots began in France, a country where, in the past, people were well used to taking the law into their own hands. In the Place de la Concorde, a large open space, with a history of sharpened steel and the rumble of tumbrel wheels over granite cobbles, a crowd was reacting to the announcement by Lars Knudsen that the End Time mission had to be aborted.

At first, there was stunned silence and then a low murmur gradually grew into a roar of anger. The Police Nationale were present only in small numbers around the perimeter of the gathering. Because of the air of goodwill over the past days at public gatherings as they followed the Condor VI, it wasn't considered necessary to have a show of force.

In the Gardien de la Paix, Jean-Pierre Lapointe sensed the crowd was turning ugly. The Brigadier to his right was on the Tetrapol comms calling for reinforcements when there was a burst of automatic fire from somewhere in the crowd. It shattered one of the large screens. The crowd took it as a sign to surge forward and outward in a release of wild energy and noise.

Trompé de nouveau, someone shouted, *cheated again*. The cry was taken up by the crowd. Within an hour trompé de nouveau spread virally on the internet and became the rallying cry amongst people far and wide, not only in France. With much of the population across continents, a what the hell mentality drove them. With hope gone and Nibiru four months away restraint disappeared.

The air of oncoming doom swayed the resolve of previously loyal-to-government uniformed law enforcement. Many of them joined in the cries of trompé de nouveau with the surging crowds. Amongst the minority remaining loyal to governments, rubber bullets and tear gas were put aside for the real thing that brought death to the streets and blood swilling down gutters. Through it all, *trompé de nouveau* was the watchword as men and women took the law into their own hands, pillaged what they could and began a battle for survival. Offices and shops were targeted, plate glass windows smashed easily with anger as the catalyst. Food halls and malls were pillaged. Panic, fire and lawlessness reigned.

The riots in the southern states of America, India, China and Russia were bad. In the African countries where folk lived at destitution level, they had little to lose to begin with, and the little they did have was going to be wrenched from them within a short space of time. *Trompé de nouveau* . . . cheated again.

UN internal security assigned armed guards to protect Lars Knudsen after threats were made to his life. He was a man who couldn't win. People wanted someone to blame for the situation they were in, and his was the public face who fitted the bill.

* * *

There was no preamble when Dearden lifted the secure phone in the great hall. He switched to speaker mode and Knudsen's terse tone of voice grabbed everyone's attention. He asked for Sir Willoughby Pierpoint. Dearden handed the phone over.

"What's happening about Plan B?" Knudsen asked.

"That is conditional. When we have disposed of the End Time weapon we can commence with Plan B. We're watching events at Turaroa on the television and we have a secure direct link on the internet. As soon as MODCOM diverts End Time we will commence with the next option. It's set up and ready to go."

"Don't you think it's about time you gave me some details about this so-called Plan B. A lot of people are putting an awful lot of trust that there is a Plan B. I want some facts."

Mitch Doughty turned the volume down on the television news. Pierpoint nodded his thanks. "Lars, I was going to ring you. We want you here as one of the representatives of Earth."

"What the hell does that mean?"

"Jem Dearden will give you the details when you arrive. Just get here . . . and make it quick."

* * *

On Turaroa, the public address came to life with a siren that told the workforce that an important announcement was coming. There was an uneasy silence for a minute, and then;

"This is Evan Blake. Firstly, I want to thank you all for the superb effort you have made from the planning stage through to launch and delivery of the End Time weapon. As you have no doubt heard, because it is all over the news and the internet, there is strong evidence our original target, Nibiru, is inhabited. Because of this, we have had to initiate a redirect of the weapon.

"What has complicated matters is that one of the actuator servos to the trigger mechanism of the bomb has failed to respond to a disengage command. The weapon is now armed. It is primed to detonate at a one-half mile above the surface of its target, so unless we destroy it, it will be an ever-present threat to the cosmos.

"Because of that, after consultation with astrophysicists, we have made a decision to redirect the End Time weapon to the asteroid belt. The redirect is now downloaded into the guidance computers of the module. The new target is an asteroid with the name Brinkman 1. The Brinkman series are fifteen of the largest asteroids in the Sigma 270 section of the asteroid belt. This group had begun to show erratic behaviour in recent years and at various times in the future, all fifteen asteroids will pose the worst collision danger to Earth of any object in the solar system. Of those fifteen, Brinkman 1 is the most likely to cause us trouble. We are going to take it out. FLIGHT, you now have control."

A few seconds went by, and then,

"This is FLIGHT . . . we have control. MODCOM, RETRO, FIDO, GUIDO, planned redirect is on my mark. 10 . . . 9 . . . 8 . . . 7 . . . 6 . . ."

*   *   *

Twelve hours later, the MiG-29 Fulcrum was wheels-down above Kineton Base after a sub-orbital flight at Mach 2.25. Through Will Pierpoint, Knudsen had engaged the services of Colonel Ryan Lindhoff, *a man who is useful to know when you're in a tight spot*, as Pierpoint had said. The touchdown came with the rumble of wheels on runway 04-22. The flared parachute for braking was discarded and Lindhoff was guided to the holding area. Pierpoint was waiting. He was there in his Bentley Mulsanne and he drove Knudsen to Dearden Hall.

61

They convoyed through the forest in Dearden's Range Rover and Julia's Jeep Grand Cherokee. Mitch Doughty was next to Rowan, who was next to Dearden, who was driving. Knudsen was in the back with Harry and Esma. Julia was following with Clive Fraser up front and Pierpoint, Matt Roberts, Storm Petrel and Lee Wynter in the back. The track was now tarmacked through to the Hub. It was smooth, not fast because of the bends and just wide enough for one vehicle.

"What is this place?" Knudsen asked. They had come to a halt in the clearing at the foot of the hill with the Hub on the plateau at the top. They hadn't elaborated the details for Knudsen's visit, other than to say that it was vital for what was to follow with Plan B. The Hub would speak for itself during his encounter with it.

"This place is alien. It's where Plan B starts, we're going to get some serious help," Harry announced, as the group walked through the tunnel leading to the lower entrance of the Hub. As they entered, Knudsen glanced at Harry with a look half between disbelief and cynicism. His attention was fixed on the bizarre surroundings he was walking through and was inclined to believe what Harry said without question. He missed his footing. Harry steadied him and he muttered his thanks. The group climbed the steep stairs with Harry explaining to Knudsen the function of each level, as they passed through them.

"Does contact take place here?" Knudsen asked.

"It does."

"Who are they?"

"They call themselves the Wasiri-Chanchiya, The Dawn People, The People at the Beginning of Time."

Knudsen snorted, and then grinned.

They came to the control room and Harry took the commander's seat, his feet dangling in the air in the seat made for the beings taller than him.

"Sit here," Harry said, indicating the chair to his left. Dearden sat to the right. When Knudsen sat he looked at the floor and then his feet. He was a tall man, but like Harry and Dearden his feet were off the floor.

The others crowded round and Dearden spoke. "Take note of what happens, Lars. This is going to be a crash course on the potential of the Hub. You need an introduction because of what's to follow." Dearden inserted the key given to him by Lan-Si-Nu and turned it.

The central screen on the wall in front illuminated with a split scene. On the left a double sun was bright in the sky, whilst to the right a distance shot of a planet that looked blue and green, with smudges of brown, dominated the darkness of space. Knudsen thought it looked like the photographs taken of Earth from space, but it was different. There were surface markings on the planet that were the outline of continents, but the shapes were definitely not the continents of Earth.

"Where is that place?" Knudsen asked.

Harry answered, "We don't know, but it is in a different galaxy to ours. It is old in cosmic time. The inhabitants of that planet are voyagers. They are the Wasiri-Chanchiya and they have been travelling the universe using the Grid from times before man was created. Their world is called Wasiri-Poya . . . the World at the Beginning of Time."

"How do you know all this?"

Dearden interrupted, "By accident, it's a long story." He glanced at Rowan and Esma. "Just accept that they are going to help us if we present a case to them stating that the people of Earth are prepared to renounce their ways of violence. The Wasiri-Chanchiya are a peaceful race, as are the other Travellers of the Grid. Technologically, they are millions of years in advance of us."

"Prove it," Knudsen scoffed. "How the hell can I come here and accept this outlandish stuff? If this is your plan B, and you want me to get involved, give me evidence that it's real." He was getting annoyed.

They had anticipated such a reaction and planned to give him the full works.

"Come with me," Dearden said to Knudsen. He headed to the spiral stairs at the edge of the room. Rowan followed close behind. The others sat in the seats on raised rows behind the commander's seat at the controls on the first row. Esma took a seat where the Secretary-General had been sitting next to Harry. She put her hand on his arm and he turned to look at her. His smile told her all she needed to know, that they were close, like Rowan and Dearden. Harry turned away from her and prepared to operate the mainframe controls.

When Knudsen stepped into the Portal, he looked around at the layout. The great crystal in the centre dominated the space and massive cables soared like flying buttresses from a metallic ring surrounding the crystal. Questions flooded in to Knudsen's mind., but the team didn't give him time to ask them.

"Are you ready Harry?" Dearden asked over the comms.

"Any time you are."

"Lars, be prepared for some changes . . . OK Harry, commence."

There was a deep humming noise and at the same time, a vibration those in the Portal felt deep inside. Knudsen flinched in surprise as he noticed a change in the outside wall – it appeared to be growing transparent and, as if through a veil, he could see the forest outside through the wall. There was a change in the landscape, the forest was huge; there was nothing but forest outside. Through the trees Knudsen glimpsed a large building in the distance reflecting the sunlight. And there was lightning and writhing black clouds high above.

* * *

"GUIDO, we confirm redirect. Course is on the nail with planned trajectory."

"MODCOM, Magellan EB 7 coming on stream on my mark . . . 5 . . . 4 . . . 3 . . . 2 . . . 1 Mark . . . Magellan on stream . . . speed ramping. Nibiru is now safe."

"And now we're not," Virgil Wright, the Flight Director said quietly to his backup sitting at his side. Then he spoke up. "MODCOM, report speed and condition of the module."

"Speed is now ten percent of c, the speed of light, and rising. We now have the fastest spacecraft ever launched from Earth. Condition of module is green. Sensors show payload condition to be stable. Speed now thirty-eight percent c and rising, we are not, repeat NOT near the throttle-stop."

"This is FLIGHT . . . give me the time to Brinkman 1."

"MODCOM, In Earth-time, we have one point five hours. Do you want the max projected speed as a percentage of c?"

"No, just get on with it."

* * *

Dearden and Rowan walked to the exit door of the Portal and pushed. There was a slight snick as the door opened to the outside world. Knudsen followed them out and hesitated just outside the door. He looked around. From the top of the hill, inside which all but the portal of the Hub was buried, he looked at the virgin forest. There was no clearing now. No tarmac. An overgrown lane led away toward the sunlit building he had seen from inside the Portal. And the air smelt so fresh. He breathed in deeply and scrambled after Dearden and Rowan, down the hill to the forest floor, where they were waiting.

"Do you think he will come?" Rowan asked Dearden.

"He will. He's bound to have seen the atmospheric disturbance. He will wonder if it is us." She nodded and looked expectantly in the direction of the great hall.

Dearden and Rowan went to a large tree and sat down by it. Knudsen joined them.

"What's going to happen?" Knudsen asked. There was a slight noise in the distance, a bell ringing rapidly that Rowan and Dearden recognised.

"He has seen the activity over the forest," Rowan said, standing and looking down the lane . . . waiting. Dearden stood and joined her, took hold of her hand.

Knudsen heard movement from somewhere down the lane, it sounded metallic and he could hear the sound of voices calling in the distance, and hoof-beats. He couldn't quite catch what they were saying, but then through the overgrown lane came a wild looking bunch of individuals on horseback, led by a big blond-haired man dressed in resplendent clothing. They dismounted.

"Rowan, Jem, you are here again." The man sounded over-joyed as he shouted in a mixture of English, and a language that to Knudsen had familiar intonations to his own Norwegian.

Rowan rushed to Leofwin, tears in her eyes. He clasped her to him and held her tight.

"Uncle, oh dear uncle Leofwin, it is good to see you—how are you and how is Aelfryth, is she well, and Ingwulf and Blythe?" There was a torrent of questions without a break where he could answer.

"Slowly, Rowan, be slow with your questions. They are all well, child. I am slightly older, and you?" Leofwin held Rowan at arm's length and looked at her clothing. He shook his head in disbelief at the changes, smiled broadly, and laughed. "How is your life with Jem, are you happy?"

"I am happy, more than I ever thought I would be, and there are so many things that are different in the time where we live."

"So I see," Leofwin nodded. He looked at Lars Knudsen's clothes, then at Dearden.

"Jem Dearden, it is good to see you, my friend," Leofwin spoke in a mixture of Anglo-Saxon and the modern English he had learned when Dearden, Mitch Doughty and Julia Linden-Barthorpe were previously in his time-frame. Leofwin looked Lars Knudsen up and down. "Who is your friend?" he asked Dearden.

"This is Lars Knudsen, a friend who has great influence, and he needs convincing of the power locked within the House of the West Wind."

"Ah, the House of the West Wind . . . I might look inside it with you one day myself. Are you staying?" The look in Leofwin's eyes said how much he wanted Rowan and Jem to remain for a while.

"Not this time, yet another dangerous situation draws us back."

"Again? You are a friend of danger, I think."

"I am afraid it comes looking for me."

Knudsen stepped forward. "Tell me Jem, what year is this?"

"Harry locked us on to 1064."

"1064?"

"This is Anglo-Saxon England."

There was silence, and then, "Why are you showing me this?"

"It is your injection of confidence. We have lived with this knowledge for well over a year now, you haven't. With what's to follow you need proof that what's happening is real."

"You said we would represent Earth; what exactly is to follow?"

"A long trip. But first, to somewhere local. We must go, Leofwin, but we will return. Probably next time we will stay for a while."

"Our lives are full of partings. Come back soon, before I am an old man."

Rowan and Knudsen stepped back into the Portal and Dearden closed the door on the Anglo-Saxon world.

"Where to now?" Knudsen asked.

"Just a short way from here, but almost a thousand years into the future, back in our own time. Harry—"

"Yes, Jem." Harry Stanway's voice came from somewhere near the junction of the wall and the ceiling.

"As we planned . . . do the transfer now."

The forest scene outside began to blur, and Knudsen looked away from the group of warriors who were running down the track through the trees away from the House of the West Wind. The ceiling and walls of the Portal were losing their transparency. And again, lightning tore through the dark clouds swirling above.

Knudsen had the feeling of softness surrounding him, gripping him firmly but gently and he lost sight of everything around him apart from Dearden and Rowan. The remarkable thing was that Rowan had been speaking to the warrior chief as if she knew him intimately. They obviously had great affection for each other.

Whatever the process was that the three of them were undergoing – Dearden said they had travelled through time – Lars Knudsen could see that the process was familiar to Dearden and Rowan. To him, it was incomprehensible, a step into the unknown.

* * *

Bill Templestone stepped through the door into the Knights' Sanctuary and locked it behind him. He was taking no chances, he had his Smith and Wesson in his combats pocket. He looked at his watch . . . twenty-five minutes to go. The event was to be in the room at the back, the one to the right, so he went to check it out. He removed some chairs from the room so that the floor space was clear, and then went back in.

Harry had tutored him about how to use the instrument he had with him, the Co-Orditrax. He stood in the middle of the room and glanced at the three co-ordinates on the screen which were related to the position of the Hub in Leofwin's Hundred. He pressed the button marked *Fix*.

Harry answered the expected call from Templestone's mobile.

"Locked on and ready for the temporal and dimensional shift, ten minutes to activation, get out of the room Bill."

"Don't worry, I'm on my way."

Templestone walked up the centre aisle, past the slab covering the entrance to the vault where Ramon Tailleur de Pierre's tomb lay. He sat in the furthest misericord from the room he had prepared, and he waited.

* * *

The sound of urgent talking came from the room at the bottom right of the sanctuary. Templestone looked at his watch. Dead on time. The door opened and Jem Dearden walked out first, followed by Rowan and Lars Knudsen, who looked serious.

"How did it go," Templestone asked. The question was aimed at Knudsen.

"I need time to think about that," Knudsen said. He sat down heavily on one of the misericords.

"All went well, but I think Lars has had enough for one day," Knudsen nodded to Dearden that he had.

"You've had an introduction to both a temporal and a geographical shift," Dearden said.

"I take it there's more of this to come." Knudsen stood up and looked around the ancient building.

"Correct. There's far more to come than you can even imagine. Remember you were told you would be part of a team that would be representing Earth?"

"I don't know if I believe that, but yes, that's what was said. So why are we in this place?"

"Because there are no third chances, no Plan C. We need to give you a shot of confidence in this process. The outcome for Earth is going to depend on the success of our mission. Why we are in this place begins with an event involving a man named Sho'mer that took place over four thousand years ago. We found his scroll in a vault over there." Dearden pointed to the area covered with a rug. "What we found was a record of Nibiru's first pass. You can read about the result in the book of Genesis."

62

Evan Blake was sitting close to Flight Director Virgil Wright, who had the overall responsibility to act on the telemetry feeding back from the End Time module. It was a far weightier responsibility than any other he had experienced in his career. He had to dispose of a weapon that could wipe out a planet.

The view from the forward-facing cameras showed the rapidly increasing size of Brinkman 1 as the End Time module made its final approach.

"RETRO, Magellan reverse thrust engaged. Orbital insertion will be on my mark, 3 . . . 2 . . . 1 . . . MARK. Guido, the spacecraft is now yours."

"GUIDO, thank you, we are monitoring progress."

"MODCOM, trigger actuators one and two should now have re-engaged. Trigger actuator number three is operational."

Virgil Wright turned away from his screen showing the summary of data from his systems managers and looked to the screen on his right. The mountainous, cratered surface of Brinkman 1 was passing by five hundred miles below. The telemetry on the screen to his left reported all systems nominal. Wright was feeling uneasy. Uppermost in his mind was Charles Villiers and his End Time test. Although in micro format, it had destroyed an island which was ten miles by three and a half. It was a comforting thought that the destruction had been finite. Nevertheless, the Flight Director was sweating more than he had when the prototype Condor VI Heavy Lift first arose on a column of fire.

"Is the drop system nominal?" Evan Blake's voice cut through Wright's thoughts.

"Telemetry indicates that is so. End Time module is programmed to drop ten minutes after stabilisation of orbit. The package will shortly be on its way down." There was a slight tremor in Wright's hand as he took out his handkerchief and wiped his forehead.

Three fifty-eight in the morning and the team controlling the Gemini South telescope had Brinkman 1 in their field of view. They were in direct contact with Flight Control on Turaroa and Sir Willoughby Pierpoint and his team at the Portal in Leofwin's Hundred. The astronomers were waiting for a visual of the drop which had been programmed into the End Time module's computers. The voiceover from Flight Control in real time, preceded visual and audio signal acquisition from the cameras on board the module by eighteen minutes.

Gemini heard Module Communications announce the start of the drop sequence.

"MODCOM, do not forget, there is an eighteen-minute delay between receipt of telemetry and the event at Brinkman 1. End Time deorbit burn is underway. Drop initiated . . . altitude now four hundred eighty miles. Present rate of controlled descent, one point five miles per second."

"FIDO, Signal acquired. Dynamic loading parameters are acceptable."

"GUIDO, tracking is on the nail to the geographical centre of Brinkman 1."

"MODCOM, shields jettisoned . . . altitude forty-two miles, altitude sensors have engaged End Time trigger."

"GUIDO, slight drift, auto-corrected by cryogenic thrusters, geographic centre of target re-acquired."

"MODCOM, altitude twenty-one miles . . . rate of descent zero point five miles per second."

"RETRO, cryogenic braking initiated to acquire approach velocity."

"MODCOM, altitude ten miles, rate of descent, five hundred feet per second."

"GUIDO, target still nominal."

"RETRO, cryogenic braking final burn complete."

"MODCOM, altitude zero point nine miles. Approach velocity two-zero MPH."

In the Gemini South observatory nine thousand feet up on Cerro Pachon, the video recorders were running and broadcasting. Filters were set. Eyes were red-rimmed with tiredness and concentration on the Adaptive Optics screen.

Excitement and apprehension sharpened the silence as the scientists in Carlos Mendulas' team awaited the outcome of the drop, and then Flight Dynamics' voice at Turaroa said the signal was acquired. Light from Brinkman 1 was reflecting down through the optics and the astronomers eyeballed the image on the screen.

The team in the Control Room at the Portal followed the drop process from the on board videocams, as did the billions of people worldwide who were watching the broadcast.

"This is MODCOM; impact will be in five seconds from my mark, 5 . . . 4 . . . 3 . . ."

And sixteen seconds later, two seconds early, the screen went black.

Carlos Mendulas and the other six scientists at Gemini South followed the real-time commentary from Turaroa, describing the End Time weapon's descent onto Brinkman 1. At the same time, they viewed the asteroid through the 'scope. The magnification of the telescope was insufficient to pick up the descent of the End Time weapon, but the asteroid's crater-scarred surface suddenly dissolved into chaos and then there was nothing but blackness.

There was a collective of comments that Carlos heard as he ran outside. From his position on the plateau at the top of Cerro Pachon, the night sky was filled with the luminescence of countless stars and galaxies. He peered into the sky in the direction the telescope was facing and there it was. The Brinkman area was unmistakable because of its absence of background luminosity and an overlay of a deeper shade of black than the surrounding night sky. From where Carlos viewed the phenomenon the effect was small, but noticeable. He shivered and went back inside.

"Come and look at this," the Australian astrophysicist Jamie Anderson called, as Carlos came through the door. Anderson's skin looked a shade paler than his normal tanned good looks. The image on the screen alarmed Carlos. Previously there had been Brinkman 1, crater strewn and barren. Now there was an absence of background stars and galaxies. In place of the asteroid, a mass was rotating. Intense flashes of light displaying violent energy betrayed its clockwise direction. The shape and movement of the phenomenon was similar to a vicious tornado Carlos had once experienced in central Mississippi's Tornado Alley. He was at a loss to estimate the true size of the event, other than it being on a colossal scale. He licked his lips. They were suddenly dry. He reached for a nearby bottle of water, uncapped it and drank.

"Professor Villiers weapon has created a black hole, I think," a scientist at his side suggested.

"I do believe it has," Carlos said. He thumbed Harry Stanway's number into his mobile.

Harry picked up on the second ring. He switched his mobile to speaker mode so the others in the Hub could hear.

"What do you have, Carlos?" Harry's tone of voice was clipped. There was a lot at stake. Pierpoint looked pensive, Lars Knudsen, expectant.

"It looks as though your Professor Villiers' End Time weapon has created a black hole," Carlos said.

"I had a suspicion that was what his research was leading to. Is it fading?"

"Looks as though the energy is decreasing."

"Also as I expected. What's it like now?"

"The mass has lost seventeen percent of its original size. Our instrumentation shows its size is now decreasing at a rate of one percent every twenty-two seconds."

"Are you getting spectrometer readings?"

"Every instrument we have has been brought to bear. This is a once in a lifetime opportunity."

Harry heard Dearden whisper, "He might be surprised."

"What about Brinkman 1?" Harry asked Carlos.

"I'll tell you when we have a clear field of view. Looks as though that will be in thirty minutes if the size continues to decrease at the same rate."

"Ring me back, will you?"

* * *

"What happens now, Harry?" Templestone asked. Harry looked self-assured . . . not in an arrogant way, but quietly confident.

"Looks as though End Time has done its job, although to what extent we will find out when we get the call back from Gemini South."

"Our time has come now, Jem," Knudsen said to Dearden.

"No doubt about that. We'll get on with it after Carlos calls Harry."

*　*　*

Harry's phone rang. Carlos Mendulas gave unexpected news.

"End Time has helped out more than we expected. It's taken out the whole of the Brinkman group and more besides. A whole tract of the Asteroid Belt has disappeared."

"OK, at least that's ensured damage limitation for Earth from the Asteroid belt in the future. Anything negative occurred?"

"Nothing immediately obvious. We are studying all of the feedback from our instruments, but the data will take months to analyse. From a visual point of view, nothing has happened that is detrimental to Earth."

Observatories locked onto the area previously occupied by the Brinkman group of asteroids. The Very Large Array in the Atacama Desert of New Mexico confirmed the findings of Gemini South. It also picked up a fast burst radio signal that they termed FRB 100938, at 2 GHz, indicating the presence of a rotating radio signal sometimes associated with a black hole.

Parkes, the large dish in New South Wales, also picked up the signal, and when Jodrell Bank locked on they confirmed the disappearance of not only the Brinkman group, but also the destruction of asteroids in the range of plus and minus nine-point seven-five square degrees of arc about Brinkman 1. They assumed that the destruction followed the same pattern in the cube dimension. A swathe of matter had disappeared from the asteroid belt.

Observatory after observatory confirmed the same results. *What the hell*, shouted the people who were consumed with anger. Confidence in the outcome of the Nibiru program amongst the general public had disintegrated. *Trompé de nouveau* was the cry and it echoed over villages and towns. The anger was getting out of control and it was expressed by the knife, the gun and petrol.

*   *   *

Entered into the Great Annals of the Wasiri Chanchiya was how one particularly courageous Earth, who went by the name of Nathaniel Devenish, spent many hours digging away the soil to expose the entrance to the Portal lying at the level of the forest floor which had been long out of use.

In the time period that the Earths called the early eighteenth century, the Devenish Earth wrote many notes. The adventurers traversing the Grid, who were present in the portal when Devenish was working, decided to test him. They let him dig through the soil to the disused ancient entrance on the forest floor, and they left the door unlocked on the inside so that he could enter.

As soon as he saw the reconstructions of the creatures in the room of exhibits, the Devenish Earth screamed loudly and ran at speed from the Portal, not even looking behind him. Two Earth-days later he came back with three Earths and some weapons, and they filled in the digging. Five and a half Earth years went by, and then the Devenish returned and dug his way to the entrance once again. This time he had four of the Earths with him, and an arsenal of vicious weapons.

When Lan-Si-Nu was in his youth, the tutor spoke of the interest sparked off by the complexity of the aliens called Earths. They possessed intelligence, but more importantly, they possessed an inbuilt moral code that made them special. Lan-Si-Nu developed an interest in the people. Not that he liked how they looked from the images gathered by the Travellers. They looked disgusting, and the returning Travellers told of how the Earths stunk. *They are foul*, recorded Sar-Theit-Nos, an ancient who was recognised as one of the greatest of all the Travellers and one of the first who walked on the Second One.

Lan-Si-Nu was determined to find out more about the Earths and specialised in them when he grew out of the Primary Learning. He gained the Cap of Distinction, Growth Three, and devoted the next years to learning everything he could about the Earths and the planet where they lived, the Second One.

In the building housing the Great Annals, row upon row of volumes contained records stretching back years without number. The volumes described the exploration of galaxies by means of the Grid and the Annals were accessed through mind–links placed around the perimeter of the room.

Due to his study, Lan-Si-Nu developed great affection for the Earths, which grew more so when he and his crew became marooned on their planet. As time went by they met Jeremiah Dearden and his group of people who were determined to right the wrongs on Earth as much as they could. This drew Jem

Dearden and the others close to Lan-Si-Nu's heart, particularly when the Harry Stanway Earth reverse-engineered the Portal to enable the Wasiri-Chanchiyans to return home.

Now the Earths needed urgent help and Lan-Si-Nu awaited the outcome of how they dealt with planet Chakrakan.

* * *

Evan Blake's phone rang. It was Harry Stanway and Jem Dearden on a conference line. Pierpoint was there too, along with Lars Knudsen. Through the speakers, Blake heard conversation amongst a group of people in the background. Blake's effort with the Condor VI heavy Lift was successful in a way, in that a target which would have been a threat to Earth in the future was destroyed and the Magellan engine had superseded all performance expectations, achieving a major proportion of the speed of light. Blake returned the data to its folder with the written memo to his molecular engineers to concentrate on the refinement of the antiproton element, which would probably increase Magellan's performance to attain the speed of light. He turned his attention to the call. But then, there was the Grid. Would that eliminate all current modes of motive power?

"Jem, there has been moderate success with Plan A with the destruction of the Brinkman group. It looks as though Charles Villiers' weapon has produced an unexpected side effect."

"That was not altogether unexpected," Harry intervened. His leisure time had been spent following up the research he found in Villiers' briefcase.

"I trust you have your Plan B ready for action?" Blake asked Dearden.

"We have, that's why we called you. We are ready to make contact with the Wasiri-Chanchiya. We want you and your team to be in on it. How are they at keeping the process under wraps?"

"They can be trusted implicitly."

63

The gentle heat from a double sun began to burn off an early morning mist from the temperate land. The mist was typical, but by the time this day developed into full suns-light it would be far from ordinary for the Hnioss. The individual members of the Hnioss, Hnion, originated from many different planets in diverse galaxies, but they all resided on the world where all things began, Wasiri-Poya, in a land called Ahra-Than.

In the middle of the day, the Hnioss was summoned to consider a developing emergency. This was unusual because the affairs of the administration normally followed a similar pattern, the dissemination of new knowledge found during grid exploration. Emergencies would occur maybe once in a lifetime.

The Preceptor of the Hnioss, Krel-Rahn sat in the ornate Chair of Focus and raised his right hand for silence. The silence was slow to develop because of the anticipation of what was to follow. Excitement echoed from the roof of the vast chamber, but gradually the chatter died down and there was silence amongst the Hnion.

Krel-Rahn lowered his hand and put on his cap of office to give him the right to speak.

"We need to inform you of a development to do with the planet Chakrakan, which is orbiting the Sun, Neros, in the 'E' type spiral Galaxy Phaelon 23057C. Background information needs to be explained for you of the Hnioss to understand the events taking place.

"Deep in the Great Annals, there is an account of a rebellion that occurred on Chakrakan. It spread to the nearby planet, Earth when some of the Chakrakans migrated there. Earth, the Second One, in turn became full of violence. The Chakrakans rejected all dialogue and were ruthless in their pursuit of power. They destroyed all the life on another planet in the Neros system in order to extract its minerals.

"The Hnioss, those many, many years ago, discussed the issue in depth. They concluded that Chakrakan had to be cocooned and re-orbited for the safety of the remaining planets in the Neros system. A well-tested system was to be used. Twice previously our Engineers of the Grid had been called upon to use the forces of the Grid to re-orbit minor planets which were in dangerous orbits. The first two operations were successful. At the time they were described as a triumph of Macro-Cosmic Engineering."

There was rapt attention throughout the auditorium. Hearing parts of the Great Annals repeated enthralled the Hnion, particularly when Krel-Rahn spoke. It was rare that he did so. When he did speak, his basso profundo words always had great significance when they reached the ears of those listening. His intonation of voice projected meaning and beauty, even with the most mundane subjects.

"But then a problem occurred with re-orbiting Chakrakan. The engineers and the other learned Wasiri applied the identical procedures that were successful in the previous orbital engineering challenges. The mathematics and the physical laws to be manipulated were identical, but Chakrakan assumed an orbit that was described at the time as pre-defined. The planet could not be synchronised to the orbit that the forces applied to it defined. The processes used were re-examined many times, and they proved to be correct in every detail.

"The learned ones did manage to cocoon the planet, which protected its population and also prevented them from causing others harm. We read in the Great Annals that when the ancients understood that the orbital situation was out of their control, they left Chakrakan alone, and were content to observe the events that took place.

"All of the Chakrakans remaining on the planet Earth were removed by the continents being inundated by water. A small number of Earths survived who had no hatred. Grid Commander Lan-Si-Nu will explain what happened next."

Krel-Rahn removed his cap of office and indicated the illustrious space in front of the Chair of Focus where speakers stood to address the Hnioss. There was a rustling of movement in the ranks of seated Hnion as they prepared to listen to the adventurer who had recently been promoted to Grid Commander because of his service to the planet, Earth, the Second One. He looked around the ranks of Hnion, at the diverse galactic races of Dimension One. As they settled into silence he put on his cap of office as a mark of respect, allowing him to speak to the Hnioss.

"In our marooning on the Second One we became close to a group of the Earths who live close to the Portal NJA 4902385. These men, as they call the male of the species, and some females, the ones who give birth, show special qualities because they pursue justice wherever they can exert their influence. They call their group SHaFT. Their approach to issues of criminality is imperfect because they are primitive in their learning, but their core belief is to right the wrongs of their world if they can.

"The Earths recently discovered that Chakrakan is on a near-collision course with their planet and they planned to annihilate the threat with a weapon that one of their learned men devised some of their years ago. Subsequently, their instrumentation revealed to them that Chakrakan is populated and their initial plan of destruction has been aborted.

"The Earths' motives have been proved to be benign because they have destroyed the weapon that they intended to use against Chakrakan. They made this decision when they realised that the planet is populated. This action proves that some of the Earths align themselves with the Higher Ethic, the preservation of life. I recommend, because of their alignment, that they represent their case to us in preparation for assistance and for membership of the Hnioss. I particularly recommend the Earth whose name is Harry Stanway to attain recognition for his services to Wasiri-Poya. He enabled us to return home." Lan-Si-Nu removed his cap of office and returned to his place. There was a murmur of assent and then enthusiastic applause.

The Preceptor prepared to speak again. When his cap was replaced, he stood. "The beings of the planet, Earth, request advancement to galactic recognition. This would also allow them full use of the Grid and to have due representation in the Hnioss. Do we stand?" The assembly stood as one.

"Then it is agreed that they make a representation before the Hnioss for assistance." There was a cacophony of assent. The Preceptor gazed around the chamber and said, "We will communicate with the Earths and set a time for their transfer."

64

Secretary-General Knudsen, used to negotiation at the highest level, headed-up the team at Dearden Hall as they revised the draft of the form of words to put before the Hnioss. Pierpoint was there, Dearden and Doughty, Harry, Templestone, Jules and Lee Wynter. The new ones were there too, Rowan and Esma, Clive Fraser and Storm Petrel. By two thirty in the morning they had thrashed all the ideas around. The draft was written up into a final copy and they went to snatch a few hours' sleep.

It was nine o'clock in the morning. Nervous tension was at an all-time high as the team selected for the transfer readied themselves in the Hub. The others were there, each with a predefined function. There was a large television on a table placed temporarily at the front of the Control Room. The Nibiru Channel, whose ratings had overtaken all the other news channels, was receiving a live broadcast from Gemini South, three hours earlier in their day.

The sky was remarkably clear on the summit of Cerro Pachon and by the magnification of the telescope the view of Nibiru filled the screen. Apart from a slight ghosting of the image, the planet's appearance looked very similar to the Earth when viewed from space. There was the blue of oceans. There were continents, drifting cloud formations and the green of forests. Connie Rios from the SETI Institute, was giving a voiceover. A news ticker with the words *Plan B, keep tuned for updates*, was stationery at the bottom of the screen.

It had become a habit for people to look into the sky. Nibiru had moved away from the immediate vicinity of the sun and was in plain view. The last Doppler Shift calculation put it at twenty-four and a half million miles from arrival, marginally over twelve days to closest encounter. As people the world over looked up and saw the bright object growing in the sky, fear took over and people entreated the old gods for support. Just as it had been years before machinery and high tech, raw fear of the unknown stalked the world and the gods were called on.

The commentators did well. Some of them had been in combat zones under incoming fire. This was different. There was always an end to war. Maybe a war's time of ending was further in the future than the most able commanders prophesied, but there was always a silver lining to look forward to at the end of a conflict. This was different. Naked fear of the end was ever present with the approaching threat in the heavens.

Mitch Doughty had constructed some stands which he had placed on the floor in front of the seats in the Control Room so that their feet didn't dangle. These things mattered to Harry Stanway. He was still young enough to take himself too seriously at times. How he looked, particularly with Esma close by was important and his feet swinging about off the floor as he sat in the seat made for a far taller being, was not cool.

"It's almost time," Harry said, from his position in the commander's chair. They gathered around, expectant, waiting for twelve mid-day on the Caruthers Chrono clock fixed to the wall. Harry turned the key, one, two, and on the third pressure the large centre screen in front of them illuminated.

The recorded information stopped and Lan-Si-Nu took its place. He was with another person, shorter in stature, who looked creased up and ugly. They were seated together on a small flat area at the centre of the huge room Dearden and the others had seen when they spoke to La-Si-Nu a few days previously. The room was colourful. It resembled an amphitheatre with seats rising in tiers all around.

The shorter being at Lan-Si-Nu's side had a visage as if set in a perpetual frown. Lan-Si-Nu said some words of greeting in the language those in the Hub remembered for its beautiful cadences, and the other being's features became mobile and contorted into a parody of a smile.

"This is Krel-Rahn, he is the current Preceptor of the Hnioss," Lan-Si-Nu said. "He is from your own galaxy, the Milky Way, that we know as Phaelon 23057C. Krel-Rahn's world is in the ninth sector, on your own turf, I think you would say." Krel-Rahn nodded in a slow sort of way.

"Hey man, can you see us?" Lee Wynter challenged.

"We can. Matter decoding cells are implanted into the walls of the Portal. We are viewing you in String Code Transmission."

"String Code Transmission?" Harry's curiosity was tugging at the words.

"It has to do with DNA pseudo replication."

Krel-Rahn leant toward Lan-Si-Nu and said a few words in a quiet basso voice. Lan-Si-Nu nodded and said, "There is urgency in your situation. Questions can be answered when times are less critical. Krel-Rahn asks if you have selected those who will appear before the Hnioss."

"We have," Dearden replied. "We have our highest elected representative here, Lars Knudsen. He will lead our party. There are five others. Sir Willoughby Pierpoint, Mitch Doughty, Julia Linden-Barthorpe, me and Harry Stanway. You want Harry to come, don't you?"

"We do." Lan-Si-Nu whispered in Krel-Rahn's ear. The Preceptor whispered back.

"The Preceptor said that Harry Stanway's name should be first on your list, not last." Lan-Si-Nu saw questioning in the eyes of the Earths.

"Harry Stanway has deeper insight into our ways than the rest of you have. His mind has no pre-conceived notions." Lan-Si-Nu shot straight from the hip.

"Of all the damn ch—"

"Jules, shut it," Dearden sliced the air with his hand for silence. It wasn't the time for temperament.

"Harry has made great progress understanding the Hub and the Nibiru situation," Dearden said to the two aliens.

"He has. Now, there is much to do and little time to do it in. Great forces are to be brought into operation if your plea to the Hnioss is successful. The sooner we begin the process, the better the chance of success will be."

"What shall we bring with us?" Dearden asked, after a moment of thought.

"There is no need to bring anything. Just come here and be yourselves. When before the Hnioss, speak of your desire to see justice done on your world with no harm to others. Cite the example of how you have recently dealt with Nibiru, you diverted the End Time weapon when you discovered the planet was populated. When you have done that, make your request for assistance. The Hnioss will detect your motives, as I have done."

Knudsen asked, "When can we travel the Grid? It is desperately urgent, our planet, Earth is descending into chaos." Another portable screen in the Control-Room tuned to Sky News showed burning and looting in place after place across the continents.

"We need three of your hours to prepare the Hnioss. What is your time on Earth?"

"Zero eleven twenty GMT."

"Make the transfer at fifteen hundred hours GMT. I will shortly explain how you will do that. First, I will tell you the location of our planet, Wasiri-Poya."

"We wanted to know that a long while back," Harry said.

"I know. We are many light-years distant from your planet. Our position from Earth lies in the direction of the constellation you know as Ursa Major. Our galaxy is out of the range of even your best telescopes and it was the beginning of the work of the First Cause.

"You will not need positioning information for the transfer. The Super-quantum will construct the node-chain for you and you will be transported over the Grid to the destination automatically. You will travel to the Home Portal of the entire Grid, which is on our planet, Wasiri-Poya. The Home Portal is identified by the symbol, Onnoth, which carries the meaning, The First One, in Wasiri-Chanchiyan.

"Listen to this information, all of you. For the transfer, you will need to follow these instructions. Harry, from where you are sitting in the Commander's chair, you will see a separate panel which has a circle of twenty-one keys to the right of the main central panel. Do not touch any of them yet. There is a key at the centre marked with a symbol similar to your mathematical infinity sign, which we call the Onnoth."

Harry saw the twenty keys, with the Onnoth key, marked ∾, at the centre.

"When you press any of those keys, the Portal auto-sets the destination rather than having to enter the cosmic position manually. The central key cannot be altered. It is pre-set to the

Wasiri-Poya Home-Portal. All the outer keys of the circle can be pre-set to other destinations. For your transfer to appear before the Hnioss, you will first of all activate the Portal and then you must only use the Onnoth key. Press it once. Who is taking charge of the Control-Room during your journey?"

"That will be Matt Roberts." Roberts acknowledged his role with a movement of his hand.

*　*　*

1455 hours. With five minutes to go the tension in the Control-Room reached an all-time high. Conversation was minimal and then there was silence.

It was broken by Lan-Si-Nu with three minutes to go. "A word of advice, Jem. During Nibiru's closet approach those of your people who are not coming to the Hnioss are best to be in the Portal. If necessary they could escape by using the Grid. Remember, using the Onnoth key would bring them to Wasiri-Poya."

Dearden looked at the team, saw them respond.

With one minute to go. Lan-Si-Nu came back on the central screen. "Harry, the first intergalactic crossing over the grid is always the most thrilling; it will be strong in your memories. Are you people of Earth ready?"

"We are ready." Harry spoke for all seven in the Portal who were ready to go. They were standing one side of the great crystal, facing the outer wall. Matt Roberts thumbed the large button which brought the Portal from latent to full power. A deep hum filled the cavernous space. The familiar dark clouds rapidly gathered overhead and lightning ripped through the sky. Roberts' finger hovered over the Onnoth.

65

The Caruthers Chrono registered 1500 hours. Roberts stabbed the Onnoth button and the transfer from node to node across intergalactic space began. Rowan saw Jem and the others fade and then disappear.

Dearden recognised the cushioning effect. The crystal at the centre of the Portal was coruscating violently with an internal fire and movement more than he had observed in previous transfers. This time, instead of the forest outside changing to how it had been a thousand years ago, as it had with the temporal transfers, the scene outside morphed to a deep velvet blue, interlaced with the myriad stars and galaxies of the cosmos.

Dearden surveyed the team; Mitch Doughty, always dependable, hands by his side, ready for action and Lee Wynter, whose presence reassured him. Harry Stanway, easy with the bizarre situation. Julia, enthralled at the scene beyond the protective cocooning. Lars Knudsen, pointing to Norway. He said he could just make out Trondheim. Pierpoint spoke quietly to him and they laughed.

The Portal rotated and the Earth was in view, jewel-like against the background of interstellar space. Lan-Si-Nu must have planned the transfer that way to show them their home in its setting. A few more degrees of rotation and the reason for the mission, Nibiru, now half the size of a full Moon, came into view. Apart from a haze surrounding the planet it looked remarkably like Earth, blue overlaid in places with a patchy white cloud cover and there was the outline of continents, but no polar ice.

The whole scene changed and the star field of the Milky Way lensed, elongated and disappeared. They came to a brief standstill on the surface of a different, frozen world with a cyclonic wind tearing at a barely discernible icy landscape. A screen near to the exit door from the Portal illuminated and writing in English characters appeared, Erigon System 5, Nihar.

"Be interesting to know the route, Mitch." Julia Linden-Barthorpe leant over to Mitch Doughty. Her voice was up-tight. "I noticed that we were facing Ursa Major, so this world could be anywhere in the direction of that star-field."

"It's impossible to gauge what the route is, or where we are."

"Maybe they'll tell us, we could ask . . . just for the record," she said.

And then they were on the move again. They remained at each node for a sufficient amount of time to observe the great diversity and in some cases, the bizarre nature of the environments. Harry was particularly interested when the progression across the grid stopped briefly on one particular planet. Immense irregular masses of writhing matter were scudding about the landscape. Harry likened the phenomenon to two poles of a bar magnet, like or unlike, reacting due to their close proximity and he noticed that the surface of the masses was covered with moving tendril-like appendages, which implied they were organic.

After twelve such increments when the Portal paused in different landscapes, they finally came to a halt and the powerful electronic hum that had accompanied them during the transfer shut down. The window and ceiling remained transparent so they were able to see outside.

They were in a large open space, surrounded by elegant looking structures and trees, some of which looked similar to those on Earth, and other life-forms which were totally unrecognisable, being long and cylindrical with twig-like projections at the top along which were regularly placed spines. They had movement, which indicated they were a mix of both plant and animal.

"I think they are a macro form of a Euglena," Harry said. "If I'm right they would function by photosynthesis and ingestion. Instead of a flagellum providing movement, they possess those appendages at the base; see how they glide like a centipede?"

They took his word for it.

Harry looked skyward and shielded his eyes against the brilliance of the double-sun core of the planetary system. He recognised Lan-Si-Nu's voice speaking in his native language, and then he welcomed them in perfect English. The information screen above the door displayed the destination in English characters. The galaxy, Thar-Thellin spiral. The solar system, Stessar Tharon. Planet 7, Wasiri-Poya.

The outer door clicked open and they stepped out into a busy area where there were beings of all manner of shapes and colours. There he stood, a few yards away, Lan-Si-Nu, his hands outstretched in welcome, with the Preceptor of the Hnioss, Krel-Rahn, standing by his side. The Preceptor was wearing colourful regalia hung loosely about his person. Fen-Nu and Thal-Nar were there. And a number of other individuals of diverse races were standing at the rear, dignitaries by the look of their ornamented dress.

It was difficult to tell the mood of the occasion amongst the aliens ranged in front of them. There was obvious interest because some of the shorter ones were shifting position to get a better view of the visitors from Earth.

"We did not expect you to communicate with us so soon after we left your planet," Lan-Si-Nu said to Dearden.

"I'd rather it had been in different circumstances."

"I'm sure you would. But I said we would help you if we could."

The Preceptor spoke. He had a surprisingly loud basso profundo voice, for someone so small and squat. "So, you are Harry Stanway," Krel-Rahn was on a mobile platform. He came close to Harry. The alien touched a small lever and the platform extended so that he could look into Harry's eyes.

"Yes, I see it now, you have a questing spirit, Harry. You thirst for knowledge. You will have much of interest lying before you in your life . . . welcome. All of you are very welcome." The Preceptor's platform sank down. "Now you can go to your lodging." Krel-Rahn motioned for them to follow.

After a few yards, they entered a tall structure with a colourful façade. A moving staircase, surprisingly like one to be found in a department store on Earth, apart from it being stationary and that it had vertical poles to hold, was waiting to take them underground. Lan-Si-Nu led the way onto the escalator and as soon as the last of the dignitaries stepped on board the vehicle began to move, gaining speed rapidly downward. It soon levelled out and came to a halt in a busy intersection where there was line after line of long tubular vehicles.

Harry thought the waiting vehicles had a similar appearance to worms. He could see annular segmentation and as they approached the nearest vehicle, there was a slow expansion along its length, as if growing to accommodate a specific number of travellers.

A door swished open in the glistening surface. Seats were ranged along the length of the vehicle. Each of the aliens, after they were seated, pressed a button on a panel let into the wall and their seat adjusted to their individual frame.

Lan-Si-Nu sat next to Harry and smiled at Harry's puzzled expression. "An extension to virtual reality," he explained.

"Ah, you are full of surprises. We are going to learn so much from you." Harry thumbed his seat button. The seat enclosed him and became ultra-comfortable.

The vehicle began to move. The sense of forward motion was intense and Will Pierpoint felt himself being pressed into his seat.

"What do you think of all this, Lars?" Knudsen didn't respond immediately. Pierpoint glanced at him. "Are you OK?"

"Sure, I'm OK. This is what we do every day."

Before long the sensation of motion stopped. The seats expanded but retained the height signature of the wearer. The door swished open.

"How far have we travelled?" Harry asked Lan-Si-Nu.

"On Wasiri-Poya, a little over two hundred of your kilometres. Over the Grid, you travelled seven hundred and fifty-three million light years. With the discovery of travel across the Grid we learned that the formulaic use of t, time became fluid. Harry, your concept of the barrier of light-speed is archaic, the barrier can be bypassed. Barriers exist in the mind. The physics of this universe and others is malleable and the achievement of spectacular results depend upon the ingenuity of original thinking. Come, the others are waiting for us. We are at the land of Ahra-Than, where exists the Hnioss and your lodgings."

After what seemed a short journey, the group mounted an upward escalator. Above ground, the dignitaries, apart from Lan-Si-Nu, separated and made their way toward a tall, wide building with large lettering in the Wasiri-Chanchiyan language displayed above an ornate entranceway. Harry, familiar now with the alien lettering, translated.

"That's the Hnioss."

Dearden scanned the building. "Yeah. And let's hope we can convince these guys to help us," he said.

Lan-Si-Nu led the group along a wide pathway that wound through luxuriant shrubs in an area laid out with dense, short leafed foliage similar to grass. Many life-forms, obviously intelligent because of their directed conversation and responses, were making their way in the opposite direction. Some, but not all of them were humanoid in form and visage.

The party from Earth arrived at a long, low building that appeared to be made of a similar ceramic material to the Hub, back on Earth. The tall entrance door swung open and they entered a brightly-lit hall with many exits. Lan-Si-Nu indicated for them to gather in front of him. "This building has a dual function. The level above ground and the five levels below serve as an administration, library and archive centre. Much of the structure for living accommodation on Wasiri-Poya lies below-ground and that accommodation begins on level six. Above ground we work with the planet's potential to be self-sustaining; in our distant past, we eventually learned not to interfere with the process." The tall alien indicated for them to follow. "Your accommodation is on the sixty-eighth level; to reach that we will use the Sarath."

"What is the Sarath?" Harry asked.

"It is a gravity lens which allows transport up or down in a vertical direction."

Knudsen and Pierpoint walked side by side with Lan-Si-Nu.
"When is our case to be heard?" Pierpoint asked.

"Tomorrow. There is a special sitting due to the urgency of your situation. I shall stay with you overnight and help with your preparations. I shall also be at your side during the hearing, as your advocate."

They entered a car somewhat similar to an elevator and covered the downward distance in a matter of seconds, without any sensation of discomfort. When they exited the Sarath the area on level sixty-eight opened into a wide vista as far as the eye could see. It was punctuated by Sarath shafts every hundred yards or so and walkways moved in the four directions of the compass from a central staging platform. Again, beings of all different forms and sizes were going about their tasks. None appeared to be hurried.

"Come, your accommodation is in the Sector of the Artisans. It translates as 54, The Astro, 10. We will take the northerly walkway."

* * *

Discussions finalised with a satisfactory nod from Lan-Si-Nu. "You are ready," he said.

The representatives of Earth shifted restlessly in their seats. It had been a long session. Lee Wynter hummed a quiet tune. He was usually ebullient but now, not surprisingly, he was in a reflective mood. He went to Mitch Doughty, who stretched and yawned and they chatted.

"This is bizarre, man," Wynter said. "Apart from the Nibiru thing, we could be on holiday in some Dorchester Hotel place with all things laid on. The only thing is that there is no sea . . . anyone seen any sea around here?"

Sir Willoughby Pierpoint stood. He looked tired, Dearden thought. They all did, no doubt, after everything they had been through, the responsibility, venturing into the unknown. But Dearden still saw the strength of the man who headed up SHaFT. Pierpoint still had fighting spirit tempered with strength of character, good nature and courage, but he looked exhausted and was showing his age. Maybe Will Pierpoint's time had come to take a step back. He had been Dearden's friend and mentor and of late he had been preparing him to take the reins of SHaFT.

* * *

Morning. In her apartment, an artificial picture window showed a double sunrise and a lowering red-coloured moon of massive size, a live display of the scene above ground. Julia luxuriated in the comfort of the softest bed she had ever experienced. At least, that is how it seemed. She had been dog-tired after the grid experience followed by the introduction to the city under the ground on Wasiri-Poya. She had floated into a soft oblivion, somewhat surreal in itself considering the excitement of the past few hours.

When Jem inserted the key into the control panel in the Hub Julia had no idea how the forward progression of events would transpire, the snapshot of scenes viewed from the portals as they traversed the Grid. Lan-SI-Nu told them he had sent them on a tour, slowed the transit down to give them a taste of the Grid.

Julia's sleep had been restless. At one point her dream was strong. She was there in full preparation for Shotokan combat because she knew a challenge was coming. Her fiery expertise had coiled like spring-tempered steel, ready for action because Nibiru had staring eyes. It took on the quasi-human form of an ogre in the maw of an ancient stone bridge, from where gushed a wild stream.

The ogre slowly emerged, a giant of a beast . . . Julia leapt into the water, swam to the surface in easy strokes and challenged the ogre who caught her defiance and retreated into the shelter of the bridge. She followed into the shadows.

"Jules." There was a knock on her door. Her heart was hammering. Dearden's voice came again, was more insistent.

"Jules, we've got half an hour before we have to go."

"OK — OK, I'm awake. She roused herself and clambered out of bed. She looked at the window. The suns were still low on the horizon, one was yellow and the other a bright orange, and clouds were wispy in an azure blue sky.

Lan-Si-Nu told them that the proceedings would be translated into the tongues of the galactic entities present and the team were supplied with earpieces. They entered the Hnioss through an elaborate doorway, Lan-Si-Nu leading the way. He insisted that Harry was to follow him.

"Lars, you come next and then Sir Willoughby. Jem, you must enter next with Lee Wynter. Mitch, you come into the Hnioss with Jules." Lan-Si-Nu had taken to using the shortened form of Julia's name. "When we get into the Hnioss you will see the Chair of Focus in front of us. You will take your position there, Lars. The chair will adjust to your shape; I will stand at your side. The rest of you will sit on the row of seats behind the Chair of Focus. Lars, if at any point you need my help, ask for it."

The entrance subway led into the centre of the Hnioss, where seating was arranged for the new arrivals. All the members of the Hnioss were seated when they walked into the vast indoor space and an expectant silence reigned. Lan-Si Nu indicated where they were to sit and he pointed to the place for Knudsen, the Chair of Focus, which had a podium before it. A few paces away another podium, occupied by Krel-Rahn on his mobile platform, faced the travellers from Earth. He raised his hand and all in the auditorium became quiet.

66

Lars Knudsen put the case of the danger to the Earth eloquently, and then asked for help from those gathered in the Hnioss. As Knudsen was speaking, the translation of his words into the languages of those in attendance had a marked effect. There was a definite reaction, but whether positive or negative was impossible to discern.

Pierpoint surveyed the scene. The colourful array of many different biological forms was seated or standing, depending on physiological structure. They were grouped in sections according to their place of origin and form. Some were giant, some miniscule, but all were quite obviously engaged in the proceedings judging by their reaction as Knudsen concluded the case for Earth. As he finished speaking and sat down the thronged amphitheatre of the Hnioss, previously quiet, erupted into a cacophony of noise throughout the audible spectrum.

Krel-Rahn stood and all in the great auditorium quietened. "We will now adjourn and consider the case put by representative Knudsen," his sonorous voice informed the Hnioss. The preceptor and his podium sank into the floor. The space was filled by a section of floor that blended into the rest, and no sign was left of the previous occupant.

Lan-Si-Nu accompanied them back to their lodgings.

"What happens now?" Doughty asked.

"The ethics of the situation will be discussed first, and then you will have to agree to the long-term implications."

"I hope your esteemed colleagues of the Hnioss come to a quick decision; the Earth is running out of time," Julia said.

"There will be a quick decision, Jules. The science is already in place for the manoeuvre. As soon as Jem's original plea for help was heard by the Hnioss there was overwhelming support to provide the resources. However, the procedure has to follow a set format. There is an historic problem, however. It was a problem that affected Earth some thousands of your years ago. The Chakrakan invaded your planet—"

"They what?" Julia, the archaeologist, latched onto the alien's words.

"You have legends of giants in your Earth cultures—"

"The mighty men of old?" Julia quoted a Hebrew scripture she was familiar with. "And there were the giant skeletons—"

"We will talk about this some other time but accept the fact that the giants in your Earth's history are absolute fact. Way back in the past our ancestors had to take action. The Chakrakan race is not a peaceful one and even now we must be certain that their cocooning remains tightly in place. They are a law unto themselves and cannot be trusted."

"Why not get rid of them?" Lee Wynter asked.

"Lee, you must not pursue that line of thinking. The preservation of life is paramount throughout our universe of Dimension One, and in the other dimensions too. If the Higher Ethic is followed there are always alternative methods, other than the ways of violence, with which you will be able to work through problems that arise." Lee was quiet and nodded his understanding, although the understanding was only partial.

"It seems to me that Earth's population has to enter a new phase, with this growing away from aggression," Harry said.

"That is exactly right. Unfortunately, your race has had plenty of practice with aggression; it comes as second nature to some of you, but there is hope. The danger to Earth from Chakrakan, Nibiru as you call it, will convince many to change their ways, particularly when you inform them of how we helped you to overcome the problem. Experience tells us that, when a race learns that it is not alone in the universe, it causes a fundamental change in attitudes, often for the better."

"You say the science is in place?" Harry asked. Lan-Si-Nu said nothing. He knew what would follow. Inquisitiveness was dominant in intelligent species.

"Can we look at your science?"

"You can. Before that we wull eat, and then we will go to the Q-phase Generator. I have been informed that the Hnioss will re-sit later this day and then, when they return, you will have the answer to your request for help."

* * *

The door opened automatically onto a balcony which was railed at the edge. Grid Commander Lan-Si-Nu led them to the edge, which hung out over a cavernous space. Julia Linden-Barthorpe grasped the railing, keeping it at arm's length. She had pluck and was prepared to face most challenges, but heights were a challenge too far.

Harry gasped and held the rail for a different reason. He looked in awe at the immense crystal extending many storey's both above and below the balcony where he stood. The crystal's inner depths, observable through its nearest facet, were writhing and twisting violently in bursts of intense carmine, coruscating through a range of purple from darkest tones to lightest. He stood near the rail and could see the ring placed around the outer profile, from which, similar to the structure in the portal in Leofwin's Hundred, immense cables arched to the outer wall.

He felt Lan-Si-Nu's eyes searching him for a response.

"Resonant harmonics?" Harry asked.

The alien nodded. "The Q-phase Generator was the culmination of a thousand years of the brightest invention in our history. Never before or since has there been such advancement; now, we simply maintain it. Oh, our advancement continues, but this," his hand swept across the vision in front of them, "This was the gateway that has taken us to the stars and beyond."

"To dimensions other than our own?" Harry asked.

"Yes."

The others in the team were silent, each of them, in their own way trying to assimilate the scale and complexity of the structure before them, its purpose and the intellect of the beings that built it.

"Where did it come from . . . the crystal?" Mitch Doughty asked.

"In the Great Annals, it is stated that an asteroid had arrived in our solar system. It took up residence in a peculiar orbit. At the time, our ancestors had advanced technologically to a level some years in advance of where you are at present We had begun to colonise some of the planets in our solar system so our space vehicles were capable of handling complex tasks.

"There was no warning about the asteroid's arrival but one of our freighters had a close encounter with it, a near miss. The object's internal structure was in stasis and it was invisible against the blackness of space because of its colour. When we examined it, we found it to have the unique crystalline composition you see before you. The crystal had been formed somewhere in the immensity of the cosmos and some say it arrived in our vicinity by design, not by chance. The Wasiri-Chanchiya crew of the freighter involved felt an affinity with it. They claimed that it was as if they had been meant to find it, so they took it in tow and brought it home.

"During the landing procedure, with the increase in dynamic pressure on the surface of the crystal it became energised. The intense internal movement you see now began and a minor time-shift occurred. It was totally unexpected and the crew of the spacecraft had great difficulty with the landing. With the time difference, the landing site was at an earlier age. They also had difficulty with the size of the asteroid. You can see the immensity of it; the crew had to attach retro thrusters and a control capsule to the crystal to enable the landing.

"How did you learn about the force-field of the Grid and the crystal's link to it?" Dearden asked.

"It was an accidental discovery, but the clue came from the time-shift during the landing and the lines of force of the grid that became briefly illuminated." Lan-Si-Nu broke off. He was deep in thought. "There are many things that you Earths will learn in the course of time. You need a steady influx of knowledge to understand the science involved. Give it time. If you exercise patience you will be rewarded. Your place within the universe will gain a whole new meaning." The tall alien headed to the exit from the viewing area.

"Come, it is time to go to the Hnioss to hear the result of your plea for help." Harry trailed along last. He took a backward glance at the colossal structure and its fiery movement and felt an affinity with it.

*   *   *

A hush hung over the assembly of the Hnioss as they waited for Krel-Rahn to appear. Lars Knudsen was sitting in the seat of Focus. His foot, tapping a nervous beat.

"I don't like the silence; it doesn't bode well," Mitch said to Dearden.

"It's difficult to read the outcome."

"What do you think?" Mitch asked.

"They don't like our history of violence. It won't do us any favours."

"They might understand that at times we have had no choices," Wynter said.

"On that point, they would reason that we have had choices; but wait, something's happening." Harry raised a finger for silence.

The area of floor opened up and the Preceptor arose on it from somewhere below, standing on his mobile platform, in front of the podium. The attention of the Hnioss focussed on Krel-Rahn as he put on his hat of office. There was a murmur of anticipation and then silence.

The Preceptor spoke in his basso profundo English, which was translated into the diversity of languages of the beings in the Hnioss. "We, the Hnioss congratulate the Earths. Their approach to us, asking for our assistance, also constituted an application for membership of the Council of the Hnioss.

Earth ambassador Lars Knudsen, your representation has been successful. Now, when you return to your home planet, you will have much work to do and sometimes it will be difficult. For this you will have guidance. The lines of communication with us are always open by means of the Portal."

As with any new application to join the Council of the Hnioss, when an acceptance was given there was a celebratory roar of applause. Preceptor Krel-Rahn waited for a short while and then held up his hand. The Hnions in the auditorium gradually lapsed into silence. The Preceptor nodded, as if in agreement. And then he turned to address Knudsen and the others from Earth, who were seated behind him

"The process for re-orbiting Chakrakan has begun. We are in the first phase of re-positioning the planet from its orbit that threatens Earth. It will still be located in your solar system, but we are moving it to a more regular orbit than the present one, which was achieved many years ago when our planetary science was in its infancy. Nibiru will be placed midway between the orbits of Mars and Jupiter. The science we now employ to manipulate the lines of force of the grid is far more accurate than it was in the previous orbital shift.

"There is an element of possible error in the current shift, but it will be accurate to plus or minus five percent of our planned orbit." The preceptor's visage took on a serious aspect.

"People of Earth, we must issue you with a warning about the inhabitants of the planet you call Nibiru. The Chakrakan race is unstable; they are determined not to learn the ways of peace. Always be aware of that and be on your guard. As they are neighbours in your solar system, they will become your responsibility."

Julia was reminded of the message that Trent Jackson, the language expert, discovered tucked in between two pages of the manual she found in the Hub. "I think it is a warning," Trent had said. She tuned back in to Krel-Rahn.

"Before you return home we will outline ways that will enable you people of the Earth planet to progress out of your infancy." The Preceptor hesitated as Lan-Si-Nu stood. The tall stature of the Wasiri-Chanchiyan drew the attention of the Hnioss.

"Preceptor, might I suggest that, when the representatives of Earth return to their planet, I accompany them to give support for a while. I am used to the ways of the Second One, the Earth planet."

"Noble Grid Commander, that suggestion has already been put forward as a resolution, and under the unusual circumstances Earth is facing at present, it has been recommended. Guidance will be needed in Earth's early days of transition. You, being lately marooned on that planet and used to its inhabitant's ways, are best placed to act as ambassador during their stages of new learning."

Harry's mind had drifted, but suddenly, and with a nudge from Wynter, he was aware that Krel Rahn had spoken his name.

"Harry Stanway accomplished feats of electro-engineering science far beyond the level of his contemporaries. That the noble Grid Commander, Lan-Si-Nu and his crew were able to return to Wasiri-Poya was the result of the Harry Stanway Earth's analytical intellect. For this, we of the Council of the Hnioss are grateful. Let this be entered into the Great Annals, that on this day of the five hundred and thirty-seventh cycle, the seventeenth day of the red moon's return, the Earth person, Harry Stanway is given the rank of Hnirath of Science, the second order."

67

The day had started out the same as any other on the planet Nibiru, but the start belied the event that was to come. The first sign that all was not well occurred around mid-day. The length of days was always in a state of flux on Nibiru because of its eccentric orbit. The inhabitants were used to that situation. Ever since the time that the cocooning began way back in history, each day's length was different to its predecessor. Each day's artificially induced light from the cloud-seeding was slightly different to the day before, but in general the days were a flat and never-ending grey.

At mid-day, the cloud-seeding that provided phased luminescence dividing day and night burst into overload. A vivid display that startled even the most fearsome warriors, caused them to flinch and shield their eyes and creep into whatever shelter they could find.

Engineers and scientists quickly gathered and argued their ideas around in displays of anger. Desperate for reasons, they focussed their instruments into the sky and tried to analyse the event. Their vision of the outer universe was limited, being hidden from view by the intense cloud cover. Within their knowledge-banks information was nested about the depths of space beyond their planet. Before the imprisonment of cocooning in their deep-history, they used ships that flew in the outer firmament to conquer other worlds.

Because of the cocooning and the accompanying shroud of deep cloud, they knew nothing of their onward orbital rush toward the planet Earth.

The giants of Nibiru were an introverted race because of their limited view of what existed beyond their own planet. Although there was clever science, much of it was rendered useless, bound by the fetters of the cocooning. History of their inventions lay on display in buildings that were old and smelt of decay. There were complex vehicles and machinery for all manner of forgotten purposes, kept shining by the wardens, but disused.

But change was afoot. The radio waves carrying news became overloaded as reports speculated on the likely cause of the increased level of daylight illumination.

"It is electro-magnetic in nature," shouted one who taught in a palace of learning. He pulled the news microphone closer and sniffed the air loudly. "I can smell the ozone from an intense electrical discharge; this is a planet-wide occurrence. Others have concurred that fact," he shouted again, trying to make himself heard above the screech of chaotic noise, comfortably typical of daily life.

The Watchers gathered on the heights of Gan. A fleeting gap had appeared through the massed cloud and through it appeared a brief brilliance of stars. The watchers gasped at the infinitesimal peeling away of the cocoon and argued about what to do next. The Thung, half again the height of the others, raised his hand for silence. There was silence, for his word was law.

"This may give us the opportunity we have wanted since the Wasiri-Chanchiya forced us to quit our ascendancy," he spat at the other watchers. They recoiled at his anger and were impressed. He had been chosen as Thung for his anger and his hatred and here he was, spilling it out in full measure. He signalled for them to follow him down the crooked pathway as the radiance from above closed up. They felt more comfortable when the fissure showing the outer universe disappeared. The immensity was difficult for them to deal with after lifelong enclosure by the grey cocoon.

The Thung felt uneasy with the great beyond that had opened up fleetingly, but he fought through the weakness. "Come on, you cowards," he shouted back as he ran, belittling the other Watchers, for that was the Thung's way and the way of Nibiru. "Quickly now. I am superior to you, a better athlete by far. If I lose you we shall meet in the Halls of Historical Artefacts." The other Watchers tried to catch up with him. Failing to do, so their jealousy brimmed to the surface.

*   *   *

If anyone from Earth heard the name of the planet Nibiru spoken in the language of the inhabitants and tried to repeat it, they would have failed miserably. The language was full of clicks, sibilants and gutturals strung together in a complexity absurd to the human ear. The sudden increase in radio traffic from Nibiru was picked up on Earth by those hardy scientists who had the commitment and the courage to stay at their radio telescope posts during the approach of the planet. Connie Rios was one of those and she heard the strange noises over the radio waves picked up by SETI using the Allen Telescope Array. She could tell from her instrumentation that the transmission was intelligent and vocal because of certain repeats and intonations in the onrush of organic noise.

*   *   *

The Thung felt movement around him. A wind, susurrating through the great thorn bushes buffeted him as he approached the Halls of Historical Artefacts. The weather was growing wild and he had never experienced such a phenomenon before. The atmosphere should be stable, unchanging. He had heard of the time before the cocooning when winds and water from the skies and a phenomenon called sunlight assailed the planet. *That must have been hell to deal with*, he thought.

He reached the hall housing the ancient artefacts and slipped quietly inside. A Watcher slightly taller than him with a weapon in his hand challenged his entry. He was quickly taken care of and the Thung stepped over the body. He took a right, rushed to the Hall of Astrophysical Engineering and headed to where the Pad, a small flat exhibit he had gazed at in awe many times, rested behind its clear housing. He smashed through the protection, extracted the Pad and placed it safely in his pocket and then ran onward into the centre of the hall.

He heard the roaring of the storm for a spell as the outer door opened and then the sound abated. Shortly, his fellow Watchers ran into the spacious room and gathered behind him where he stood contemplating the sleek, shining vehicle that towered above them. It was one of the few undestroyed after the cocooning.

"We will take our chance," he shouted. He had prepared for such a moment as this. Much of his life as a mature Nibiruan had been taken up with study of this class of vehicle and he was a recognised expert in the field. Until this moment it had been theory; now he would put his learning to the test.

"Open the roll-out doorways," he shouted. "The biggest of the two buttons over there . . . hurry, and you two, pull over the step-gantry."

"Where to?"

"Where do you think . . . there." He pointed to a door only just discernible in the vehicle's side. The great door to outside slid open and the storm roared in, making it difficult to stand. Lightning flashed again and again in incandescent arcs and the punishing sound of thunder hit their ears. The chaos was new to them and filled them with boundless joy.

The Thung ran up the gantry steps with the others following and he reached into the deep pocket of his tunic. He removed the Pad and touched a symbol on the door with it. The door opened inward, and he indicated for the Watchers to enter. After they filed past him they waited for the Thung's next move. He entered the vehicle, kicked the gantry away and touched the symbol on the inside of the doorframe with the Pad. The vehicle's door closed and shut out the comfort of the raging storm.

68

"How long will the process take?" Mitch Doughty asked Lan-Si-Nu. They were back on the viewing balcony overlooking the Q-phase Generator.

"The re-direction shunt is now being applied by three nodes, including the one in Leofwin's Hundred. It will take six of your hours to build sufficient energy to feed a controlled Gravity-Wave Tsunami. After twelve of your hours Chakrakan will be progressing toward its new orbit."

"Come and look, Jules," Sir Will Pierpoint said. Julia was hanging back at the rear of the balcony. She shook her head.

Dearden moved to the back and took her hand, he pulled, and they stood next to Mitch Doughty and Harry.

"You will never see the like of this again, Jules," he said. "The mover of worlds." She kept hold of the railings and trying to ignore the abyss, she looked way up and she could see, towering above them, to the top of the immense crystal. Daring quickly to glance down into the depths she took in its awesome size. The crystal was shimmering with an inner fire and the lines of force of the Grid were plain to see as streams of plasma, bending from the heavens, arced as if alive onto the surface of the crystal.

"Your work here is done for the time being," Lan-Si-Nu said to Knudsen and Pierpoint. "You need to return to Earth, to convey the news to the people of your planet that the threat has passed."

"What will they see at present, the people on Earth? Pierpoint asked.

"During the next day, there will be wild winds and storm surges. Some may notice the recession of Chakrakan as it flows into its new orbit. The majority of your people will be fearful. They will not comprehend that the danger has been removed. Lars and Sir Willoughby, now is the time when your reassurance will be most valuable. I fear that there will be widespread breakdown in communication due to large-scale electromagnetic interference. It must be restored. After this event, the people of your planet will be in prime condition for a fresh start."

"A big job," Knudsen said.

"Maybe so, but I will be with you to give you support, and you have experienced the nature of our support in numerous ways."

"We have that," Pierpoint confirmed.

*   *   *

Over the past hour the gale force wind was gathering in its intensity and was whipping the trees of Leofwin's Hundred into distorted shapes that gave the impression of elemental life. Another stab of lightning burst through the skies, illuminating the dark glades surrounding the Hub. The electromagnetic storm was worldwide and caused radio to go down, quickly followed by television. The last news broadcast on the Nibiru Channel and Sky before the screens blacked out was a sign-off by Marsha Sefton, the science correspondent. Her mouth quivered as she wished her viewers the best of luck. It was the only sign of emotion anyone had ever seen from her.

Many people at that moment felt the end was near. The event that confirmed the situation was desperate was the loneliness that came when television screens went blank. Television, long part of everyday life, was the other person in the room who kept the hours together with inane chatter, documentaries, news both good and bad and films both old and new. But television was dead.

* * *

All was quiet away from the storm, but soon the wind could be heard inside as the elements grew violent. In the room at the top of the Hub, the Portal, Bill Templestone had overall command of the operation. He would keep at his post as Jem had asked him to do before he left with Pierpoint, Knudsen and the rest in their attempt to avert disaster.

"I think we've got to face it, we're running out of time." Clive Fraser said. His knuckles were white as he grasped the table laden with emergency rations.

"You don't know Jem Dearden and Will Pierpoint like we do," Templestone said. Templestone was always encouraging, even under live fire. Deep down Bill knew this was as bad as it could get but he had to keep his spirits up and be positive for the others' sake.

Matt Roberts, with Storm Petrel at his side on one of the benches, was sharpening his Bowie. He tested its edge on the ace of spades. The cards had helped them while away the hours as they waited. Templestone was ready for another game. A pile of coins and a few notes were close to his hand. Storm took the pack of cards and shuffled them.

"Who's for another hand?" she asked, dealing out the pack into eight places around the table.

"Count me out this time," Fraser said. He looked pale and his hands shook slightly. His chair rattled as he pushed it away from the table and stood up. He walked to the edge of the room and stood by the wall with his back to the others.

"Get back to the table."

"What was that?" Fraser asked.

Robert's voice was firm. "I said, get back to the table." Templestone could see where Roberts was coming from. This was no time for weakness to creep in. Roberts lived life on the edge; he was a man of the outside. The wilderness and the forest suited him. He also understood the human psyche. A bit of anger drawn from the depths worked well on occasions. Fraser turned and faced Roberts, who flicked some stray hair from his bandana away from his face. Roberts stood slowly and stuck his Bowie into the table, where it stood, quivering.

"Listen," Rowan shouted. Her keen hearing picked out a noise she recognised and she had to shout to be heard above the noise outside. She stood quickly, and as she held up her hand for silence the others around the table quietened down.

"What's goin' on?" Storm Petrel asked.

"I heard relay engage . . . we must go to Control Room." Rowan headed over to the stairs. Wynter and Roberts forgot the cards and the knife, and Fraser forgot his outburst of anger that had snapped him back into focus. They ran after Rowan, who was already half-way down the spiral stairs. Templestone was only a second slower. "Things are about to happen," he yelled. He felt like a young man again as he took the tall steps down two at a time.

As Roberts got to the commander's chair and sat in it, a deep electronic hum reverberated through the Hub. Storm Petrel could feel it as she reached the bottom of the stairway and turned into the Control Room. She remembered Concorde taking off from John F Kennedy International when she saw her dad off on a business trip. The noise from the engines punched the air when the afterburners blazed their power. Storm recalled how the aircraft had set off the alarms in scores of cars parked up around the airfield; how the noise pulsed through her body and she gloried in the release of power from the aircraft. She had felt the pulsation from the Hub in the same way, deep inside. Matt pressed the button for a Shift Reception, the humming ceased and Storm ran up the stairs, following Matt back into the Portal.

*   *   *

Carlos Mendulas, on the high peak of Cerro Pachon, was determined to remain in front of the viewing screen. There were power outages and many countries were in darkness, or where they lay in daylight, cities and the thrust of commerce had ground to a halt. Gemini South, however, was on emergency generators and all was working.

Carlos was a cool customer. His father had been a bullfighter back in Spain and was bringing his son up to face the almost impossible odds of the bull. "Stare the beast out," his father had said. "Face your fears and more times than not you will win out." Two years later his father had been gored to death but the training had remained with the young Carlos. It wasn't long before his mother wanted to cut all ties with Spain and the matador set, so they emigrated to Chile, to a place near the observatory peaks, where they could still use their Spanish and he had learned astronomy.

Carlos Mendulas was a matador in how he faced life. A challenge didn't faze him. Even if the challenge was like a snorting red-eyed bull a metre in front of his face he stayed focussed. So, he stayed in front of the screens as Nibiru rushed on its orbit toward Earth. Over a period of two hours the threat appeared to slow down and then become stationary. Carlos rubbed his eyes to combat the tiredness. When he opened them again he caught a fleeting movement near the surface of the planet. It had happened so quickly that he thought he might have imagined the sunlight reflecting off sleek surfaces. It was a vision straight out of science fiction that had blazed with light, distorted lengthwise and then disappeared. He rubbed his eyes again, leaned back in his chair and went to sleep.

* * *

"Hey, kid, it's good to see you," Dearden whispered to Rowan as he pulled her close. "What's happening here?"

"It is bad. The news that we have managed to get says that everywhere has fierce winds and floods and lightning. High tides flooding sea-towns. People are going to hills, to be safe. What is news from your mission?"

"Lan-Si-Nu's people accepted our request for help and the rescue is under way . . . the next few hours will be critical because of the forces involved. There will be widespread damage. Maybe many will die, but the Earth will survive."

"The storm is worse than anything I have known before. I am frightened, Jem. Maybe the world is ending."

He shook his head. "Remember how Lan-Si-Nu helped you. You were near death and they brought you back. We will be alright." Rowan remembered how the light had been bright in her mind as she was regaining consciousness. She studied the expression on Jem's face. She was glad to have him back.

69

The wind had died down to a few desultory gusts. Through the transparent wall of the Hub they surveyed a scene of devastation, with fallen trees littering the landscape of Leofwin's Hundred. Lan-Si-Nu went to the door and opened it. He stepped outside and the others cautiously followed. The air seemed remarkably fresh and Julia commented that she could smell the ozone from a high tension electrical discharge.

"It is a by-product of the re-orbiting process," the alien said.

Templestone looked through the transparent ceiling into the sky, which was clearing, and bright sunlight appeared through the parting clouds. "There's Nibiru," he said. And then, "They've done it, look it's getting smaller." There were cheers and laughter, and a great sense of relief. The great orb was there, its land masses and oceans could vaguely be seen through a shimmering haze surrounding the planet and it was visibly receding.

* * *

"Looks as though there's a lot of clearing up to do," Storm Petrel said to Roberts as they scrambled down the hill containing the lower levels of the Hub. She reached the base of the hill and surveyed the swathe of fallen trees.

From the top of the hill Dearden and Rowan looked out across Leofwin's Hundred. "I wonder if Old Jack has survived," Dearden said to her.

"I hope he has. He is like a friend," she said. She had known the tree in Anglo-Saxon times when it had no name and was of moderate girth. It was known far and wide, having been the marker planted in a grove where a hermit once lived who had returned from Jerusalem. Rowan and Jem followed the others down the slope to where Julia's Grand Cherokee stood, crushed by a fallen ash tree at the edge of the clearing around the Hub.

"I'm glad we weren't in that," Julia said to Clive.

He grimaced; "I'm thinking that a lot of folks will be looking at what they've got left. Maybe it won't be much."

"More to the point, how many people are left?" Wynter speculated. Clive picked his way over an uprooted tree covered with moss on one side. "You've got a good supply of firewood here, Jem," he called.

"More than I need. Let's go and see if there's a fireplace left to burn it in," he said, as he made for Dearden Hall with Rowan trying to keep up with him.

Lan-Si-Nu and his fellow aliens were taking one pace to the others' two. "You must be prepared to face widespread damage," he said to Lars Knudsen and Will Pierpoint, "And there will be much reorganisation. But it is a fresh start and you can look to the future with optimism. Make the most of it."

"We will," Pierpoint said. "But the first thing I'll do is to contact all the SHaFT operatives. We'll get together in Kineton to see where the organisation goes from here. I fancy we will go very far afield."

*   *   *

Shadow Brook was running high, with debris from the forest borne along on the swirling current. The reinforced bridge had survived and the water from the forest was gurgling through the channel below it. Old Jack was still standing, although one of the lower boughs had been ripped off by another falling tree. They skirted the obstruction and headed on.

Templestone caught up with Dearden.

"Where are the Heskins, and Tomahawk," Dearden asked.

"In the basement, along with Harry's cat and Titch."

"That could be amusing."

"Yeah, I hope the Heskins can handle Tomahawk, but they did volunteer."

"What did Red and Possum Chaser do?"

"There's some old mine workings on their land. Apparently, they were used in Roman times. Red has made something of them, living quarters of sorts, and a place for the wolves. They have a connection with the place, with the land and they were determined to sit it out or die there. They've been in touch and all's OK with them."

"Good. Anything else you need to tell me?"

Templestone thought about the question. "We do need to see what communication we've got. There has been disruption of services on a massive scale. Electro-generators all over the place have been destroyed. Before Sky went off air they reported that the Nuclear reactor at Hinckley Point was going critical because of a power failure. An emergency team had been sent in to tackle the problem. Lord knows what else has occurred in other continents."

"Maybe we'll return to the wild," Roberts said. He didn't seem too bothered with that. He wouldn't be, but Mitch Doughty wondered how Storm Petrel would cope with living at subsistence level with Roberts in the forest. Then Mitch remembered Storm's damn-you attitude when they first met in New York.

Storm would get by and with Julia Linden-Barthorpe on-side too, two strong characters, and with the rest of the SHaFT team close by the chance of survival was better than eighty percent, even with world-wide disruption of all the systems of modern life.

"What else has happened?" Dearden asked.

"Things were getting really bad in the last day and a half. As Nibiru was getting larger, tides were getting higher. There were earthquakes where none had happened before. One was centred on Lower Gornal."

"Where's Lower Gornal?"

"Dudley, in Staffordshire. There was a minor quake there some years back, but this one was major, 7.2 on the Richter scale. There was panic, fire and riots. Folks are scared, Jem. Civilisation is collapsing. Apparently, the churches were full."

Dearden laughed. "They would be. Most people only turn to God when things get too hot to handle."

"Yeah . . . anyway, a few hours before you got back a wobble was noticed in the approaching planet. Minutes after that the news blacked out and now conditions out there are guesswork."

*   *   *

Everyone on Earth who could do so was staring into the heavens, wishing, hoping and praying that what they saw happening was a turn for the better, that the threat was lifting. Nibiru was definitely smaller. In the space of six hours, the planet had diminished to half the size it had been previously.

Apart from the most hardened criminals and warmongers, people were reassessing their lives, thankful, indeed to be alive even with cities and villages in a state of ruin. Rescue teams were trying to consolidate their efforts, but with many of the geostationary satellites knocked out of orbit, organisation was, at best, primitive. Where fuel was available, bulldozers and tracked vehicles were trying to shift rubble to reach those trapped beneath. Cries and screams were heard and bare hands clawed at masonry to reach the victims when there was no machinery.

Hydroelectric generators that suffered least damage had begun pumping the megawatts through a disordered network of supply services and cabling. Televisions that had been left on at the time of outage blinked into half-powered flickering life. It suddenly became obvious that money counted for nothing. Within the space of hours, Wall street, the Hang-Seng and the other stock exchanges had been relegated to memory and weren't people pleased!

In the UK, the interim government under the leadership of Stephen Marston, had begun a rationing scheme. Food, bedding and fuel, in that order, were the essentials and the vast majority of people accepted the restrictions. After all, they had life, where previously hope of life had gone.

The United Kingdom, through an accident of geography had suffered less damage than elsewhere. There was still smoke day and night from crematoria, with a morbid black pall floating before the winds of change, which blew cold from the prevailing north.

Things quickly settled down at Dearden Hall. Mitch Doughty and Matt Roberts began the repairs to the house and within a month of Nibiru's receding, an air of normality had returned. The thick stone walls of the ancient structure had ensured that damage was minimal. Frieda Heskin related how, at the peak of the disaster, Tomahawk had howled with the tempestuous wind, as if at one with it, but they were all safe in the arched cavern of the basement way below the wild weather.

Pierpoint telephoned Stephen Marston and demanded a meeting. Marston, in a bunker below the destroyed Houses of Parliament, had been reminded of the existence of an organisation called SHaFT by Fenton Bull's private secretary, who remained loyal to his post through succeeding premierships.

"If they have survived they will get in touch with you, we really need them now," the private secretary said to Marston. Within hours the secure phone rang and sure enough it was Pierpoint making his demand to meet. The call from Pierpoint came only hours after Nibiru began to shift away.

"I am rather busy, Sir Willoughby," Premier Marston said, "But I will be very glad to meet."

"Stephen, there is nothing more important than this meeting. It is most urgent that you come to Dearden Hall here in Warwickshire as soon as is possible. What we have to show and tell you is going to alter all of our lives radically. Come with armed security, if you wish."

They met, without armed security and Sir Willoughby, who, unusually for him, was feeling his age, explained what had taken place with Plan B. They also met with Dearden and Harry Stanway, who accompanied Marston to the Hub. Lan-Si-Nu was there to meet them in the lower level and once the premier had got over the shock of his contact with the alien he was treated to a tour of Earth's home galaxy, the Milky Way, over the Grid.

Lars Knudsen set up his new headquarters at Bletchley Park and became firm friends with Professor Trent Jackson. Knudsen, using what remained of his team at the UN and the SHaFT team, drew them around him as the basis of Earth's members of the Hnioss. Using the infant, but powerful broadcasting unit at Bletchley, Knudsen outlined to the listening public how the threat of Nibiru had been lifted.

They had the television on in the great hall to watch Knudsen.

"I have to tell you now, we have been helped out of what could easily have been a doomsday event by a race of extra-terrestrial people called the Wasiri-Chanchiya. Their planet, Wasiri-Poya, lies beyond the constellation of Ursa Major, part of which most of you will know as the Big Dipper, or the Plough. This race of aliens, contrary to all previous concepts of inhabitants of the universe other than ourselves, are dedicated to peace and harmony.

"People of the Good Earth, we have to learn new ways. Our future life and advancement depends upon it. But I do assure you, if we work with our alien friends, we will have a remarkable future. We have a period of exciting learning in front of us and I can also assure you of this, that it will be a time of fulfilment such as has never yet been experienced by the human race. We will communicate with you in due course about the next stage of our development.

"For now, I want to inaugurate a period of celebration that will be called Second Pass. It will last for one week and will be repeated on this same date every year. This date will henceforth be written in the Great Annals as the time that the human race finally shed the ways of violence and looked outward, in peace, to the stars."

Knudsen said nothing about the way SHaFT had been involved; he said nothing about the place hidden in Leofwin's Hundred, the Hub, the House of the West Wind, that had enabled the saving of Earth.

Time, the onward progression of events, would demonstrate the reality, without Knudsen having to detail the process.

Those of SHaFT who had been involved dispersed to their various homes to do what repairs were necessary. Templestone moved out of his accommodation above the stained-glass studio at Dearden Hall and took up his role as Keeper of the Knight's Sanctuary and the HaMabuwl scroll, that was back in the vault made by his ancestor, Ramon Tailleur de Pierre. Templestone added his own record of the Second Pass into the cedar wood box and moved into Keeper's Cottage in Temple Balsall.

* * *

"Let us go to the bank of Shadow Brook, Jem, where we used to go when we lived in Leofwin's time," Rowan of Maldon said. They walked hand in hand through the primeval forest which had begun to repair itself, and as they walked they talked about what they thought the next years would bring.

"The world has become a strange place, Rowan," Jem said. "I sometimes question what reality is and what is fanciful."

"I thought of those things when you first came out of the House of the West Wind," Rowan said, using the name the forest dwellers of Heanton in the Arden in Anglo-Saxon times called the alien building. "Life is so strange," she said.

"I am glad we are not alone in the universe," Jem said. He felt very close to Rowan, and she was the person that made sense of it all. Love, the predominant force binding all things together, was theirs.

The Wasiri-Chanchiya had realised that truth many millennia in the past and had relinquished violence and hatred. Now Earth was set on the same course and the time of new learning was at hand. What did the future hold for them, where would it take them?

Jem and Rowan came to Old Jack, the ancient denizen of the forest in whose watch, measured in the oak's slowness of time, events both small and great had taken place. The moon had risen when they reached the place on the bank of Shadow Brook. Here, a thousand years ago, Jem had spoken to Rowan of Maldon about Shakespeare and his words of a moonlit streambank in a forest called Arden.

"We have the whole universe to go to, Rowan," Dearden said, looking upward into the great beyond. "And with the Hub we have all the time in the universe in which to do it."

Rowan followed his gaze and saw the brilliance of the Milky Way. Through the branches of the ancient trees she fancied she saw a shadow, a dark presence in the sky that flashed across the surface of the moon.

"I want to go back now, Jem," she said. "Let's light the fire in the great hall and sit close to it."

"Why, what's the matter?"

"I thought I saw something very dark . . . up there." She pointed to the heavens.

"What was it?"

"I don't know . . . maybe it was from Nibiru," she tried to laugh, and then she shivered.

70

Harry Stanway's mind had settled after the tumultuous days when he and the others travelled the Grid outward past the constellation of Ursa Major to Wasiri-Poya, the planet where all things began. Now, along with all the other survivors, he was trying to adjust to the great changes that had re-shaped life on Earth.

The world was quieter now and slower. The shape of continents had altered. The familiar outline of lands such as the boot-shape of Italy and the re-claimed land known as The Wash, in the United Kingdom, were altered beyond recognition. The eastern seaboard of the United States had likewise altered. Low-lying land the world over had flooded when the Arctic and Antarctic icecaps had undergone stress changes. Calving icebergs floated into warmer climates and added to the highest tides ever experienced.

As the news of survival accumulated and news channels' signal strength was amplified, people across the continents heard epic stories of bravery, survival and loss. In the final hours of the week-long Second Pass celebration, Lars Knudsen made another television appearance. He announced the commencement of weekly broadcasts to help people adjust to the changes in their lives caused by Nibiru. The highlight of this broadcast was the introduction to the general public of the ambassador of the alien race who were instrumental in removing the threat of the rogue planet.

Lan-Si-Nu gave an eloquent explanation of the recent event in layman's terms. He expressed sorrow over the great loss of life. The feedback received after the broadcast was positive and great respect was shown for the Wasiri-Poyan. People were excited, although not too surprised by the fact that finally there was proof-positive of the existence of life on other worlds.

Optimism began to grow out of the chaos and out of the darkest of times there was supplanted a bright hope for the future. A Second Renaissance began to be spoken of, another week of celebration in addition to Second Pass, to occur annually, dividing the year. Added to those words, an image of Lan-Si-Nu was incorporated into a logo which sported the words, *Second Pass*.

*   *   *

Harry relished mysteries, but all the more so did he relish solving them. Before the Second Pass of Nibiru, he and Esma would sometimes walk to The Green Man with Titch and they would spend an evening together in a quiet corner of the bar. They considered themselves fortunate. The death toll was impossible to calculate accurately. Figures being estimated were in the billions, calculated in rough terms by previous earthquake and tsunami disasters.

After the near miss of Nibiru and the catastrophic environmental upheaval there were a number of survivors in Hampton in Arden and Ken Tillman, the owner of The Green Man was one of them. He tried to get the public house up and running again, back to a semblance of normality.

Tillman began to brew his own beer in mash tuns in an outbuilding at the back of the pub. At first the beer was rough so he bartered it as best he could. But then he added more malt to the brew and the result was good. Sometimes the bar was lit by candle light and Esma said she liked it that way because it was softer to her eyes and it reminded her of her own time in Mercia.

"Would you prefer to go back to your own time?" Harry asked one evening after they settled into their corner.

"No. This time we live is exciting. New things to learn every day. Wide-open space of thinking is good. We are not closed-in here." Harry turned to look at her. In profile, her lips had a look of determination, which was similar to her character.

Sometimes Esma would persuade Harry to tell her about the things he found interesting. She liked the sound of his voice and as her command of modern English grew and he listened to her responses, he learned that Esma, like him, was very intelligent. He thought that, given time for her to learn, she could be his equal intellectually and not only did he love her above all else, but he also developed a great deal of respect for her.

He couldn't forget, or more accurately, didn't want to forget Professor Charles Villiers' laboratory, which lay at the end of the tunnel leading away from Repository One at MoD Kineton. It irked him; drew him like a magnet. What interested him most of all was the sealed-in doorway at the top of the steps at the far end of the lab. And there was the faint noise coming from the other side of the stonework that definitely didn't come from the Castle Inn which lay directly above the laboratory through 380 feet of Warwickshire Red-Marlstone rock. Even if a stairway led upwards to the Inn beyond the blocked-off doorway, the noises he heard the other side were definitely not those of a public house. They were noises he associated with a world of open space, which was odd.

Esma liked mysteries too. She often used a colour wash from the local chemist on her hair so that Harry never knew what she would look like when he met her next time. She wanted to be a mystery to Harry so that he would notice her and want her all the more. She walked into the village one day, where she had noticed a newly opened tattoo artist shop which was staffed by a husband and wife team. In her mix of modern English and a few Anglo-Saxon words, she explained to the woman tattooist that she wanted an H in the middle of a robust-looking heart.

"Here." She indicated the secret place where she wanted it. Harry would like it when he saw it, but until they were husband and wife, secret it would stay.

"I'll have another pint, Ken," Harry said. He had his own glass behind the bar. It had a handle which was shaped in such a way that it reminded Harry of an algebraic expression. He had seen the glass in an antique shop amongst the bric-a-brac. In reality, it must have been a mis-shape, thrown out as scrap, or an apprentice piece, but it appealed to Harry and it now lodged on a hook behind the bar in The Green Man.

In their corner, Harry quietly told Esma about the tunnel and the laboratory with the weird noises beyond the blocked-up entrance and she was all for scouting it out. They told no-one else about the plan, which, in hindsight, was a bad mistake.

They packed a tote-bag with simple things. Bread, a newly baked cob loaf and some cheese, both of which were made by Frieda Heskin. They took two bottles of water. A sheath-knife, a cigarette lighter and a can of lighter fuel, although Harry abhorred smoking, but the lighter could be useful. He had a set of lock-picks and a pick-gun to hold them with, a lump-hammer, a bolster chisel, which had been newly sharpened in the workshop by Templestone and a plugging chisel. A powerful Maglite with spare batteries, and a wind-up radio, completed the kit. The difficulty was to convince Dearden to get him access to Repository One.

*   *   *

Harry thought that it would be in the interest of everyone to find out the full extent of Charles Villiers' work, after all, he had devised the End Time weapon, but more importantly he had sent strong warnings out about Nibiru. It could be conjectured that he may have been working on parallel, or maybe even divergent fields of science. Villiers was at the forefront of physics and had an original mind that ran tangentially to recognised thinking. There was a need to know, so Harry told Dearden that he wanted to speak to him privately.

"I need to get into Repository One," Harry said to Dearden when they sat in the privacy of Harry's upstairs pad at Dearden Hall.

"What on earth do you want to get in there for?"

"We need to find out what exactly Professor Villiers was experimenting with. His science was original and it could be useful to see what he was up to. There are filing cabinets in his lab; he was very organised in what he was doing so there are bound to be records of his work. I think it shouldn't be hidden, so I need to see it."

Harry was uncomfortable using subterfuge with Dearden to get what he wanted. He would justify his request by checking through Villiers' records. That was a legitimate request for gaining entry into the secure site, to see what Villiers was up to. The blocked off exit from his lab was a secondary reason which would be investigated at the same time. There was no need to say anything about that.

"OK, I agree that it would be wise to look at his records. I'll speak to Lieutenant Colonel Ramsay." Dearden glanced at his watch. "It's late now, I'll phone him tomorrow."

* * *

It took some thoughtful persuasion by Harry to convince Dearden and Ramsay to allow Esma to accompany him into Repository One. Mike Ramsay was impressed with how Harry had deduced the whereabouts of the End Time weapon, and Dearden explained Harry's role in the communication with the now famous Lan-Si-Nu. The persuasion worked. Ramsay gave the go-ahead for entry into Repository One on the condition that two armed guards were posted outside the personnel entry door.

"Give us eight hours and we should be out of here," Harry said to Ramsay and the guards.

"If you're not we'll be coming in after you," Ramsay called, as they walked into the cavernous storage area that reeked of army surplus. Five minutes later, Harry and Esma were standing at the steel gates at the entrance of the tunnel leading to where the End Time weapon had been stored.

Harry undid the padlock and Esma got close as they walked through into the dark. He found the light switch in the beam from his Maglite, switched it on and with their way dimly illuminated they set off toward Villiers' laboratory.

"This is interesting," Harry said to Esma as he rifled through the folders in the 'D' section of the filing cabinet. 'Dimension Research, I'll look through these later." He put the folders on Villiers' desk.

"That's what I'm really interested in." He pointed to the doorway at the top of the six steps. Esma thought it looked interesting too.

There was a small landing area in front of the door where Harry put the tote-bag with the tools. He got out the lump hammer and coursing chisel, opened the door and surveyed the stonework, looking for the most open joint where he could start work. Esma put her hand on his arm to attract his attention. Her other hand touched the metal panel which was part of a complex looking door frame. It was warm to the touch.

"Listen," she said. She was frowning. "I hear talk, and birds."

"Really, can you?" Harry was silent, listening. Again, the sense of space came to mind from beyond the blockage. He held the head of the lump hammer onto the stonework and placed his ear on the end of the handle, a crude stethoscope, but it transmitted the sound from the other side.

"You're right, it is conversation and there is birdsong . . . listen." He stepped to one side, still holding the hammer onto the stone and Esma put her ear to the handle.

"Yes . . . we knock through?"

"Let's do it. Put these on, they'll stop your eyes getting hurt." He handed Esma a pair of protective goggles and put some on himself. She fiddled around with them, trying to do the same as him. "Here, let me help," he said. He brushed some hair away from her face and slipped the goggles on. "They make you look great," he complimented her and she smiled.

The first stone was the worst to get out, but after half an hour's effort he handed Esma the hammer and with the chisel he levered the stone side to side, inch by inch out of its position. The sound from whatever was happening the other side was louder.

"Mind out, it's going to fall." Esma stepped back. Harry gave a final push on the coursing chisel and the block teetered on the edge of the stonework and then it fell to the floor in a cloud of dust. There was another door beyond the stonework, which was still blocking the view to the other side.

An hour and three quarters later a pile of stone blocks were stacked in the laboratory. Harry and Esma stood in front of the next door, a solid oak four panelled door one might see in a house of the nineteen forties. Esma tried the handle, but the door was locked. Harry remembered seeing a large key in one of the drawers in Villiers' desk.

"Hold on, there's a key over there, I'll get it." He dashed over to the desk and came back with a key that was showing signs of surface rust. He pushed it into the mortice lock, turned the key and the latch grated open.

"OK, let's go for it." Harry twisted the door knob and pushed the door slightly ajar.

Daylight streamed through the opening, which was weird, because they were three hundred feet below the top of Edge Hill. Harry knew the calculations about their position were correct, so he wondered why there was daylight.

As they stepped through the doorway they heard a shout. Unable to hear clearly what was said they stepped through a little further and shut the door behind them.

"No, don't shut it," the man, who was running toward them, shouted. When he reached them, he saw the door was shut. "Oh, you young fools, that's torn it."

Harry recognised the apparition from the photograph on the desk. He stepped back and gasped, "Professor Villiers . . . but you disappeared."

"Good observation; I did disappear, along with my colleague here, Dick Martell." Another man arrived. He was short of breath after running. "Dick was the Keeper of the Knight's Sanctuary. I ought to have been pleased to see you, Young man," Villiers said. His voice sounded cultured, like the BBC English of the nineteen-forties. "But now you have added your own problem to ours."

"What problem—"

"The doorway, man. The doorway you've just come through that is now shut again. It happens to be a gateway to another universe, this one, and we can't get back home." He reached for the handle and jerked the door back open. Where the old laboratory had been a minute back there was utter blackness, set with the brilliance of stars.

John James Overton.
The West Midlands of England,
2017

What will happen to Harry Stanway and Esma? Are they locked into the alien dimension that opened up through the door in Professor Charles Villiers' laboratory?

What do they experience . . . will they ever return home?

Can Jem Dearden and SHaFT help, tied up as they are with the destruction, and the world-wide changes caused by the second pass of the planet Nibiru?

Find out in . . .

A QUESTION OF REALITIES

Book Three of The Grid Saga

J. J. Overton

Here is a taster

1

1959

Professor Charles Villiers noticed something weird going on in the hollow core of the high-frequency induction coil. The eight-foot diameter coil was part of a state of the art circuit involving magnetism. It had been placed, for convenience while it was on test, some three feet away from a lead-lined cupboard where a small amount of antimatter was stored. The chance combination of antimatter and magnetism produced the side effect of a vortex in the centre of the coil. Villiers and his assistants peered into it and glimpsed the landscape of an alien world.

Over the following months Charles Villiers and his team experimented. They only had a sight of the other world once more during that time, but it had fascinated them.

"Notice anything odd about that place?" Villiers said to his assistant, Professor Robbie Cranford.

"Do you mean how the movement taking place is in slow motion?"

"Yes . . . un-naturally so, don't you think?"

They built on the empirical knowledge that their experimentation revealed, and commissioned sheet metal fabricators to build a housing in the general shape of a doorframe.

There was no other way of describing the completed device other than by calling it a switch, but the importance of its function ensured that the first letter of its name ought to be capitalised. The Switch, plain and simple, and it was capitalised because it *switched* into a reality different to the one in which the Earth existed.

*   *   *

One evening, after dark, Villiers took his close friend, Richard Martell, the Keeper of the Knight's Sanctuary in Temple Balsall, to his laboratory in an obscure part of MoD Kineton. Villiers did this because he craved support for his ideas and he needed to show Martell the device he had been working on. It started off as an innocent excursion, but afterwards an excursion both of them bitterly regretted.

The team had fitted the last of the panels to the face of the doorframe during that day. Switch-on was planned for the following morning. Villiers was usually meticulous with procedures, particularly when working close to the boundaries of current knowledge. Every system was usually triple-checked to ensure that its function was fail-safe. However, in a moment of foolhardiness, he overlooked a vital decision he had stipulated, that the newly installed doorway apparatus would only be used for observation.

The professor switched on the high-tension supply and soon afterwards, above the slight buzz of the electronics, he heard what he thought was birdsong. He opened the door and was captivated by the vision.

"Where on earth is that?" Villiers said, in a hushed sort of tone. He and Martell peered at the land they could see through the doorway and, without thinking, walked forward.

It only took half a dozen paces past the doorway for them to realise that the place they walked into bore no resemblance to anything they had experienced before. Even the breeze was strange. There was a cloying feel to it as it touched their skin, as if the moving air had more viscosity to it than there should have been. Villiers looked around, saw small colourless masses that made no sense at all. He was trying to analyse them, when the wind gusted, and the door slammed shut behind them. Villiers, in a moment of panic, rushed back to the door and tugged it open. The panic turned to terror, because all he could see through the doorway was blackness, interspersed with countless stars.

*   *   *

Robert Styles Cranford, an assistant professor of Villiers, had been the last to leave the laboratory the previous evening and he was the first in next day. All the lights were switched on and Cranford knew for certain that he had switched off the lights before he left. At first, he had suspected a break-in. The laboratory was full of data, and the End Time Weapon, crated up and under wraps, was a prize any rogue government would be prepared to bargain millions for.

At the far end of the laboratory a light above the apparatus door was illuminated. Switch-on of the trial was to be at ten o'clock A.M., so the light should be off. One of the machinists, Ted Roper, who traditionally brewed tea for everyone in the morning, came into the lab and asked Cranford if he wanted a brew.

"I do, but before that will you come to the Switch with me. All the lights were on when I came in, and that warning light above the door shouldn't be on."

It was obvious the gear had been switched on when they got close to the doorframe because not only was ambient heat radiating from it but they could also hear the distinctive buzz of HT current. Cranford carefully opened the metallic door, saw blackness and stars, slammed the door shut and stepped back quickly.

"What the hell was that?" Roper asked.

"A star-field."

"But how can it be . . . in this place?"

'I have no real answer to that; I wish I did."

Roper stepped back another couple of paces. "What is it, the doorway?"

"A type of switch . . . it goes to other places."

"You can say that again."

"Yes, I guess I can. The point is, Villiers stipulated that we only make observations through the Switch, and now the idiot's stepped through it."

Robbie Cranford did his best with further research. It was highly theoretical, and in time he and the team ran out of ideas. The technology to produce mapping of the places the Switch accessed was difficult to devise. Cranford gave it six months. Once a week, always with two or three of the team present, he opened the door, but obtained no result that would help them to rescue Villiers. There was nothing beyond the door but the black void and the stars.

* * *

"We've done all we can here, Villiers has had it," Cranford announced to the team one day in August. Money that Villiers had siphoned off from government sources to pay for the End Time Weapon only had a month and a few days to run.

"Before we leave we must seal that thing up," Cranford said. There were objections because Villiers was still someplace beyond the doorway, but as the senior man Cranford's word was law. He ordered in lead sheet, a quantity of dressed Hornton Ironstone blocks, cement and sand for mortar, and they sealed the opening against outside meddling. To finish the job, one of the machinists, who was also a carpenter, installed another door in a wooden frame in front of the stone blocks.

2

There was a period of anger and confusion after Harry and Esma walked through the door from the laboratory and saw Villiers, and another man further away who was running toward them. Villiers had been trying for some years to figure out a construct of information and technology to get him and Dick Martel back home. He had plausible theories and had been able to devise some tools. The tools were primitive, but sufficient to help him and Martell build an elaborate shelter. It had two separate living quarters because there were times when they got sick of each other and argued violently. But Villiers, clever as he was, could not make the tools and the instruments to help him figure out the way back home.

Apart from the occasional exploratory journey which would last for a few days when the adventurous spirit took over, he and Martell never moved far away from the door. The door was their link to home, although, as time passed, home became a distant ~mory. When they opened the door, which they did quite regu- ᵃw a different place each time, usually a view of the ~ occasions, although they were seldom, when ~nge new world, always an unfamiliar

man and woman, he, maybe in his ᵉr, probably by ten years or so, burst through the door. Villiers had yelled at them urgently not to shut the door, but they did so before what he had shouted registered, and the way back was lost again.

Charles Villiers had an edgy temperament. People had said that it went with his creative nature. Sometimes his sheer brilliance of invention was subsumed by periods of rage over the slightest of challenges.

"Oh, you stupid young fools, that's torn it," he shouted. And then he broke into a chain of expletives, some of which the Anglo-Saxon girl, Esma, recognised. Esma retreated behind Harry, and peeped over his shoulder at the man who was purple with rage.

Harry's immediate reaction at seeing the apparition of someone he thought was dead was to step back and gasp,

"Professor Villiers . . . but you disappeared."

"Good observation; I did disappear, along with my colleague, Dick Martell." He started ranting again and then the other man arrived, short of breath after running.

"Shut your damn mouth or I'll shut it for you," the other man said to Villiers, at which Villiers shut his mouth, simmered down, and then looked embarrassed.

"I am Sorry. Dick has to keep me in control. Sometimes things get out of hand. This is my colleague, Richard Martell. He was the Keeper of the Knight's Sanctuary. My apologies, young man. I ought to have been pleased to see you; and you, young lady." Villiers' change of mood was uncanny. Harry thought he probably had some sort of bi-polar disorder. Now he was calm his voice sounded cultured, like the BBC English of the nineteen-forties.

"I am afraid you have added your own problem to ours."

"What problem—"

"The damn doorway. The doorway you have just come through is now shut again. The link is variable and we can't get back home. We could have done if you had kept the door open."

Harry had a sense of being in control. Although he was easy going, had a smile for most people most times, he never let anyone mess him about. Out of habit he looked at his watch. It was digital, with hands. It had developed a fault. The hands were moving far quicker than they ought to be. He unstrapped it and put it in his pocket. He would see to it later.

"Professor Villiers, I would suggest that, if we are going to get through *our problem*, we should get together and work on it in a constructive way. What do you think to that idea?" The professor looked at the ground. Nodded.

"Point taken, young man . . . shall we talk things through?"

They went to the place Villiers and Martell had built. There was a communal area. The tools in Harry's tote-bag rattled when he put it down and sat on the ground. Esma sat by his side and when Harry began to ask probing questions about their surroundings Villiers became prickly. After a while Martell grew impatient with Villiers. He stomped off to a container and came back with drinks and after a while the atmosphere lightened. The liquid was surprisingly good. Definitely alcoholic. Served in purple earthenware vessels.

"There's a preponderance of manganese in the rocks and soil here. That's what has given these drinking vessels a purple hue," Villiers said.

Harry studied his vessel. Rough-made, still with thumb and finger marks, but rock-hard. "It's not bad as a colour. I'd prefer clear glass to drink from, but the drink's good, whatever the colour of the container."

They got to talking about their situations. Villiers about the planet he and Martell had ended up on. They had taken to calling Earth 2. Harry told them about Earth 1 and its second encounter with Nibiru. Villiers was immediately interested in what Harry was saying and questioned him enthusiastically.

"So, a delivery system was developed in time?"

"It was, but only just in time." Harry told them how it was discovered that Nibiru was inhabited, and because of that the End Time weapon had to be diverted.

*   *   *

When the trauma of the entry into Villiers' world had passed, Harry's incisive mind began to analyse the observations he had been storing up mentally. Vegetation was wildly different to all the species of Earth vegetation Harry was familiar with. Not that he was a botanist, but he had a photographic memory and his retention of information gave him a prolific amount of data at his disposal and he could reason on it in a refined way.

There was a time when the four of them were sitting in the communal area of the hut when Harry launched into an explanation of how he had understood his observations. He spoke about the various life-forms he had seen, and the physical attributes of the surroundings.

"What I can see of the vegetation reminds me of some research I did after one of the Controversial TV programs."

"Controversial TV?"

"Yeh. It was a television channel that always broadcasted challenging information. Things the establishment didn't want in the public domain. One of the programs was about Mycorrizal life and its connectivity. But before I tell you about this, have you heard of the internet?"

"The inter what?"

"The internet. I'll explain that in detail later. Let me just say that Mycorrizal life resembles the internet, which is a worldwide provision of information that can be accessed by anyone at any time. The internet is accessed by the end user using a computer."

"Come on Harry. You are telling us things we have no clue about."

"So, listen and learn. Mycorrizal fungal life is conjectured to provide widespread communication between tree species. It is a network that exists below soil level. Sometimes it spreads for miles underground. The internet, for we people of Earth, is a wireless network that is now a major means of data exchange and communication. I think what we see demonstrated by the vegetation here may be a similar phenomenon to the internet."

"What makes you conclude that?"

"See how the vegetation bunches up in groups, and the foliage of each separate tree, or whatever lifeform they are, moves in an identical way. And then a distant group responds. Think of the movement of a flock of starlings, how they appear to instantly communicate when they are on the wing. That's what I'm seeing with these lifeforms. Communication." Villiers scanned the emerald green foliage and saw how the movement was being replicated. Group to group the complicated movement was identical.

"Where will knowing about that get us?"

"I don't know . . . yet. There's something else. See what's happening now?" The others looked at the vegetation. Villiers shook his head. "Well, at the moment, the foliage is pointing toward us. Even those in the distance."

Martell shielded his eyes against the light of the Sun. "Are you thinking the same as I am," he asked Harry.

"That depends what you're thinking."

"Trees know we are here," Esma said.

Harry nodded. "Exactly. That is my first major observation, take it or leave it. To what extent it will fit in I don't know. But don't you think what we see smacks of communication?"

"Maybe it does. I reserve judgment," Villiers said.

"I have wondered why we see no sign of animal life," Martell interjected. He was astute in his comments. He said little but thought a lot. Only when there was a real need did he comment. "I do think that the life created here is different to anything we know."

Harry was surprised at Martell's comment. It should have come from the scientist.

"There is something else, come to think of it," Harry said. He seemed at a loss for words, embarrassed, which was unusual for Harry. He and Esma had talked about this one time when they were out of earshot of the other two. *"They have been here for nearly fifty years, why don't they show their age?* Harry had said.

"How old they are?" Her modern English response had been slightly wrong again.

"Counting in Earth-years I think Villiers would be more than a hundred years old."

"He is no looking sixty years."

"And that raises an interesting proposition about aging in this place," Harry had said.

He took his watch out of his pocket and held it up for Villiers and Martell to see. The hands were still moving far too quickly.

"I think that the aging process is slowed right down here. This watch is still showing Earth-time. I don't know why this is happening yet, but I have ideas about it." Villiers looked at him, nodded knowingly. Smiled slightly.

Esma liked Harry's ideas. She liked to hear his voice when he explained them. Often, she did not understand the things he said, but she trusted him. Trusted his honest eyes. She knew that, when he told her his ideas, they were true. So, when Harry was embarrassed to speak about the age of the two men, Esma took over. With her upbringing she didn't give a damn about what other people thought of her.

"How old are you?" Her gaze was direct. First at Villiers, then at Martell.

John James Overton
www.jjoverton.com
Twitter: @JJOvertonAuthor

Follow Dearden and the others in The Grid Saga.
Nos Successio Procul Totus Sumptus.
'We succeed at all costs.'

Made in the USA
Lexington, KY
29 March 2018